LUCKY CHANCE

R. C. WELCH

ISBN: 978-1-7336158-4-6

Welch. R.C.
Lucky Chance

Edited by: Allie Coker

Published by Warren Publishing
Charlotte, NC
www.warrenpublishing.net
Printed in the United States

LUCKY CHANCE

ACKNOWLEDGMENTS

I would like to express loving gratitude to my wife, Dr. Cherrie Dawn Welch, for inspiring me to write this story. She has been tenacious in that regard. She says that I tend to forget one thing and the next, from one day to the next. To clarify, I should say that during the process of writing, I found myself quite pleased with the story on numerous days, but on others, I was convinced that nothing I had written was worth the ink and paper. She has also served as my first editor. She has gifted her precious time, dedicated attention, and persistent encouragement through long reading sessions that often left her feeling confused, and sometimes, shocked. The gifts she has bestowed upon me and my work are irreplaceable.

I would also like to thank my sister, Juliet Cecile Welch. She has offered a constant stream of encouragement, and a compassionate ear with regard toward my new endeavor.

I also owe a debt of gratitude to all the authors and thinkers who, through their published works, have influenced my life in one way or another. I am grateful to various works involving the Judeo-Christian conception of human endeavor beneath a transcendent God. I am also indebted to various works which involve those same issues, governed under the suggestions commonly associated with addiction recovery programs. In addition, I have taken two particular notions from two influential thinkers. Dr. Walter E. Williams of George Mason University has inspired my notions of marriage as an exclusive club, and Dr. Alfred North Whitehead has encouraged me to consider judging a life through a series of moving images, rather than awarding such a verdict to any single snapshot image excerpted from the running film.

PROLOGUE

Who can tell what a day might bring? My wife advises that fortune telling, card-reading, crystal ball gazing, and foretelling in general, are forbidden pursuits, and have been since the first revelations of God. Nevertheless, I have attempted to perform that very task across most of my life. I wonder, in secret, how God might judge a child who attempts to divine his fate, underneath the watch of an active alcoholic. Interestingly, the Bible introduces the word divination to describe the craft of predicting the future. Without relying upon actual research, the word, divination, by simple appearance, suggests that the action being categorized has something to do with the divine. Surprisingly, I felt that exact sensation when I was young. Despite being routinely tormented and occasionally tortured, I, Jack Weatherlow, thought that I could, indeed, see and know exactly what my future held.

I needed to become proficient at soothsaying during my formative years. I needed a source of power to defend my otherwise powerless childhood. I became quite skilled at observing and discerning from certain mannerisms and telltale clues. I could tell, and I could see, the type and temperature of the day or evening that lay ahead. Most of the time, I was powerless to do anything but endure the wrath of a predicted storm. However, on various occasions, I could alter the prevailing currents by shifting certain preferred behaviors, or performing an uncharacteristic task or chore. As a child, such power, underneath a highly unpredictable parent, suggests pure divinity.

I wonder whether the original prohibition of such a craft was intended as counsel rather than condemnation. I never really knew, nor could I foresee, the actual trials that would transpire. I only suspected the measure and magnitude of misery and mayhem that might be expected. Every day of my young life was the same, but every day was also different in some unpredictable way. Nevertheless, I was seduced, and I was convicted, by the power of my craft, and to this day, my thinking along these lines is somewhat warped. I find the task of accepting the fact that I cannot truly know the future to be as elusive as the actual events that will inevitably unfold. Therefore, I choose to view the original proscription as God's way of warning us of the consequences of such wayward occupations.

I think we all dabble in the forbidden art of divination, to some degree. Looking ahead, we might anticipate the dawning of our new day with expectant enthusiasm, or we may peek forward, reluctantly, out of a fog of dreary dread. Most days will arrive, languish and pass as if glancing through the pages of an unillustrated book, black and white in a limitless string of banal routine. However, there are still those days which promise a predictable parade, but produce events and episodes that defy all practical prognostication.

Indeed, my life began to unfold following one of those shockingly unpredictable days. I was four years old. That day was a summer day in 1961, an anticipated day, by all accounts. My family had enthusiastic plans for a wonderful gathering of friends and relatives. Regardless, things changed. There was a telephone call. The caller informed my family that my grandparents had been killed. They were in route to our event. There had been an automobile accident of unimaginable horror. That accident made the front page of the paper, below the fold, in my home town of Atlanta, Georgia. My father became an orphan that day. He was twenty-four years old.

I would argue that my mother also became an orphan on that day. She became an orphan through unpremeditated abandonment and overwhelming responsibility. She lost a husband that day, through a type of spiritual and emotional withdrawal, and she gained a teenaged son, my uncle. She became the matriarch of a peculiar family, unexpectedly, and I suppose, grudgingly. Her status shifted from postgraduate ingénue to head of the family over the course of a single telephone call. She was also twenty-four years old.

In fact, I think each member of the surviving Weatherlow clan became an orphan on the day of that accident. Perhaps, love, and nurture, compassion, and understanding blossom from the connections supplied through spiritual and emotional linkages in far greater capacity than through physical proximity. It may be that physical nearness only becomes a reliable method of assurance when the gap that separates one from another diminishes to the point of contact. We did not touch one another in my family. I can't recall a single physical exchange of affection between my parents and me. I was swiped by a physical blow of sorts, on occasion, but even that was inspired by disgust, rather than correction.

After the accident, I think we all adopted a way of living, which might be described as 'present absence.' We gathered and lived, together, but we were not linked by reliable cords of assurance and comfort. I believe that my mother looked toward my father as her vital point of connection. My father was fully husband and dad in every visible way, but he was also missing in all the spiritual and emotional duties assigned to those roles. My father was an exceedingly devoted man, of a responsible nature, as far as provisioning goes. We had anything and everything one might imagine, but we were alone in the midst of those treasures.

Before long, my mother found a friend to keep her company. That friend was loyal and dependable, providing comfort and camaraderie. However, her companion was not formed from altruistic elements, but was a rather stern landlord of her care. The friend my mother chose, over every member of her household, and the world, was Vodka. And, as memories of passing days go, I don't recall a single day in which my mother was completely sober.

My mother held the lamentable title of alcoholic overlord of my young life. She was, more than anything, decidedly destructive in all her movements. She is guilty by my experience, but also innocent, by my learned appraisal. She chose a path, but she was also forcibly given to a situation that she could never have predicted. Her condition was undoubtedly formed from choice, but also, I think, inspired by inescapable duty.

I recall another summer day, many years displaced from the accident of 1961. I was seventeen. The day was a Saturday.

I answered the telephone before anyone was awake. The identity of the caller was unexpected and alarming. I spoke careful words to the father of my beloved girlfriend. He and I did not share telephone conversations. He informed me of another telephone call, which had arrived at his house during the latter shank of the previous evening. My mother had called to offer her sodden opinion of his glorious daughter. That morning, he asked me to drop by in order to help him make things right.

A vital part of my life was stolen that day. I did not recover for many years. That day was something of a small scale Pearl Harbor event. There was a surprise attack upon a sleepy port, which produced devastating destruction, and took precious casualties. That morning was, to me, personally, almost like the wreck of 1961. It was devastating, and shockingly unpredictable, but this time, not accidental. That morning was something along the lines of an unlucky chance.

I suppose that I retired from active duty following that event. I withdrew gradually, but more precisely, I adopted my mother's form of retirement. I chose a new companion, one that was devoted and trustworthy, almost exactly as my mother had done after the original tragedy. I devoted my life to this new relationship for a not so lengthy, but incomprehensibly, critical period of time. I managed for a while. Over the ensuing years, however, my projections for the future hung underneath a gloomy overcast, with periods of unsettling terror. For example, I acquired a rather common presence before various magistrates of my life, those of a legal degree, those of medical necessity, and those of business evaluation. In other words, I spent a few nights in jail. I spent a few weeks in the hospital, and I spent more time than I care to remember attempting to maintain gainful employment.

In May of 1987, I awoke, or rather, I should say, 'came to.' I rose from the floor of a hotel room. I was lying between the double beds of a standard room, inside a fine hotel. That hotel and that room happened to be located in Kansas City. I had taken that room by invitation and expectation of my most recent employer. Inside those dawning moments of bleary consciousness, the darkened room seemed to foreshadow a dismal future.

I could not recall my movements across an indiscernible span of time, and I was possessed of a type of malady that was viciously afflicting my mind, my body and my spirit. I was four months shy of my thirtieth birthday, AWOL from work, distantly displaced from home, out of money, and out of Vodka.

Based upon my record at that point in life, I cannot determine how I summoned the will or the energy to call for help. I deserved nothing resembling assistance. My previous record of failure gave dreary testimony, and my own mother had predicted my ultimate disgrace on many occasions. Nevertheless, I placed a telephone call from a strange room, in a strange town, to a strange hospital that cared for strange people who drank liquor for common reasons. They came to fetch me. They took me in. They sobered me up, and they sent me out, but something happened in that hospital. And, to this day, I look back upon that first day in Kansas City as the last day of my inebriated retirement. On that day, the gloomy expectation of dreary dread transformed, into an enthusiastic memory of unexpected liberation and undeserved renewal.

Approximately fifteen months after that spectacularly unusual day, I was looking out upon a crisp autumn morning. I was living in my acquired 'home' town, gainfully employed and practicing my life in recovery. I might say that my outlook, for that day, was much the same as many previous days. By comparison, I was expecting to turn another page in an unillustrated book. However, there was no dread haunting those particular pages in my history of sober living. In fact, most days were energized by a prevailing sense of gratitude. Those early days were pleasant, but purposely uneventful. I had designed and ordered them as suggested, and I expected manageable similarity.

That particular day happened to be wash day. I took my dirty clothes to the laundry room at my apartment complex, and there I met Samantha Davis Morris. We met under a situation that seems like fantasy, excerpted from an old Hollywood movie script. At the time, we were living in the same apartment complex, but unaware of each other's existence. And, while I was still a relative newcomer to Kansas City, Samantha was, as they say, 'fresh off the boat.' She was living with her parents, newly arrived from her hometown, Paris, France.

We were alone that day. She was already in place when I arrived. Sam turned when I entered. She spun around quickly, startled by my entrance. I had apparently interrupted some secret contemplation. She gave a little jerk with her head. She blew smoke into the air, while throwing her hair out of her eyes. We shared a brief, but natural, greeting as I entered the steamy, chlorine-scented room. I remember a glinting instant of eye contact, which remained in place for a moment longer than might be expected. The only sound filling the room was the methodical whirring of the machines.

When I first saw her, I recall feeling flushed by a sense of confusion, or a nervous anxiety. I became inextricably distracted. I was struck stupid, all of a sudden. I couldn't focus on my work. I fumbled with simple tasks that I had executed quite proficiently for the better part of my life. I was no stranger to laundry duties, but in those few moments, I appeared dumbfounded by the simple chore of loading a washer. I had trouble putting a quarter in the machine. I cast the very real appearance of someone who needed help, and Samantha took the opportunity to lend a hand. Clumsy male struggling with laundry duty, adept female coming to the rescue; the scene seems ludicrously formulaic and fraudulent, but it is nonetheless our story.

That event fits the description of a lucky chance. Two disparate lives were emerging from certain similarly traumatic histories, and whether by sheer chance, or by statistical probability, those lives intersected, and a rather mundane day transformed into one of the more remarkably enthusiastic memories of our lives. We have been together, as a couple, ever since.

Samantha and I share similarly profound episodes of tragic upheaval inside our separate histories. However, while my story involves a recovery from the disconnection, resulting from a series of tragic events, Samantha's story concerns the concentrating powers of connected recovery, inspired by a single tragedy. Sam was born in Kansas City. Her father was full-blooded American, but her mother was full-blooded French. Her parents met during World War II. Samantha's original given name is Savanne Davier Morris.

Her biological parents were lost in an unexpectedly tragic automobile accident a few months after her first birthday.

In 1961, Samantha was adopted by her father's brother and his wife. They were unable to have children of their own. At her adoption, she was given, by way of love and outlook upon the future, an Americanized version of her original name. Savanne became Samantha, Davier, became Davis, and her surname remained in place in remembrance of both sets of parents. Like me, Samantha retains no active memory of the tragedy that disrupted her life, but unlike me, she had been embraced by a substitute set of parents who were relatively unaffected by the loss of a sibling and an in-law. Samantha knows a sense of permanency about her life, while I tend to think of all things as a temporary state of affairs. I might say that, while Savanne is an orphan, Samantha is fully connected.

Her adoptive parents were living in France at the time of the accident. Samantha's adoptive father was associated with the foreign services branch of the United States Government and stationed in Paris. Her adoptive mother worked as a teacher of English in one of the private schools of that city. Consequently, Samantha was raised in France. She is composed of half American and half French stock, and she was raised by Americans, living in France. She lived within an American household, but was immersed in French culture. She is fully half of both in every conceivable way. She answers to both names, French and American, yet by my observation, she is whole, in mind, body and spirit.

As for me, I have rarely felt a sense of wholeness about my life, at least until I met Samantha. Through patient coaching and subtle demand, she shares her sense of peace, which is, for me, an absence of restless searching.

Under diplomatic prestige, Samantha attended the best schools in Paris. Her curiosities and academic acumens led her toward advanced degrees in religion, specializing in Historical Theologies and Church History. She is classically trained in all aspects of her chosen subjects, but she leans heavily upon the traditions of the Roman Catholic persuasion. Over time, I have become inculcated by ranging tracts of that particular philosophy, but somewhat adjusted and tempered by Samantha's particular and, sometimes, peculiar interpretations.

Samantha is exceptionally amenable toward the subject of her personal history. I have been somewhat less forthcoming. Her stories are, for the most part, familiar. She has a past, as they say. However, she is here, and at this point, she is my wife.

A few years back, we looked upon one of our days together, energized by an expectant enthusiasm. We had planned to celebrate the one-month anniversary of our courtship, by cooking supper together in my apartment. Prior to that day, and by purposeful design, we had never shared time alone together inside my apartment. Nevertheless, for this event, our shared sense of enthusiasm had been formed from disparate forecasts. In other words, I was feeling anxious and guarded, while Samantha was feeling curious and eager.

At that time, I was protecting what we were enjoying in the present, by withholding certain information about my unsavory past. I was simply playing the part I had been given by my family. I was a diviner of possibility, on one hand, and a protector of the realm, on the other. I held all information about our family in strict confidence, and I manipulated certain obvious misadventures in favor of the queen and her court. Among many things, I am an accomplished actor, but out of duty and necessity, rather than by actual stage work. Samantha simply wanted to meet the actual man, behind the delightful character, who was providing the entertainment.

In painful irony, Samantha was forecasting a glorious future, based upon a rather odd form of disclosure. In fact, that evening, I came to understand another recovery slogan. 'You're only as sick as the secrets you keep.' She had predicted who I was, beneath and behind the enigma, who was presently acting like a good guy, in order to cover for my conception of a bad guy, who needed to remain hidden in the past.

In short, Samantha was prepared to accept my story, and me, I think, just as I was, grizzled history and all. At the time, I had no awareness of her goal, and I doubt that I would ever have realized, without the aid of two simple virtues. Samantha was faithfully accepting, and I was cautiously willing.

The steps in our anniversary event were simple, but also delicate, and therefore, surprisingly difficult to perform. That evening was about beginning a future by disclosing the past, and resigning from the role that kept that old story fresh and alive in the present. We had our evening in my apartment, and despite several moments of alarming dissension, we came to 'know' one another, in the Biblical sense, for the first time.

This practice of 'knowing' involves a type of surrender, or giving of oneself to the other. Under that light, Samantha's process of merging with me is oddly similar to my understanding of recovery. Both occupations often leave me feeling confused and amazed by simple tasks, which are difficult to perform. Regardless, I have found that, since that first day, in the laundry room, the majority of our days suggest at least a sense of expectant enthusiasm, and despite the normal routines and regimens that tend to dissolve into that unillustrated book of similar page-turning chores, every day with Samantha Weatherlow harbors the possibility of unveiling something along the lines of a lucky chance.

CHAPTER 1

The Art of Taking

....

I called out into the general atmosphere from my standing position, in front of the bathroom sink.

"Hey Sam, did you take my razor blades?"

She responded to the alarm, rather than my inquisition. I find that we often begin our interactions much like how I imagine prehistoric people may have communicated. We react and reply to intonation and inflection, rather than by a truly comprehended word. The opening of this repartee was no different. Her answer was carried upon a melodious voice that caressed my ear and fluttered into my brain. I heard the sweet sounds, which composed historically foreign words.

"Qu'est-ce que c'est?"

I called again, sweetly sarcastic, "There was one left in the sleeve, and now it's gone... I always put the old blade back in the sleeve, upside down. I never throw them away by themselves."

In the next second, Samantha was standing in the doorway of our bathroom.

She asserted, "Mon Chéri, I did not take your razor blade, but I have it, nonetheless."

I instantly understood, but I still felt the sting, which results from a petty larceny.

Sam continued, "Chéri, I needed to change my razor last night in order to prepare for our celebration. I shaved my legs, if you remember. Hmmm...? I recall you saying something about them."

Since the outset of our relationship, Samantha and I have celebrated a number of personally significant occasions. We do this alone, but together, in our apartment. The event under consideration was no different, although the inspiration for the festivities was somewhat unusual. We celebrated the fifth anniversary of the last day of my drinking career, or underneath a different light, the first day of my recovered life. Among several activities exclusively designed to honor my achievement, Sam prepared a French supper, complete with caviar and champagne. Samantha always celebrates with French champagne. I am restricted to popping the cork, and pouring, while she raises her flute in cheer. I have come to enjoy that odd chore.

I recognize that day but without a corresponding sense of enthusiasm. My equanimity toward this marker was installed by a single question that I received from my grandfather, early along the course of my renewed journey in life. He asked, quite frankly, 'Why would you celebrate something that you should have been doing all along?' I have never forgotten that painfully astute piece of logic. Nevertheless, Samantha assigns a type of honor to my day that seems to match any of her religious holidays. In addition, my guide through recovery and mentor for renewed life has insisted that I celebrate my success in meetings. He says the recognition is meant to inspire the newcomers, rather than me. His stalwart advice remains in my mind alongside my grandfather's question. That counsel is also rather simple; 'It's not about you, pal.'

I declared in hopeless defense, "I don't think the effect justifies the theft, in this case."

"Mon Dieu, Chéri, I did not take your razor blades."

"Seems to me that, since it was here before, and now it's gone, and since I had no part in its disappearance, and since you admit to having it, then you had to have taken it."

"Mon Amour, I did not take your razor blades, I accepted them as your gift to me."

My case was lost. Even the evidence miraculously betrayed my cause.

Shifting gears I searched for a report on my standing. "Sam, honey, I…I mean that…I certainly would've given them to you, but I didn't…I mean, how far does this giving and receiving thing go?"

Through a cherubic smile I heard, "Tout ma vie, Chéri."

I stood there, momentarily appraising this last comment, and my wife, as she stood in the doorway to our master bath. When I use the term, wife, to describe my Samantha, my meaning extends beyond a common definition. We were legally married on April 27, 1990, a Friday, to be exact. This date exists in my mind as if it had been inscribed with a welder's torch. I see its emblazoned image quite clearly, and at all times, much like the occasions of my real birthday and Christmas or the Fourth of July. However, it tends to wander rather carelessly through the synapses of my Samantha's memory. I might describe this situation as a striking anomaly when compared to the stereotypical understanding of paying record and honor to such a momentous occasion. Throughout our culture the male is depicted almost without exception as the party who forgets or overlooks the anniversary of his contractual agreement to cherish and hold his mate, 'until death do they part.'

I happen to remember that particular date for several obvious and remarkable reasons. First of all, we were married in the same church where Samantha's mother and father were married, The Oratory of Old St. Patrick. That particular church is an extremely lovely house of God, which has been dedicated to the Roman Catholic persuasion. Our wedding ceremony was very small. My father and my sister came from home. My recovery mentor, Grant, attended. Samantha's parents were there, and Samantha's oldest friends, Manette and Paul, came all the way from Paris. Those nine persons, less the celebrant and his attendants, composed the entire coterie of witnesses to our legal marriage. Nevertheless, those few souls, set apart from the larger world by the cavernous grandeur of that beautiful church, transformed our simple event into an occasion of glorious splendor.

Notably, I received my first official reprimands from the church that day. Both were tendered in response to apparent acts of wandering attention, clearly demonstrated during the ceremony, from my side of the aisle. The first was inspired by Samantha, and the second by a scene from an old movie. Both oversights were recognized by eyes, belonging to an official legate of God. A menacing squint, silently ordered mandatory restitutions for my transgressions, and I paid my penance in currencies of fear and shame.

My first official liturgical oversight was inspired by Samantha's wedding attire. The ensemble she had prepared was a closely guarded secret, about which I was forbidden to know of the first stitch. As I mentioned, our wedding ceremony was small and private. We did not have attendants, with the exception of Samantha's father, who was required to officially transfer ownership to me. She wanted to be given away by her father, and she wanted to supply and arrange all the flowers. I was our wedding planner for the remaining elements of the ceremony. We did not ask our guests to wear formal attire. However, Samantha and I had previously decided to stand for our ceremony in the guise of figurines, which typically adorn the top layer of the wedding cake. For my part, I was wearing a simple black tuxedo with notched lapels. I was allowed to wear my own tux slippers. They were the real thing.

Sam materialized at the end of the nave in an A-line dress, rather than a gown. At first glance, she and her dress appeared to have been summoned across time itself, for our special event. Her ensemble featured a fitted silk charmeuse bodice and accompanying skirt in diaphanous tulle. The dress hugged her abdomen, but billowed and soughed like powdered snow as she stepped. Below barely covered knees, she wore white hosiery, and white satin heels, which featured a tiny black bow across the vamp. However, the most mind-bending article of her surprise raiment was covering her lovely head. This separate artifact, also in white, appeared to have been liberated from the hidden vaults of an ancient order of the church. She was veiled by what appeared to be, at least for her diminutive size, a cacophonous medieval hood, which fell about her neck and shoulders in a softly layered cowling effect, like a mantle or cape. I have no idea how, or from where, she acquired these items.

She was white and wispy, soft and shiny, small and silent, and somewhat sinister, as she placed each approaching footstep upon the wooden aisle. She moved as if she were skating instead of walking. I found her image to be deliciously mischievous, feminine holiness, moving through a cloud of suspicion. I recall craning my neck in several odd contortions in order to look upon her shrouded face. Soon enough, I found her lapis-colored hawk's eyes glowing out of a retracted darkness. She was unshakably fixed upon my station. I was transfixed by that gaze and her image, and I failed to heed my call after she arrived. I may have been drooling slightly at the time of my summons, but more truly from stupefaction, rather than lusty greed or hunger.

The second lapse of attention occurred following the ceremonial move that took us from the altar to the tabernacle. I faded into a moment of common reflection, albeit somewhat illicit in this instance. I wandered into a set of remembered images, which had been installed by the first Godfather movie. I recalled the scene, near the very end of the production, which features a shifting of images. That scene might be entitled the Baptism of Michael Corleone's Son, but that principal event, ensconced within the highest degree of Catholic splendor, was interrupted by a montage of grisly murder scenes, in which the captains of the other prominent syndicate families were being simultaneously dispatched. Lost in my momentary adoption of the character of Michael Corleone, I once again failed to respond to an official summons.

I remember my wife at our wedding for obvious reasons. I remember the church and the ceremony and the silent reprimands, for reasons that flow from the fact that I am not well versed in matters of religion. My memory of our official marriage is partly a product of academic retention.

I could not simply marry my Samantha in her parents' Catholic Church. I had to undergo a sort of initiation ritual, beforehand. In other words, I had to be confirmed. I had to become a Catholic. That endeavor is a sort of exchange of acceptance, mine being focused upon the practices of the faith, and theirs, in evaluation of my expressions of learning, and confession of loyalty.

Prior to my induction into the Roman Catholic faith, I had never been a member of any church, nor had I added any significant wear and tear to the pews of any religious establishment. This is a product of inadvertence rather than aversion. Emerging from this mildly hedonistic background, I suppose that I felt rather enthused by the thought of being accepted as an official member of an organization which is founded upon such profoundly remarkable history. On the other hand, Sam is well versed and, I should add, has been classically trained in the smallest nuances of the Catholic faith. Prior to meeting Samantha, I can honestly say that my experience with members of the Catholic faith was extremely limited. I might recall one young lady, if pressed. Consequently, Samantha has moved me from a loosely tethered life of casual abstinence to active membership in the most prominent faith in the history of the world. She is, in my biased opinion, an active, but unacknowledged priest, and, in my opinion, a legitimate candidate for sainthood.

For all the above reasons, and because I am, at base, a devoted follower of certain established rules, our official church wedding date holds a prominent place in my memory. However, I don't mean to imply that this date is meaningless to my Samantha. She thinks of our church wedding as her gift to me, but the date of that particular bequest doesn't really matter. To Samantha, marriage is synonymous with the notion of becoming 'one flesh.' That holy process of amalgamation involves and requires far more than verbal pledges and stated vows. Therefore, while the church is a fine stage from which to proclaim these noble intentions before faithful witnesses, the public act of professing does not necessarily guarantee or accomplish the necessary merger. She simply wants to 'know' all of me, mind, body and soul. And that desire issues from a purely and distinctly biblical sense.

If asked, I have no doubt that Samantha would offer the date of November 8, 1988, as her legitimate wedding date. She says that she gave herself, mind, body and spirit, to me on that auspicious evening. In addition, she will offer that my real wedding date is November 8, 1989. I made my official proposal that evening, and through the method, and certain obvious expenses which were involved, she accepted that particular overture as my gift, of mind, body and soul, to her. These former dates are markers of spiritual conception.

Sam says that we came to 'know' one another on those dates, a very special type of knowing, as in the Adam and Eve sense. Quite candidly, I was unaware of what was really happening. I suppose that I was doing 'x,' while Sam was doing 'y,' but that's the point, according to Samantha. Through a chromosomal commitment, we were apparently chaperoning an elemental merger between mind, body and soul. For Samantha, God alone presides over this transaction.

The marriage contract takes effect when one or both parties freely and fully agree to 'know' their chosen partner. In addition, there is no effective divorce from this consensual accord. Under these guidelines, marriage appears to be a one and done sort of event. However, the 'done' condition doesn't seem to prevail. On the contrary, every day, with my Samantha includes a hearty measure of confabulation concerning our wedding. Nevertheless, she has her date, I have my date, and we share the church date, together. All in all, when I look upon my wife, I could say that I have married her three times, or I might also say that I do my best to marry her every day that we are together.

Through my appraisal, I noticed that Samantha was wearing a pair of jeans, well-worn and settled softly at every appropriate place. Her hands were buried in the back pockets. She was barefoot, and she was also wearing a periwinkle, banded-sleeve sport shirt, hers in this case, rather than mine. The left breast sported a logo, embroidered with pink and orange thread. It was a depiction of an Iris bloom, underscored with the name of a flower shop; L'Hôtel des Fleurs dans La Ville; The Hotel of Flowers in the City.

By my way of thinking, Samantha came to settle in this city because of that shop. She, however, presents a vastly different view of her summons or calling. The Hotel of Flowers in the City is, in legal deed, and practical operation, her shop. She owns it outright, and she runs it her way. Nevertheless, that same shop once belonged to her biological mother, and before her mother, that flower shop belonged to Samantha's maternal grandparents. Samantha has never known any of her shop's previous owners, yet they are all inseparably intertwined.

That shop and my Samantha share a curious sort of history. The Hotel of Flowers in the City was born in Paris, France, but lives its life in Kansas City, USA. It was named after its original location along the Quai de l'Hotel de

Ville just off the Seine River. My Samantha was born in Kansas City, but has lived most of her life in Paris, France. She carries the names which descend from her ancestral homelands in Brittany or Bretagne. I might say that they have both traded locations, and parents, throughout their lives. In effect, they, the shop and my Samantha, are both, orphans of two generations.

The Hotel of Flowers in the City was conceived by original parents, but has been reconceived, moved and maintained by adoptive parents. My Samantha was also conceived by authentic parents, but she has been reconceived and moved and maintained by adoptive parents. That shop and my Samantha persist and thrive despite shared histories of daunting tragedy. There is a peculiar sense of enduring presence about that shop, and my Samantha. Nevertheless, my thoughts along these lines tend to emphasize the remarkable absences, over and above the obvious presences, which remain. I am often reprimanded for my conception of this history, but I keep close watch over that shop and my Samantha, just in case.

For my part, I cannot boast of a journey that shifts between international locales. I have never left America, but I am well-traveled and presently displaced from my birthright home. I acquired two careers for a time. I worked and I drank. I liked to drink liquor but I had to work. Therefore, I worked and I drank, but I soon worked, in order to drink, and before long, I drank in order to live, and after that, I began to move, and change jobs in an attempt to survive. At this point, I can honestly say that I am grateful for the eventual collapse of a rather sinister juggling act that I never desired to perform.

I have a new career now. I hold the title of Rooms Manager at a giant, downtown hotel. I suppose that I chose this job, but I was under orders at the time, and I was in need of funds, by which I might support my recovered life. Quite surprisingly, I feel a certain sense of gratitude for my new career, and I might even say that I enjoy my new life. Samantha delights in the fact that I work at the hotel of people, while she works at the hotel of flowers. That odd bit of information is one of our connecting points, by her way of thinking.

In fact, Samantha savors each ingredient that composes the spiritual alchemy, which has connected our previously disparate lives. Despite having evolved from vastly different physical beginnings, Samantha thinks we have been blended together inside one, common, spiritual flow. For example, Samantha is, by technical definition, a legitimate orphan. Her biological parents were taken in a tragic accident just after her first birthday. I, on the other hand, was raised to legal age by two biologically connected parents. I knew, more or less, a full line of distant relatives. I also had a host of friends with whom I spent the formative years of my life in close association. Nevertheless, while my heritage appears integrated and connected, I feel the enduring sense of separation and detachment that yearns from an orphaned soul. In glaring contrast, Samantha apparently pays absolutely no toll whatsoever for her legitimate status as an orphan, but instead, she moves through her life within the ethereal embrace of unshakeable acceptance and welcome.

In Samantha's words, I move through life under an assumed warrant, offered to a prospective affiliate, or as a guest of the larger world. She, on the other hand, belongs to God, and correspondingly, she moves about her life within the ranging bounds of the surrounding world. She does not need a particular place or people within which to find connection or fulfillment. Samantha says that I belong to her at present. She says that she is God's representative, and that she is God's appointed watchman for my journey. Samantha is a sort of mystical preceptor who is helping me negotiate the various chores and duties which are attached to a self-imposed initiation ritual. She wants me to 'know' the peace and security of place and belonging in something immutable and inseparable. Intellectually, I know that she is right, but my internal wiring system prefers the reassurance of physical sensation. Quite candidly, I find touch and taste and tone and sight and smell to be far more appealing and reassuring than the ineffable associations of her heart and soul. Nevertheless, she says that my temporary status rests upon tentative things.

Sam and I live in Kansas City. However, my original home, along with every physical thing to which I have ever felt linked, lives in Atlanta, Georgia. That declaration is, by Samantha's way of thinking, a description of the heart of my problem. Samantha's effort at refocusing my life just happens to involve the surrender of that place, those people, and all the things that I have ever embraced across all life. I suppose that I have been more or less willingly accommodating that pervasive submission since the day we met.

I suppose there exists a hidden benefit to our arrangement. I am no longer truly alone in my search or my surrender. Samantha is always with me; she and I move together, or as a team, in my quest for an ultimate place of fit and belonging with the God of my understanding. I'm glad that she is with me, and I think that, she is glad that, I am with her. I'm not quite sure why she accepts such a role in life, but I am no stranger to loyalty, nor am I a foreigner to a sense of gratitude. I cherish my new journey and my place beside my indomitable bride, even if a passing glance returns a slightly different appearance.

I might add one additional thought about our connection. I believe that Samantha and I share a mutual experience with the biblical concept, commonly known as becoming lost and being found. We are like her flower shop in this regard. While I have said that that shop was conceived and reconceived, I might also say that it has been lost and found, time after time. I was, most definitively, lost for a time, but wrecked or derelict might be a better description. I have also been displaced or lost, as if a casualty of a type of war, involving a healthy portion of tragedy. Nevertheless, and despite a personal ledger that lacks a significant number of entries that pertain to earned merit and practical reasoning, I have also been found by Samantha Morris Weatherlow.

While I don't believe that Samantha's detour ever threatened her physical status on this earth, she suggests that we have negotiated similar thickets and brambles, in terms of spiritual and emotional direction. Sam says that we have all been lost and found, in order that we might be together for the remainder of our lives. I am uncharacteristically soothed and, I suppose, warmly embraced by that thought. In my opinion, our peculiar blending of being and feeling in terms of lost and found is her favorite drop of relational glue.

At the moment, Sam was peering at me with her head angled slightly to the left. Her heathery hair was tied back in a thickly gathered ponytail. Her cornflower eyes appeared as if they were splashing heavy droplets of Pacific Ocean water in my direction. The expression she wore was pregnant; the image of imploring innocence, preparing to give birth to a wholly different emotion.

In clear view of my appraiser, I was compelled to take stock of my intentions. We were, or I was, preparing to do battle over a single razor blade cartridge. I was ready. The facts were on my side, and beneath the clear light of that truth, I was right. I wasn't playing at the moment, but neither was Sam's disarming repose a product of playful gamesmanship. She was inspecting me as I was inspecting her.

In addition to 'becoming found' and 'knowing' one another, over the past few years, we had also been practicing a cooperative relationship, partially empowered by the notions of giving and receiving. Sam has been teaching me to understand that taking and keeping, or hoarding, does not require the presence, participation, or the cooperation, of another party. She prefers my presence in her company. We are not takers or keepers, unless certain circumstances prevail.

An image came to mind as I was reflecting upon our respective positions in this simmering debate. I tend to view confrontational events in terms of predator and prey. In matters of relational jurisprudence, we are like the snake and the mongoose. On most occasions, I show my fangs, and express a few drops of pernicious poison, but Samantha is fearless, cunning and quick. My strikes are a product of conditioned reflex, rather than deadly purpose. Samantha says that I am not who I think I am. Her proof for that claim stems from observations of my proclivity to listen and consider, despite boastful arguments in my defense. More often than not, I accept defeat, and the compulsory counsel, against my position. Surprisingly, I rarely feel diminished by the outcome. At present, and, underneath the radiant effulgence of truly beseeching intimacy, I retracted my fangs of predatory truculence, and swallowed the poison that I was dripping.

I returned, haphazardly; "What if I had decided that I wanted your toothbrush or cigarettes, or your lipstick?"

Sam giggled, "Mon Chéri, if you had taken any those things, then I suppose that our conversation would be quite different."

"Same principal…no difference!"

"You may have any of my things, Chéri, even those things."

"Sam, you're making me mad, and I was almost ready to quit. Just stop it…I should be able to have my own razor blades."

"Mon Chéri, would you give me your razor blades?"

"Of course, but my blades are old, and I needed a new one."

"Oui, yes, but we will buy some new blades at the store today."

"You mean, I will buy some new blades at the store today."

"C'est dommage, Chéri, you are going out today, oui?"

"Yes, I am, but…."

"You said that you would shop for some things for our supper after finishing at the golf course, oui?"

"Yes, yes, Ok! Just forget it. I'll get some at the store on the way home. Maybe I'll buy you one of those lady razors that takes those special lady blades."

"But, I like using your old razor."

"Of course you do….good grief. I keep forgetting that you cherish the possibility of mixing our blood cells along the keen edge of chromium steel."

Sam giggled, again. I was glad. Her role as the mongoose in these affairs generally followed a pattern of live and let live. In other words, she was patient with my posturing. I suppose my tendencies in this regard developed quite naturally. My formative years were spent in actively reluctant conflict with a destructive alcoholic. She was a busy predator, constantly attempting to shape her life to fit inside some measure of peace, while perpetually inspiring the misery and torment that she desired to escape.

Mom came by her trade honestly. She and my father faced more than their share of tragedy and trauma early along their united pairing in life. As far as I'm concerned, my entire family was shaped, and fired, and molded, by a single traffic accident, which took the lives of my paternal grandparents. For my parents, that tragedy reconfigured a forward-looking appraisal of life, and afterward, the methods that they chose to employ in an attempt to accommodate that horror and the radiating loss, shaped my siblings and me.

My family acquired two peculiar distinctions in the aftermath of that accident. First of all, truth became an inspiration for insult and outage, and illusion provided the road to peace and safety. Natural aptitudes for perception and understanding became provocative occasions for confusion or hostility. We did not trust what we felt, saw or heard in my family. Subsequently, acceptance, compassion and understanding became rare commodities in my home. I was an unsuspecting recipient, but I am a repentant practitioner of those dubious traits.

I might describe my family as a lovely sailing regatta, peacefully tacking across a sea of gasoline. Our public appearance was different than our private operations.

Nevertheless, the first, smallest spark of controversy or conflict always ignited a raging conflagration. I can recall that, failing to return the ironing board to its proper closet inspired long days of seething turmoil. That small oversight remains with me to this day as an infamous standard for attending to simple chores. My soul sustains the permanent postmarks of temporary torridities.

Actively avoiding or obviously accepting responsibility for certain offensive missteps met with similar forms of retaliation, which was, more often than not, devastating. All of life became a crime in my mother's eyes. As far as predators and prey go, under my mother's watch, the assumed predator always became wounded prey.

I believe that my mother saw me as an offensive predator. That depiction is also a product of natural, but highly convoluted, logic. Inside my childhood home, typically accepted roles tended to become wildly skewed from commonly accepted norms. Such a thing seems to follow, when the rules of engagement are based upon illusion, rather than truth and honesty. I had a legitimate mother, who was an adult, but she was, in equal measure, an unpredictable and unmerciful tyrant and fiend. I thought I saw my mom enter my bedroom at night, but I always engaged with a monster, instead.

Reconciling this sinister conundrum installed a type of internal courtroom scene in my heart, mind and soul. I visit that court of inquisition quite regularly, and I have done so, throughout all remembered life. I stand trial for crimes relating to common actions and simple decisions. The charges I face are modest. I am accused of being less than I might have been. The verdict is, always, guilty. The sentence is humble. I don't think very highly of myself.

That courtroom is the second distinction which hails from childhood days with my alcoholic mother.

Nevertheless, I learned to defend myself inside my home. I developed a dependable set of tactical engagement routines. Most of the time, they are stored away like cleaned guns, quiet and harmless, but they are also ready for loading, and aiming, and firing when needed. Sam is attempting to discourage the practice of opening my arsenal. I actually love her for that, and quite fittingly, I feel the scorch of shame whenever I begin to jingle the keys to my heirloom gun cabinet.

Alongside a picture of innocence, I was gazing upon the personification of patience. I am gradually coming to understand that Samantha accepts the fact that certain learned behaviors are not going to disappear without a trace. Certain episodes of controversy and conflict inspire reflexive reactions. I am consistent in this regard, and over time, she has become prepared. I attempt to honor her patience and understanding through a legitimate willingness to amend old behaviors. Mostly, I apologize after the fact. She is also especially gracious in this regard.

Sam asked with tender concern, "Where will you be golfing today?"

Still prideful, I stated, "I'm not playing. I'm only practicing. I'm going out to Sunflower, to hit balls and practice my short game around their greens."

"And your tournament is next week, oui, yes?"

"It's not a tournament, it's a qualifier round."

She asked, "Quelle est la différence?"

My sensory accusers took this small request as an opportunity to renew an offensive position. I felt an electrical frisson shimmer through by body. However, the sweetly inquisitive tone of Samantha's words grounded that imbedded shock, and allowed a rational response to follow. In other words, I retreated once again, favoring my new home, over my old.

"Well, I suppose that a tournament is final, while a qualifier is a preliminary event, which weeds out the weakest players so that no 'hacks' make it to the real tournament."

"Then why do you need to play in the tournament if the best player is revealed by the qualifier?"

"Honey, it's like seeding in a tennis tournament. You have to keep winning in order to play for the grand title."

Samantha knows about the sport of tennis, but is less familiar with the nuances that surround tournament golf. She is, by my assessment, an accomplished tennis player. She played for her school team throughout her formative years. We play together, often. Our matches are surprisingly competitive. I use the term, surprising, quite honestly, but also somewhat shamefully. I was not raised to compete for athletic supremacy against women. Samantha says that we play for fun and exercise and also for companionship. I don't, or didn't, play for any of those reasons, until I met Samantha. We're also working on the issue of competitive performance.

Knowingly, Sam announced, "Voilà! Now I see."

I could not resist the urge. I said, "I suppose that I'll just go off to the course unshaven."

This small note of sarcasm raised no alarm, nor did it appear to incite the first note of concern.

Sam continued, "I do not know the Sunflower Golf Course. Will you be playing the qualifying event there next week?"

"No, that's going to be held out at Wolf Creek Country Club."

"I am confused again, Chéri? You are always telling me that the changes in the course make each round of golf new and different from the previous. It seems to me that you would feel more confident in your play if you knew something about the course that you will be playing for your event. Why aren't you going to practice at Wolf Creek?"

"Well, I don't have time, really. They're allowing practice rounds next Monday, but I've already arranged for the day of the tournament, and I don't want to take another vacation day to play the practice round."

"Why would you not go out there today?"

"Wolf Creek is private, and I'm not a member. Besides, I've been there before with Grant. He's a member, and I've played as his guest, several times."

"Mon Chéri, you mean you feel like a guest, even when you are doing what you love to do?"

Her comment inspired a mild alarm, which warned of a wholly new, but equally involved, interview regarding my association with guest status in the world at large. I instantly forecasted an undesirable delay in my practice session.

I spoke carefully, "Sam, honey, do we have to discuss this right now?"

With that question, Sam had breached the temporary buffer zone that protected potential combatants. She stepped toward my position in front of my bathroom sink. Before I realized, she was standing immediately in front of me. I felt the tips of her toes teasing the tips of my toes. Apparently, the rules governing the rights of personal space were being suspended for the moment. I felt her hands take me by the waist just above my hip bones. They moved lightly upward along my sides. They fluttered over the crests of my scapula bones and came around and under my arms to rest on my clavicles at both shoulders. I looked down into small indigo pools, slightly hidden behind a few wayward reeds of vanilla hair. I watched the image of golf begin to slip away, as if the lens of my mental telescope had been suddenly inverted.

Softly, I heard, "Dis-moi, s'il te plait."

"No… I mean, yes, sometimes… I mean, some courses are private. You can't belong everywhere. You have to be a guest sometimes. I mean, it's nice to be a guest sometimes. Like at Wolf Creek. You have to be invited. That's not so bad. It's not the same as you're thinking. Let's let this go, so I can go, Ok…?"

I felt Sam's hands slide off my shoulders and around my back. With her arms, she pulled me closer in an embrace that suggested a note of urgency. Reflexively, I encircled her small frame with my arms. I felt her hair and her head warming against my chest.

"Je t'aime beaucoup, Chéri."

"I love you too, Sam."

"I understand, you know. I have played tennis at many private clubs when I was in school. Sometimes the clubs were very lovely, and sometimes the courts were different, too."

"Well, see… we're the same. We're both guests sometimes. It's not so bad. Sometimes it's sort of a luxury to be a guest. In fact, if miracles do exist, mine have come in the shape of several utterly fantastic guest appearances at flashy golf clubs. I felt pretty cool on those occasions. Being a guest doesn't have to be a spiritual catastrophe."

Pushing back, Sam aborted our reconciliation nuzzle and resumed a posture of determined examination.

She stated, "Mon Chéri, you are an endless puzzle. Knowing you is like trying to follow Ariadne's Thread. You find an answer, but then you forget, and you begin your search all over again. There are many paths but, in each case, the final product is the same."

"What does that mean?"

Samantha took my face in her hands, and kissed my lips ever so softly. She murmured, "Oublie, Mon Amour, go play your game, but come home to me, s'il te plaît."

CHAPTER 2

A Day at the Range

....

I had decided to practice at Sunflower Golf Club for several reasons. In my opinion, they offer one of the best public practice facilities in the town. The driving range is huge. It's long and flat, and the turf is always hearty. There are an ample number of yardage markers downrange, and their positioning is fairly consistent with the actual distances. They offer a large practice green and a workable chipping area, featuring two new bunkers that have actual sand in the bottom. In addition, they also provide fairly decent practice balls and the option of purchasing a giant practice basket. In other words, Sunflower supports an actual practice activity, rather than simply providing a space for warming up before a round.

I suppose that you must acquire a taste for practice.

Quite frankly, I can't conceive of any activity across the span of my life to which I have invested considerable measures of time and attention without the hope of an immediately recognizable return. Don't get me wrong, I understand the purpose and the need for practice. I simply prefer the clarity of standing provided by a final outcome.

There are no scores in practice. I've played superbly on many occasions, after having arrived at the course five minutes before tee time, and still reeling from the previous evening's less-than-noble sporting endeavors. Then again, I've played terrible after having practiced and prepared diligently over an extended period of time, preceding my event. In the past, I've termed myself a player, rather than one who spends his time practicing. At other times, I've been grateful to swipe a few balls out of a small bucket during a stolen moment of time.

In terms of time, or devoted attention, I would say that golf has been far better to me than I have been to her. I use the feminine pronoun pointedly. As Samantha, and others, may well attest, I think of golf as my original bride. We share a bond that has existed for most of my remembered life. However, the feminine ascription and the marital imagery may seem highly disrespectful. I do not intend to demean my actual bride, or the institution of marriage. Nevertheless, while my sentiment in this regard touches upon my feminine partner, it actually reaches even further, toward notions of the divine.

When I say that golf has been better to me than I to her, my meaning is, at base, that she has never left my side. She willingly gives and receives in whatever capacity I choose to engage. Her embrace is always available. She has enticed and inveigled, and she has comforted and accepted. She has taught me. She has encouraged my effort, and she has soothed my pain. She is relentlessly forthright and faithful.

In return, I have embraced her charm and pledged my devotion. I have chased her and caressed her, and I have lusted for her pleasures. I have boasted of her nobility and beauty. I have shared my deepest intimacy with her. I have adored her. Nonetheless, I have been wantonly inattentive and frequently unfaithful. I have tried to change her and bend her to suit my will. I have felt scalding fires of jealousy in her company. I have accused her. I judged her aloof and callous, if not brutally unfair and deliberately insulting. I have cursed her. And, I have tendered my petition for divorce on multiple occasions.

In spite of these atrocities, we have remained betrothed or connected, but our relationship has changed over the years. I am the primary recipient of change, in this case. I have evolved, while she has remained pretty much the same. More succinctly, I have acquired a taste for practice, or rather, a willful desire to be consciously present in her company. I might offer that practice is a state of being which involves listening in equal proportion to speaking. It requires a willingness to give and an openness to receive. It is a time of nurture and support provided and accepted by both parties. In this regard, practice is much like an intimate conversation with my human bride on a Sunday morning. It is like discussing our plans for the future. It is like sharing a personal problem at work, or celebrating the other's success. It is like speaking of feeling like a guest at a golf club, and it is like accepting one more scrape from an old razor blade. Practice is spending time together, and practice is exactly, as my Samantha says, the process of coming to 'know' one another, better.

Prior to my most recent promotion, I could practice my golf game most any morning that I chose. I worked second shift at the hotel. I simply needed to finish and refresh myself prior to three in the afternoon. These days, and considering the added responsibilities owing to my new posting, I have to plan my practice sessions more carefully, and always on my off days. This being a Monday, I didn't expect too much traffic on the range. Nevertheless, you never know what might transpire at a public range.

I purchased a large bucket of balls and settled in a spot near the far edge of the designated hitting area. A large bucket contains approximately 130 balls. Long ago, I recognized that this number was fairly consistent among each bucket. Subsequently, I devised a practice regimen that allows me to hit thirteen balls with ten different clubs. I am somewhat compulsive in this way. Such a session requires just under an hour and a half. Afterward, I usually putt and chip for an additional thirty minutes. I find that I can maintain my golf marriage, and my human marriage, by exercising myself in this way once or twice each week.

I am always wary on the practice range. There is something about me or about my game that certain practitioners find attractive. This statement is not intended as a boast of any kind. Apparently, I don't seem to project an image which appears repellent or suggests that I prefer privacy. For example, during a session not long ago, I was approached by a gentleman who appeared more like an aging farmer than a senior golfer. He abandoned his practice routine, lit up a smoke and sauntered over to my position. He spoke as if we were old friends, and without the slightest regard for my status in mid-swing.

He said, "You, hit'n them balls real good. Is them new clubs ya got there?"

I hit the ball that I had been addressing in the forehead, which resulted in a sort of screaming missile that left the tee in a line drive trajectory, and never rose above a foot from turf. It skittered to a stop somewhere near the one hundred yard marker. I turned to address my unassuming assailant. He was wearing denim overalls, faded from use, rather than fashion, a golf shirt with a huge collar and an ancient pair of Nike sneakers.

Before I could respond, he asked, "Can I see one of them clubs?"

Apparently, he was a humble victim of braggadocios golf marketing, and simply thought that the club was producing what he had judged as admirable golf shots. The player, in this case, had little to do with the demonstration.

I said, obligingly, "Sure, hit one if you like…."

Without further invitation, he took the Two Iron from my bag.

He offered, "Hoo wee, this thing is thin as a butter knife! Can you hit it?"

I play with traditional clubs. My clubs are commonly described as muscle back blades. The description comes from the rounded shape across backside of the irons. They are not old in my book, but they are not new, either. I had purchased them in conjunction with a golf shop credit that I had won in a tournament, not long after I graduated from college. My clubs are ten years old. However, the design for my clubs had been in play since the first stroke was launched from a Scottish cow patty. There was nothing new to see in my bag. As a matter of fact, I had not changed the styling of my clubs since I was awarded with my first set. My brother and I split my dad's old set of Wilson Staff irons. He got the even numbers and I got the odds.

I said, "I can."

"Lemme see ya."

His request inspired an imaginary comparison, which placed my game on par with the likes of Ben Hogan. Hogan was a famous professional golfer, well-known for his exceedingly meticulous practice with the long irons. I was instantly percolating upon an effervescing pride. I took the club from my odd attendant, as would a player from a caddy. I carefully positioned a ball for the strike, and took my address.

For me, the awareness of an attentive audience creates a sensation, much like that which is produced by a drink of liquor or some type of drug. I change. The feeling is euphorically agreeable. There is a fresh sense of freedom, but the type or condition of bondage which has been removed is a mystery. I suppose the change in persona has something to do with the apparent fact that someone cares about what I am doing. I am a showman at heart, and simply relish any opportunity to reveal my true identity. Perhaps, I am simply describing the burden of vanity. Regardless, the prevailing sensation of freedom seems to inspire a higher level of performance than when I am the only person holding a ticket to the show.

My secret assessment of this change effect is that I am a better man when released from the unknowable chains that tether my true soul. For instance, I hold no doubt that I could, and did, perform every occasioned task, better, after having a drink of liquor. This assessment lies in direct conflict with every conceivable guideline. We have laws that condemn drinking and driving, for example. Nevertheless, every sensory-driven response to external stimuli seems to be tuned or enhanced during this initial state of release and freedom. I believe that this momentary reprieve is the underlying reason behind every drink or drug that is ever consumed.

My problem is that I am not satisfied with performing better. I prefer to perform at my very best, and in an attempt to inspire this noble outcome, I add another drink or two to the promising formula. I never had just one drink. This supplementary desire seems to be the more serious factor in the supervening problem. The equation that I believe, in my heart of hearts, to be true is patently false. One drink may render a positive alteration, but two does not inspire my best. An imperceptible shift of being takes place after the first drink. I am no longer simply showing off, but rather, taking command. Quite possibly, there exists an elusive point at which innocuous vanity transforms into baleful pride. While I might swim with the sharks in an ocean of vanity, I risk drowning in the slightest trickle of pride. If I were to suggest an image by which to associate my attempts at chemically inspired performance, it might include a diver's graceful bounce from the end of the board, followed by a botched swan maneuver, which plummets toward a non-existent pool. I have abandoned my experiments with chemical enhancement, but I cannot avoid the inevitable, but uninvited, curtain call that beckons for my presence.

In preparation for this particular performance, my primary swing focus was defensive. I preferred to avoid executing the dreaded 'mousetrap.' That swing designation is precisely appropriate. It involves a protracted take away or backswing coupled with an inconceivably reckless downswing and ball strike, exactly along the lines of carefully attempting to set the hammer on a mouse trap, but accidently letting it go before securing it under the hold bar. There is a momentary lapse of consciousness involved in this type of swing. All practiced poise prodigious planning, and preliminary preparation, is abandoned in favor of a banshee attack upon the unsuspecting golf ball. The result is rarely profitable.

Regardless of my efforts, I executed a controlled version of the mousetrap. I hit the ball almost squarely, but nearer the toe of the clubface than the center. The resulting shot flew away from the teeing ground as would a better shot, but rather than soaring as expected, the ball fluttered along an abbreviated flight path, powered by the grace of torsion mechanics. In other words, I had produced a shot that is commonly known as a fabulous fake. The ball landed just beyond the 150 yard marker, some sixty yards short of its intended spot.

My observer was, apparently, none the wiser. He remarked, "Hoo Wee, I cain't believe you can hit that thing!"

In my mind, I hadn't, but I could, and I would. With my club head, I corralled a second ball from the remaining pile, and prepared for my next attempt. This subsequent swing was much better, something that might have been recorded by a common camera, rather than the devices which are used to capture still shots of hummingbird wings. I struck this second ball, dead, solid, perfect, as they say, right in the middle of the clubface. It flew fast and straight, and high and far, well beyond the 200 yard marker sign. I held the follow-through until the ball had completely stopped moving. I turned toward my observer anticipating his celebratory congratulation. I found him examining my golf bag. Neither shot seemed to have mattered.

He spoke from his position of inspection. "Say, are you from around here? I mean, I ain't seen ya out here before, and I come out here to hit them balls, pretty frequent. The doctor told me to take some exercise when I can. He says I need to quit smokin' too. I thought I might try to play one day, sometime soon. I thought that, maybe, if you was from around here, that you and me could play. I have to walk though. I cain't ride one of them little cars. I need the exercise, 'cause the doctor says so."

This statement inspired a gaggle of simultaneous sensations. I felt the warmth of flattery. I sensed the weight of sadness. I felt the alarm of fear. I felt a desperate chill of guilt. I felt the constraint of responsibility, and I felt the pinch of violation. And, I was immediately swept into the ethereal courtrooms of my mind. I took the stand for questioning. Testimony in my defense was weak, and the subsequent verdict was quick and simple. Consistent with that judgment, I deflected my ingratiatory associate's request with a series of questions about his health, and his regimen of golf exercise. We spoke together for over thirty minutes. I left half my practice balls on the range that day. Mercifully, for my case, I have not seen him again, nor have we ever played together.

On another occasion I found myself on that very same practice range, but absolutely alone. I took my usual spot at the far end of the hitting area. The day was perfect. It was summer. The air was clear and very hot. I like hitting underneath a magnifying glass heat being projected by the sun. I had acquired a pleasing rhythm in my routine. I felt peaceful and satisfied. Nevertheless, in the midst of a short break, I noticed a rather large gentleman headed my way. He was apparently impeded by a pronounced limp, and his torso angled noticeably to the left, as if the bucket of balls that he was carrying was extremely heavy. I imagined an aging lineman from the more leathery days of the National Football League. In his other hand, he carried one golf club. I could not determine which club. Of the twenty-some odd open spaces on the range, he claimed the spot immediately adjacent to mine. Instantly, the huge range became oppressively crowded, by two souls.

This gentleman was apparently fixed upon mastering the one club he had selected for the day. He had purchased the large bucket containing 130 balls. He said nothing, as he began his session. I watched him dump the contents of the bucket on the turf. He took a moment to assess both the hitting area and the landing field. He pointed his club downrange, as if he were mimicking the famous home run image, immortalized by Babe Ruth. That particular pose of grand assurance was actually an integral step in his address. He repeated this targeting challenge to the world with each swat. His actual swing followed the aforementioned pattern of a practiced mousetrap, complete with fantastic speed and wicked violence.

The first slashing strike skittered along the ground for about fifty yards. He instantly pulled another ball from the pile and hacked again. He did this again and again and again, without any apparent consideration. With each swing, he expelled an exclamatory grunt that seemed to communicate equal measures of satisfaction and disgust. He did this repeatedly, until he had hit all 130 balls. He took no break during the entire melee. After the last ball had come to rest, somewhere among the settled hoard of wounded projectiles, he picked up his bucket and made his way back to the shop, limping and angled to the left. He hadn't been on the range for longer than fifteen minutes.

I attempted to remain inconspicuous but attentive during his visit to the range. If pressed, I might admit to authoring a strategy for personal defense. I considered having to defend myself, in a sort swashbuckling duel, using our clubs as swords. I calmed after his departure, and I completed my practice session. I asked the guys in the shop about this gentleman, as I was returning my own empty bucket.

"Hey, Curt, what's the world record time for hitting a large bucket of balls?"

"What?"

"Really, how long to hit all the balls in that bucket?"

"I have no idea. Why?"

"How 'bout fifteen minutes?"

"What the hell are you talking about?"

"That older gentleman that was just in here. You know him?"

"No, not really, but I've seen him. What'd you do, sit down there and watch his whole routine?"

"Didn't have to, he set up right next to me, down there on the end."

"What? The range is wide open!"

"Right! I took a break to plan my defense against an attack from the mad slasher."

"You're crazy...."

"Maybe—but I'm not alone."

I happen to believe that whether practicing or playing, golf reveals a glimpse of the status of my soul. In my view, my existing disposition within the world influences the shape of my game. This notion has nothing to do with the final score, but rather, with the journey that carries me to that end point.

If I am feeling settled and peaceful, the round or practice session might simply unfold in one way or another. If I were feeling slighted or wronged in a general manner, the round or session will be more deliberate or forced. In addition, the aspects of the game which lie beyond my control, such as 'The Rub of the Green,' the way the ball bounces on the ground, or flies through the air, seem to synchronize with my mood and affect. Nevertheless, I took note of my range associate that day, and I wondered what type of pains and frustrations he may have been experiencing outside and beyond the game of golf.

In keeping with my notions of a chance audience, a different, but similar, gentleman interrupted a previous practice session by asking if I might try his driver. Through a pronounced sheepishness, he offered that he thought the club might be defective. He knew better, but apparently needed some proof. I didn't even take a practice swing with his club. I teed a ball, and performed the most peacefully arcing strike of my entire life. The ball flew straight and high and long. I was pleased, while he was dismayed. The club was not the problem. I attempted to maintain an attitude of humble nonchalance. This episode was as much a lesson for me as for him. I have spent my share of time accusing clubs of defective status.

During my formative years with the game, I developed a wicked slice from the tee. I knew, without doubt, that my old driver was the culprit. Nevertheless, I went to the practice range out of an attempt to rectify the problem. I toiled away, hitting ball after ball, using the same swing with the same club. Despite this dedicated effort, I found myself failing to effect any improvement. I finally reached a point of hair-pulling insensibility, and I slammed the club to the ground out of violent disgust. Following this demonstration, I was approached by a gentleman whom I knew to be an accomplished player and a member of the Georgia Tech Collegiate Golf Team. He asked about my problem. I told him, in no uncertain terms, that I simply could not play with such crappy clubs. He asked me if he could try my driver. I was confused. I play right handed, but I knew that he was a 'south paw.' Nevertheless, he took my club, and teed a ball. I watched him turn my old club, toe-down inverted. He never took the first practice swing. He hit a gargantuan shot that sailed far and long and perfectly straight. Afterward, he handed me the club, and offered me a smile. He said, "Keep practicing, you'll work it out." I have never forgotten that lesson.

I acquired a different kind of audience, on another day. A middle-aged gentleman interrupted my session, asking if I might allow his charges to watch me hit fairway wood shots. He had two small children in his company. I just happened to be hitting that type of shot with my thirteen ball regimen. I was also hitting them very well that day. When properly played, that particular stroke is, conceivably, the most beautiful of all golf shots. The ball leaves the ground rather than a tee, but flies along a path, which is much like that of a driver. The contrasting whiteness of the ball rising against a cerulean sky is a captivating image. I hit several lovely shots for his children that day. He thanked me for the impromptu clinic. I offered that I was pleased to oblige.

On a different note, I was once interrupted by a decidedly frantic gentleman who announced a type of emergency situation. In this case, he simply inserted an exclamatory remark in between my practice shots.

He bellowed, "I can't decide whether to buy this driver!"

He continued, "It hits good, but it costs a lot."

Moreover, "I can't decide, and now, I'm out of balls."

Finally, "Do you mind if I take a few of yours to make sure?"

What does one say in this instance?

"Hell no! Get your own balls."

"Sure, I'm not doing anything. Make yourself comfortable."

"By all means, take all you want. That's a big decision. You shouldn't have to decide on your own."

"Better yet, why don't I just buy it for you? Then, your troubles are over."

I said none of these things, but I did offer a few balls in support of his dilemma. He took a handful, offered a small verbal gratuity and returned to his deliberations. I watched him depart after he had hit my balls. He went directly to his car. I have no idea which way he decided to go with the driver purchase.

For a game that, for many, presents an image of brutal exclusion and haughty snobbishness, I have seen the practice range accommodate a wide assortment of human nuance and diversity. In addition, for every remembered event of odd camaraderie or intrusive interruption on the public driving range, I can match it on the private range with an event of equal, if not greater, measure of outrageous entitlement and bizarre connection.

I was once approached by an aging curmudgeon, while practicing on a private range. I knew him by sight, but not by acquaintance. Through a resolute confidence, he proceeded to inform me that I was hitting from his spot. He stated that he always hit from this spot on Wednesday. Although startled by the accusation, I posted no debate, and immediately slid over, by a distance of two unnamed and unclaimed slots. The required shift is almost transparent, except for the loss of rhythm. That range was almost always empty, and practice balls are simply provided without an obvious exchange of currency. I watched the older man stand in my former spot for a time. For my part, I was assessing the possibility of being reported for the misdemeanor.

Before long, the caddy master arrived, carrying the man's huge leather golf bag. I was well acquainted with this gentleman. He set the bag on a stand, prepared a towel, and handed the member two clubs for the warmup routine. As the caddy master turned to leave, we shared a brief moment of communion. I rolled my eyes, but he smiled broadly, winked affectionately and twitched his head downrange. He knew, and I knew, but he seemed to say, 'Get over it and get on with it.' I forgot that lesson for a long time, but it has been returned to me over these past few years.

I suppose that I learned how to hit the golf ball on a public range, but I learned how to play the game on a private range. There's a difference. Hitting the ball requires some athletic aptitude, a measure of skill or talent, and a willingness to perfect certain mechanics over time. However, actually playing the game requires far more than the ability to propel the ball in a desired direction. There are rules that govern how and when that ball may be moved, and there are chores and timings and respects and favors and gratuities that must be learned and implemented throughout the progress of a game.

I learned how to hit golf balls at a public facility called Par 56. It was a combination driving range and golf course. They had a huge range and a small golf course. Scoring all pars on all holes added up to 56. That place was located across the street from an Air Force base. The general ambiance of "Par 56" mandated a type of militaristic poise under fire. Every few minutes the solitude of the range was bombarded by the soul stealing whine of heavy jet engines that propelled creaking transports and nimble fighters off of their field, and over ours, in route to mysterious destinations and secret missions.

Dad took my brother and I to that place on various occasions. I went there a few times on my own, when I was older. They also had a bar that featured cheap pitchers of beer and an indiscriminate eye toward legal drinking age. Nevertheless, I liked to hit from the top tier of their modern concrete teeing structure. We hit from formed slots that offered a padded green carpet with a rubber tee. I liked the benefit of the elevated launch pad, at that time. Back then, I had to hit with one of the 'house' clubs. I had no set of my own, and Dad used full sized, adult clubs. I always chose a three wood club that wasn't actually made of wood, but rather, solid aluminum. I knew it was aluminum because it was coated in a crusty white glaze of elemental oxidation, rather than rust. In contrast, the steel shaft was mostly brown rust, but not the head. In addition, the leather grip featured frayed indentions that fit my fingers perfectly. For some reason, that club was always available for borrowing.

Dad moved us to a private course, with a private range before too long. The private range was accessible and available to members' kids. I could go there on my own. I could hit all the golf balls I wanted without need for cash money. At that time, kids, or juniors, as we were called, weren't allowed to play the actual course until we passed the head professional's proficiency test. His test didn't have anything to do with how far or how straight we could hit a golf ball. It had to do with how to carry and rest our golf bags, how to rake a sand trap, a basic understanding of the critical rules of the game, and how to respect the course and our fellow players. Strangely, his final exam included finishing nine holes of golf in less than two hours. We had to walk and carry our own bag. That task is fairly easy if you're playing golf and not doing too many other things along the way.

Nevertheless, once approved and sanctioned, regular, junior play on the real course became available, but at severely rationed intervals, something like before sunrise, and after sunset, and never on Wednesdays or Saturdays. But, we could hit all the balls we wanted on the range. I hit thousands of balls while waiting for an authorized opening to play the game that I had learned from my secret mentor, and head professional golfer at our club. I suppose that I developed my game as an incidental result of the process of killing time. However, I learned something else while waiting at the private range. I began to think that the private range was better. I translated a bestowed quantity into a perceivable quality. However, that equation is one of any number of improper calculations that I have, throughout my life, employed as markers and guides for the sound judgment.

At this point, I can say without doubt that there is little difference in a public practice facility and a private driving range. I have seen both in pristine condition, complete with lush turf, miles of open landing fields, lovely white practice balls and accurate distance markers. I have also seen both, at certain points in time, when they appeared to have been strafed by napalm. Both have offered balls that 'buzzed' along their intended flight, but only at a private range have

I hit 'floater' balls into a lake, due to a shortage of available property. Nevertheless, before I underwent my change of mind, or my awakening, I acquired a contemptuous pride of right and privilege that precluded my presence at certain locations. I forgot that I had once enjoyed slashing balls from the upper deck of a concrete launchpad with an aluminum three wood. In fact, I quit playing for a long stretch of time when I no longer possessed a credential that would allow me to perform within the bounds of a respected private facility. That was, of course, to my detriment rather than the game.

This decision is the basis for my previous confession regarding the effective equanimity of the game in the face of blatant snobbery. As I said, the game has been better to me than I to her. I also mentioned that there is something else about golf that extends beyond the image of devoted spousal support. Golf is also, in itself, as an entity, beyond the grass and holes, and clubs and scores, and competition, quite god-like in its nature. The game seems to inspire a sense, or hope, or determination, to create something wonderful. It arouses a dawning effulgence, composed of sparks of freedom and invitation. There is an enveloping atmosphere of goodness, and grace, and honor. The air is freighted with possibility and obligation and responsibility. And, if I am being honest, I sense a weighty musk that reminds of certain poverties, suffering, and the chance of disaster. I have heard it said that a round of golf is like a life lived in full. You are born on the first tee, and you end on the eighteenth green, but the most important part is not so much the final score, but rather, how you negotiate the path between those two points. I believe this to be true.

In addition, through the teachings of my recovered life, and my bride, I have come to know and accept a god who is eternally present. All I ever have to do is join in his eternal presence. I have always thought of golf in this way. Making the switch was simple.

To this point, I've played many games of golf along the floor of my living room, and I've played the game throughout my own backyard. In fact, I have played a hundred golf games along the ground of my childhood yard, using a stick and a pine cone. Despite my youth, and my rudimentary implements, immediately following the inspiration of the challenge, every critical aspect of the game presented itself for guidance and evaluation. For instance, I remember feeling a twinge of guilt, following an intentional adjustment added to the lie of my pine cone. I recall wondering whether I could count a certain shot that didn't appear clearly successful. All I was doing was trying to hit that pine cone at the trunk of a chosen tree. Through the magic of imagination, these rudimentary forms of the game are often no less challenging or rewarding than a round played along a famous old course or as a contestant in the grandest tournament. What was happening underneath the notion of hitting that pine cone toward a determined goal? What was invited into that childhood game, if not the spirit of honor and goodness and grace that radiates from a divinely eternal presence that exists beyond and higher than me?

Moreover, the game is not simply managed or regulated by rules that govern play, but also by a set of rules that govern my behavior during that activity. These rules for behaving are termed, 'etiquette of the game.' In my mind, I observe the rules of etiquette for the benefit of my fellow players, regardless of whether they are physically present or potential followers. For instance, I rake bunkers for the benefit of following players, not for myself. I am called to assist, and to defer, and to provide support or counsel, and to commiserate and encourage. These rules for behavior, or etiquette, also magically appear and prevail when the game begins. I might offer, for the sake of brevity, that the rules of etiquette are simply the measure and means of caring for my fellow man. Overall, I suppose that to honor the rules that govern play is a form of loving God, 'with all my heart and soul and mind,' and to honor the rules of etiquette is to 'love my neighbor as myself.'

Finally, I suppose that the mystical materialization of this sense of righteousness and glory provides the basis for the notion that golf is a gentleman's game, and in this sense, is something that lies beyond the reach of a common folk. I believe that, the notion of exclusion often attached to the game is a persistent residue, which clings to the original understanding of the term, gentleman. In the beginning, gentleman was an indicator of societal title and status, and conveyed ownership of certain esoteric privileges. I might compare this to what I know of the church in general, where only a select few have been afforded a type of discriminating revelation regarding the presence and preferences of God. These early interpretations may have prevailed in the beginning, but they are not, in my opinion, a true distinction of the game or of God. Like God, golf exists and is available to all humanity.

Ever since I hit that first pine cone through the back yard or that aluminum three wood off that concrete deck, I have seen things in this way, but before meeting my Sam,

I was unaware of what I felt and believed. She has taught me that God prefers my companionship over my worship. And, that Jesus was far more concerned about teaching how to live and practicing how to behave than proper methods of paying tribute. In addition, Samantha and recovery have taught me that the founding principles of creation are love, forgiveness, grace and mercy. And, those notions come in handy when I realize that I am human, and I tend to wander from the assigned rules, both kinds, those that govern the game, and those that govern my behavior before my fellows. Therefore, I practice my life and my recovery by playing golf. I walk along the path of my game wrapped in the spirit of God, and I attempt to practice behaving in ways that might please God.

I returned to our apartment after a fairly profitable practice session, which proceeded without interruption from my fellow man. I also stopped off at the grocery store, where I purchased a whole chicken for our supper, and a triple-sleeve pack of razor blades. I was home just before my appointed time. I performed at home as I would in my golf game. I honored the rules of our game of life, and the rules of etiquette, which provide favor and grace to my beloved playing partner, Samantha.

CHAPTER 3

Post-Practice Reconnaissance

....

Samantha was not at home when I returned from my practice session. I was momentarily puzzled, but not alarmed. I felt my mind shrug. I sensed the slightest grip of tension sluice from my shoulders like water from a shower. Even with Samantha, I prefer to transition from one engagement to another without entertaining a human audience. This is an acquired trait, from which I've been unable to detach. During my formative years, returning to my home, following some type of appointment, which took me away for any considerable period of time, was always met with a probing inquisition. More often than not, my mother asked intimate questions, surrounding a particular set of private activities. Her interrogations were designed to divulge a suspected agenda, which breached the bounds of her personally permitted persuasions. I was never mindfully innocent, but I was not always actively guilty. I learned to expect officious prying, rather than affiliated concern. I was taught to operate on the grace bestowed by a reluctant pardon, rather than the peace which was granted by a certified acquittal. Samantha is patient with me, in this regard. She expresses a warm delight and a charitable concern on every occasion of my return.

I was fully expecting to find Samantha's smiling face, inside our apartment, upon this particular return. We had the day off together. Samantha prefers to synchronize our days away from our respective working engagements. This scheduling activity is something of a chore in our case. We are servants of the public market. In other words, our 'weekends' do not always correspond with the commonly observed weekend days. For instance, one of Samantha's busiest days in the shop is Saturday. She works most Saturdays. On the other hand, 'The Hotel of Flowers' is closed on Sundays, but 'The Hotel of People' is always open for business. I often work on Sundays. Playing host to large conferences and conventions often requires a full complement of housekeeping chores on Sundays. Groups disperse, and the house needs to be prepared and waiting for the upcoming business week. Neither of us enjoys the dependable regimen provided by a forty-hour, Monday through Friday, work week, so our arrangements work out well.

I was taking my 'weekend' on Monday and Tuesday of this week, and she had followed suit, at least, with the Monday part. Samantha wasn't officially working on this day, but she's the boss, and her presence is by her preference. I suppose that the surrounding loneliness sparked my memory. Moving through the empty silence of our small apartment, I recalled the probable reason for her unexpected absence. Sam had developed the notion of holding a flower-arranging class at her store. This was an unusual event for her, and her shop, and I assumed that she had been called away in order to attend to some final preparations.

This conception had evolved quite naturally over time. She was always telling me that she was just as much a salesman as she was a florist. She lamented the fact that she often sold more loose flowers than constructed arrangements, and that she spent a considerable amount of time suggesting methods and ways in which various types of cut flowers might add a touch of beauty and peace inside a home. These accounts continued for a period of time as a type of extended news report. I mostly tried to be a good listener. Then one day, out of obvious, but uncharacteristic exasperation, I heard:

"Je suis devenu un enseignant à la place d'un fleuriste!"

Alerted by the French and the tone, I followed, attentively.

"Traduire, s'il te plaît."

"C'est dommage, Chéri. I have become a teacher instead of a florist."

I attempted to affirm her observation. "Why don't you just give a class?"

"Je devrais enseigner une classe."

"Right...I think."

"Qu'est-ce que tu penses?"

I encouraged the notion, wholeheartedly, but I added that she might also think of her class as a type of honorable publicity event for the store, and one that would add revenue to the bottom line, if she chose to charge for the service. My astute attempt at warm affiliation was rewarded with a signature smack, which stung the deltoid of my left shoulder. Vulgar capitalism had incited the wrath of virgin altruism. In my opinion, Samantha was feeling a little anxious about the prospect of teaching an artform that she understood through sheer talent, as opposed to legitimately credentialed authority. She was, after all, the more officially recognized academic in our pairing. I held no doubt that she would perform the duties befitting an excellent teacher, and without the slightest difficulty. In the end, practical measures prevailed and the idea began to take shape, as a class, first, a clandestine act of publicity, second, and a nominal revenue stream, lastly.

Moving toward the shower, I recalled that her first class was scheduled to meet on Tuesday evening of this week. This recollection inspired a sparking frisson, which shuddered through my body. Earlier, I mentioned that the class idea had evolved, but like the more famous process, it did not simply end with the notion of the class. The current mutation had occurred during my watch, but without the slightest hint of awareness or invited counsel. I was simply swallowed up by the flow.

I suppose that the notion of a class hints at the idea of a social gathering. I should have expected something from the beginning, but I was resting proudly upon my original contributions, rather than thinking of improving my reputation with new thoughts. Nevertheless, the event was redesigned before it ever began. It became a couples' occasion, at some point in time, between the original proposition and the printing of the official invitations. Due to certain foresights and delights that elude my scope of vision, Samantha's class had been opened to the men, who were attached, in one way or another, to prospective female students. I learned of this change through a type of mandatory invitation. There is but one RSVP check box on such a request, and it is pre-checked, and underscored with the word 'Attending' emblazoned in blood ink. Samantha said that the class was the perfect occasion to inspire a measure of shared intimacy between promised couples. I was to be an integral part of the promotion aspect; a type of male fertilizer, so to speak, which was being sprinkled about in hopes of germinating a fecund crop of spousal support.

I was toweling my hair after my shower, when I sensed a change in the atmosphere. Despite the vigor and fluff of that routine, I knew that Samantha had returned. I felt her presence, as if the warmth of her soul was dispersing the chilly emptiness inside our apartment. I did not, however, expect her to be watching my chores.

In the next moment, I heard, "Comme c'est beau!"

I turned to face her, but casually, as if I were wearing clothes. I took my time, before tucking the towel around my waist. Sam was standing in the bathroom doorway, exactly as she had begun our day in negotiations over the misappropriated razor blade cartridge. As I hoped, she was startled by this unexpected offering of performance art. We are not typically exhibitionists in our home.

She exclaimed, "Oh la la, Chéri!"

"Girls shouldn't be spying on boys in the locker room."

Sam crossed her arms, feigning a serious expression. She chirped, "I wasn't spying!"

Coolly, I asked, "Well, do you…I mean, are you planning on supervising all my bathroom activities in the future?"

Still resolute but giggling, she said, "Peut-être."

I smiled, adding, "Well then, I might just return the favor from time to time."

"Ma oui, Chéri, and you might find me sitting next to the sink to do my makeup!"

"What?"

"Oui, yes, and sometimes I use your razor instead of mine."

"You wouldn't."

"Voilà! There are many things that you do not know."

"So, you think that I haven't been paying attention in class?"

"Oui, yes, perhaps you are distracted."

"Maybe the teacher skips around too much."

With that comment, I watched Sam give a subtle shake to each foot. She stepped out of her sandals, and padded across the floor tiles toward my position. I have a habit of noticing her footwork. In this case, I was efficiently enchanted. I felt primordial engines ignite. She took me by the waist. I idled. She tenderly maneuvered her hands upward, along my sides, over the crooks and bends of bone and muscle. They rested about my neck and shoulders. She pulled herself up on her toes, and gazed through dusty vanilla reeds of tousled bangs. I pulled her close, and bent to meet her. I touched my forehead against hers. We stood breath to breath as ancient gears engaged.

I whispered, "I've been missing you."

"I've been at the shop, preparing for our other class."

Emboldened by the quickening hum, I took a chance.

"I thought that you smelled a little funny...."

She instantly dropped her head and attempted to push back.

I held her firmly, while I continued, "...like chlorophyll and rose petals."

The struggling was replaced by one chuff of laughter. Her face came back to meet mine.

I added, "You should take a shower."

I watched lapis pools become cobalt oceans. She appealed with one phrase.

"S'il te plait?"

"I will."

Sometime later, I was lying, right side down, between the sheets of our new bed. I was pleasantly entwined and entangled with my bride. My face was snuggled into the crook of her neck. I was blowing damp strands of saffron hair. My only agenda was to prevent being tickled by an obstinate filament. I felt Sam stir.

She said, "Mon Chéri, do you think that the class will be successful?"

"I thought it went well, but we can try again in a minute if you want."

I felt a pinching sting on the top of my left thigh. Apparently, the sheets prevented the more common notice of correction. I was pleased, but adequately adjusted, and I replied appropriately.

"How can you be worried? As far as I'm concerned, you're the best florist in town. And The Hotel of Flowers is the best shop. What can go wrong?"

Sam rustled herself, which disengaged our limbs. She sat up and shifted toward the headboard. She fluffed a pillow for her back and head, rearranged the covers, and pulled her legs up. I was left alone, lying on my back, inspecting the ceiling. We were beginning another class of a different type.

"Mon Chéri, I have not been taught, yet I am becoming a teacher. I do not know the proper words."

"What words?"

"The words! The words that describe techniques for constructing and arranging and for the flowers."

"Come on…just do the whole class in French. Everyone will think that you are a genius, and sexy too! What's the

French word for Rose?"

"Arrête-ça, s'il te plaît. I should know…if I am going to teach."

"You cannot teach what you don't know. Good grief, I'm starting to sound like you."

"Oui, yes. That is the problem."

"Honey, I would have no problem teaching someone to play golf, but I'm not a professional, nor have I had many official lessons. I would just tell them about what I know."

"But, would you accept their money for the lesson?"

"In a minute!"

"La vache! You are being silly."

"Honey, what are you trying to do? You're not handing out degrees in horticulture. You're trying to help people who want to use your flowers. That's a pretty good thing to do, and you happen to be a busy woman with a successful business. You're spending your time, and you're opening up a pretty cool shop for people to come and hang out for a while. You're giving and you're receiving. Sound familiar?"

"Merci, Mon Amour."

"Look…as far as the teaching words go, just let them do their thing with the flowers. That's kinda what you do… right? And, for the flowers, I'd bet that you know the name of every single flower in your shop. Just talk about what's in play. You can't be expected to know the Latin name for every type of flower in the world. I think that you're all set. Now, who's coming?"

"My friends from the tennis club are coming with their husbands, and they have invited two other ladies from the club, but I only know them by acquaintance. I expect ten, and, with you and me, that makes twelve. I have arranged separate workstations, on my tables in the back of the shop. The class is full."

"Are the husbands tennis guys?"

"I only know two of the husbands, but yes, I suppose that they are tennis guys, as you say. They play in the men's division at the tennis center, near the plaza. Does that matter?"

"Not really, but I'm not sure that I know tennis people."

"Qu'est-ce que c'est?"

"I can know someone fairly well from watching their golf game. I mean that, after playing a round of golf with someone, I can pretty much tell you what they are like in the other parts of their life."

"Mon Amour, you sound as if you are judging books by their covers."

"No, I'm not. I said that I have to play with them to know."

"Give me an example, s'il te plaît."

"Ok, here's an example. Not long ago, I played with a guy who was dressed in a wild-looking outfit. He looked almost like a professional from television. His slacks were of a bold plaid, and the color of his shirt was a perfect match for the one thread of color that seemed to organize the geometry of the plaid. He wore a real hat that was banded around the crown with a strip of fabric, which matched the plaid of his pants. You could not miss him. Truth be told, I felt a touch of envy. However, his shoes were plain old black and white saddles that he'd probably worn for years. They didn't match anything."

"Mon Chéri, this story is about you."

"No it's not."

"Why were you looking so closely?"

"I said that you couldn't miss him. An outfit like that says something. You don't just wake up and throw that stuff on your back and head out to the course. For all I know, he thinks that if he dresses appropriately, he can play like one of the pros from television, or maybe he is a pro golfer, and he's run across a patch of bad luck. I mean, he's out there with the rest of us for some reason. He's a mystery, at first. Maybe he has a flamboyant personality, or he's a clothes horse. Then again, what about the shoes? Why match everything but the shoes? But, who has shoes to match every outfit?"

"I do."

"What? Oh yeah, right, and I love you for that, but it's a little different."

"You love me for my shoes?"

"No. Can we pretend that I didn't just say what I said?"

"Non, nous ne pouvon pas!"

"Really?"

"Non, I will not pretend, but, I will wait. You may finish your story. I want to know how you judge people from their golf game, and how you judge me for my shoes. Vas-y s'il te plaît."

"Ummm…yeah, well, here goes. So, I'm sitting in the cart with my sartorial partner. We're waiting for the starter to release our group. At that point, all I know about him is his name, and of course, the way he is dressed. In the meantime, two other guys pass by in a different golf cart. They are apparently well acquainted with my partner.

"One of these guys barks, 'Hey Ron, nice outfit, your wife been shopping again?'"

"To which Ron returned, 'Yeah, I'll tell her you noticed. Maybe she can help your wife pick out something for you. Hey, try to keep it in the fairway, and don't hold us up!'"

"Then Ron looks at me and says, 'My wife likes to buy my clothes. She likes me to look nice, like they do on TV.'"

"I say, 'No worries here, looks good to me.'"

"Now, I have to spend the next four hours in the immediate company of this man. To one degree or another, we are forced to share the fluctuations of emotion, which are inspired by the results of our endeavors on the golf course. In the end, Ron turned out to be a pretty good player. He was even tempered across good shots and bad. He was appropriately focused on his game the entire day. He wasn't too chatty or overly needy. He also seemed honest and forthright with the rules of the game, and that includes me. He was not overbearing or intrusive toward my play. Overall, I thought that he was a better playing partner than I might have drawn. As for the fancy outfit, I never saw him show the first note of concern. His shirttail was half untucked at the end of the round, and his pants were a tad muddy from an unfortunate incident near one of the creeks.

"All in all, I felt like I spent the afternoon with myself, almost. Here is my point. Each of the characteristics that Ron demonstrated on the golf course probably translates to the other aspects of his life. He is most likely even-tempered and personable. He is probably honest and fair. He is socially astute and not overly concerned with his image. In fact, he leaves that part of his life to his wife. What I don't know is if he delights in pleasing his wife, or whether he simply indulges her fantasy. I wouldn't go so far to say that he is dominated by his wife, but he definitely trusts her. He is not what he wears. He is Ron underneath the outfit that his wife prefers.

"The difference with me is I'm not going to dress like that unless I have a chance of playing the part. To me, if you look flashy, you had better be able to play flashy."

"Why does that matter, Mon Chéri?"

"When I was a kid, I used to watch the better players. I mean the men who were real members of the club, but also the guys that played better than most of the other men. And, I watched the pros playing on television. They all seemed to demonstrate a confident swagger, which was set off by what I thought was a sharp outfit. I suppose that I simply coupled the two; look sharp and play well. Therefore, at least in my mind, to truly belong within the game, I had to do both."

"That sounds exactly like something that you would do, but that is not the intention of the game."

"And…I know that, but I don't feel that."

"And, you watch what other people do, in order to predict your competitors."

"That's right. You can tell a lot about someone from just simple mannerisms, claimed liberties and preferred practices. For example, some men use head covers for their iron clubs. That's all well and good, but it tells me something about that person. I'm fairly meticulous about things. I like to look sharp, I try to play by the rules, and not least, I try to swing the club smoothly with each strike. That's not as easy as it sounds. Nevertheless, I would never consider head covers for my irons. The thought of removing those things, and replacing them, before and after every shot is a mind-boggling chore, in my mind. The man that can do that is different than me. He is meticulous in a different way. I'm not saying that that's bad, but it is a notable trait that might affect a future negotiation session, over a ruling, or a score, or something."

"Perhaps he has great respect for his possessions."

"Possibly, but still, those things are made out of steel, and they are intended to strike a hard object that is lying on the ground, and that ground might be rocky. They're called irons for a reason. Tough tools are intended to do rough things. They can't possibly remain in pristine condition."

"I've seen leather covers used for knives and axes."

"Yes, I have too, but I always thought of those scabbards as protection for me, rather than the blade. I might drop it on my leg or hand or something."

"Oui, yes, peut-être."

"What do you think?"

"But, Chéri, unlike tennis, when you play golf, your opponent is really the golf course, and perhaps, you, rather than the other players…"

"Right again, but still, these amateur competitions are filled with a diverse group of men who bring a range of unexpected human intrigue into the game."

"Qu-est-ce que c'est?"

"I once played with a gentleman who timed my shot routine. He said, 'Do you realize that it takes you eleven seconds to hit the ball?' I'll never forget it. And, I never forgot that remark throughout that entire round. I mean, I wondered, and I considered, and I became frustrated, and finally, stirred to anger by that odd announcement. His comment affected my play to some degree. And, by the way, that guy was a tax auditor."

"What do they say in your recovery program?"

"Yes, I know. Let it go, but that's easier said than done."

"I understand."

"Another time, a competitor, a complete stranger, stepped over to my position on the tee. He spoke with the solemnity of a doctor, sharing a vital concern for my health. He said, 'I hate to hit a hook off this tee. That rough over there on the left is a jungle.' That remark did not fit the speaker in this case. Up until that point, I would have characterized him as somewhat proud, or entitled. Sharing a personal fear, or expressing concern for a competitor, did not seem consistent with my passing assessment. Consequently, I interpreted his remark as a rather obvious and somewhat sinister act of gamesmanship. I thought that he intended to inspire that very shot from my next swing. However, while his suggestion succeeded in disturbing me, I wasn't focused on that particular type of shot, but rather, I began to pay closer attention to his game, throughout the remainder of the day. In fact, I noticed that he availed himself of certain questionable liberties, concerning the whereabouts and general lie of his golf ball. You see, this makes my point, as well. His gamesmanship told me something about his person, and I suspect that this trait carries over, in one form or another, in the general conduct of his life."

"Oui, yes, I do not like him."

"See?

"Back when I was a kid, I used to play in local junior tournaments. And, for some reason, I seemed to be paired with the same kids, time after time. I came to know them in tournament golf, but not through school or any type of social occasion. One of kids, with whom I was paired on multiple occasions, was always accompanied by his mother. She walked along with our group. We had to carry our own bags at the time.

"First of all, try to imagine that scene. Try to imagine, me, a teenaged boy, attempting to demonstrate certain skills and talent, in the midst of a critical performance, while a strange mom was overseeing the whole operation. Hell, back then, all moms possessed a certain Carte Blanche. There was no telling what she might say, or do, and I would have paid attention. In addition, there was this mystical tug of filial allegiance that wanted something from this substitute mom. I mean that a part of me wanted to avail myself of some type of motherly service or commiseration. Was I hoping that she might hand out sandwiches, or just a slice of motherly praise, for good shots, here and there? I don't know. The whole thing was bizarre.

"Nevertheless, this kid, the son, experienced some kind of emotional crisis during every round. He would throw a tantrum and collapse into a wild crying jag. His mother never sympathized, but rather, like a drill sergeant, she commanded the kid to shape up and get with the program. Hell, I tried to shape up, but from what condition I don't know. I simply felt guilty. I can still see the spectacle, her carrying his bag down the fairway, and the kid, wailing away, in tow. She sort of dragged him along by the sinews of motherly will. Those rounds involved far more than swing mechanics. I sometimes wonder whatever happened to that kid. But, to be fair, I suppose that I walked a similar fairway with my own mother."

I noticed that Sam had turned her face away and to the right. She was laughing, albeit reservedly. I saw the covers of the bed vibrating, evenly. I actually enjoyed coaxing her in this way. I loved her, in part, for her peculiar ability to express sympathy through amusement. She commands a keen appreciation for the coexistent presence of comedy and tragedy.

I queried, playfully, "What is so funny? I'm right here. You're not hiding very well."

"Mon Chéri, you are funny."

"That is not the point!"

"Oui, yes, and I have seen similar things on the tennis court, as well, but I never thought to consider the person behind my competitor. Perhaps, a tennis match moves too quickly. But, we will be with my friends tomorrow. We are not competing. No one is bringing their mother, nor do I expect to see any mischievous floral psychology."

"I think that I'll wait and see about that last notion."

"Mon Amour, now I want to know about the shoes. You promised to tell me about the shoes."

"The shoes? Oh, yeah, well, shoes are like a fifteenth golf club. I think that most people think of them as equipment, rather than attire. You can't just buy a pair of golf shoes for every outfit. You have to order special shoes. That effort takes some time and thought. I suppose that Ron's wife doesn't think to go that far, or he has told her that shoes are, indeed, equipment, and not clothing."

"Non, Chéri, not those shoes, my shoes."

"I thought we were going to discuss that later, or just forget it."

"C'est plus tard!"

"Ok, your shoes.

"Hmmm…here's an idea. If you'll go slip on that pair of red suede pumps, and come back here, I'll show you."

This remark ignited a small firestorm of activity, which emerged from the neighboring position on the bed. I had anticipated this very response. However, rather than attempting to escape from the conflagration, I rolled over, in an attempt to smother the sparking flames of affront and disgust. I laid myself lengthwise, on top of Samantha's body. I tucked my face into her chest just underneath her chin. I received one glancing swipe across my right shoulder, while I gathered her around with my arms. A quick review of my mental scorecard showed that we were now even.

I spoke mindful words, which were somewhat muffled by my defensive position.

"Are you mad?"

"Chéri, do you think of my shoes as, equipment, as you say?"

"I do not."

"But, Chéri, do you think that I am what I wear, as you say?"

"I do not."

"But Chéri, do you judge me, as if I were one of your golf partners?"

"Maybe, but not exactly. You practice a type of inadvertent gamesmanship, which works in reverse. I mean that, in our game, you tend to inspire, rather than discourage, my ability to play well."

I felt Samantha relax, almost as if a sore tooth had been splashed with Novocain. I slowly raised my face to meet hers. I found sapphire lasers, focused precisely upon my sheepish grin. I felt her arms surround my back. I also felt a collection of sensations, which were vaguely similar to bee stings, but arranged in the curved symmetry belonging to the fingernails of small hands.

"I like my shoes, Mon Amour."

"I know you do, and so do I."

"But, you said that you loved me for my shoes."

"That is true, but that is not the only truth."

"Pourquoi dirais-tu ça?"

"My comments pertain to me, rather than you. I am revealing myself to you, My Love."

"Je vois."

"We have a game in progress here. We are the only players, and we make all the rules. And, I might even say that I am winning, for today, at least."

"Que gagnez-tu?"

"You, of course."

"Merci."

"You have taught me everything I know."

"C'est dommage. Like I said in the beginning, I am not sure that I am a good teacher."

I released my weight upon Sam after this comment, and I kissed her softly on the lips. She returned my gesture, but reapplied the bee stings. I couldn't tell whether this reaction was meant to inspire or discourage my advance. I held my place and the kiss. Momentarily, prickly pains were replaced by pleasant pressures. We disengaged after a time, but we retained our places.

I asked softly, "Am I too heavy?"

"Non, Mon Amour, I like you there."

"Good, I may not move for the rest of the evening."

"But, you said that you were cooking tonight."

"I did, and I will, but later. I may have another assessment to perform, first."

Sam giggled, and added, "Je t'aime beaucoup, Jackson Weatherlow."

"Jet t'aime, Mrs. Weatherlow."

"Mon Chéri, did you see the note that I left for you?"

"I did not, where is it?"

"C'est dommage, Chéri. I left it on the bar, in clear view."

"Is it a love note?"

"Non, Chéri, you received a telephone call."

"Telephone call? Who was it?"

"Chéri, you must call them back. I do not know."

"Who was it? Did they sound serious?"

"We should get up. You can see the note, and you can begin our supper. I will help you. I am feeling hungry."

"Was it from work?"

"Up, Chéri. Let me up, s'il te plaît."

CHAPTER 4

Fantastic Invitations

....

A s was our custom, I heard concerned words wafting from a different room.

"Mon Chéri, you did not sleep well last night."

"I'm sorry, did I keep you awake, as well?"

"Non, merci, but I knew that you were not at peace."

"It's that phone call."

"You might have called last night."

"It was too late. That area code is from Atlanta. They were already an hour later than us. Besides, Mr. H.D. Woodson, sounds serious."

"You are imagining professional attire, and you are judging his game and his person to be superior in some way, oui, yes?"

"Yes, but I think that you need the word, 'court,' in there somewhere."

"Mon Chéri, why are you so worried? You have been dedicated in your recovery. Have you not cleaned up the past, and made amends, to the best of your ability?"

"Yes, Mrs. Wilson," I playfully mocked.

"Qu'est-ce que c'est?"

Sam emerged from the bedroom in the next instant. She met me in the corner of our kitchen, at the counter, near the refrigerator. I was preparing a light breakfast. By our standards, we had not slept late, but the hour was not early per common practice. Our careers do not require the pre-dawn regimen of farmers.

She was wearing a top that was cut from a wispy chambray fabric, muted by a sage green color. The bodice was appointed by vertical pleats, which gave a fitted appearance to the upper portion, while the tail section flared away like a skirt. She wore billowy slacks, which appeared as linen, but without the wrinkles. They were the color of sand. I pictured a beach on the Atlantic Ocean, rather than the sugar-white stuff along the Southern Gulf Coast. I became aware of the fact that Sam and I had never been in any ocean together. She was also holding an additional garment. This piece was periwinkle in color, and appeared to be cut from a cotton poplin fabric. She held it draped over her left arm. Her shoes were hidden from my view, underneath the wide hem of her slacks.

If one were to categorize women, in terms of hair color, Sam would belong to the blonde group. However, her hair color is a salt and pepper version of blonde, where the salt is pearl, but the pepper is bone. The result yields a soft humming hue that calls to mind the color of a vanilla milkshake. Beneath the falling mane, but above the drapes of her delicate outfit, she appeared as a face moving through mist or fog.

"Tell me again, s'il te plaît. I did not understand your last words."

"Never mind…it was nothing, really. You look lovely, by the way, sort of soft and gauzy, and touchable."

I stepped toward her, and took her with my hands. I settled them along her sides, in the curve of flesh that rests above her hip bones. I have no doubt that, that particular spot was specifically designed to fit my precise grip. Sam peered into my eyes.

"Merci beaucoup, Chéri."

"If this is a teacher outfit, I'm gonna be distracted in class."

"Easy, please. When are you going to call?"

Instantly reoriented to the occasion, I answered, like a student to a teacher.

"I'll call before I leave. I promise."

"What do they say about the past?"

"Listen, trying to shut the door on that stuff is foolish. Someone is always knocking."

"Mon Chéri, if you look for goodness and grace, instead of disaster, you will feel better."

"I know, I know. God didn't bring me this far just to throw me in the ditch…."

"Non, Chéri, you are practicing for life and golf today. You are going to become better at both games."

"You know what? That's actually helpful."

"Oui, yes, we are all practicing to become better at all our games."

"Hey, what's this jacket on your arm?"

"This is one of the smocks that I ordered for the shop. I brought it home last night. I wanted to spend some time together, but that hasn't helped. I do not like it."

"So, you're breaking up with your jacket?"

"La Vache! I ordered the shirts and the smocks together. I ordered the same colors, periwinkle with the embroidered logo in pink and yellow. The shirts are fine, but the smocks will not match."

"Match what?"

"My outfit! Or, my guests' outfits!"

"What? Isn't that thing supposed to protect your clothes from plant juice or sap or something?"

"Oui, bien sûr, but the ladies may not wear them, if they do not match."

"Honey, just let them mess up their clothes once or twice, and then they'll wear them."

"Peut-être. We will see. I cannot send them back. They have our name on the breast. Now, will you arrive at six, like I asked?"

"I will."

"You will be finished with your golf and your telephone call?"

"Oui, Madame."

"I want to hear about both, when I see you."

"I'll prepare a full report, if I'm still here, that is, and not being extradited to Georgia."

"La Vache! I will see you later. Je t'aime beaucoup, Mon Chéri. Kiss, s'il te plaît."

"What about breakfast?"

"I have to go, I am anxious too, Mon Amour."

"I know…I love you. Don't worry. The class will be great!"

"Au revoir, Chéri."

I was not kidding Samantha about making that call to Atlanta. The name that she had recorded appeared to fit the nomenclature surrounding several grim events from my former life. I was seeing lawyers and judges, and wooden benches and balustrades, and fences of various design and purpose. I hadn't been a criminal of any sort during my drinking days, but some of my decisions had led me along pathways that skewed from expected norms. I had to answer for those tangential acts, and I had been ordered to make my amends in an official capacity.

The time was nearing ten o'clock in the morning, which meant that Atlanta was nearing the lunch hour. I had to make my call. I heard the voice of my mentor barking in my head.

"You don't know what you don't know."

"Move a muscle and change a thought."

He was always right. The problem was overcoming that first step, a huge speed bump composed of trepidation and cold fright. Nevertheless, I had been walking a different road for five years. I took a breath, and my note, and I sat next to the telephone in our den.

Across the passing seconds, before I depressed the buttons on the receiver, I reflected. I wondered about the motivating energy involved in placing my call. I wondered if I was moving in the proper direction in order to appease Samantha, and I considered whether I might be attempting to please my mentor, as well. I concluded that a better man may have moved in the right direction of his own accord. Nevertheless, I placed the call. My electronic inquiry was intercepted on the first ring.

A chipper voice greeted my dismal chore. I heard a woman. Common words were delivered through a distinctly southern melody that blended sound with timing and breath. Her manner was pleasant but objective.

I heard, "B. F. W. Good morning, how may I direct your call?"

I was momentarily frozen by conjured images of automobile tires, and telemarketed flowers. I felt legitimately startled and confused.

I stammered, "I'm sorry?"

My apparent confusion provoked a practical expansion. I heard, "Breedlove, Fitzpatrick and Woodson, Attorneys at Law, how may I direct your call."

I hung up. I was instantly afflicted by a blazing fever. My heart rate and blood pressure soared. I was also frozen stiff by a chilly gust from a lonely wind. I felt heat emanating from my face and scalp, but a general sense of frostbite surrounding my soul. I felt desperation.

I became a captured witness. A condensed history of my drinking days passed through my consciousness. I watched the brilliant pageantry of a lamentable parade roll along the screens of my memory. I saw every dubious liberty, clumsy misstep, trivial infraction and glaring transgression. I was accused and convicted and alone.

I turned back toward the telephone. It seemed to have changed color. I saw a waxy grey sheen shrouding a device which was molded from lead. In that instant, I was treated to another remark that had been branded upon my brain by my mentor.

"Sometimes the telephone will seem to be the heaviest object in the world. That's a lie, pick it up, and use it, before you do something that you'll regret."

I wondered if that statement was like all the others. Did it hold true across all instances? I puzzled about how they had found me, and why, after all this time. I was 800 miles, and some 1800 days, from that tedious territory and tumult. Our marriage license came to mind. I checked myself for not accepting Samantha's definition of marriage, and thereby avoiding the official recording of my name. Next, I thought of my tax returns. I thought of the year I had innocently omitted the paltry part-time pay that I had received from a holiday stint at the men's store. I had misplaced that W-2 return form that year. I recalled that the amends for that inadvertent omission had erased most of my intentional commission.

I was extracted from this encroaching darkness by an infusion of pure grace. I recalled yet another adage that I had been given, by my journey in recovery. I recalled words that worked like a key, which unlocked the gates of an unusual type of prison.

"No one thinks as much about you as you think they do. You're not that important."

I also recalled my own notions concerning grandiosity. Grand is an adjective that modifies a sense of success, or failure, in equal measure. I took advantage of this unsolicited reprieve, and I readdressed the telephone. It was resting peacefully, on the side table, next to the sofa, and had been, during the interlude of horrors, miraculously restored to a pleasant, green hue. I lifted the receiver and I re-dialed the number for Mr. H.D. Woodson.

This second call was answered in the same manner as the first.

I heard, "B. F. W. Good morning, how may I direct your call?"

I offered, "Mr. H.D. Woodson, please."

"May I have your name, please?"

"Jackson Weatherlow."

"One moment, please. Yes, Mr. Weatherlow, I have your name on my list. Mr. Woodson is expecting your call. Please hold for a moment."

My self-induced fever returned during the brief interlude that followed. Familiar images played to a captive audience. I tried to focus on breathing.

"Mr. Weatherlow? I have Mr. Woodson. Hold for connection, please."

I heard a click, followed by silence, and then a gentleman's voice filled the void. I heard command and confidence communicated through a southern drawl. I heard the familiar sound of a past life, in the midst of coaches and dads.

"Jackson Weatherlow, I'd bet that you're wondering why I called you."

I answered meekly, as if making my report to an agitated coach. "Yes, sir."

"Please call me Henry. I'm hoping that you and I might become friends."

I was instantly and resoundingly dumbstruck. This shockingly unexpected, but believably apparent, offer of affection had completely obliterated my defenses, and my strategy for survival. I muttered through sagging chainmail. My response was a disconnected amalgam of faith and manners.

"My friends call me, Jack, sir."

"Henry, please."

"Yes, sir...Henry."

I sounded like the village idiot addressing a knight of the realm.

"Well, then, that's settled. Jack, I am calling out of respect for a recommendation that I received from my wife, of all people."

"Your wife, sir?"

"Jack, Janie's description of you was nothing less than glowing, in all respects."

"Janie?"

"Janie is my wife's name. Apparently, you rescued her from a rather unfortunate situation, while she was a guest at your hotel."

"I'm not sure that I recall such an event, sir."

"Henry, please…but, let's set that aside for a moment. I don't presume to know the first thing about you, but Janie thinks very highly of you as a person, and as a hotel man."

"That's very kind, thank you."

"Jack, you're in Kansas, right? But, do you happen to know much about the South?"

"Sir, I mean, Henry. I've only been in Kansas for the past five years. I was actually born in Atlanta, and I lived there all my life. I consider Atlanta as my real home."

"I had no idea. This is actually wonderful news. In fact, I might even say that this call is positively providential!"

"Mr. Woodson…Umm, Henry, please forgive me, but I'm not sure that I follow."

"Jack, here's the story. The reason that I called, I mean. However, first, let me ask you this: do you happen to know anything about golf?"

"I've played all my life. As a matter of fact, Dad has been a member of Atlanta Country Club since its inception. I would say that I pretty much grew up out there. I think of that place like a home, as well."

"Just more good news, I would say, and strong support for my Janie's discerning eye."

I waited for his next words. I was still feeling confused, but sunlight was beginning to peek through the hanging overcast of my self-designed storm of doom. I felt comfortable in speaking about golf, and the hotel, if those topics happened to come up again.

"Jack, I serve on the board of a distinctive golf club. I happen to love the game of golf. I've played for much of my life, but I think that I may have started somewhat later than you. Nevertheless, I have a number of associates, who are involved in various pursuits. Some years ago, I was invited to participate in a project. That project has since come to life as the golf club that I mentioned. Our idea was to establish a facility and an affiliation founded upon a mutual sense of respect, and admiration, but also a certain type of devotion to the game. I realize that such a notion is not new, or unique. But, we do think that our project has become something quite special.

"My meaning is this. We built a golf club, but we also built a retreat. Our club is not in Atlanta. It's actually located just south of Savannah. Being from Atlanta, I presume that you are familiar with the Georgia coast? Well, one of my associates offered a particular piece of property for consideration; 300 acres to be exact. Our land is south of the Moon River, and west of Delegal Creek. We're in the middle of nowhere, so to speak.

"Here's the thing. Our club features a main lodge that offers ten full-service guest rooms. In addition, we have four cabins resting along the eastern edge of our practice facility. Our busy days feature nine groups. One foursome on every other hole is the idea. Of course, our accommodations may be configured in many ways, but that's where you come into the picture.

"We like to think of ourselves as a stay and play facility. But, we do, however, entertain members only on a daily basis. Some of our associates have residences around the Savannah area, and a few come down, from as far away as Hilton Head. Our course features six holes that border the river and the creek, and twelve inland. From the tips, we stretch out just beyond 7000 yards, give or take tee placements. We have four sets of tees, but only two meaningful yardage differentiations. I might say that we have 36 holes in one layout. Our practice range has eighteen stations. We are 100 yards wide and 350 yards downrange. We have a nine-hole pitch course, complete with championship greens. We feature a pristine carpet of Tifdwarf Bermuda grass across the entire compound, with exception given to natural areas, of course. Our slogan is: 'One Lies as All Lie.'

"We are open year round. Our occupancy rate is approximately eighty five percent, with an average length of stay that shifts between two and three nights. We offer three meals a day. We have a service bungalow out on number nine. Our course is of the older style that does not come back to the main house after the ninth hole. We prefer to play all the way out, before we have to come back in.

"Our lodge features a library, a reception area, a formal bar and banquet room and locker rooms for men and women. Of course, we have full time staff, serving our dining accommodations, and housekeeping chores, but we also have dedicated attendants serving the member's needs in the locker rooms. Toilet and shower facilities accommodate ten men and four ladies, separately of course. We offer full-time shoe and club service to all our associates. Laundry is processed offsite, but we have couriers who accommodate the requirements of our lodge, and the personal requests of our associates. Counting house staff, and golf staff, we support twenty full-time employees.

"We actually built a smaller version of the big house to serve as our proshop, and associates' grill. We manage all the needs of the game from that standalone location. We are more formal in the main lodge. The proshop occupies the creek side of the structure, and a full service dining bar, and a patio area, overlooks the eighteenth green on the course side. Oh, we call our club Wambaw. So, what do you think?"

"Mr. Woodson, I think your club sounds spectacular, however, and forgive me if I sound a bit obtuse, but I'm not sure you care to hear about my opinion of your golf club. In other words, I'm not certain that I understand the nature of your question?"

"Jack, once again, I am beginning to see the things that Janie saw at the hotel out there in Kansas. Jack, I am asking if you might consider a position with our club. I need a full-time facilities manager, someone who can ensure that our physical accommodations are always operating at peak performance. I see your role as, perhaps, acting partner to the greens keeper. I might say that you would be our inside man, while Mr. Goddard cares for the outside. You would be the Assistant Secretary of the club. Perhaps, you might feel more comfortable thinking of this role as the general manager of our little golf hotel. We can discuss the details of responsibilities and reports when you come for a visit."

Mr. Woodson's words expressed themselves into my head, like helium into a child's balloon. I felt as if my skull was expanding, and I felt as if my whole body was beginning to float, above the sofa, upon which I was sitting. However, this unexpected infusion of ebullience was quickly strapped and tackled by a constricting sense of abject terror. A complete stranger was apparently asking me to take command of his personal ship. He was extending a full measure of credit and faith to me, Jack Weatherlow, a hotel man of enigmatic regard.

I sat for a moment, while the courtroom of my mind contested and refuted the words which had been delivered across the telephone line. After a time, I responded, in a manner to which I had become adept over the course of my life. I produced my own report, which was actually a type of sleight-of-hand magic trick that was intended to create the illusion of confidence and enthusiasm.

On a deeper level, I pictured my words as colorful autumn leaves, floating upon a fresh wind. They lilted on the prevailing gust, but were ultimately destined to rest upon the ground. They were appropriate and lovely, hopefully captivating, but intentionally distracting. Quite honestly, I hoped to keep them afloat long enough to develop a legitimate system of propulsion.

I said, "Mr. Woodson, please forgive me, but your proposition sounds too good to be true. I've always loved golf, and I won't shy from saying that I've developed an affinity for my work at the hotel. An opportunity to combine the two seems unbelievably perfect."

"Jack, that sounds supah. I'm delighted. So, when do you think that you can get away for a visit? We want to get to know you, of course. I want you to meet the board. But, we also want you to get to know us. I mean, the board, and some of our prominent associates, and all the facilities, and the golf course, as well. I was thinking that you might come out for at least two nights. Spend a day on the golf course, and a day inspecting the facilities. I thought we might hold our official meetings across the table at meal time; breakfast, or dinner, perhaps. We want the fit to be exactly right for both sides. Please check your schedule and I'll do my very best to match it with our availability. Just let me know, and I'll have my people make all the arrangements."

"Mr. Woodson, I don't suppose that you know, but I'm married. I'd like to share your news with Samantha, before I confirm with you."

"By all means, do you have children?"

"No sir, you might say that Samantha and I are newlyweds. We celebrated our second anniversary this past April."

"Congratulations! Please, Jack, I want your wife to feel included. Please invite Samantha along for the visit. She is most welcome. In fact, I'll invite Janie and her crowd down from Atlanta. We don't want Samantha to feel lonely. Does she play golf?"

"Yes sir, but not exactly, she plays with me, but not on her own. She's a tennis…never mind, I'm grateful for your generosity. I'll check on things from my side and get back to you. Will tomorrow afternoon be alright?"

"Supah news is all I can say. Jack I'm delighted to have had this opportunity, and I feel assured of the future; yours and ours, to put a point on the matter. I'll look forward to your call."

"Mr. Woodson, before we go, would you mind sharing a few details about the incident that introduced Janie and me? I meet many people at the hotel, and sometimes those meetings occur during hectic circumstances."

I heard a sincere chuckle preceding the next words. "Jack, I've often tried to picture a scene that has been reported many times. Janie and her crowd were visiting Kansas City, last fall for a game between the Falcons and the Chiefs. Janie loves football. I have tickets for all the teams, Falcons, Jackets, and the Bulldogs too. I'm a fan, but I'm involved with the club during that season of the year. Janie goes with or without me. I'm sorry, I tend to wander.

"Anyway, Janie was staying in one of your suites, which makes the matter all the more incredible. Apparently, she was in the bathroom, when a geyser of black sludge suddenly spouted up from the toilet. The image of an oil strike comes to mind. Jack, she was simply frightened out of her wits. Black muck was everywhere. In her mind, she feared for her life, and her things, but you came to the rescue. You resettled her in a new room, before any real harm was done. She has told that story over and over, and you are her knight in shining armor, every time. I hope that rings a bell of some sort, but no matter, I'll be waiting to hear from you. Let me know. So long, Jack."

"Thank you, Mr. Woodson. I'll speak with you tomorrow. Goodbye."

I placed the receiver in the cradle and I sat back, deeply, as if I were extremely heavy. I relaxed. A tight smile pulled my lips across my teeth. I remembered that incident in the hotel. The 'black sludge' remark served as the unmistakable memory cue.

I recalled that particular incident, clearly. The time wasn't extremely late—somewhere around 10 p.m. I was moving along one of the middle-floor hallways. I was alerted to an odd squawk from my voice pager. I actually heard a shrill whining noise that was an electronic reproduction of a human scream. I set out for the room number, which had been indicated on the notification panel. After a few moments, I arrived at the thirty-sixth floor via the North stairwell. Entering the hallway, I heard a verbal scream coming from the opposing side of the building. I ran toward the scream and the suite that occupied that end of the floor. The door to the room was open. I entered without voicing the customary announcement.

Inside, I met my evening housekeeper, and Janie, the tenant in residence. They were both screaming and pointing toward the bathroom. I rounded the corner, took a step, but froze in the frame of the doorway. I looked inside one of our luxury lavatories. I saw a room, which displayed the detritus resulting from the detonation of a chocolate bomb. However, I was not bearing witness to chocolate, but rather, a slurry of hotel plumbing residue, which was being regurgitated through the system and into this very room. Surprisingly, I do not recall feeling offended by noxious odors. By all recollection, I was simply mesmerized by the spectacle.

I do recall the peculiar sound which emanated from this bathroom. I remember hearing a deep rolling moan, like that which might be produced by a giant internal combustion engine, attempting to fire. I heard it circulate three times, before another fountain of black goo exploded from the toilet bowl.

This strange exhibition inspired a host of emotions. I might describe by first impressions as a temporary pang of madness. I experienced a collection of sensations, stewing together, and all at the same time. There was a tremulous fear, a stultifying sense of shock, the thrumming vibrations of explosive hilarity, and a profound aura of awe. I revealed none of this to my concerned onlookers. By what power, I do not know, but I collected myself after a moment, and I began to attend to the needs that had arisen out of this odd circumstance.

First, I relieved my housekeeper of her remaining duties. She seemed to be the more unhinged party in that moment. Next, I assured our guest that I would remedy her plight, immediately. I recall asking if I could recover her articles from the bathroom. She agreed. I remember taking care in handling certain delicates that suggested various degrees of intimacy. In the midst of this recovery effort, I called hotel security. We needed to cordon the scene of the crime to the best of our ability. I also called engineering to evaluate the technical aspects of the problem. Not least, I called the front desk to have our guest transferred. I moved her, personally, without bell staff support, to a replacement suite, just above, on the thirty-eighth floor. Finally, I recall summoning my most trusted evening associate. I understood that, at that late hour, the inevitable and gruesome cleaning duties would fall upon me and my helper.

Our guest was safely, and satisfactorily, resettled within twenty minutes. Over the next few hours, I learned that the plumbing issue had been resolved, and over the course of the following hour, the room was sufficiently scoured, scrubbed, and sanitized by the hands of yours truly and my indispensable partner, Ms. Chou. I returned home that evening just after two o'clock in the morning. I remembered feeling energized by an unusual sense of compassion during that event. That night, I simply tried to do what was right and good. I suppose that I made an amends of sorts, in effort to rectify the unjust sufferings of my guest, and my hotel. I had no idea that anyone would take notice.

I was on the golf course, shortly after assimilating the imports of my telephone call with Mr. H. D. Woodson of Atlanta, Georgia. I played an actual round, as part of my preparation for the qualifying event, which would take place on Wednesday of the following week. I was practicing, but over a real course, and through actual play. Beating balls into the wide open spaces only takes you part of the way.

I joined the late morning gangsome, which is really a school of sharks, masquerading as a friendly gathering of senior golfers. I played exceptionally well, and from the back tees, as required by rite of privilege, accruing to my age and handicap. Regardless, I hold no doubt that my performance was motivated by the lingering glow of recognition. Mr. Woodson had offered me a precious gift. In other words, I had accepted praise for my performance in life, from a personally accredited approver. I took no encouragement from his offer of employment. I had filed and forgone the mental debate which was due to commence over that volatile issue. I was good at that chore. I suppose that such a talent or skill might be categorized in the folder, marked as denial. I have practiced that particular acumen for most of my life. In addition, at least for that afternoon, I took what I liked, and I left the rest, for later.

Following my round, I returned to an unoccupied apartment. This time, the vacancy was expected. I knew that Samantha would be at the flower shop. I showered, and readied myself for the next appointment of the day. I wore a new pair of old khakis. I had purchased them at my favorite Army Surplus store. They kept a few tables of rerun garments. There were piles of slacks, board stiff with starch, stacked like dinner plates and arranged by waist size.

They had to be torn open like glued envelopes, in order to assess their condition and fit. I preferred the fabric and the fit that was used for officer slacks. They were full through the legs, but snug at the waist and hips. Samantha always expressed chagrin, at my proclivity to cherish another man's pants. I actually preferred the pre-worn drape provided by the second-hand condition. I added a bottle-green, banded-sleeve sport shirt to the top, a frazzled alligator belt, and oxblood penny loafers on my feet. I had been advised to wear a casual outfit.

Having readied myself for the flower class, I sat for a moment before departing for the shop. I was timing my arrival by delaying my departure. However, while that short interval of time may have seemed as luxurious moments of relaxation, I was alone, but also in the company of my mind. My mentor says that going into your own head, alone, is like going into a bad neighborhood. You can expect to get beat up. The innocence of my timing event quickly transformed into a courtroom session of evidentiary evaluation and accusation.

CHAPTER 5

Trophies

....

In the instant that my worn twill backside touched against the chenille tapestry front-side of our sofa, a vast panorama of visual history was submitted for consideration and evaluation. I was treated to colors of emotion and images with temperatures. I felt sound by remembered intensity. I perceived taste through visions of texture. I experienced the sensation of movement and speed, although I sat quietly inside a dead stillness. I was being reminded and prepared for a mandatory math test.

In the midst of this numberless procession of unfolding impressions, I beheld my wife for the first time in that day. I saw her through an aroma of her flowers, the warmth of her eyes, and the reassuring tug of her love. Her image slowly dissolved into that of my first girlfriend. I saw her by feeling rather than hearing her voice. She was quickly replaced by my mother. Her figure took shape from tweaking twinges of every possible emotion. All these sensations resolved and formed and held and dissolved over the course of seconds.

In short order, the notion of my employment offer was displayed as if a diploma of notable regard inside a frame constructed from gilded bands of irrefutable perfection. In the background, I observed a shadowy image of The Hotel of Flowers being consumed by a lush tangle of budding liana. I began to project and predict the future, using the data which was being presented. Finally, I was treated to a simple mathematical equation, which added something here and subtracted something there. I instantly understood. The opportunistic equation, which I had interpreted as a potential gain, would not balance without Samantha's necessary loss. I sank back heavily.

In the next instant, the curtains of my memory stage opened upon an episode from my past life. I understood immediately. That single memory play encapsulated my entire understanding of familial math tests involving gains and losses.

The event that came to mind occurred during the summer before college. I was an active teenage boy and a recent graduate of high school. Near the time of graduation, I had received two invitations by which I might spend my summer days in profitable adventure.

One opportunity was self-solicited and desirable, but the other was unsolicited and far less appealing. In the first case, I was looking forward to spending my summer as an assistant to the head professional at one of the finer golf clubs in town. I would be acting as a sort of apprentice to the master. The other offer appeared unexpectedly. Through various connections, my mother had arranged a job at one of the hospitals in town. Mom preferred a doctor-son to a golfer-son. She envisioned her opportunity as a sort of apprentice role to doctors and surgeons. I looked upon that particular job as if I were becoming an assistant to the janitorial staff. I took the job at the country club against my mother's firm counsel and intense desire. I offered kind regrets to the position at the hospital.

The truth of the matter is that my mother and I share a certain measure of guilt in this particular incident. I was guilty of a crime which resulted from omission of information. During the first weeks of that long ago summer, I went to work each morning, but I did not reveal which of the two jobs I had decided to perform. My mother was informed by accident, by a mere acquaintance, who wanted to extend a word of praise in favor of a young man who was exceptionally efficient and delightfully cordial in his work at the country club. I suppose a lie is a lie regardless of its method of delivery.

My mother's guilt evolved over that summer. Through the years, my role in conflict with my mother might be accurately characterized by the notions of stamina and fortitude. I prefer the term 'active-surrender' to describe my battle strategy. I quickly learned that an active opposition to my mother's fury simply fueled her fires for conflagration and guaranteed a more grisly outcome. If I weathered the blows, without rising to draw an equivalent measure of damage, I considered the clash a success. Looking back, I suppose that my life in general was my primary offense.

Of all the images, which might be selected to provide clarity to those clashes, I prefer a picture of a medieval castle, preparing to defend against a siege, poised and populated by an angry mob of thousands. I play the part of the castle, and my mother the part of the mob. In my case, the goal of the castle is to outlast the onslaught rather than to defeat the enemy. Victory, if such a thing can be claimed, is achieved through fatigue and waning interest in the fight.

As I sat there in that silent apartment, reviewing my opportunity and waiting for my appointed departure time, I heard my mother's voice ringing out of her makeshift courtroom in our family kitchen.

"You're a liar and a traitor! Just get out of here…I'm so mad! I can't stand you!"

I returned in defense, "Mom, will you listen just a second?"

Louder this time, "Your father is a liar, your brother is a liar, and now you. I should have known. I hate all of y'all. Just get out of my sight."

During those years, I will freely admit to my share of side-stepping. I had avoided full disclosure on many occasions. I was also guilty of blatant obfuscation over the course of many conversations with my mother. Manipulating the truth was an acquired skill, designed to protect and defend the welfare of myself and that of my family.

My mother was an avid drinker. However, while she apparently drank alcohol out of an effort to inspire a sense of peace, her preferred means of lubrication had a tendency to inspire violent raging and highly irrational behaviors. Over the years, a state of alcoholic anesthetization became the standard for all daily operations. Mom's notions and apprehensions about her family, and about the world in general, became misshapen and misdirected. Beneath such a watch, my family members and I lived as if tinder box homes precariously poised in the path of a potential wildfire. I came to realize that any arcane topic or esoteric information might inspire a blazing flare of uncontrollable fury. Under all circumstances, I had learned to shape my words and stories in a manner which was designed to keep the peace. While my mother saw deception and betrayal, I saw diffusion through intentional distraction.

I never discovered the true source of her fits of anger or her irrational suspicions and paranoia, but I was a constant victim of her vengeful furies. Which came first; the lying or unbridled rage? Which was worse; the deceit or the immeasurable casualties that resulted from her drunken tirades? This endlessly looping program of dishonesty and abuse enslaved my family. Who started it? Who knows? How do you terminate an eternally orbiting dance that promenades in perceptions of deception and betrayal and sashays in acts of violence and revenge? Who steps first? Who trusts their partner? Anyone who stood up was crucified. We all participated, and we all allowed it wane. We lived in the interludes of peace. We endured the hurtful harangues and physical threats and tried to move on with our lives, grateful for the peaceful pauses, but perpetually preparing the fortifications of our own castles.

Once again, I heard Mom shrieking out of the corner of my mind.

"I tried to help you, and you might just as well have slapped me in the face."

I pleaded, "Mom—please...."

"I just want to slap you in the face!"

"Mom...."

I suppose I became somewhat unusually distracted through an uncharacteristic attempt to assert myself into the evolving skirmish. I failed to realize the import of my mother rising from her chair. As she rose, she cocked her arm in preparation to accomplish the threat communicated through her last remark. Not that my focus mattered; I had to accept the physical blows along with the mental lashings. She brought her hand to my face in a full round-house swipe. Her palm connected almost dead on my cheek. The impact of her hand sent a stunning electric pain shattering through the left side of my head. I could hear the resounding percussive smack echo throughout the house.

The memory of that swipe, calls to mind a common exclamation—'Wow, she slapped the shit out of you!' That's not what leaves. The shit stays, but a trustworthy grasp of self-control becomes extremely tenuous. That type of out-of-control gesture was extremely frightening, not because it was painful, although it usually was, and not because it was damaging, although it usually wasn't, but because the unexpected strike inspired a searing fury, which seemed, of itself, barely containable and bent upon an immediate reflexive retaliation. Although I cannot say why, I can say that through each and every similar instance some ineffable force always held me in check. I look backward with gratitude, knowing that I never returned a blow with a blow in conflict with my mother.

Inside my apartment, I re-experienced the unhinging sense of desperation that rose up after that volley. I remembered the oppressive desire to run for cover, but I also recalled holding myself together and remaining in my position. I almost felt the sizzling of my cheek, and I recalled the energy of will required to maintain an image of unaffected composure.

I saw my mother returning to her seat. She took a long drag off her burning cigarette, a deep pull from the twin straws that serviced her afternoon highball. She dismissed me by directing her attention toward the television set. Both rooms, past and present, began to settle as if nothing had happened.

However, my memory play continued with a feeble proclamation.

"Mom, can I tell you what I want?"

"Go ahead, it doesn't matter what you say when you're a liar."

"Mom, I think I can make a living doing what I love."

Once again, I saw my mother's head begin to rotate, much like that of an owl or something far more macabre. And, in the presence of the appearance of focused attention, I recalled my final words.

"I'm really glad you tried to help me, but I had the club thing already set up."

I saw it all, in that moment, as clearly as I had during the original episode. At the sound of my voice, my mother seemed to change. At a glance, she appeared to be paying attention to my words, but a closer inspection revealed that she was a million miles away. Her boozy elixir instigated wild, irrational tirades, but also enabled a weird type of mental detachment. Seemingly at will, my mother could assume a vapid, expressionless, facial countenance which was tuned ever so slightly to appear present and engaged, while her actual consciousness had withdrawn into the secret privacies of her tippled mind. Within the twinkling span of that brief moment, Mom had transformed into a freaky, creepy thing. It was like addressing a waxen mannequin. In those instances, I never knew what was happening behind her glassy eyes.

From the displaced safety of my sofa seat, I heard my mother's final remark. It was delivered through a burst of maniacal laughter.

"Ha, ha, ha, ha, ha!"

She ballyhooed her amusement like an insane person. She laughed for a good long while and, finally, almost light-heartedly, she dismissed the whole affair.

"Get out of here! I don't care."

Memory was reality in those moments. I felt a barren emptiness then and inside my apartment. For a moment, no particular image formed. In place of picture memories, I reviewed the thoughts which had been eternally etched by those long ago proceedings. My history with Mom was brushed up by vibrant paints from an artist's palette. Angry magenta and vivid yellow blended and mixed with melancholy blue and sorrowful black to craft a sweeping panorama of human drama.

I often wondered about the finer details which shaped my mother's journey in life. I imagine that she began her role as a parent as one person, possibly a reluctant person, but still more whole than not and rightly directed for the most part. At some point in time, I presume that she met with an irresolvable division in her conception of that original role or her identity in general. I suspect that the horrific accident that killed my dad's parents inspired the initial separation. However, I wonder if the imports of that tragedy were simply the last drops of a sinister reagent which had long been burning away the reigns that held her in the middle of the road.

Regardless of the cause, my mother salved her injuries with an anesthetic rather than an antiseptic. She chose relief rather than cure. I don't suppose that she ever realized there was a difference. Nevertheless, the relief became the food or fuel which energized and promoted the process of her separation. She grew ever closer and more identified with her torment, and she grew evermore distant from her peace. I watched the transformation occur across my young life, such that I found myself more often despised and attacked by the tortured and tormented monster of trauma and tragedy, and less and less nurtured or treasured by the compassionate and caring mother of my imagination.

As I ruminated over these mournful recollections, I saw the curtains of my memory open upon the final act of this regrettable episode. Sitting there on my sofa I became the young man I had been almost half a lifetime in the past. I recalled the entire incident as if I were stepping through the unfolding act of reprisal.

The retaliatory note that my mother was holding for my crimes of betrayal came due, very late one evening, just before I left for college. I recalled springing to attention that night for no apparent reason. I recalled my sense of confusion. At that time, I didn't know whether I was awakened by a sound, an intuition, or a dream. At that time, I roomed with my brother. He and I heard many sounds in the dark of night. We had shared many seemingly endless evenings which had been interrupted or decorated with boisterous harangues and contentious dealings. Anomaly in our nighttime was difficult to define.

I might describe my sleep in those days as a sort of resting idle. I reclined in my bed, half asleep and half alert. My brain was like the CPU of a computer polling its environment for an imminent task. I slept, as I imagined that a spy might sleep, in enemy territory—resting, but anticipating discovery.

A summons to provide testimony in the middle of the night is another prominent image emblazoned among the memory files of my formative years.

Regardless of the reason, that night I woke from my light slumber feeling more curious than afraid or anxious. I sat up, still half covered by my blanket, trying to focus on the suspicious innuendo which was calling for my attention. The beckoning was indefinite, but still I could not shake the feeling that something was awry. I felt tempted to investigate, but the prospects of being apprehended during a clandestine inspection of the situation held me in place. We did not move around our house after bedtime without good reason. Mostly, I remember hoping that the strange beckoning from the dark would disappear.

Despite a multitude of reservations, on that fateful occasion I rose from my bed. I was painstakingly careful. I did not want to arouse my brother. I made no attempt to dress but padded out of our room. I moved down the hallway toward the stairs. I stopped there to wait and listen. There was no light, except for the refracted illumination of a late evening, a dim glimmer at best, but then shaded by the pine trees outside and once again degraded by the angles of the room. I waited in a faintly flickering cobalt glow.

I heard the television from upstairs—a dull conglomeration of sound which was muffled by the double doors of the foyer but also diminished by the angular path that led to my attuned ear poised in the lower realm of the house. Still I heard or detected more than what was apparent to my senses. The sound from the television was not a real clue. Mom left that thing going well into the morning of the following day on a regular basis. On most evenings, she dozed under the spell of her anesthetic coma in the midst of full lights and blaring television. Although her goal seemed to be the blissful escape of unconsciousness, she never chose her time to clock out for the day. I imagined that the final condition befell her like a black hood unexpectedly cinched over the head of a captured victim.

For some unexplainable reason, I felt compelled on that night. I was invigorated by a strange courage which moved me forward in semi-heroic curiosity rather than backward in shameful retreat. I moved up the stairs to the foyer. I waited at the double doors listening for something out of the ordinary. I didn't know the exact time, but I did not hear Johnny Carson's voice coming from the television. I presumed that the hour was beyond one o'clock in the morning— Johnny's scheduled bedtime. At that point, I actually heard a peculiar, out of the ordinary sound. The noise was not emanating from the enclosure of the den, but seemed to be coming in from the lawn in the distance.

I checked myself, remaining perfectly still and deadly silent. Next, I detected the familiar report provided by an automobile engine. I realized that this adventitious vibration had served as my alarm signal rather than any particular sound that was emanating from the gloom. I wondered why a car would be running at this late hour. This likelihood was odd, but well within a range of comprehensible possibilities. I abandoned my plans to inspect the backyard, and I turned to focus my attention toward the driveway. I fell back a few steps and peered across the front room which ran parallel to the den. The summons that I had detected was wafting through the wall of large plate glass windows looking out onto the wooded property that fronted our house. I took a relaxing breath, knowing that I could investigate further without having to enter my mother's chamber.

I made my way through the front room, crossing the formal living area and navigating the dining room. I paused at the doorway which provided access to the kitchen. After a moment, the vibration became actual sound. I clearly heard the engine that powered my dad's Buick Electra Limited. It was rumbling in the drive. I also heard the clanking of the transmission engaging the gears.

I felt safe to move through the kitchen and into the alcove at our back door. There, I rose and peered through the windows in the door. Looking out, I saw no headlights, but I noticed the white nose of the car passing by the vertical horizon established by the exterior brick wall of our garage. I watched as the car retreated from my field of vision. I watched this same scene repeat itself several times. The car was apparently moving back and forth over a short distance as if it were being rocked in order to break free of a mud-slick which had stolen the friction from the tires.

While observing, I heard a new sound occurring in conjunction with the revving engine and grumbling transmission. This noise was like rubber tires on a gravel road. There was a distinctive crunching—something vague like the snapping of wooden sticks and an occasional pinging ricochet as if the pressure of the tires on the small stones had sent one sailing off into the distance. This was not ordinary. Our drive was smooth asphalt. I was irrepressibly drawn to pay closer inspection to this odd circumstance.

I left the relative safety of the house through the kitchen door. I committed myself to my precarious errand. Outside the house, I became a crepuscular creature stealing into the night. I slithered along the brick wall of the garage like a summer lizard. I slowly inched my way toward the asphalt drive which served as our basketball court and parking area for extra cars. I heard the engine rev, the gears clank, and the ground crunch. I saw the front bumper pass by the corner and then slowly withdraw from view. Very carefully, I made my way to the edge of the back walk where I could obtain a full view of the drive. I sucked back against the wall hoping the downspout of the gutter might hide me from view.

Peering around the safety of my hollow metal camouflage, I saw my dad's car slowly coming my way for another pass. Through the clear windshield, but shadowed in a deep blue haze, I could see my mother inside the car. Her hands were at two and ten on the steering wheel. She was hunched close, as if driving in severe rain or heavy traffic. She was focused on her work.

The asphalt below the vehicle was littered with bits and pieces of objects that twinkled in phosphorescent sparks. These shards of debris reflected the hazy metallic hues of gold and silver. I also noticed other, darker objects lying in her path, but they were crushed and broken beyond recognition. I was puzzled, not by the fact that my mother was using the car in the middle of the night as a Caterpillar roller machine, but by the articles that she was decimating. This is the type of information that demarcated normal behavior from curious or abnormal errands of the night.

As she backed the automobile in preparation for another pass, the front tire connected with something large. I heard a snap, then the clacking ricochet sound. A piece of metal skittered from underneath the car and clanked against the bricks below my position on the back walkway. I shifted my focus. I gazed upon a golden piece of shrapnel. Having grown accustomed to the dim light of the waxing morning, I gave closer inspection to the metallic object lying at my feet. I took a moment to focus, and gradually the figure of a small golden man began to register in my mind. My sense of confusion remained in place.

In the next moment, the car made another pass, crunching through its small field of destruction. I drew back, reflexively, sliding behind the protective cover of my gutter. The car stopped. The transmission disengaged, and the engine was silenced. Stark terror glued me to the bricks. Seconds ticked, but I did not move. I heard the car door open and close. In the next instant, my mother was standing before my frozen countenance.

Beneath an image that I might describe as classically disheveled noir, I detected the radiant aura of smug satisfaction. My presence in the middle of the night, flat and suctioned against the brick wall along the back walkway to the house, raised no start or alarm whatsoever. In fact, Mom reacted to my presence as if we were passing one another on a calm afternoon in the midst of unloading groceries.

She looked at me coldly through one eye and said, "They were mine."

I watched her pass unsteadily, and I watched her enter the house.

I thought, What were mine?

In that instant, I recognized the significance of that golden piece of man-shaped shrapnel. I was finally and immediately consumed by an alarming fright. I felt it blazing up as if I had been doused and fired beneath a shower of gasoline. I hooked around my corner at the gutter, terrified to see but compelled to know. I took in the small vista of carnage littered with the pieces of silver and gold. In the next moment, the other previously undefinable debris began to take shape. Mixed together in the general clutter were pieces of splintered wood, like broken furniture, and variously sized shards of polished granite. All these chips and splinters, flecks and pieces, of gold and silver, wood and rock, had been dashed and broken by the tires of the car.

I stooped low in order to peer underneath the vehicle. Through the blackness, I found a collection of twisted metal cup-like objects and several more broken and orphaned men of gold and silver. Slowly I returned to a standing position. I rose as if lifting a barbell. The weight that I felt was composed of utter defeat, bitter anguish, searing pain, and irretrievable loss. Underneath this weight, and through a feeling like confused panic, the image of the first man of gold became totally clear. My mother had been using my dad's car to destroy my golf trophies. I realized then that I was also underneath that car. I was unexpectedly, but not accidentally, murdered on our driveway that same night.

Even resting safely on the sofa in my apartment, displaced by half a lifetime and separated by hundreds of miles, I revisited the shock of that episode. I felt certain elements of vitality draining from my body. I was surrounded and gripped by a familiar sense of mortification. Mostly, I felt shame—shame of having delighted and hoped and invested myself in something that could be destroyed so easily and so thoroughly.

I considered the gains and the losses associated with that long ago evening, and I began to realize that the real casualty of that event was the loss of a sense of fulfillment. My physical death had been symbolic, but my sense of freedom to act or choose had, indeed, been quite literally annihilated. Not that I could no longer choose to do as I preferred, but that every future choice and action would be exposed to my mathematical equation which measured the potential loss embedded inside the perception of gain.

Momentarily, I began to realize that since that event and those days, I had always expected an imminent, but unknowable, penalty for going my own way. I had guarded all sense of the rightful pride of success and any sneaking hope for the future. Those vital commodities of existence had become reserved and leaked, or dripped, along a journey that was tyrannized by apprehension. And finally, I recognized that when I looked back and across the halcyon days of youth and coming of age, I saw a pattern of similar episodes, all illuminated by the glow of a similar horror. Whenever I took a measure of liberty, my mother had taken a measure of revenge.

I saw my mother in those moments of introspective deliberation. The notion of hatred seeped into my consciousness. I recognized that feeling, but instantly recoiled in shameful disgust. She was, after all, my mother, the vessel and provider of my existence in this world. Between us, the hatred and disgust, the pain and helplessness, could not prevail. Cold contemptuous separation would not stand, and our relationship and interaction would eventually return and resume. It always did, but always more tentative and alert or, sadly, more aloof and reticent. We were never set free or absolutely untethered by the final divisiveness of indefatigable hatred. Within an atmosphere of grave risk and scattered reward, governed by the inescapable laws of our peculiar mathematical equation, Mom and I defied the design of eternal creation. We shrank and constricted together instead of growing and blooming and becoming who, and what, we were intended.

Once again, I returned to that scene from half a lifetime passed. I stood before my mother for the final confrontation and feeble attempt at rectitude. Mom was casually luxuriating on the corner of the sofa. She peered at me through a haze of menthol smoke. She held one eye closed in order to keep my image stable. One sleek black lock of disheveled hair hooked below that eye. She drew from the ever-present pairing of straws submerged in her glass tumbler. I stood still, quietly gazing, but trembling slightly, not from cold, but in an effort to retain a raging effervescence.

I heard her words clearly.

"The trophies were mine, and I got tired of them."

I bellowed—less from affront than out of an escaping energy, desperately willing to retain an outburst of far more hideous import.

"How can you possibly say that my golf trophies were yours?"

I recalled a return that was almost casual.

"Because! I took you to the golf course every time. Every day of my life, I got out of bed. Every day I drug you to the golf course, and for that reason—for taking you, every day— they were mine! I can do anything I want with my stuff!"

Those words echoed through my mind as my memory theater dimmed and the curtains closed. I heard the clock tick and realized the hands had moved. The time for my departure arrived. I thought of Samantha. I felt anxious, afraid, and sad. Foolishly, I considered saying nothing about the transpirations of this morning's telephone call. More astutely, I observed that Sam would never accept such a status. Either way, and against my preferred intentions, I noticed that my familial scoreboard had been illuminated. I saw it materialize above and behind the previous procession of remembered events. It hung there waiting for its own form of input. I understood that all forthcoming decisions regarding today's telephone call would be reflected, in one way or another, by the garish radiance projected by that regrettable device.

My familial scoreboard is the memory computer which manages, for selected opponents, the mathematical equations which reconcile perceived gains and losses within the ranks of conscripted warriors. The output from this type of scoreboard doesn't inspire the amiable tension derived from a respectable contest, but rather, a type of wanting sorrow attached to uninvited surrender or outright theft. All in all, I wasn't feeling afraid of having to give my report about the offer, but I was grievously alarmed by the prospect of posting numbers on this particular machine. My mother invented this device, and she installed it in my mind without awareness or permission on my part.

In route to the shop, I reviewed my life with Samantha. I decided that, across the span of over three years, I couldn't recall ever having seen that old device, much less possessing a desire or need to post a number. As I pulled my car into the parking lot, I recalled Samantha's assessment of my earthly status. She was attempting to move me from a station defined by notions of temporary and mobile to a position of permanence and foundation.

That old scoreboard was, and is, a permanent fixture inside my temporary life. In those moments of contemplative reflection, I watched a permanent past invade a temporary present. My fortuitous job opportunity became a lamentable scoring event. I felt fearful and anxious about an inevitable posting of regrettable values above our precious relationship, and I was, quite frankly, terrified by the remembered history of former games.

CHAPTER 6

Class

....

I parked in the rear lot, behind the shop, which is not exactly a designated parking area, but rather a square of blacktop asphalt, from which several essential services are performed for the store. For the most part, delivery trucks rest there while various products are off-loaded, and refuse trucks enter there to collect waste products. Sam parks her vehicle back there, but Mrs. Peverall parks on the side street. She drives a Cadillac, and prefers to preserve its condition by parking in the relative safety of the wide open spaces, as opposed to risking a ricochet inside the self-defined 'shooting range,' behind the store. I planned my entrance into The Hotel of Flowers, through the rear service door. I have my own key.

Samantha beams with delight whenever I enter the shop through the back door. She also celebrates the fact that I have used 'my' key. She thinks of The Hotel of Flowers as our shop. I suppose that this transfiguration of ownership was a product of evolution. It didn't simply happen, and no official papers have been signed. First notice of the change began to appear through a simple alteration in verbal address. The Hotel of Flowers began to be classified as 'our shop' whenever it was not being identified as 'the shop.' On the opposite hand, Samantha noticed the change by the fact that I did not make a similar switch in my vocabulary. Apparently, I always address the shop as 'her shop' whenever it was not 'the shop.'

Samantha says that this anomaly of speech is an example of seeing life as a series of temporary engagements, rather than as one permanent journey. She also says that I look at life through a series of still photographs, rather than as one long moving film. These observations are prominent points in her coaching repertoire. Nevertheless, the practical impact of our apparent difference in thought is, in my view, negligible. In my mind, her shop is my shop, by reason that it is her shop. Sam is my shop, in my mind. I will care for her, and protect her, and accommodate her needs and wants, in any way that those callings might take shape. If I am asked to work in the shop, I shall. If I am asked to move things around in the shop, I do. If I am asked to participate in flower arranging classes, I will. I am like a faithful dog in this respect. I will care for and protect her things, but they are not, at the same time, my things.

This mode of operation raises another coaching issue for my Samantha. She worries that, through the performance of these services, I might be attempting to legitimize or earn my place beside her. Her concern has an irrefutable foundation in past fact, and presents a considerable probability for a forecasted truth, but does not, in this case, prevail. I suppose that the difference is subtle. I perform my chores, on her behalf, out of a desire to please her and make her happy. Her happiness and joy are my ultimate pursuits. The route by which those goals are achieved doesn't really matter in my mind. Samantha would prefer that I find a measure of joy from the entire process, but that has not been my inculcated practice over a relatively short, but somewhat tumultuous, lifetime. She is always telling me to have fun at the golf course. I do not play for that reason, although happiness is often gifted to me in the process.

I am not an automaton inside her store. She often asks for my cerebral or emotional participation. In fact, one section of the store carries the distinctive signature of my last suggestion. While most of the shop is, by Samantha's definition, a faithful reproduction of how nature might arrange and display her flora, my section features flowers and plants that have been tamed and trimmed, and ordered and arranged, as if they might be poised for transfer to a planned landscape display. My vision in this regard is a product of involved experience with the manicured lawns and fairways, and 'natural areas' which adorn the golf club. I sometimes pause to admire an exceptionally well-raked bunker. I prefer this type of careful attention to a rising sentiment, which tends toward the notion of 'waste area,' where anything and everything seems to pass for perfection.

The Hotel of Flowers occupies a small corner of property within the district of town known as Country Club Plaza. This area is, in my opinion, the finest upscale shopping and dining area in town. Sam owns the building and the ground beneath, through certain grandfather contract clauses, which date back nearly fifty years. In order to achieve my goals in making my bride happy, I have had to learn something about commercial real estate. Nevertheless, the store rests upon a small corner, one block south of the main artery that feeds the area. The shop opens toward the east, facing a secondary street that offers curbside parking. The south side of the building is bordered by the road where Mrs. Peverall, the unofficial manager of the store, parks her Cadillac. I think of that road as a cut-through or service lane for other businesses.

We updated the shop this past year. As expected, I acquired a range of duties for the project. I was an eager architectural-materials consultant, a hopeful contract adviser, a meek funding assistant, a dutiful mover, and the menacing image of a suspicious guard dog. In other words, I offered my opinion regarding which building materials should be selected. We agreed to replace the old windows with slick-looking, green-tinted glass. I thought that installing a revolving door for the front entrance might add a touch of panache, and carry the name of the shop. I mean that all nice hotels feature revolving doors, why not The Hotel of Flowers, too? I was overruled on this suggestion, due to a price point issue on my part, and an exclusionary point on Samantha's part. The door that I liked was tremendously expensive, and Sam said that some of her customers could not use the door without serious hardship. As for my other roles, I accompanied Samantha to the bank for funding negotiations. I signed nothing, but offered an opinion, which was based upon occasional experiences, across a variable history, involving large monetary transactions. I also assisted in moving whatever needed to be moved, in order to provide access to the workers, and I performed in ways that informed those workers that Samantha and Mrs. Peverall belonged to me, and were not hunting game or menu items.

Basically, the changes that we made were cosmetic in nature. We replaced the refrigerators, the interior lighting and an HVAC component, necessary for humidity, but we were primarily focused upon refining the appearance of the shop. The store is a flat roofed, single story building. We are now enveloped by the green tinted glass on two sides. We have a double swinging door, front entrance, and the exterior façade is now stacked stone cladding. This effect wraps the windowed sides of the building, but also covers the northern interior wall. We also banded the roofline with a solid strip of copper flashing. The copper roofline, against the green windows and the golden cast from the stone, makes The Hotel for Flowers look like something from a 1950s exhibition of the future. Samantha has been thrilled with the result; however, we're still waiting for the sign.

We ordered a neon sign. French Script spells the French name of the store, L'Hôtel des Fleurs dans La Ville, in clear glass tubing, three-quarters inch in diameter, twelve inches tall and ten feet across. This sign is a beloved article for Samantha and a lingering headache for me. I recall listening to technical specifications across multiple telephone conferences. During one call, I was placed on hold rather abruptly, and in the middle part of concentrated effort to comprehend something like synchronizing ionization processes across supplementary transformers. On that occasion, my representative simply laid the receiver down and picked up the other telephone. I listened, while he gushed over a different order. I heard the words, 'Las Vegas' and casino, clearly, and I instantly realized that I was a small fish, attempting to swim with whales, in an odd ocean filled with Noble Gases. Hopefully, after our sign arrives, and after it is installed and electrified, it will, indeed, glow as promised, like a trained periwinkle snake.

As I crossed the threshold of the back entrance, I felt as if that sign had been cracked across the top of my head. I heard a silent admonishment barking within my skull. 'What the hell are you thinking!? You can't take that job. You're an idiot!' I answered audibly to no one, 'Right….'

I had arrived at the requested time, but still an hour before the class was to begin. Mrs. Peverall leaned into the arched passageway that separates the public shop from the private shop. The store front provides the showroom for all the merchandise, and the rear portion serves as a work area for staging all the orders. Mrs. Peverall was actually staging herself. She was not looking my way.

She asked, confidently, "Jack, is that you, honey?"

I answered, out of my southern training, "Yes, ma'am! Are y'all ready? Can I do anything?"

"Just about, you might want to ask Samantha. Just don't touch anything back there."

The last part of that remark was a given. I almost never extracted my hands from my pockets, while on my own, inside the shop. I felt like I was ten years old most of the time. In the next moment, I was formally greeted by Mrs. Peverall, with the customary peck on the cheek.

Mrs. Peverall has been with this shop, across two owners, and for over twenty years. She actually knew Samantha's biological mother. If forced to divulge my secret presumptions, I would approximate her age at just north of sixty years. She is a refined, attractive and energetic woman. She works out of her love for flowers, and at this point, I would add, a love for Samantha. She has no children of her own, and once again, if pressed, I might say that Mrs. Peverall has secretly adopted my Samantha. This is a coincidence of nature that I find extraordinarily providential.

I easily endow her account with mom credit. She is like some of the mothers that I have known over the course of my life, but still different. She is familiar, on one hand, and an enigma, on the other. She demonstrates a level of energy and enthusiasm that seems to belong to younger women, but she expresses a motherly type of affection and encouragement. She fashions herself in the image of a contemporary set, but carries herself within an aura of peace and poise that can only be acquired through age and experience. She is clever and wise. Rare demonstrations of anger or frustration emerge from precisely targeted rifles, instead of sawed-off shotguns that blast the general vicinity. But, most of all, she has yet to pose a legitimate threat to the little boy that watches her from inside my heart. She cooked dinner for Samantha and me one night. She served a beautifully delicious meal, around authentic Osso Buco. I am constantly intrigued while in her company.

I don't suppose that Mrs. Peverall needs to work, although she projects a miser's eye upon her weekly wage computations. I assume that she has been taught to review the numbers. Her husband is a prominent banker in town. She is, by all appearances, an active member of the Country Club social set. She moves within and among a company of regular patrons with flair, and easy affection. Some of Sam's biggest orders arrive in uncanny coincidence with Mrs. Peverall's predictions. She has officially retired from her managerial title, but she has retained her role as Samantha's trusted mentor. She is also my immediate supervisor, whenever I am called in for duty. In my view, The Hotel of Flowers is a family affair.

I surveyed the front of the store in hopes of locating my wayward bride, but I heard her voice calling from the back of the shop.

"Mon Chéri, come and see, s'il te plaît."

"What? How did I miss you? Where were you?"

"Qu'est-ce que tu penses, Chéri?"

I turned, using a basketball pivot, keeping one foot stationary to avoid an unnecessary traveling penalty. I saw Sam rise from beneath one of the tables in the back. Through an intake of breath, she smiled broadly, but instantly shrugged it off.

"What are you doing underneath that table?"

"This one is not level, Chéri. I am shimming the short leg with doilies."

"I didn't realize that you could shim with a doily."

"La Vache, we are being serious tonight."

"Oui, Madame, what am I looking at?"

"Chéri, we are working on these tables. I have three stations at each table. Everyone will receive a vase or a tray and all the flowers and ferns and decorative materials will be available in these staging buckets that I have placed around the room. Everyone will be free to design anything that they like, using these selections. I have…"

"Sam, honey, this looks absolutely perfect."

"Merci beaucoup."

"And, I can see the perfect job for me. I'll be the bartender, and the water boy or the resupply guy. I'll keep these buckets and all the students' glasses from running low. I'll do my hotel thing, inside your hotel thing."

"Non, Chéri, I am most excited about seeing your arrangement."

This last comment inspired a more formal type of greeting. I received a robust hug and a hard kiss on the lips, which I returned with matching enthusiasm. After the kiss, we stood there together, facing one another. I was looking down and Sam was looking up at me.

I affirmed, "Honey, you've done a beautiful job. Everything looks great! The class will be a huge success."

"Merci, Chéri, but setting up has been a bigger job than I anticipated, and we've been busy all day. I have not been able to help Carol with customers. I feel badly about that."

"Hey, is Mrs. Peverall staying for the class?"

"I have invited her, and I have saved a place for her at your table, but she has a dinner engagement tonight."

"Well, we'll treat her to another dinner later this week, to make up for the extra work."

"Oh la la, Chéri, tell me about your telephone call!"

"Oh yeah, well…I'm pleased to say that it was nothing like I imagined."

"J'en ètais sûr! You always imagine the worst, but things never turn out that way."

"It's always good to be prepared."

"Le Vache! Dis-moi, s'il te plaît."

"I think that we should wait until later."

That suggestion came off exactly like a particular type of poor golf shot. In both cases, the golf shot and the remark are faithfully attempted, almost as intended and necessary, but the execution is slightly off the mark. In either case, immediately following the launch, you instantly realize the shortcoming, and in a frenzied attempt to compensate for the misstep, you replace what has been omitted with an enthusiastic burst of hope. The hope is applied as a sort of supplementary energy, which is intended to replace the missing kinetic force in the golf shot, or a more comprehensive consideration in the suggestion. Hoping for success is fine, but that ethereal energy does not substitute for rocket fuel, nor does it exchange feeble words for those with deeper meaning. In this case, my wounded suggestion fell short of its intended target, and I was left to hope for the miraculous consolation. As is the case with most golf shots, I was rewarded appropriately.

Sam spoke through an assertive tone, "Dis-moi, s'il te plaît."

I watched her acquire a familiar repose. She cocked her head slightly to the left. Her brows shifted toward one another. Her eye lids opened like a lens shutters in the dark. Her lips puffed and absorbed the commas that frame her mouth. Behind vanilla bangs, hickory nut brows, lapis eyes, blush lips and sun-bronzed skin, I saw concerned resolve. I was instantly disarmed and compelled to answer.

"Sam, Mr. Woodson offered me a job."

"A job, Chéri?"

"Yes, a new job."

"What type of job, Chéri?"

"A hotel job, but at a golf club, rather than a giant building."

"I do not understand."

"That's why I wanted to tell you later."

"Mon Chéri, why would he do this?"

"Well, I'm not some schlub at work. Maybe Mr. Woodson recognizes true talent when he sees it."

"La Vache, how does he know you?"

"He doesn't, really, except for today, on the telephone. His wife told him to call."

"His wife? Mon Chéri, I am very confused."

"I was too, at first, but then he explained about his wife, and I understood the inspiration behind his offer. Nothing is settled. He wants me to visit his club, and you too. He wants to hold a sort of double interview, us about them, and them about us, I suppose."

"Where is this golf club hotel, Chéri?"

"Sam, look, all I did was listen. I didn't say anything. I didn't do anything, either."

"Where, Chéri?"

"Sam, it's in Savannah. Savannah, Georgia, to be exact, but outside the city, to the south, but inland from the ocean."

"Ocean! I thought Mr. Woodson was calling from Atlanta?"

"He did, but the club is in Savannah."

"Is Savannah near Atlanta?"

"Looking from here, maybe, but from Atlanta, not really."

I felt Samantha sag in my arms. She placed her forehead heavily against my sternum. I felt a forlorn guilt intermingling with the humid air. Breathing became a chore.

I said, "Sam, all I did was make a telephone call. Everything's alright. Nothing has changed."

Downcast, I heard, "Mon Chéri, I think everything has changed."

I tipped her face toward mine with a crooked forefinger of my right hand. I saw one giant crystalline tear welling in the corner of her right eye. I took it, with a gentle touch of my thumb.

"Listen, I did what I was supposed to do, right? I returned the telephone call, even though I was afraid. I practiced doing the right thing. That's all that happened. All I have to do now is call back, and say thank you, but no thank you. See? Back to normal. Easy."

"Mon Chéri, we cannot simply let this go. I know you, Mon Amour. I know your mind, and I know your heart, and I know your soul. I am you, and you are me. We must see this to the end, together."

"Sam, really, the last thing in the world that I want to do is hurt you, or us. I love you, honey. I can let it go. I will let it go. Please don't be upset."

"Someone has called for you, Chéri. Someone has recognized you with respect and trust. Someone has offered you something that touches your oldest desire. I will not allow you to add this to your list of losses, as you say. If you have been called, I have been called, and we will respond together. We have met a detour in our journey on God's river. We have steps to take, and perhaps, a future destination that I did not expect. That is why I am upset, but I am not angry. We will adjust, and we will follow our road, and in the end, we will be settled and grateful for Mr. Woodson's call."

This pastoral edification was followed by an unexpected peck on the lips.

"I am proud of you, Mon Amour."

"Sam, we don't…"

"Tais-toi, s'il te plait. I forgive you, Chéri, now and always."

Before I could ask why I was being forgiven, I heard Mrs. Peverall calling from the front of the store.

Her voice lilted into our pairing. "Savanne, may I see you for a moment, please, dear."

Sam was Sam, as always, but she is more appropriately, Savanne. I had been informed of the existence of this name, by accident. I asked a question, and I was rewarded with a history lesson. Savanne is Samantha's original French name. Her birth mother had chosen that specific name, as a tribute to God, in return for the gift of her daughter. Savanne means, literally, 'In Service to God.' That name was and is uncannily authentic, whether inside this French flower store or outside, in negotiations with her wandering husband.

I was gathered by embracing arms before Sam answered the summons from Mrs. Peverall. The hug was brief, but intense. When she released my torso, our faces met again. I was peering down, and she was gazing upward. In this instance, I was the one with the welling eye. Once again, my question was interrupted.

Sam whispered through a smile, framed by tiny commas, "I can hear what you are hearing, Mon Chéri. You are being accused, but I am the judge overseeing your trial. Through my forgiveness, I pronounce you not guilty."

"Sam, really, I can…"

"Tais-toi, s'il te plait. I forgive you, but you are not free to go. You have community service to perform. You may begin tonight, but you may have a head start on the others. Look through my buckets and decide which flowers you want to use for your arrangement. I'll check on you in a minute."

She applied a final kiss and departed. I remained in my position. I suppose that I was momentarily stunned by the remarkable marvel of absence. I felt no pain. I sensed no hurt. I was not agitated by anxiety, nor was I stinging from humiliation. There was no darkening sadness, nor a swelling tension from bridled anger.

On the contrary, I felt rather peaceful and, I might even say, whole—with slight exceptions allowed for two issues that captured my attention. First of all, I puzzled over the fact that I had failed to predict, within the smallest range of accuracy, a single response, offered by Samantha's imaginary negotiations team. Secondly, I began to wonder whether I would ever come to know my bride, in the manner, or at the depth, at which she apparently knows me.

Stranger still, I did not feel diminished by these observations. I was not reeling from sorrowful regret. If anything, I felt an idling energy of encouragement, which brightened my outlook for us, and the job offer, and this evening's class. Best of all, I noticed that the old scoreboard, which had accompanied me into this establishment, was dark. Not a single bulb flickered. No value or credit had been recorded or illuminated for either of my self-designated teams. I began to understand that Samantha's view of wedded partners as one flesh, or one team, eliminates the concept of scoring points through competition.

My mother's scoreboard records peculiar values. It assigns and records an irregular type of credit, which is always negative in value. Scores result from various pains and insults, which are caused by activities that do not align with certain standards. Positive commendation for adherence to the rule of law and approved achievement was expected, and therefore, not recognized.

All recorded value indicates a type of reverse credit, which affords the recipient certain rights of revenge. When I did something or chose something that deviated from the approved guidelines and expectations, my mother posted a value on her side of the board. In return, and at some unknowable time in the future, she would use that value as authorization to exact an equivalent measure of pain and affront upon my life. In the process and afterward, I received a value on my side of the board. This circle of inadvertent attack and premeditated revenge was known as balancing the scoreboard.

During my formative years, I understood that my most egregious and enduring offense was to show favor to a special young lady from school. My affections in this regard kept my mother's side of the scoreboard spinning up points like a Las Vegas slot machine after a robust pull of the handle, and her concerted attempts to undermine my affaire d'amour kept my side of the board, blazing in white hot glory.

I remember those years, under my mother's watch, as an arduous process of trial and error. The problem was that, my preferred trials were most frequently recognized as treasonable errors. We spent our lives together, posting evil numbers on a sinister display board that only we could see.

I can't imagine that either of us set out to perform in such a lamentable contest. I remember my mother as an effective tyrant, but not as a determined despot, and I hope that she saw me as an aggravating adversary, rather than a wanton criminal. In the end, I suppose we accepted a truce through separation. I followed my own road, but I carried papers that announced a dishonorable discharge, and for that reason, our tournament of wills is unforgettable. I don't believe that Samantha is aware that such a game exists.

Before long, Samantha's floral students began to arrive. I decided to project an image that balanced opposing airs of attraction and aversion. In other words, I planned to connect with the female guests through an element of charming enthusiasm, and I planned to side with the men, by sharing a mutual, but covert, sense of resigned bother. Both personas were honest. Training, through trial and error, encourages the ability to perform well in many roles.

As expected, Samantha proved to be a delightful hostess, and an attentive professor of floral engineering. In fact, throughout the evening, she offered a series of short lectures, advising her class about the basic requirements for a proper arrangement. I learned that we might enhance the shape of our design by developing an element of flow. I had never thought of describing a stationary flower arrangement in terms typically reserved for movement. I did not intend to venture down that curvy road. She also offered a refresher course on color combination, in terms of blending and contrast.

Something about her delivery of that particular topic inspired old images of certain performances inside my high school chemistry class. I could not resist stealing a moment of vainglorious stage work. In response to these invigorating energies, I offered an unsolicited discourse on the evils of blending plaids and contrasting stripes. I described textile mayhem using Samantha's named flower selections. I shaped my words such that they might appear to flow between charm and scandal. I meant to inspire humor, rather than harm. I would say that my remarks were successful. I was the class clown again, but a smart one, I made straight A's in that chemistry class. Being that we were in a public arena, I was not disciplined in the customary manner. Instead, I received a poised glare from narrowed eyes and tight lips that curled down at the corners.

Undaunted, Samantha moved forward with suggestions for combining textures, and she offered cautionary notes concerning aromatics. She concluded her lecture series by describing a host of foliage that did not seem to belong in the flower family. She offered names and descriptions for various items that I might have described as moss and sticks, or leaves and brambles. She also featured a host of odd ornaments that appeared to have been models for the unique artistry adorning Dr. Seuss books. They were like giant dandelion puffs offered in weird hues that defied proper categorization.

Nearing the conclusion of class, Samantha suddenly called attention to my arrangement. She invited an encore performance of my earlier stage work. I recognized this particular notoriety as a type of revenge, being exacted in return for my episode of comedic impertinence. I might have expected this move, but I was distracted by my creation. I suppose that, under certain circumstances, Samantha and I do, indeed, operate underneath our own type of scoreboard. However, the mild pain and breezy insult that we trade, through quips and quirks, is intended as playful mischief, rather than degradation or demolition. I suppose that I simply fail to take notice due to other remembered engagements with my opponent.

I had chosen to work from one of her trays. As instructed, I fastened a block of that spongy green material to the bottom. I covered that with tufts of moss. I inserted several stems of the tallest dandelion flowers into the sponge. Their puffy blooms stood tall above the moss. Next, I affixed a row of fully open rose blossoms, in pink, and I backed that with a row of silver thistle heads. My inspiration came from a recollection of a section of landscape greenery that I had seen at the golf course, earlier in the day. My dandelion stems were trees in my mind, and the roses and thistles were neatly trimmed hedges. The moss served as my imaginary grass. I thought that I done a good job in blending and contrasting colors and textures. I also considered that my creation projected a pleasing aroma. The only shortcoming, to which I might submit, was a lack of flow. My display was fixed in straight lines, top to bottom. Overall, I thought that I had done an admirable job in replicating my vision, in miniature.

Nevertheless, my reverie was interrupted by a syrupy chirp. "Jack, Chéri, would you mind describing your arrangement to the class, s'il te plaît?"

I was startled, but recovered quickly, "Not at all, what would you like to know?"

"Perhaps, a theme would be nice."

Through parading naivety, I offered, "Well, I was actually trying to create a golf motif."

My response inspired a general sense of amusement and a varied collection of jibes.

One of the husbands asked, "Yeah, what is that, the woods behind thirteen at Augusta?"

I was impressed.

One of the wives offered, "I think it's kind of cute."

I was delighted.

Samantha asked, "And, how would you use your arrangement?"

Startled once again, I said, "I don't know... on a table or something."

Another husband inserted, "I get it! It's a trophy...the consolation prize for the Rose Bowl of golf!"

I was humbled.

I gazed at my inquisitor. She was chuckling softly, behind a narrow cover provided by two pink nailed fingers. She removed them from her lips after seeing my face. She smiled warmly, and tilted her head slightly to the left. I saw pure endearment through her expression. I was renewed, and I knew that I had done my duty.

I had dedicated my evening in support of my wife. My focus was upon her, rather than me. This demeanor rendered me free to participate and fairly impervious to witty commentaries. If anything, I expected an even exchange of pleasure, Sam's for my faithful presence, and mine for her success and happiness.

While Samantha was offering her closing comments, I reflected on my role. I considered that I had been playing this particular part with the special women of my life for as long as I could remember. In fact, I recalled a similar episode, or rather, the original performance, in this capacity. I was fifteen years old at the time. I simply agreed to accompany my girlfriend's band of princess goblins on their annual Halloween foray. I was the only male. I committed myself to her pleasure. I was focused on her, rather than me. However, the sacrifice suggested by such an assessment is not pure. On that night, as on this evening, I was rewarded with an expression of endearment, from which I accept a luxurious sense of satisfaction. I gazed at my bride making her final round of the tables, and I recalled her remark about my recovered life.

"Mon Chéri, you have not changed. You are who you were. By the Grace of God, you have been restored, and the life that was intended has been returned."

This is another example of uncanny authenticity that seems to oversee our pairing.

After our guests had departed I helped Samantha straighten the classroom. While she disassembled the teaching buckets, I policed the workstation tables and the surrounding area. In the midst of these proceedings, Sam floated an unexpected commendation.

"Merci beaucoup, Mon Amour."

"You don't have to thank me. I had a good time, actually. I think things went very well."

"Oui, yes… Mon Petit Malin!"

"I'm sorry. What is petit malin?"

"Perhaps, I should say, c'est un frimeur?"

"I was trying to be a good sport, if you don't mind."

"Oui, yes, Monsieur Je-Sais-Tout!"

This series of unintelligible remarks called the hanging job offer to mind. I did not typically misread her signals, but this entire evening had been something quite new, and unique, to our team. I revisited my cavalier performance from earlier in the evening. The air seemed to acquire a chill.

"OK, whatever you're doing doesn't sound good. Just say it, please. Are you angry?"

Sam said, "Non, je suis aussi, Une Petit Malin."

"Look, I still don't get it. We don't have to go. I promise."

Sam giggled her words, "Ah oui, Mon Chéri is no longer the smart-ass in class. You have revealed something new this evening. I am simply returning the favor, oui, merci."

I laughed, and I relaxed, grateful for my misinterpretation.

I offered, "Now, I see. You know what? I used to like my smart-ass teachers, and I think that they liked me, too. I made good grades in their classes."

"We shall see."

"We shall see? What does that mean? What do you have in mind, homework or something?"

"Perhaps you will be taking my exam."

"I'm sorry, but it's time for me to go home."

"C'est la vie. I will give my exam there."

"I don't think students are supposed to go home with teachers."

"We may stay here if you prefer, but you will be taking my exam, regardless."

"In that case, I think I might feel smarter at home. Can I study first?"

"Non. If you have paid attention in class, you should do well."

"What happens if I don't pass?"

"You will have to repeat the class, and the exam."

"Well, this might be a long night. We should get going."

Sam bounced her brows, shrugged and smiled. She tucked away the teaching buckets, and locked up, while I collected the trash. The shop was ready for the Wednesday orders. We turned out the lights, and we exited through the rear service door. I accompanied Samantha to her car, which was angled into a back corner of the small blacktop service area. At her car door, she tipped up on her toes and kissed my lips.

"Mon Chéri, you have made me happy tonight. Je t'aime."

"Je t'aime aussi, Teach. The class was great, and so were you."

"Don't try to be cute. Your class is not finis."

"I'm trying for extra credit, not cute."

"Come right home, you will need extra time for extra credit."

"Oui, Madame."

"Au revoir, Chéri."

CHAPTER 7

The Qualifier

....

I was up early. The day of my qualifying event had finally arrived. I had thirty-six holes of medal-play golf, waiting. Medal Play is the official name for counting every proper stroke of the golf ball, and penalty strokes, which are incurred and added as a result of various improper strokes of the golf ball, plus all the peculiar oversights and mishaps that tend to plague tournament competition. I held two official tee times for this event. My entry acceptance letter listed my times as 7:20 a.m. for the morning round, and 12:30 p.m. for the afternoon round. I had been focused upon that morning golf time during my morning home time. I planned to be at the course at just after six o'clock. I would already be at the course for the afternoon time, and barring any issue, outside the category of force majeure, meaning, violent thunderstorms, tornadoes, or earthquakes, I would be waiting on the tee, when my name was called, for both times.

This being a qualifier event for an official, nationally sanctioned, amateur tournament, I understood those tee times to be exacting, and critical. I also understood that my play, and my behavior, throughout the span of this grueling day, would be scrutinized and policed by ominous figures, wearing blue sport coats, and white hats. As far as I'm concerned, those dignitaries are the supreme guardians of the game. The association that they represent hangs in my mind like an image of Mount Olympus, and the officially adorned men and women who descend into the realms of earthly competition are like gods and goddesses, who oversee and guide, and—on occasion, torment, the temporal participants of their golf tournaments. Nevertheless, I feel quite privileged to play in their officially sanctioned events. In fact, being accepted as a competitor, and seeing my name on their stationary, is a delightfully rewarding experience. In return for that grace, I offer them my respect, and my submission. I consider them to be faithful watchmen, but unnerving observers.

I had prepared a traditional childhood breakfast for my nourishment. I had two slices of white toast slathered with a mixture composed of two boiled eggs and two pats of butter. I was almost finished when Samantha emerged from our bedroom.

Behind non-seeing eyes, being rubbed by delicate fists, I heard, "Mon Chéri, why do you have to go so early? Even the sun is still sleeping. You cannot possibly see to play."

"Honey, the sun will be up when I get to the course. I can't be late."

"Mon Dieu, Chéri."

"Sam, the penalty for being late is DQ."

"Qu'est-ce que c'est, DQ?"

"Disqualification, my love. I have never before seen that mark beside my name, and I don't intend to today."

"Mon Chéri, you are never late for any of your appointments."

"Merci, but, I carry the mark, even though I've never been hit with the stick."

"La Vache, I cannot speak with you like this so early in the morning."

"Go back to bed, my love."

"When should I arrive, and how will I find you?"

"Honey, you don't have to come. Just finish at the store, and I'll meet you back here, after I finish at the course."

I had settled the job interview with Mr. Woodson and Samantha. As things stood, Sam and I would be spending the upcoming weekend in residence at the Wambaw Club. Apparently, both my overseers were anxious to evaluate the prospective participants of a potential merger. We were holding confirmed seats on the eight o'clock Delta flight from Kansas City to Atlanta. We planned to overnight at a sister property of my hotel chain, which served the Atlanta Airport. I had a car reserved through the weekend. Thursday morning Sam and I were scheduled to drive from Atlanta to Savannah, and then, on to Wambaw. We were expected for dinner at the club that evening.

I felt secure with these plans, but hardly peaceful. Prior to our departure, I had to play thirty-six holes of golf, transfer, to and from the golf course, twice, steal a shower, and eat a bite of something. I imagined Sam and I reenacting the famous O.J. Simpson airport commercial, except that, in my version, she and I would be leaping over baggage and passengers in an effort to reach an ever-diminishing doorway, which was surrounded by a giant clock. I saw the doorway shrinking away with every tick that clicked huge hands toward 8:00 p.m. I kept these thoughts to myself, of course. I mean that the next few days had been specifically devoted to my personal persuasions, after all, and the newly envisioned disasters seemed to blend well with the usual soul-unhinging fermentations that arise whenever I realize that my name is listed on a formal tournament tee sheet.

In response to my offer of mercy, Sam said, "Non, Chéri, I want to see you play."

"Yes, well, I can promise that you'll see me, but as far as the rest is concerned, you'll need to keep an open mind."

"Arrête ça, Chéri. You have prepared and you will be rewarded."

"That sounds nice, honey, but it doesn't seem to work that way. I feel sort of proud that you want to come, but a little nervous too. Let's just say that I plan to do my best, and we'll see how things turn out."

"Très bien, Mon Amour."

"I'll leave your name at the gate. But, after you enter the facility, park somewhere, and go around the front of the clubhouse. Don't try to go inside, just come around the building. Ask someone to direct you to the first tee. You need to be on the tee before 12:30, or finding me will be more difficult."

"Who should I ask?"

"It doesn't matter, just someone. Whoever is standing around will know. But, don't worry about crowds of people or anything. It's not going to be like you've seen on TV. You'll be the only member of my gallery."

"Mon Chéri, I thought that I could be your caddie. I have never known you to play twice in one day. I want to help, so that you will not be too tired for the remainder of our evening."

I chuckled, but cautiously. Samantha's offer was puzzling. I could recall being assisted, quite graciously, by my recovery friends, but in those cases, I obviously needed some type of help. There was nothing needful or necessary about this golf tournament. It was, at best, an indulgence. I couldn't recall a single person from my past who had voluntarily pledged their personal service in support of my preferred pursuits. I was simply bearing witness to an unconditional act of loving concern. I had seen that from friends, but never from family. In the end, I felt warmed, but also somewhat frozen. I experienced a mild sense of shock, which was composed of equal parts lilting flattery, sentimental gratitude and shameful suspicion. Following her offer, I instantly wondered whether Samantha could carry the bag for eighteen holes.

My response was a cover and a hedge; "Thank you, honey, but can we wait and see how that goes? I'll be delighted to have you by my side, either way."

"Chéri, will the other players have people watching?"

"Some, but as I mentioned, it's not like on TV. Some of the younger players will have parents following. A collection of guys from the club are always around. I've seen a wife or girlfriend following, on occasion. There will be a smattering of caddies. And, some players do, indeed, have friends that come out to watch their play.

"As a matter of fact, I once played against a gentleman who had a legitimate gallery following him around the course. He was sort of famous around the local amateur circuit. Once again, he wasn't TV famous, but still, a legendary figure in the eyes of the resident golf community. I had never met him before that tournament. As usual, I was already on the tee, waiting for our time, that day. I introduced myself to the other members of our group as they approached. The Legend arrived last."

"Legend? Chéri…."

"That's right. He was, indeed, legendary in that area. Now, that tournament was not like today's event. It wasn't nationally sanctioned. I mean that the rules for play were observed and enforced, but, let's just say that the general atmosphere around the course was less formal. Anyway, when the Legend finally appeared, he was riding in a golf cart, followed by ten men in other golf carts. They had six carts altogether. They swung around the tee in a sort of Airforce squadron maneuver, which left them positioned side by side, on an embankment, overlooking the first tee. The Legend had a caddie for this event. He was also the driver of their golf cart. I was walking, by the way.

"Like I said, I had heard of the Legend before that day, but I had never met him. He went by a surprising name. In other words, the name didn't seem to fit with my image of legendary status. He introduced himself as 'Poochie' Corlis. I can't imagine that that was his real name."

Sam laughed, " 'Poochie'? Chéri…."

"Right, do you see? Nevertheless, there he was, easily fifteen years my senior, sort of a refined, sunbaked, grizzle of a man, but standing in at six foot three, and carrying two hundred and some odd pounds of 'Poochie.' And please don't ask, because I didn't ask about that name. Anyway, this unexpected stampede simply served to ratchet my normal dose of tournament anxiety, until I felt as if I were a tuning fork, emitting an audible thrum.

"Poochie's gallery was composed of a raucous crowd of wooly men, who looked better suited for benches at a football game than along the fairways of a golf match. They all carried large coolers on their carts, and everyone, that I saw, had a beer in hand. While we were exchanging scorecards and deciding the honor on the tee, one of Poochie's outlaw fans hollered down from one of the carts. I had my back turned against the insulting remark.

"I heard, 'Hey, Slick, I'll give you ten bucks for them shoes when we're finished!'

"I held no doubt that that wisecrack was intended for my ear. I was wearing my tournament shoes. You know…the red-white-and-blue ones?"

"Oui, yes, I like those fancy shoes, Chéri. Will you wear them today?"

"Ummm… no, I'm wearing the brown-and-white saddles, but never mind. That day, after that remark, I did something far from ordinary. I don't know, really. My reaction was a type of offensive play intended as a defensive strategy inside a threatening atmosphere. I met his derogatory comment with an impromptu story that rolled off my tongue, as if I were reciting the pledge of allegiance.

"Without delay, or hint of derision, I said, 'Thanks, but I can't do it. Johnny Miller gave me these shoes after his last round in the 1975 Atlanta Classic. I was a shoe shine kid for the pros that day. Mr. Miller said that I should keep them nice, and only wear them for tournaments.'

"Is that true, Chéri?"

"Not even close, honey.…Listen to what happened.

"A voice from the gallery said, 'No shit? For real?'

"Before I could respond, all six golf carts were empty, and I was surrounded by a crowd of admirers, gawking over my famous shoes. In fact, one guy spilled some beer on the tip of my left shoe and almost started a fight."

"Mon Chéri, that is another story?"

"No it's not. For real, that really happened. The good part is that the shoe issue was instantly forgotten."

"Did you play well that day, Chéri?"

"Yes and no. Something about 'Poochie' and his renegade gallery made me sort of crazy. I actually played terrible over the course of the front nine. I made small, unforeseeable mistakes on every hole. I was six over par when we made the turn. Then, on the tenth tee, I noticed that the whipping on my driver had broken loose. Like I said, weird things happen in tournaments."

"Qu'est-ce que c'est, whipping?"

"Oh, that's that black cord that wraps around the club head, where the shaft is inserted. It's supposed to stabilize the wood, against the vibration of the steel. Anyway, after playing terrible on the front nine, and dealing with the rabble rousers the entire time, I suppose that I went a little insane, again.

"Once again, I don't know why I said what I said. I might say that the unexpected shock of seeing my wounded club simply detonated my fizzing emotions. Anyway, on the tee at ten, I just blurted out a statement, which appeared as a brazen accusation. I was feeling frustrated, but as I said, a little crazy too.

"I addressed the gallery in particular, but rather boldly. I said, 'You know what? I was starting to like you guys, but I guess that y'all had me totally fooled. I out-drive everybody on nine, and then, after the turn, and while I'm in the clubhouse, somebody cuts the whip on my driver. You're nothing but a bunch of cheaters. Who did it?!'

"I held my driver aloft as proof. Now, under normal circumstances, to say that that remark was daring is at best an understatement. Foolhardy and reckless, or just plain stupid is more fitting. Like I said, that gallery was composed of men who appeared as if they were a reunion group of professional football players. And, they were also well-fueled for the second half of our game.

"I attempted to appear defiant, underneath a frosty shower of abject fear, while I waited for the expected attack. However, and once again, something quite extraordinary happened. I heard a hearty round of laughter burst forth from the riders in the gallery. I credit my saving grace to a weird sort of antagonistic camaraderie that had enveloped our group. In fact, the same guy who made the original comment about my shoes offered the return. He left the seat of his ride, speaking, as he approached me and my disheveled golf club.

"He said, 'What the hell, Slick? We've been pulling for your sorry-ass and them Johnny Miller shoes, since the first hole. We didn't touch your club. Gimme that thing!'

"He snatched my club from my hand, and extracted a giant knife from the leather scabbard attached to the military belt that was holding his canvas work pants. He turned the driver up, and with the sun glinting off a blade that appeared more like a Persian scimitar than a folding knife, he slashed through the loose windings of the whip. He pulled the remnants away, threw them to the ground, twirled the naked driver once, and handed it back to me.

Turning to leave, he said, 'Now it's fixed. Hit it, 'Slick', let's get this thing going. I gotta get down to the beach before dark, or Mama's gonna chew my sorry ass off."

"Mon Chéri, perhaps, I should just wait for you at home."

"I'm sorry, honey, I got kind of carried away. Please don't think of that story as a common depiction of the game. It's kind of funny though. Something about that guy, or that gallery, and 'Poochie,' I mean that, he fixed me, as well as the club, through that strange gesture of kindness. I shot two under par on the back nine. I carded a 76 for that round. I finished one stroke behind, 'Poochie.' That score wasn't good enough to win, but I was left feeling quite proud. The course and the tournament weren't my only competitors that day. Listen, don't be afraid. Please come, I want you to."

Once again, this last comment was issued from an engine that was running rich, but stuck in second gear. I was committing myself out of a combination of hopeful desire and boastful vanity. I wanted to perform for my bride, but she would be witnessing a show, which would be decorated with improvisational acts, inspired by unexpected prompts and incidental cues, rather than an orchestrated production that moved along practiced lines and designated scenes. In other words, I understood that Samantha would be watching a patently authentic version of me. Golf, in general, and tournament golf, in particular, produces a stage, from which the performers are inevitably, and inescapably, disrobed of costume and disarmed of pretense. I was actually giving her an especially beloved gift, which she did not expect to receive. In Samantha's mind, she would know me a little better, following the upcoming round of golf.

Sam said, "Oui, yes, I am coming, and I will help you manage unruly spectators."

"Thank you, but we'll wait and see about that, too. Look, the weather report looks good for the entire day, but it's going to be hot. Don't wear anything heavy and don't wear jeans. You can't wear jeans at the club."

"Ç'est dommage. I was planning to come barefoot, in my short jeans and a bathing suit top. Now, I'll have to plan something totally different. Bon sang, Chéri! Why do you think I wear white at the tennis club? We have rules too, you know…."

"Ok, ok, I'm sorry. I'm a little rule crazy today. 'No Jeans Allowed' just seems to be the first rule at every club that I've ever known."

"Mon Chéri, You have not shown such a keen interest for the rules of behavior in any of your previous events. Why is this one different?"

"It's not really, other than the fact that it is nationally sanctioned. And, that's a fact, not a wisecrack. We'll be supervised and observed by certified officials of the game. You'll see them. They'll be wearing blue sport coats and white hats.

"You're right, though, I haven't participated in this type of event since we've been together. You know how I tend to retain the behaviors, which have been conditioned by past programming. I played in one of these qualifiers when I was much younger. I was playing well, too. Bradley Janes was my caddie that day. During the afternoon round, on the back nine, we came to a par four hole that turned to the left off the tee; a dog leg, in golf parlance. Anyway, that hole looks good to my eye. I feel comfortable envisioning the flight of my ball from the tee. Earlier in the day, I hit my drive, such that it flew straight for a distance, but turned at the corner. That shot followed the exact course of the fairway. I hit a going hook, as they say. I hit that ball with just the right touch of counter-clockwise spin."

"I know about spinning the ball, Mon Chéri."

"I know that, honey, but you're left-handed, and we do spin in opposite directions sometimes."

"You might be spinning around out there all alone today."

"Look, let's forget about the stories for now. I'm making you angry, and it's early, and I don't really mean to upset you. I should just get going, before I'm late...."

"Dis-moi, s'il te plaît."

"Ok, but quickly. When I came to that same hole, during the afternoon round, I noticed that one of our observers was watching from a golf cart. He was parked in the distance, at the corner of the fairway, away from the green, on the outside portion of the turn. I could see the blue coat and the white hat, behind the wheel. I planned to hit my tee ball along the same flight path that I had used during the morning round. However, on this subsequent occasion, my swing was disjointed. I hit the ball in a manner which was exactly opposite of my intention. I hit what is known as a double cross, only in reverse. I was too quick from the top, and my clubface slid across the ball, imparting a clockwise spin. My golf ball whirled away from the tee, following a course that was opposite to the direction of the fairway turn. I hit an inadvertent slice. I don't think that happens in tennis. I mean, I accept the fact that you can hit a poor shot, but you don't attempt one type of shot, and then hit the ball in direct contradiction to your plan."

"Oublie, Chéri. Continuez, s'il te plait."

"Well, that shot went sailing over the observer's head, and continued flying deep into the woods. It was the worst tee ball of my entire day. By rule, I had to play a second ball from the tee, as a provisional shot, in case I couldn't find my first ball. Anyway, as Janes and I followed the trail of my wayward slice, we passed by the observer's cart. He said nothing, but exited his ride, and followed Janes and me into the woods.

"On foot, in the woods, I turned, and remarked, 'I appreciate your help, but we can find it.'

"He replied, rather coldly, 'I'm not here to help you find your ball.'

"Now, besides being rattled by tournament nerves, and the simmering fright of having to add a penalty shot for a lost ball, I was shocked by a remark that was, in reality, an implied accusation. I mean that, if that gentleman was not helping me locate my ball, he must be following along in the capacity of a detective. He was looking for a slight of hand maneuver, a foot wedge, or the old, hole-in-the-pocket-down-the-pant-leg, miraculous golf ball materialization trick."

Through laughter, Samantha giggled, "Mon Chéri, you cannot be serious!"

"Oh contraire, Madame."

"Dis-moi."

"I actually found my ball, before long. I felt relieved, but of what burden, I did not know. I remained feeling chain-locked guilty, despite the astonishing find. My ball was resting on a luxurious bed of pine needles. It was precariously poised for an easily observed, and ever more damaging disaster. I was afraid to get near the thing. The ball lay there, as if throbbing in radioactive menace."

"Arrête-ça, Chéri."

"I'm not kidding, in the least. That ball needed to remain perfectly still while I positioned myself and my club, atop four inches of vacillating pine needle purgatory.

"I remember attempting to dispel some of the tension by promoting a note of honesty. I sent Janes out of the woods to work as a spotter for the escape attempt. I peered over the ball, as if it were the last egg of an extinct bird.

"I offered, 'This is my ball.'

"The observer cautioned, 'Make sure.'

"I said, 'It has a red dot, under the three. This is my ball, for sure.'

"My attendant responded, 'I believe you.' But, I didn't believe him. We were twenty yards off the fairway, standing together, like Lewis and Clark, peering out of a primordial wilderness, and he was wearing a sport coat.

"As I took my address, standing on fluffy clouds of brittle brown straw, I could feel his eyes burning laser holes through my back. I hovered the club head of my four iron an entire inch above the webbing that suspended my precious orb. I had a half swing worth of unencumbered air, within which to generate enough punch to propel the ball through a warren of woodland horror that made a professional football prevent defense look like a Saturday morning opener for the Jr. Pee Wees. I took a breath, focused my mental eye on the round white underbelly of the egg, nested beneath my perch, and I swung the club. I don't think I opened my eyes until I heard Janes exclaim, 'I got it!' I didn't relax until I heard the official say, 'Nice play, son.'"

Sam said, "I think that I will wait for you at home, Chéri."

"Oh no, you're not. I'll be waiting for you at 12:30."

"You make golf sound scary."

"It's only a game, my love, and I need my teammate."

"Oui, yes, I will come, but you may need more than I can offer."

"I'll be looking for you. Don't be late, je t'aime…."

"How could I be late, after hearing these stories? Au revoir, Mon Amour."

The conversation with Samantha had delayed my personal schedule by several minutes, but I wasn't severely off my game. I arrived at the course just past 6:00AM, and as I had predicted, there was plenty of sunlight beaming through the tree leaves. I could see just fine. I had no trouble settling my vehicle and myself.

My car had served as a mobile locker room for as long as I had been driving. I stored all my golf equipment in the trunk. My recovery mentor, Grant, calls me a 'Trunk Jockey.' I take no offense from that remark. He also says that no longer having need to live out of the trunk of his car serves as a pleasant reminder of a successful journey in recovery. I have appropriated that notion as a future goal for my own journey. I had, indeed, lived out of the trunk of my car for the span of two days, when I had first landed in Kansas. However, laying sole claim to a clubhouse locker is not nearly the driving force of my recovered life. Like Grant, I am encouraged by a familiar vision that exists as an attainable prize.

I made my way to the course, clicking along on the tops of brand-new cleats, affixed to my old, brown-and-white saddle shoes. I was wearing a pair of slacks, cut from a summer-weight poplin, dyed in the deeper tan color which is typically described by the words British Khaki. I thought they matched the saddle of my shoes. I wore a white, banded-sleeve, polo shirt with an alligator on the left breast. I had packed a similar shirt in pine green and an extra pair of white socks to use as a refreshment outfit for the afternoon round. On my head, I wore an ancient, white, high-hat visor, with the logo of my old Atlanta club embroidered on the front strap. I thought of my appearance as respectfully appropriate, but inconspicuous. I had dressed myself to match my mood. I need a touch of forward-looking confidence, in order to add the preferred notes of swagger and flash to my wardrobe and my feet. Accordingly, I was not wearing my red-white-and-blue, Johnny Miller tournament shoes.

Before long, I was pitching warmup shots onto a seemingly endless carpet of verdant grass, barely speckled with the usual white glitter provided by other golf balls. I paused before changing clubs, to survey the vista that lay before my eyes. I saw tractor mowers moving in synchronized pairs, along distant fairways. I saw busy workers moving in and out snowy bunkers like ants over picnic napkins. I saw walking men, pushing mowers, across lush greens, and sweeping men, trailing behind, whipping the fresh cut surface with long pliable rods. In that moment, I reviewed my history with the game of golf, and I reflected upon my history with the game of life.

I smiled, genuinely, as I recalled Samantha's words, about being restored, rather than changed. She says, 'You are who you were in the beginning.' I wasn't seeing myself as someone who had acquired a higher station in life. I wasn't thinking of myself as someone who had stepped above, or beyond, my previous experiences, as if I had physically moved or transferred to an upscale neighborhood. I was, in that moment, the same man that I had been, in a former time. I had always been invited and welcomed into the game.

Holding present images, against past memories, I wondered if, from the very outset of our pairing, the game of golf hadn't served as a primary vehicle by which grace had been bestowed upon my life. Standing there, in the midst of opulent golfing glory, I issued a prayer of sorts. I mouthed a silent thank-you, and I sent it aloft. I expressed the previously elusive notion of gratitude toward the god of my understanding, and I reflected.

I had spent the greater portion of my golfing history on a course, and within the bounds of a club, which was very much like the one that I was presently overseeing. That club and that golf course were my home away from home for many years. That association was an oasis of peaceful hospitality, but outside the inhospitable desert of my chaotic home. I was welcome at the club. I was encouraged. I was trained. I was recognized and celebrated, but I was also taught and disciplined, appropriately. Moreover, and more significantly, I was accepted, regardless of my performance report, be that exceptional, or rather wanting.

At the club, I found my place on the golf course. However, I suppose that I afforded that perceived sense of belonging, to the club, rather than the game. As a kid, I did not realize that the attributes, which I enjoyed at the club, were conditional. Nor did I recognize that those same attributes were being afforded by the game of golf on an unconditional basis.

I only learned of the difference through my choices for life and recovery. After I outgrew my rights as a junior member, I was relieved of my oasis. I set out to restore that blissful refuge, but I did not possess the proper means. Against that deficit, I retired into a different type of sanctuary, which might be better described as bedlam. The benefits seemed comparable, but proved, over time, to require a far more exorbitant fee.

Nevertheless, throughout my endeavors, using the booze club, as a substitute for the golf club, I played the game that connected and persisted, through and across, lives and memberships. However, during those some odd years, and in addition to my clubs, I carried the attitude of an exiled king. I played through a sense of denied entitlement or cheated vitriol, and I raged against a theft of title and territory. Nevertheless, the game always took me. I was accepted at my worst and my lowest. At this point, I am certain that I could not know the game of golf until I gave up my reverence of the club, and in a similar manner, I could not know God until I surrendered my worship of liquor.

Not long into my journey of sobriety I was corrected by a club pro, in the exact manner in which I was coming to know teaching and discipline from my recovery mentor. I had participated in the annual championship tournament, sponsored by the local golf league. We had played through a steady rain for the entire day. Conditions were deplorable and so were the scores. I remarked, albeit absentmindedly, as I looked over the leaderboard.

'I can't believe that 78 is low medalist. Hell, I could have shot that with my eyes closed.'

'Pro' turned, in recognition of my comment, and although he was looking at me, he spoke toward the general crowd of onlookers.

He said, 'Well, if you can shoot 78 with your eyes closed, I hate to think of what caused you to post that 84 I just recorded, next to your name. But, please, keep that information private. I don't want to know.'

That remark was a hit among the players who were watching the leaderboard. I was somewhat less enthused, but I recognized that acerbic wit as recovery talk. I suppose that I see most clearly through contrast. In other words, while recovery has taught me to see the truth, my former journey provides the contrast, which enables the clear vision. From that formula, I need both, in order to proceed along the right path. As far as golf is concerned, I can now look, out and over, any golf club or course, through grateful eyes.

I have also been told that the vision through which I have been taught to see is simply a form of acceptance. Recovery has taught me to apply the words of a particularly appropriate prayer to the circumstances of my life. In recovery, that verse is known as the Serenity Prayer. The words are: 'God, grant me the serenity to accept the things that I cannot change, the courage to change the things that I can, and the wisdom to know the difference.' I suppose that golf first taught me the underlying notion of that prayer, through the words, 'Play the ball as it lies.'

I recall that prayer whenever I need to hole a par putt across a patch of dried green fungus, which is, quite literally, better compared to the flakey layers of fine French pastry than closely mown turf grass. I lift that prayer whenever I watch my golf ball careen away from a fairway that hasn't seen a drop of water since God removed the flood, and, I offer that prayer whenever I watch my shot dissolve within the confines of a bunker, as if it had been injected through a high powered syringe. When I can accept these events without transforming into a fountain of profanity or a club-slinging banshee, then I can say that I am playing the game of golf, rather than lamenting my lost privileges at the club. I could not express such thoughts before sobriety tuned my vision.

Along a different path, I have had to learn that pristine agronomic splendor does not preclude the possibility of disaster. For most of my life, I assumed that better course conditioning at the club translated into lower scores, a finer performance and a larger helping of grace. However, just like practice can't promise a perfect round on every occasion, pool table greens, sugary bunkers, checkerboard fairways, and surgical cuts of rough don't guarantee peaceful rounds and lower scores. In light of these revelations, I have discovered that acceptance simply substitutes a willingness to participate for the right to determine the outcome.

Nevertheless, despite a long history of presiding from the self-appointed stations of judge and jury, the game of golf has never turned me away. I have always been accepted, but also taught and disciplined, appropriately. Despite a proliferation of punctuation, provided by unjustifiable question marks, and inconceivable exclamation points, the game has allowed me to write my story. I am a better man, by pure grace. The grace bestowed through recovery, and the grace afforded through the game of golf. However, the recipient of those gifts is, quite feasibly, the same man that God intended in the first place.

I made my way to the first tee, after completing my regimen of practice putts. I was given my scorecard for the morning round, behind the tee, and underneath an official tent. I watched a gentleman in a blue sport coat check my name on his starter's sheet. I also greeted my companions for the event. We would be living together over the next eight or nine hours of life. I did not know my playing partners, but I was not surprised when we introduced ourselves. I had already picked them out of the crowd of possible candidates who were preparing for the day. For my own relative safety and security, my formative years had forced me to watch, and review, and perceive, and predict.

I can't decide if this ability is a learned skill, a gifted talent, a malevolent curse, or simply the result of certain inbred insecurities. Nevertheless, I rarely miss my guess. I had chosen two candidates while on the practice tee, and I had identified the third on the putting green.

During the introductions, we exchanged our scorecards. I would be scoring for Lenny Mullen. At a glance, Lenny appeared to be older than me, but by an indefinite number of years. He was somewhat thick, although my judgment pertained to musculature rather than mental capacity. He wore a bushy mane and shaggy brows. The unruly darkness of his hair seemed to match the exterior aura that he cast over our foursome. His look was intense and focused. He had a caddie playing for his team. His name was, simply, Bob. Lenny offered that he was a member of a club that resided some odd number of miles south of the city, and of which I was unfamiliar.

Our partner competitors introduced themselves as David, and 'Trip.' These names were attached to men who appeared to be brothers, although David was tall and thin, while 'Trip' was rather diminutive both in height and weight. Nevertheless, these young men offered that they were summering college students. With that fact in mind, I fixed myself in the middle position, on a range of ages, which spanned, approximately, twenty years. 'Trip' freely offered that his father was a member of our host club. He added that he played here regularly, except for the occasions when he played with David at his other course, which just happened to belong to one of the finer clubs, nearer to town. This information served to resolve the curious introductory moniker. 'Trip' was a nickname indicating the fact that he was the third male in possession of a longer name, which I did not attempt to discover.

We all hit acceptable drives off the first tee. Along that initial stroll together toward our shots, Trip posted a question of sorts.

He said, "Hey man, are you gonna carry your own bag all day? Who are you, Iron Man or something?"

My vanity enjoyed the unexpected stroke. My age prompted me to look toward Lenny. I saw that he was moving down the far right hand side of the fairway, well ahead of the common luggage bearers. Bob was hanging back, just off my right. I saw him laugh, but turn away.

Through an amiable chuckle, I offered, "Sure, it's no big deal. I've even been known to carry double on occasion. Kinda balances the load. Lemme know if you get tired, and we'll work out a fee."

This remark was intended as a defense of my ground, but also to break the ice. The younger men appeared to accept the comedy and the insult as an appropriately balanced wisecrack. I actually heard Bob laughing. I didn't think that Lenny was concerned with friendly relations. This snapshot frame of time would serve as the general model, which would accurately depict our intergroup relations throughout the span of this long day. Lenny kept to himself, mostly, focusing upon his game and achieving an elusive and long-suffered goal. David was a polite young gentleman throughout the day, also focused on his game, but looking toward a goal that seemed to fall into the category of expected result, rather than astonishing achievement. Trip would hold true to his first remark. He was the most expressive member of our group. I would say that expectation and entitlement were synonyms inside his game. He often called our attention to certain denials and outright thefts that were being credited to his account by obtuse fates.

I suppose that my appearance on the course also suggests a sense of entitlement. I am frequently questioned about certain announcements of anger and displeasure that follow a shot which has ended its journey inside an obviously respectable circumstance. In my defense, I prefer to accept what I deserve, rather than to take what I can get. If I plan to hit a butter-cut slider as an approach shot, but double-cross that swing, instead, I judge myself as undeserving of an acceptable result, in spite of the fact that my golf ball is lying on the putting surface.

I found myself returning to Trip's initial comment, throughout the morning round. Basically, I wondered who I was. I saw myself taking steps toward major commitments to mutually exclusive endeavors. I was attempting to qualify for the right to change my life through the prestige attached to a nationally recognized golf tournament, and a nationally recognized job opportunity. I didn't think of Samantha until we made the turn. I remembered her, while we waited for the tenth fairway to clear. Of all things, she would be arriving before long, to support a battle between self-conflicting interests, and I considered that she would be paying the bill for the war. I kept seeing her beaming smile behind carefully arranged work tables and flower buckets. I completed the morning round, under the merciful grace provided by justifiable distraction. In other words, my body played, while my mind wandered.

A seasoned tournament golfer might point out that I carry around a set of personal distractions like another set of clubs. Among this peculiar set of weird tools is a proclivity to remember scores. I have a tendency to recall every shot that has been hit by all members of my group. I can also calculate, without vigorous effort, every score that has been officially penciled. This is not police work intended to ensure honesty among potential thieves, but a gauge of my personal status. I like to know where I stand with my immediate competitors. I also perfected this particular acumen, at home, when I was a kid.

Before we signed our cards, I already knew that David was our medalist, with a score of 73. Lenny was one shot back, carding a 74. Trip and I were four strokes off the group lead, posting rounds of 77. We had a strong foursome, by all remembered standards. Everyone played fairly well, given the venue and occasion. Remarkably, our group was unscathed by notable incidents of unjustifiable assault, and unprecedented glory. I carded the only double bogey of our day. I hit my approach to the par five, fourteenth hole, slightly heavy. My ball found the pond, which fronts that green. I dropped out of that lateral hazard, and adding the mandatory penalty stroke, I hit my fifth shot on the green, and proceeded to two putt, for a seven. Nevertheless, I was officially recorded, and preparing for the afternoon round, at high noon.

CHAPTER 8

To Caddie or Not to Caddie

....

I watched a gentleman, wearing a white hat and blue sport coat, verify the fact that all the carefully recorded numbers did, indeed, tally to match a final score of 77. He touched a pencil against each marking, as if he were soaking up the data through the lead point. With each recorded figure, the pencil tapped against the card, twice, apparently indicating the calculation in progress. I couldn't decide who was looking closer. After he applied the much desired checkmark, and handed the card to one of the practiced calligraphers, who would eventually etch that number beside my name on the tournament leaderboard, I went to my car.

I wanted to change for the afternoon round. The temperature was a toasty 88 degrees. I gauged the humidity in the air by the adhesion of my shirt. I felt as if I had passed through a heat tunnel and was now enveloped by a skintight wrapper, made of cellophane, rather than cotton pique.

The final verdict over the morning round left me feeling rather blasé. I hadn't bothered to inspect the big board for my position in the field. At best, I suppose that I was feeling unembarrassed. I knew that I had to cover at least four strokes during the afternoon round, to approach David, but that also meant that he had to falter, and this scenario of gain and loss would certainly hold true against the other competitors, who I had yet to see. Nevertheless, digging out of a hole can be a respectable occupation. However, there is a point, the embarrassing point, as a matter of fact, where the digging seems to turn into mining. Once your particular hole becomes so deep that the only visible light appears as a vague glow over the edge of the rim, your business becomes somewhat blurry. I suppose that, as golfers, we are more closely aligned with diggers than miners. I have spent my time mining for hidden gold in dark shafts of unfathomable depth, but I have also been known as a fairly proficient digger, as well.

My other predominant tournament concern was simply, identity. That score, which would be posted and etched, next to my name on the leaderboard, in perfectly crafted Old English Numerals, was like a medieval tribute. I saw Jack Weatherlow 77 as my new, or more definitive, name. As simply Jack Weatherlow I might have been anybody, but by adding the numbers beside the letters, I became identified and situated within the classes and ranks of our small leaderboard society. As things stood, I was being classified as someone of mediocre skill but inoffensive occupation.

The effect of the process was like watching a parade of citizens being reviewed by the royal court. The men in blue sport coats and white hats would be knighting various contenders, crowning potential kings, but also, banishing hordes of peasants to the mines for digging practice. At least, for the morning round, I was grateful of the fact that I was not Jack Weatherlow 84, a name that had frequented my past, and a name which was synonymous with mining, rather than golfing. Without seeing, I knew that I had retained the right to carry my clubs, instead of mining tools, for the afternoon round.

Safely secured behind the solid veil of my trunk, I began the process of changing costumes. I was shirtless, but shifting, when I heard a familiar voice.

"Oh la la. S'il te plaît, Monsieur, je suis perdu. Can you direct me to the first tee?"

Pulling the shirt down over my shoulders, I said, "Mademoiselle, have you ever heard of big American men who kidnap small French girls by throwing them into the trunks of their cars?"

I felt small hands encircling my chest, underneath my shirt. They pulled me close, just as I heard new words floating across my right ear.

"Non, Monsieur. Is that why the guards of fancy golf clubs are reluctant to allow French girls to enter, even though their name is on the list?"

I turned rather abruptly, "What happened?"

"Oublie, Chéri, I am here."

"Did they give you a hard time?"

"Non, Chéri, but I could tell that something was unusual."

"Just stick close to me, please."

"Oui bien sûr, that is my plan, for now and forever."

"Thank you, but don't get crazy. You need to focus. We're at a golf tournament."

"Oui je sais, as I said, I am here to be your caddie."

"Hang on, just a second. I need to change my socks, and then we'll get down to the tee. Have you had anything to eat?"

"Mon Chéri, I did not know that you would be changing outfits."

"Well, I do in the summertime, for this type of tournament. Look at my other shirt? It's completely soaked and too sticky."

Samantha angled away from her embrace and attempted to peer into the trunk. Despite remaining somewhat attached and facing one another, I took note of the maneuver. As she bent around my left shoulder, I watched the tale of her pine-green shirt rise up her back. I glimpsed a panel of warmly tanned flesh appear, below her rounded shirttail, and above the waistband of her white skirt. I was not leering by any means, but merely observing the movements, ordained by physical science. My eyes trailed over the upper edge of the skirt, and downward, along the line of one side pleat. Below the hem, I saw more sun-bronzed skin belonging to a rounded thigh, a straightened knee and a flexed calf. Below that, I saw a perfect ankle, holding an extended foot on the toes of white tennis shoes, which were marked with a figure that resembled the shape of an elongated 'U' in blue. I simply consumed this vision, as if I were enjoying a cookie, pilfered from a freshly baked batch. When Samantha returned to meet my face, I felt as if I had been caught.

"Mon Chéri, I can smell you."

"I'm sorry, but you can't take showers in the middle of golf tournaments."

"Non, Chéri, I like it."

With that comment hovering in the pungent air, Sam dipped her head away from my face. I felt the tip of her tongue touching the skin along my neck. I jumped.

She said, "You are salty."

"This has to stop!"

I watched her head fall backward. She was celebrating a minor victory, taking place inside a larger contest, in which I am the favored opponent, but a rival who lacks a ready awareness of the ongoing scrimmage, and the impulsivity of delight in the abandon. Sam laughed heartily for a moment, before coming back to meet my face. She offered a serious expression and a mock salute. I saw joy, through knitted brows, pursed lips, and the movement of a straight hand, reflecting off a touch of her forehead.

She said, "Oui, Monsieur, I will be good."

I leaned back against the trunk, demonstrating an indiscreet manner of inspection. I looked over my bride. She instantly discerned my overt intentions, and offered a discordant curtsy. However, I held my pose and my gaze for a moment longer than she expected.

Realizing my error, I quickly offered, "Honey, you look lovely."

"Merci, but something is wrong. Do you think that we are we too matchy? Our shirts are the same color."

"No, my love, I don't think that anyone will be concerned about the color of our shirts. Just remember, stay close to me this afternoon."

"Quoi, hein, c'est ce que je veux dire!"

"I'm sorry, Traduire…"

"Why are so concerned with me staying close to you?"

"I might say that I just realized that I'm wearing my flashy tournament shoes."

"But you are not. Expliquer, s'il te plaît."

"You're right, but I'm still feeling a little conspicuous."

"Perhaps, you would prefer that I wait for you at home?"

"No, no, no…I don't want you to go. Just give me a second. I'm glad you're here. Proud really, but I didn't expect…I mean, I've never… Can we, please…just let this go?"

"Non, nous ne pouvons pas!"

"Look, it's like the other day. Remember when I was trying to share some of my history with golf tournaments, but ended up confessing secret feelings about your shoes? Can we just say that I suspect that this whole day will be like that conversation?"

"I did not come to distract you!"

"I'm not distracted in the least."

My preference was to avoid describing the stew of emotions that Samantha had inspired. For instance, the typical notion of distraction calls to mind the image of wandering attention. In this case, I wasn't anywhere close to that definition. In fact, Samantha's presence had focused my attention, rather precisely. I had been enveloped by an emotional sensation that was absolutely primal. I was feeling like a king or a warrior, who was bringing the prize kill into camp. I felt a prideful sense of satisfaction, idling on a vibrant energy, which seemed identical to lust. I also felt something like greed, as if I held rightful ownership to all the valuable property. Looking forward to our arrival at the tee, I was anticipating a celebratory parade, but I was not prepared to share the bounty.

I also noticed the presence of the more customary feeling of guilt. I was being reined by a whispering suggestion, which was undeterred by the thronging court of imaginary admirers. I was being reminded of the fact that Samantha was not a trophy kill, nor was she my personal property. That notion was confusing. We had spent long hours in the practice of giving ourselves to one another in order to know the true intimacy of being, as one flesh. In addition, the notion of belonging to one another easily translated into terms of property and ownership. Nevertheless, I was extracted from my conundrum by the saving grace provided by my seductive, autonomous, dependent.

Samantha said, "Oui, je vois! You think that you need to protect me, here in your world, and you are worrying about how you might provide that service, while you play your game."

"Umm… yes, that's about right."

"La Vache! I am your caddie today. I am taking care of you this afternoon. Where are your clubs?"

Properly distractedly, I returned, "Yes, well…I mean, they're down at the clubhouse."

Sam said, "Allons-y!"

I watched her as she moved away from my car, toward the clubhouse. With each step, she rose slightly, on her toes, as was her custom. I watched a creamy milkshake-colored ponytail bounce, and flow. I watched calf muscles flexing beneath the sashay of white pleats, and I watched tan arms begin their swing. Her procession carried a militaristic air of confident determination. I caught myself, after a moment. I performed a quick step jag and quickly caught one of her hands in mine. We walked together, toward the start of the afternoon round.

A larger crowd had gathered around the clubhouse during my absence. There was also a considerable number of golf bags deposited here and there and around the general vicinity of the practice green.

Sam asked, "Mon Chéri, how will you find your clubs among all this baggage?"

I answered as I moved our team through the crowd. "Sam, it's like one of those National Geographic Documentaries on TV. You know, when all those thousands of birds are all together on that lonely island in the sea, and one of a pair is gone for weeks looking for food. They always know where to return, even though everyone looks exactly the same. It's right here, see."

My smug smile was met by a slightly scary scowl.

"Mon Chéri, I am losing hope in thinking that I will ever truly know you. Unless knowing you means that I will never know exactly how you feel."

"Come on, you know me better than anyone. Don't think like that."

"Chéri, this comment does not match your mood at the car."

"That's because, up there, I had time to think, and down here, I need to do what is necessary. You know what Grant says, 'Your mind is like a bad neighborhood. Every time you go in there alone, expect to get beat up.' That statement might sound dumb, but it speaks truth."

"Oui, yes, and that is what I am trying to help you change."

"I know that, and I am grateful, but we have other things to do right now. Let's move over to the first tee, it's almost 12:30."

"I will take the bag, s'il te plaît."

"Are you sure? You can just walk along next to me if you prefer. I don't mind."

"Non, Chéri, I am your caddie."

"Ok, but look… you're going to have to do certain things. Please don't get mad when I tell you what you need to do. I probably won't have time to explain."

"That depends upon how you tell me."

"I promise to be gentle. Just think of them as mandatory suggestions, like program stuff."

"Oui, yes, I will follow your orders."

"See there? Now, I'm confused again…But never mind, let's just go, but wait a second. Here's lesson number one. Always carry the bag with the club heads facing front. You can use either shoulder underneath the strap, but club heads always face the direction in which you are walking. Never behind."

"Is that a rule of the game, Chéri?"

"Not exactly, it's simply the way it's done."

My bag was a relic of sorts. I had bought it when I acquired my last set of clubs. I had purchased the bag, but I had used proshop credit for the clubs. Both the clubs and the bag were ten years old. My bag was a travel version of the larger staff bags. It was mostly white vinyl, but featured green trim panels, which were fashioned from real leather. The strap was fairly wide, and sufficiently padded. I thought the weight was nominal. I had removed the rain gear from the back pocket and my inventory of balls was a little less than normal. I had removed all the shag balls.

I watched her hoist the bag onto her left shoulder. The sight of her carrying my golf bag was somewhat startling. In fact, I felt verklempt, as they say. A sentimental mist was effervescing through my nose and heading toward my eyes.

Before we took a step, I said, "Hang on a second, please. I'll be right back."

I rifled through one of the big pockets. I removed a zippered pouch and headed off toward the clubhouse. I left Sam, standing with my bag. I heard her call to me in a sort of whispered exclamation. I paid no attention. I returned in less than two minutes.

While I was replacing the pouch, Sam asked, "Chéri, what is happening? Where did you need to go so suddenly?"

From underneath my arm I retrieved a white, high-hat visor, embroidered across the front strap with the logo of the club and the name of this particular event. I presented the gift to my caddie.

I said, "We're a team right? Now, we really match, and you can keep the afternoon sun off your lovely face."

I watched concerned confusion transform into simple joy. Through a beaming smile I heard, "Merci beaucoup, Mon Amour. But, where did you get this hat?"

"All these types of tournaments provide a souvenir table for the participants and spectators. I just thought that you might be more comfortable underneath a little shade."

"Merci, Chéri, and once again, knowing you is going to be my lifelong study."

"Now let's go. It's almost time."

"Attendez, s'il te plaît."

I started to offer a complaint, but instantly realized that my gift was being properly applied. I watched Sam pull her ponytail through the back strap, and I watched her use a golf tee to extract her bangs from beneath the front strap. The finished product was devilishly agreeable.

"Qu'est-ce que tu penses?"

"It's perfect. No one will ever suspect that this is your first loop."

"Qu'est-ce que c'est?"

"I'll explain later, let's go."

Along the way I asked, "Hey, where did you get that tee?"

"I took some from the bowl on that first table. I thought that you might need them."

"But, I didn't see… never mind. Thank you."

"De rien, Chéri."

Despite certain unexpected negotiations over the rules, which governed the formation and operation of this new partnership, we arrived at the first tee several minutes before my afternoon time. As expected, we also enjoyed an unofficial cushion in timing provided by the inevitable delays in progress. I checked in with the starter, and I informed him that I would be taking a caddie for the round. He paid no apparent mind to that piece of information, as he applied the customary checkmark next to my name on his paring sheet.

I passed Lenny on my return trip.

He said, "Hey, do you know if they're watering these greens in-between rounds?"

I answered, "I do not."

Lenny said, "I'd bet they are. It's hot. The speed is going to be different, just wait'n see."

I said, "Thanks, I'll keep that in mind."

I noticed Samantha surveying the first fairway. She had the bag shouldered. I also saw Bob, arriving with Lenny's bag. He appeared to be surveying my caddie. He set his bag on the ground, in close proximity to Samantha's position.

I said, "Hey Bob, looks like we're almost ready. You feeling good? Y'all played pretty well this morning."

Still distracted by his observations, Bob returned, "Hi Jack, yeah, I'm good. Lenny's feeling good too. Sorry about that double out there."

"Thanks…couldn't help it. Just hit it fat is all. Listen… Bob, I'm taking a caddie this afternoon. Hey, Samantha, this is Bob. Bob this is Samantha. Sam…Bob, is carrying for Lenny. He's over at the starter's table, checking in."

The ensuing scene unfolded, as if I were a director, overseeing my actors, performing their parts. In this case, Samantha was playing the part of daytime, and Bob the night. Sam turned in a manner that was like the dawning sun. She radiated her light through a beaming smile. Bob, on the other hand, withdrew, without moving an inch, behind a darkening chagrin.

The dialogue for this scene occurred simultaneously.

Bob exclaimed, "Holy shit! I mean … I'm sorry."

While my caddie introduced herself, politely, and in French.

"Bonjour, Monsieur. I am caddying for Monsieur Jack."

In the flickering frames of passing seconds, I watched my French Sun become confused. The words that she had heard were accepted and contemplated and understood. Her smile stretched and her face drooped. Bob, being a good man at heart, retrieved his own light and offered it to my caddie through a smile that suggested sheepish regret, and hopeful reconciliation.

Bob stumbled along through chuffing laughter, "I'm sorry. Samantha, is that right? Please forgive me, but I … I mean, I didn't expect … I mean, you don't look like most of the caddies that I know. Please, call me Bob. We'll get these guys where they need to go today, Ok? If I can help you in any way, please let me know."

With these words floating in the air, Samantha turned toward me. I saw mild despondency transform into puzzlement. I offered a consoling shrug, which was intended to communicate, 'What can I say?'

I heard Bob interject. "Hey, set that bag down. You don't want to carry that thing all the time. You'll get yourself tired out for no reason."

Sam turned back, saying, "Merci."

She removed my bag from her shoulder and set it on end, in the same manner that Bob was demonstrating. I might have said, 'Cut. That's a wrap. Print it. We're done here.' However, I knew that this same scene was scheduled to repeat itself at least three more times, for Lenny and David and Trip. With each reprisal, the play was much the same for the male actors. Samantha, being a quick study, performed her part slightly different with each new introduction. I watched her expression conform to the presumed impression of her new acquaintance.

Lenny was polite, and attempted to appear nonchalant or indifferent to the presence of my new teammate. However, in stark contrast to his accustomed focus, he made his own study of my caddie. Throughout the remainder of the afternoon, I caught him stealing a glance, here and there, for a brief second of two. I judged him to be harmless, but I wondered about disturbing his preferred level of intensity. I saw no obvious anomalies arise in his game. Samantha greeted Lenny as if she might have welcomed a male customer into her flower shop. She was polite and cordial and respectful. Her French was offered in the same manner that she and I practiced in normal conversation.

David was obviously surprised by the introduction, but quickly adopted a disposition which I assumed to have been a product of his home life. David became a young gentleman in the company of an older woman. Although, I judged that he viewed Samantha in the character of one of his teachers, rather than as a relative, or one of his mother's friends. In this case, he was polite and cordial and respectful. Samantha adopted a soft expression in his company, and her French seemed to lilt upon a note of compassion.

Trip was a different matter. He clearly saw Samantha as an attractive young woman, who had been seduced into the service of my desires. After completing the formal introduction process, he cornered me, and feigning the secret confidence of male camaraderie, asked, "Hey Jack, is that your girlfriend? You are the man! I would love to get a girl to caddie for me."

I felt that my response was somewhat deceitful, but I was operating on my own preferential understanding. I think of Samantha as my girlfriend, who just happens to be my wife.

I answered in return, "She is."

I felt a twinge of regret reaching toward Trip throughout the afternoon round. I hold no doubt that Trip was solidly enamored by Samantha's presence. For Sam's part, she met Trip's obvious enthusiasm with an attitude of playfulness. Her expression was bright and open and inviting. She sprinkled her French more liberally in his direction, and Trip lapped it up, like a bowl of his favorite ice cream. In fact, to look from a distance, he appeared to have become my best friend. However, I was hardly the object of his inspired affections. He inserted himself and his bag, between Samantha and me, as we made our way toward our shots from the first tee.

Although Samantha did not demonstrate the first hint of encouragement toward Trip, her mere presence created a distraction that was so irresistibly seductive that I had to help Trip count his strokes on the second hole. That hole is a par three, and he took five to get down. Unfortunately, four of those strokes were putts.

If I were to be brutally honest, I should claim responsibility for the incident which disturbed Trip's ability to putt. My tee shot fell short of the green, and came to rest in the front bunker. Being the only member of our group who had not reached the putting surface with my first shot, I played from the sand before anyone hit a putt. This was slightly out of sync with the schedule of honor, but agreed upon by everyone in my group. To my own amazement, I executed a miraculous short side flop, which rolled up within a foot of the cup. This satisfying marvel was immediately met by a subsequent phenomenon offering supplementary surprise. Sam was waiting, with rake in hand, to clean up my mess. This image was even more amazing than her pocket full of golf tees. I had provided no instruction in either case.

I whispered to her as I extricated myself from the bunker. "I can rake this time, if you prefer."

She returned, softly, "Non, Chéri, I am your caddie."

As if a parent to a child, I said, "Please, make it smooth for the next group."

I heard, "Comme un galçage sur un gâteau!"

I did not fully comprehend her remark, but I did understand that gâteau had something to do with birthday cake. I decided that silent trust was the best response. After I marked my ball, I positioned myself just off the far side of the bunker. My plan was to lend a hand to my caddie, should she appear to need help in climbing up the steep embankment that surrounded the hazard. This act of chivalry would not have been poised if my caddie was not also and at the same time my girlfriend-wife. Nevertheless, while she raked, Trip attempted to putt. Sam was almost hidden beneath the horizon of the bunker, but not quite. I watched Trip peeking at my caddie as she bent herself toward her raking chores. Between the lunging step that pushed the rake forward, and the return pull, her pleated skirt was swinging in rhythm with her ponytail. Trip's first putt was wide right and ten feet short. His second was five feet long. His third lipped out, and his fourth finally went down, following a twitch of the putter blade.

In the midst of this horror show, Sam appeared by my side. She actually took my sand wedge from my hand, and replaced it with my putter.

She whispered, "Why is he having so much trouble?"

My lack of response was due, in part, to mild shock but also, proper decorum. When my turn finally arrived, she offered, "Chéri, you hit a wonderful sandy shot, you will not miss your putt. I know it."

I could have putted that ball into a buried thimble. I didn't detect the first twinge of discord. I might offer that I re-married my caddie on that hole. I realized that I belonged to her out there on those fairways and greens, and I simply took her for mine, as well.

Stepping toward the third tee, I said, "Will you marry me?"

Sam said, "Oui bien sûr, always and forever."

Although I had no idea at first, Samantha's presence during that afternoon round had generated one of those rarified environments of blissful reverie. I have often heard it described as moving underneath the blue light from heaven. I was, indeed, distracted, by her companionship, but not from my game. My focus upon her welfare shifted the attention I normally applied to myself. In other words, I was distracted from me. I rarely gave any shot more than a casual assessment, before playing the exact stroke that I had envisioned. In addition, I enjoyed an endless stream of encouragement, provided by an opinion that was decidedly focused on my welfare. In this case, I hit shots that seemed to please my girlfriend-bride-caddie. We soon settled into a revolving harmony of giving and receiving simple pleasure. Before long, every shot that I hit seemed to evoke Samantha's delight, and her energetic response inspired a commensurate return from me.

During the round, I looked at her for signs of fatigue and uncertainty, and she looked at me for signs of need and approval. As for the other members of our foursome, I found that Trip was the only player about whose play I retained any memory. This state was unusual. Typically, I could remember every shot and every score without too much mental strain. As for the other members of our group, all I could say was that I thought Lenny and David were playing fairly well.

The eleventh hole was the only site where we encountered the suggestion of turmoil within our team. Eleven is a par three, featuring a green, nestled against a small stream, which fronts a wooded area that I prefer to call, 'The OllyOpps.' 'The OllyOpps' are forgotten areas of nature that certainly forbid any type of recognizable golf swing, but also tend to discourage any type of normal human traffic. Trip took a wicked lash from the tee at the eleventh hole. I watched his shot sail across the imaginary line that demarcated habitable terrain from 'The OllyOpps.' That ball was instantly consumed, but memorialized by the faint sound of a single tick, and a final swish.

One, common but often overlooked, characteristic of all golf courses, that I frequent, is that they feature strange magnetic forces. These golf course poles do not conform to the rules that govern cosmic physics, but they do exert their gravitational pull upon small orbs composed of rubber and plastic. The rules of the game demand that the location of these attractive energies be identified to the players. To that effect, they are commonly identified by wooden stakes, which are buried in the ground. These stakes typically surround or outline, a water feature, or a demarcation line for legal play, and in some cases, the impenetrable confines of 'The OllyOpps.'

While I can't honestly say that Trip's ball was an innocent victim of those ethereal powers, my tee shot at eleven seemed to sail upon an energy that I had not administered. As I watched it fly, I felt a prickly sense of electrification begin to arc and snap throughout my entire body. My ball seemed to carry along for a prodigious distance, headed toward an unmerited disaster. I have no doubt that I was saved from that ruin by an equally mysterious and unseen power. By the time my ball landed near the back edge of the elongated green, I felt the breeze belonging to an unexpected zephyr, out of the west. That unseen gust broke the spell produced by the pole, hidden within 'The OllyOpps.' The uneasy tension began to dissipate when I realized that I would be putting for birdie instead of dropping in penalty. That shot traveled a full club longer than I had planned, but before I took that swing, I thought that I was a club short.

During the short trek to the green, Samantha said, "We should help Trip find his ball."

"Honey, that ball is gone."

"Perhaps, but I will help him look. He might feel encouraged. He is not playing well, and I think that he feels lonely."

"Oh, he feels lonely alright, but not because he's playing poorly. Just let me do the encouraging, this time. Besides, you probably shouldn't go into 'The OllyOpps' in a skirt."

"Mon Chéri, I have felt very comfortable in my outfit. My skirt has not caused a single problem that I have noticed. I think that I have been a good caddie."

"That is true, my love, and your skirt has proven to be extremely functional."

"Qu'est-ce que c'est, 'OllyOpps'?

"That's my word for forbidden jungle territory, with briars, and poison ivy, and snakes, and unfindable golf balls. I'll help Trip and I'll save you from being scratched and bitten."

Over the course of our round, I had altered my engagement strategies with Trip. I had attempted to balance my initial feelings of regret, with an air of compassion. I had never considered that he presented any type of threat or competition, in terms of my relationship with Samantha, but I had not prevented his mind from wandering in that direction. In other words, I felt somewhat responsible for his erratic play and ever-ballooning score.

Sam said, "I am not worried about a few scratches, nor am I afraid of snakes."

"I know that, my love, but like I said, I would prefer that you remain unscathed and unpoisoned."

Just as we arrived at the green, we were met by an official, wearing a blue sport coat and a white hat. He was driving a golf cart and apparently engaged in a cursory inspection lap around the course. He exited his ride to oversee our adventure in 'The OllyOpps.' He stood next to Samantha, on the bank of the stream that flowed, approximately three paces from the back of the green. As expected, we did not locate Trip's ball. Luckily, the brook was marked with red stakes and a red streak of paint, which indicated an official lateral hazard. This designation allowed Trip to drop a new ball near the green. The hazard markings actually rendered the necessary penalty, less damaging than had he lost his tee shot in an unmarked area. In this case, his third shot was a pitch, rather than a second attempt at the green from the teeing ground.

Following his play, I was first to putt. I performed the typical routine of surveying the line, and I stepped off an approximate distance. For all putts of any considerable distance, I stepped the distance. I calculated length by approximating the interval of my pace as one yard. For example, ten paces equated to thirty feet. For reasons of an intuitive nature, awareness of an estimated distance provides a measure of comfort with the impending stroke. For that putt, I stepped fifteen paces for a distance of forty-five feet. In my mind, I executed a solid stroke, along the proper line and with an appropriate force. My ball came to rest some two feet short of the hole. I was pleased with the attempt.

After I marked my ball, our surprise guest motioned for my attention. I complied without delay. Upon arrival, he asked, "Son, is this young lady your caddie?"

I noticed Samantha's eyes flash.

I said, "Yes sir."

He continued, "She was standing directly behind you when you made your stroke."

"I'm sorry, I didn't notice."

"According to rule 10-2b a caddie is prohibited from standing behind the player along the extension line of the player's putt. The penalty for breach of this rule is two strokes, and you must replay the original stroke."

Hearing these words, I felt as if I had been officially electrocuted. I saw that Samantha's flashing eyes had gone dark. I stood still for a moment, smelling something like ozone being emitted from my charred body.

I heard, "However, I am tempted to believe that the configuration that I saw was inadvertent. Is that correct?"

I heard, "Oui, Monsieur, je suis vraiment désolé. This is my first caddie loop. I did not know that I was breaking the law. It will not happen again."

A different set of eyes flashed after hearing these words. Time stopped and all movement was paused. We all stood together for a long moment.

Before too long, the official offered. "Yes, well, I suspected something like that. You may play the ball as it lies. Watch your position from this point forward."

Sam glued herself to my side, as our watcher bid our group au revoir.

Sam said, "Je suis vraiment désolé, Mon Amour."

I took her hand, for the first time since we had left the parking lot. I gave a squeeze and peered into the dark blue pools hiding beneath the shadows provided by a tournament visor.

"No, my love, I will do a better job for the remainder of the afternoon. I wasn't thinking, is all. You had no way of knowing."

The final extraordinary incident at number eleven was the sight of my par putt descending into the cup. We played the following hole underneath the lingering shade of somber weather. Our skies seemed to clear on the next hole and over the course of the par five fourteenth, Sam and I had been restored to our appointed walk, bathed in the blue light from heaven.

I finished the afternoon round, carding a very respectable 72. I was delighted beyond normal bounds with respect to that particular round, and the fact that my scoreboard name would reflect an ultimate version, which read, Jack Weatherlow 149. That final number, being less than 150, represented a pleasant benchmark, in my mind, which served to separate prospective players from potential miners.

Looking over the leaderboard, Sam said, "Mon Chéri, your score is good, oui, yes?"

I said, "Well, yes and no."

"How many players will qualify, Chéri?"

"Two."

"Mon Dieu, Chéri, out of all these names, only two?"

"Yes, my love, only two."

Sam said, "Well then, we should go."

"What? We can't. We need to wait awhile."

"Mon Chéri, your score is fourth best, and only half the names are finished."

"Well, you don't have to judge that quickly, something could happen!"

"Allons, allons. We have other things to do now."

"I don't think caddies are supposed to talk like that. Where are you going?"

"Dépêche-toi, s'il te plaît!"

"So you're just leaving? Like that? What about the bag?"

"Allons-y!"

"Oh, that's great. Look, don't worry about the bag, I'll take it from here."

"Au revoir, Mon Amour. I will meet you at home."

CHAPTER 9

Reviewing the Course

....

We made our flight to Atlanta that evening, but we were not moving upon the cushion of casual comfort that I prefer. I had worked for the airlines for a number of years in a former life. During those years I enjoyed the wonderful benefit of flying for free, as they say. However, that particular gratuity was only afforded through strict adherence to a collection of rules. In those days, I felt as if my travel plans were being overseen by the blue coats and white-hat folks from tournament golf. In fact, I can recall those airline travel regulations almost as easily as I remember the rules of my preferred game. For this flight, we had breached the long-standing statute governing preflight arrival time, and I was feeling the tension, which is due for that indiscretion.

Those decrees no longer dictate my behavior for an airline flight, but they remain etched upon my mind, as would a set of Best Practices for acceptable conduct. In my opinion, flying for free is, indeed, wonderful, as long as you don't really need to go anywhere. I was welcome in a company seat, but a paying passenger was always more welcome. My promissory gift was always available for reassignment. I was often surrendering my preferred plans, along with my provisioned seat. I could never decide if I felt more satisfied or aggravated by those mandatory exchanges. On one hand, having to surrender my seat seemed appropriate and normal. I considered myself a perpetual guest moving around the surrounding world, credentialed by an imaginary permission slip. On the other, I grieved another loss. The loss was small, but nonetheless, an undesirable sacrifice of something in which I had invested a measure of my yearning soul. Ironically, this understanding of employee airline travel, as in guest status and undesirable loss, encompasses the major issues of my life, from which Samantha was helping me detach.

Safely enveloped by our full-fare seats, Samantha asked, "Mon Chéri, you played well today. You should feel pleased, oui?"

"I think shocked is a better word."

"Shocked! Why do you feel shocked?"

"I was shocked by the indifferent attitude of my caddie."

"Mon Chéri, you could not have finished first or second."

"See there? It's your utter lack of confidence that is so disturbing."

"Chéri, what could happen to change the outcome?"

"Well, nothing really, but you didn't have to be so cold about it."

"Mon Chéri, we had other things to do, like making this flight, for instance. And, I see that you are finally beginning to relax."

"I know, and I'm teasing, mainly. I'm not really upset. Those tournaments are always that way."

"Qu'est-ce que c'est?"

"Years ago, I played in a similar event. I shot 72 during the morning round. Afterward, I watched the official scorekeeper write my name on a chalkboard. They don't always have nice scoreboards recording every number for each player. I mean, I don't suppose that it really matters if you're only taking two guys. Anyway, I saw Jack Weatherlow 72, listed beneath one other name. Another guy had posted a 71. Following the completion of my afternoon round, I returned to that chalk board. At that time, the board had been distinguished by a vertical chalk stripe. There were three other names written on the right hand side of the board. They were alternates. All three had posted 73 for the morning.

"As I was surveying the scoreboard, I heard one of the Blue Coats calling my name. I reported as ordered. I handed him my card. We stood face to face. I recall that his expression was fixed and firm, as if carved from stone. I watched him as he surveyed my card. Inside a long moment, he greeted me, he inspected my card, and then he dismissed me. All I received was a shifting of blue eyes, from mine, to the card and back to me. He said nothing, but turned, and with a single swipe of a felt eraser, he removed my name from the chalkboard. I was there, and then I was gone. They call that moving from the throne to the outhouse. Like I said, it's sort of shocking."

"Mon Chéri, what did you score for the afternoon?"

"What else, the dreaded 84."

"Pourquoi Chéri? Were you feeling afraid, or anxious?"

"You'd think so, but I didn't really feel that way."

"Ce qui était faux?"

"Well, I felt sort of peaceful, really, or maybe satisfied is a better word."

"Qu'est-ce que c'est?"

"I shot even par, in the midst of a big tournament. I was pleased and delighted with that first score, and I suppose that I lost the edge, or the desire that's necessary for a repeat performance. Sometimes, when I declare myself lazy, that's what I mean."

"Mon Chéri, you are very perceptive. But, you are describing common behavior."

"Which do you prefer, my love, that I'm lazy or that I'm common? Neither seems very appealing."

"La Vache! Mon Chéri your comment is being offered by a guest, someone who does not truly belong. You must be where you are, before you can go where you prefer."

"What does that mean?"

"Why did you tell me that story about having your name erased?"

"For the shock value, of course."

"Oui, yes, but besides the shock, how did you feel in that moment?"

"How about humiliated? Better?"

"Non, you provided the answer only a moment ago. You felt validated."

"Validated! Come on, who feels that way?"

"You do, Chéri. I saw you play this afternoon. You played very well, as a matter of fact. As far as I am concerned, you performed as well as anyone, and far better than most. You belong in that tournament Chéri, but you do not know that. Once again, you are playing a different game from everyone else. You are trying to earn your place, Chéri. You are trying to belong, and that endeavor is different than winning the tournament.

"That morning round 72 score represented an accomplished goal. You had proven to yourself that you belonged. You counted yourself successful, and your play, throughout the afternoon round, was merely paying honor to a standing obligation. You play for yourself, Chéri, not for the Blue Sport Coats, as you say. When you accept the fact that you belong, you can turn your mind toward a different goal, like winning or qualifying. Accept where you are, then you may go where you prefer."

"Sam, sometimes I wonder why we're together. I mean, I wonder whether we simply exchange one pain for another, your pain from my behavior, and my pain from your observations."

"Mon Dieu, Chéri, we will never change our course without feeling some pain. We just happen to be courageous travelers. And, we are willing to consider a better road."

"Well, in spite of the pain that we are feeling, you have led me to consider an old path. I've always wondered why I tend to follow up a birdie with a bogey, or worse. I used to call that the balance of nature, but, I think you're right. After a good hole, I feel like I've done my job, and my play along the following hole loses something. At least, until I feel the need to step it up once again."

"Qu'est-ce que c'est?"

"Never mind, I'm actually agreeing with your assessment. But, I don't see how you find such a thing attractive?"

"Au contraire, Mon Amour, you are always trying to perform for me. You see yourself as a guest in my company, and you do not truly believe that you belong to me. Therefore, you are always doing things that might persuade me to accept you."

"That sounds good. So, you like to use my infirmity for your own benefit."

"Oui, yes, I enjoy the attention and care that you freely offer. However, I also worry for the day that you will count yourself successful, and become lazy, as you say. Once you feel like you have achieved your goal … that you do, actually, belong to me, perhaps you will no longer care for me, and play with me in the manner that I have come to love."

"That won't happen."

"Nous verrons, Chéri, nous verrons."

"Sam, I don't see how, telling you about a good score turned me into a bad guy?"

"Mon Chéri, you are not bad, or evil, but you have been taught to play a different game. Everyone carries something, Chéri. I just want you to understand your particular burden."

"Since we're on the subject, how did you feel today? I mean, being my caddie?"

"Be more specific, s'il te plaît?"

"Well, I know it was hot, and the bag was heavy, and I realize that the environment was odd. How did you feel being with me, but as my caddie?"

"I was delighted to spend that time with you."

"Yes, but you were my caddie. We weren't exactly lounging by the pool."

"What do you mean?"

"Did you feel like a servant?"

"Non, Chéri."

"But you did things for me, like carrying my bag, and raking sand."

"Oui, yes, but I was helping you."

"What's the difference? I mean, between helping and serving. I would say that most people think of caddying as a menial job that carries the image of indentured servitude."

"But, I am your wife, and not a regular caddie."

"I think that our bond makes my question even more relevant."

"Non, Chéri, I want to help you, because you are my husband."

"My question pertains to images and standing. Like I said, caddies are widely seen as lowly servants for the more refined players. Didn't marriage vows once require women to obey their husbands?"

"S'il te plaît, what is your point?"

"Ok, today, I thought of you and me as a team. I did not think of you as my servant, but as another player on our team. We both have positions on our team, but we have different chores to perform. I thought of us, as one, or together, working toward a common goal. Believe it or not, I thought that I was helping you today, just like you were thinking of helping me."

"But, once again, I am your wife."

"I know that, but today you were also my caddie. If you will offer a moment of grace in my favor, I will explain."

"S'il te plaît."

"I used to caddy for extra money when I was younger, but strangely, I never thought of that work as a burden. Every time I took a bag, or a loop, as a caddie, I became absorbed by the notion of participating in a common endeavor. I always seemed to know the exact chores that my player considered necessary and valuable to his game. That role provided me with an acceptable identity. It installed me within defined boundary lines and offered me agreeable terms. In other words, I knew exactly where I belonged. Thoughts of toil, or a sense of burden, never entered my mind. And, I might add that most of the caddies that I have ever taken seem to have been possessed by a similar persuasion. Most have added value to my game. The money that we exchanged for the service rarely seemed to be the primary concern.

"I realize that everyone will not see things that way. I mean that I've carried for some players who did, as far as I could tell, think of me as a servant. They rarely spoke to me, and they barked orders for this and that, throughout the day. I served their agenda, rather than our agenda. Nevertheless, whether I was carrying for a player who was engaging, or one who seemed preoccupied, I always enjoyed the satisfying sense of belonging.

"Here's why I asked for your grace. I think of myself, with you, in terms of caddying. I will perform for you because I feel like I belong with you. I am not attempting to earn my place by your side. I am at home with you, and I think that I know most of the things that you need and the things that you desire. I will provide these things to better your game and because we are together, working toward a common goal. That is what I hope that you felt today, when you were actually caddying for me. That is also why I asked you to marry me, out there on the course."

Following these words, Sam turned her head toward the window of the airplane. She moved as if she had been summoned to inspect the passing blue vista. After a moment, she returned to meet my gaze. Her eyes were brimming full, and appeared as if they might be melting into lapis puddles. I was startled. I had not foreseen this reaction.

She whispered, "Je t'aime beaucoup, Jackson Weatherlow."

The use of my full name informed me that my words had, indeed, inspired the deliquescing of her hawkish blues. Samantha only used my full name when our hearts were being traded. I also understood that my response should include her full name, in order to reduce the temperature of the fire that I had inadvertently ignited.

"Je t'aime beaucoup, Savanne Morris Weatherlow."

"Mon Chéri, I was wrong, and I am sorry."

"Nope, as a matter of fact, and as usual, you're right. I would say that my behavior is like my mission. Neither is easy to know. And, I tend to get lazy, or complacent, after I achieve my goals.

"Sam, earlier today, you noticed a change in my behavior. You mentioned that I acted differently, after we moved from the parking lot to the golf course. The reason behind that variation is that I feel at home on the golf course. I belong there, as you say. I hold no doubt about that truth, but the golf course is an unusual place to call home. I might add that, while my real home offered emptiness and hurt, the golf course provided welcome and peace.

"At home, I spent my time attempting to perform in a way that might fill the hollow and soothe the pain. In other words, I tried to earn my place, or a sense of belonging. I carried that same behavior to the golf course, where I thought that such a practice would be necessary. However, and strangely, I found that my performance didn't seem to matter. On the contrary, I was always accepted, and sometimes, celebrated. That situation was confusing. Among my friends, I saw that, home and family provided the primary environment of embrace and encouragement. No one that I knew seemed to be drawing upon a different place for their diet of peace and comfort.

"I think that you saw the remnants of that confusion today. You have described my family as a gathering of spiritual orphans. You said that we were an authentic, blood-linked family, living inside a real home, but a home in which no one seemed to belong. I suppose that, since we had a real home, I felt guilty for finding peace and comfort, elsewhere. I was legitimately linked to an inescapable void. In other words, the existence of my real home prevented me from claiming a sense of belonging, anywhere, but most especially at the golf course.

"This may sound crazy, but sometimes, my real home, invades my golf home. That usually happens on tournament days. On those days, I attempt to perform. I forget that I belong, and I resort to earning my place. That's exactly what you saw through my story.

"However, you have invited me to find my peace and comfort inside a different kind of real home. If you can accept my words about caddying, I might say that you have been attempting to carry my bag since the first day we met. Every minute of every day you add value to my life.

"I can tell you that, but sometimes, like you noticed at the golf course, my old home invades our new home, and I feel the need to perform, and to earn my place. I seem to see more clearly when I look through the images that I know from the golf course. In the end, I'm trying to say that I have accepted my place with you. I belong with you, and to you, as well. You have always been my caddie, and I hope that I can always be yours. I like the way you carry for me, honey."

"Mon Chéri, you have not spoken to me in this way before today."

"Well, I just decided to take a risk. I don't suppose that many wives could appreciate being compared to a caddie. It doesn't sound all that romantic. But, don't worry about carrying all the bags, after we land. I'll help you."

As expected, the last portion of my remark invigorated Samantha's preferred gesture of correction. I received a brushing, backhanded smack, along the top of my left shoulder. However, that amending signal was quickly followed by a luxurious osculation. For this event, her engagement with our kiss seemed to last longer than I thought acceptable for public air travel. I broke away, after reaching my imaginary time limit.

Sam asked, "Mon Cheri, now may I ask for your grace for a moment?"

"Of course, always and forever."

"If you are feeling at home with me, in our home, why are we going to Savannah?"

"That is a good question, my love, but one that I thought we had settled. I thought you said that I needed to answer the call."

"Oui, yes, but now I am thinking of this trip in terms of your golf. I am wondering whether we are seeing the same objective."

"Of course, a new job, with serious leadership responsibilities, surrounded by the occupation that I love the most."

"Oui, yes, and you have been invited to explore this opportunity without having to ask, but are you trying to win, in this case, or are you trying to belong?"

"I don't understand?"

"Mon Chéri, having been invited, you may consider that you already belong. You have already won the battle, which has kept you searching throughout your life. Mr. Woodson has asked for you. He is saying that you belong in his game. To win or qualify, in this case, means that you will accept this new job. Your name is listed on the chalkboard, Chéri. We are playing in the afternoon round."

"Wow, that's pretty sharp. I wasn't sure that you would understand the connection."

"Mon Chéri, do you want this new job?"

"Of course…I mean, maybe…if you do too. We'll have to see."

"Pourquoi, Chéri?"

"Sam, I hate to say it, but I am feeling somewhat satisfied, right now."

"Voilà!"

"And, now I feel like an idiot."

"Non, Chéri, I will not allow you to think like that! You are beginning to understand the force that drives you. You have been wounded in the past, and you spend your time attempting to repair the damage. You look for people, and activities, and things that might fill the emptiness that was created long ago."

"Sam, please don't say that. I thought we had settled all this in Atlanta, after Mom died."

"This is a different case, which comes from the same source. That space may never become completely filled in this life, Chéri."

"Sam, that's the thing. That's why I feel like an idiot. I mean, here I am, and here you are, dragging down the same road, again. Why do you do it? When will you quit? I mean, if it's never going to be fixed, why would you stay?"

"Chéri, I love you. We are one, together. I belong with you, and to you. I feel the same things that you were saying about me."

"Why, Sam? Why?"

"Mon Chéri…"

"Please don't say that you have been called to help me…."

"Bon Sang, Chéri. You may not condemn the inspiration of my heart or my faith. I have never been flippant about such things in the past, nor will I be in the future. However, I understand your feeling at the moment, and I will save you from your pity party."

"That too, Sam. Why?"

"Mon Chéri, may I tell you a story? It concerns caddies."

"By all means, let's forget about my question, altogether. Just pretend like I've moved over to a chair in the corner to reflect upon feeling sorry for myself."

"Je vais. But, I want you to listen from your chair, s'il te plaît."

"I will. Go ahead."

"Mon Chéri, do you remember the story that I told you about my life in Paris?"

"Of course, I do. I mean, oui, bien sûr. If you haven't noticed, I've been paying close attention, ever since you arrived."

"Très bien, Chéri! Merci. Do you recall my story about Nicholas?"

"Who?"

"Nicholas was my fiancée, Chéri."

"Umm, yes, I suppose, but that story resides somewhere near the bottom of my denial pile. I can retrieve it, but only if, absolutely necessary."

"Merci. At the moment, I am feeling ashamed for telling you that story."

"Honey, please don't worry. We haven't even opened that folder. Let's just slip it back into the stack of stuff that we want to forget."

"Non, Chéri, I have opened that folder. In fact, you have opened that folder for me."

"Come on, Sam. How can I become the bad guy, by telling a story that I happen to think was sort of charming?"

"Mon Chéri, now I understand the role of a caddie."

"Sam, just forget it. I do that kind of thing. It doesn't mean anything. I have a habit of making stupid connections between weird examples."

"Non, Chéri, I understand. You are correct. I see more clearly. And, I need to tell you why I feel ashamed. I was not honest about my relationship with Nicholas."

"Ok, I understand, and I forgive you. Let's let it go."

"Non, Chéri. I cannot."

"Sam…."

"If you recall, I told you that I recognized that his heart was divided between a commitment to the church and a commitment to me, and us, as a family. I told you that I saw in him a priest. Yet, I also saw that he was afraid to commit his life to that calling. I told you that I broke our engagement to set him free to follow the true calling of his heart."

"You also told me about smoking cigarettes and drinking wine, in the Latin Quarter."

"Oui, yes, I did."

"Sam, your original story seems pretty honest to me, or at least as honest as I need to see. Haven't we been talking about feeling committed to one another, about belonging to one another? I forgive you for leaving out the detailed honesty part. I promise."

"Chéri, the story that I told you was honest, in that it was a part of my mind, at the time. However, my story was not a truthful recollection of actual events. I hope that you will forgive me?"

"What does that mean?"

"Mon Chéri, your description of caddies has frightened me. I was, with Nicholas, like a caddie. I did things for him, and I tried to add value to his life, as you have described. I even saw that image, in my mind, at the time, but my heart would not allow me to see that my player was a preoccupied man."

"Please Sam, you don't…"

"I felt something special for Nicholas, at first. He was my first…"

"Sam, please, honey."

"Mon Chéri, I think I need to tell you."

"What if I said that I don't need to hear?"

"As I said, I have participated, in the past, but I have never given myself, before you. I suppose that I was willing, but I did not 'know' him, Chéri."

"Thank you, but I'm not feeling any better about this story."

"At that time, I did not understand the biblical concept of 'knowing' your partner. I did not understand the concept of becoming 'one flesh' together. Mon Chéri, that concept is the same as your common goal from golf. I did not 'know' him, Chéri, even though we had 'known' one another in that way. There was no common goal, as you said. Something was missing."

"Sam, honey, where are we going?"

"I felt that, before, but we were going to be married. We had been engaged prior to that first time. I wanted to connect. I wanted to 'know' him. I wanted to know what he needed and what he desired, and I wanted him to 'know' me. At that time in my life, I thought that the marriage ceremony would instill, in me and in us, our common goal, or your notion of belonging. Mon Chéri, when I told you that he possessed a desire to combine family life with the priesthood, that idea was a part of my mind. I saw that clearly, but I was still blind."

"Sam, I am seeing far too clearly at the moment."

"Chéri, like you said about me, I caddied for him. I did things for Nicholas. Things that I thought might dispel my conception of mutually exclusive desires. I attempted to connect us through my service. I tried to add value to his life, through my commitment to his game. I tried to manufacture our team and inspire the common goal that you described. However, I now know that I never belonged with him. I think that I always knew that we were not a team, and that we had no common goal.

"Chéri, Nicholas was the one who broke away from our engagement, not me. I was not honest with you about that detail of my story, and I am ashamed."

"Sam, that's not a big deal. I forgive you. I understand, really."

"No Chéri, I have a reason for being dishonest. And, for that reason, I am most ashamed."

"Sam, honey, I'm going to forgive you either way. It doesn't matter."

"I will never forget that event for as long as I live. We had stayed together that night, and we had been together that morning."

"Sam, really, I'm starting to feel a little crazy."

"In my bed, in my apartment, Nicholas asked if we might talk. He was very frank, but he also seemed cheerful or excited about something. I can see his face, this very instant."

"Me too, I think, but I wish I couldn't...."

"He sat up, but he held my hands. He told me, first, that he was sorry. Next, he told me that his heart belonged to the church. He told me that he had made a decision to follow the path to the priesthood. I was shocked by that announcement, and I was hurt, but I also felt something like relief. I felt, perhaps, like a child, receiving a discipline from a parent, but learning a boundary line for life, in the process.

"I recall that Nicholas seemed to measure my response. He paused before speaking again. We simply watched one another for a time. I recall seeing something like a shadow darken his expression. In the next moment, he smiled. He told me that I would be traveling with him.

"I found this remark more surprising than the first. I felt teased, and I responded with a touch of frustration. I said that such a thing was impossible. After hearing my words, he smiled again, and dipped his head to apply a kiss to my forehead. I was once again feeling like a child.

"I will never forget his next words, Chéri. He said, 'Tu as tort, Chérie. Tu seras toujours avec moi.' He was telling me that I was wrong, that it was possible for me to be with him. In fact, he was saying that I would always be with him.

"He appeared as would a compassionate parent, accepting, but also correcting, the mind of a confused child. I was not so much silent as mute. However, while I watched, I felt something change. I began to see his smile more clearly. The expression of compassionate understanding hovering above my face, transformed into an image of smug satisfaction. In that moment, I understood his remark, and our entire relationship, and I 'knew' Nicholas, for the first time in my life.

"Mon Chéri, when he told me that he was taking me into the priesthood, he was saying that he would remember me.

He wanted to possess the memory of 'knowing' a woman. He was taking the memory of me, and what we had done as a couple, into the church. I was the experience that he would use in service to the people of God. Chéri, I knew it, but I did not. I felt it, but I did nothing. I have lived every image that you described, Chéri. I carried for him. I was his servant. My name was on your chalkboard, Chéri. I was there and then I was gone. And I am wondering if the relief that I felt at first was actually validation of the fact that I had been used and discarded."

These words lit the fuse connected to a small arsenal that guarded my soul. I could feel the fizzing sizzle as I spoke.

I said, "Sam, are you telling me that your entire relationship with that…with Nicholas, was a sham? So that he could gather experience for the priesthood? Please tell me that I am way off the mark."

"Mon Chéri, I think now that I prefer to see myself as a caddie for a preoccupied man, rather than as a whore for the church."

One of the bombs detonated. I actually jerked. I could feel the seat belt cinching my waist as I blasted out of my airline seat.

I exploded in whispered rage. "Damn It, Sam, where is that sonofabitch priest? I don't care if he's God's private Pope. I'm going to add a few vivid details to his perverted church memory."

In the midst of a muzzled tirade, I noticed that Samantha's eyes were once again melting. I caught myself, first. Then, I captured her neck using my left arm as a firm, but gentle lasso. I pulled her close.

I spoke softly, "I'm sorry. I'm only making things worse, but that makes me so mad, I could bite a nail in half!"

Sam whispered into the atmosphere between the seats. "I am sorry, Chéri."

"Why are you sorry?"

"I am sorry for not being honest."

"God Almighty! I can't believe that you could be a part of such a thing?"

She lifted her face to meet mine. "I am sorry, Chéri. He asked me to marry him. I was young, and did not think...."

"Stop it, Sam, don't say another thing. Listen to me. You are a precious thing to me. You have been more loving and patient and well...more of everything to me than anyone that I have ever known. I can't believe that someone could do that to you. That has to be the creepiest piece of sorry-ness that I've ever heard. Why, why would he tell you those things? But, worse still, why would he do such a thing?"

"He said that he thought that I might be pleased to know that I would be serving God's people, even though I was a woman, and could not serve as a man."

"What the fuck...?

"...Wait.... Give me a second... please.

"Sam, I'm sorry.... I think that I'm losing my mind.

... Please forgive me. I'll try to calm down."

"I cannot be a priest, Chéri."

"Sam, I'm a living, card-carrying, curb-hugging drunk, and I know, beyond a shadow of a doubt, that I cannot live a decent life if I hurt you in the process. I don't even go to church, and I try to live by that rule. On the other hand, that sonofabitch has been knighted or christened in the shadow of God himself, and he now possesses the power to bestow

God's grace. You taught me that. How can that be!? How can I do what I do, and he do what he did, and we be seen so differently by the world. I'll never put my little toe inside any church, ever again."

"Stop it, Chéri. He is not the church. The church is composed of the people who light the candles. It does not belong to the priests who speak and bless, and open the doors of a building. I will not allow you to condemn God's church for the actions of one man."

"Do you hear yourself, right now?"

"Non Chéri, I should have known. Do not blame the church."

"Sam, honey…I don't give a damn about the church. I only care about you."

"Will you forgive me?"

"Sam, really? Please, honey, let's go to France instead. I'll make it right."

"Will you forgive my church?"

"Sam, I…ok, ok, I'm sorry. How about this: I will not project my disgust of one sorry example of manhood upon the entire church, even though I think that both have been taking advantage of my woman! Better?"

"Mon Chéri, may I finish my story?"

"You have more?"

"This part is about you."

"I'm not sure that I can take it."

"Mon Chéri, you were asking about why I love you."

"I don't care anymore. I'll never let you out of my sight, ever again, no matter what you say."

"Chéri, when I care for you, I do so from the memory of this story. I do not offer you acts of service, but I try to offer patience and understanding toward the difficulties that you have experienced in life. I hope that, if I am patient and loving, then you will keep me as your caddie, and not remove my name from your chalkboard."

"Sam, do you actually think that I might be thinking of switching partners? I mean, I'm asking you why you stay with me. Have you really considered the same question of me? Where would I go? What would I do without you?"

"Mon Chéri, there is a sweetness about you that is guarded by a mystery. The mystery is why you will not allow that sweetness to escape. However, as I said, I understand. The answer is revealed through your second question, concerning my devotion and my faith. Trust is a difficult transaction for you. You do not fully trust me. As you say, your real home invades our new home. Your suspicion is a product of your orphanage home, not ours. I see that, Chéri, and I see the person that you are, behind the person that you present.

"I have always 'known' you, Chéri. I 'knew' you, before our first time, before we 'knew' one another in that special way. I 'know' you, Chéri. I know what you need, and what you desire, but what I know is not easily described. And, in spite of what you prefer to deny, this sense of 'knowing' has called to me. You have touched me in ways that neither, you nor I, can understand. Earlier, when you were enjoying your sense of satisfaction, you revealed your true self to me. Not so much for the first time, but at a deeper level than you have ever allowed me to see.

"Only a moment ago you were telling me that you belonged to me, and that we belong together, but for some reason that connection became suspicious. Your scoreboard was calling to you. You were there one minute and gone the next. That is where you return when things become contentious. I understand these occasions. You are viewing the present through remembered images of your past. I see you in the present. I do not look at you through the past.

"Now, I will tell you why I stay, and why I will remain. You do not try to avoid your faults and misgivings. You desire to repair them. You think that you need to be perfect in order to be accepted. And, as long as you are not yet perfect, you choose to overlook my shortcomings. You consider that grace, as your balance. You will not attempt to change me, but you do struggle to change you. In other words, you are kind and generous with me, when you do not practice those same graces with yourself.

"Why would I want to escape from consideration and grace? Why would I want to escape from a man who spends his time practicing to be perfect? Why would I want to abandon a man who has adopted this chore for my benefit and pleasure? And this evening, you tell me that you do this for love, rather than belonging? Why would I abandon someone who belongs to me through the bonds of love?

"I do not need this type of attention, but it is quite glorious. Despite the hauntings from your past, I know that you do, actually, trust me, and I trust you. How many couples discuss the things that we discuss? You might be the only person who will ever know the story that I told today. We have our difficulties, but I know that we share a common goal. We are simply engaged in the process of sifting and refining our connection. Shall I continue? We have other things that we might discuss, but, as you like to point out, we are in the public domain at the moment."

"Savanne Morris Weatherlow, I believe you. And, I'm sorry. God almighty, it seems so much worse after hearing your story. What can I do for you? Anything, I promise. Listen though, I started all this because I was unexpectedly stricken by the possibility that I might be trying to resolve an old set of problems by moving to a new territory. I have a history of hitting the same kind of shot from different locations."

"Mon Chéri, you have not had me by your side in the past. That is the difference, n'est pas? As I said, you have been called. We will be looking in this case, rather than searching. Nous verrons, Chéri, but we shall see together."

After we landed, I would not allow Samantha to carry a single bag. I was feeling nauseous about my caddie comment. We retrieved our rental car, and installed ourselves inside a complementary room provided by my current employer. At first, I was feeling somewhat duplicitous, in light of the fact that I was enjoying such a benefit for the purpose of meeting a new employer, but on second thought, I considered that I was once again entertaining my bride, upon the extended grounds of my old home place. As Sam has said, we were looking, rather than searching.

Given the length and intensity of the activity which had filled the day, we spent the few short hours in our complimentary room, 'being', rather than 'doing' anything. However, in this case, the 'being' was indistinguishable from 'doing.' I suppose we finished that day as human beings, who practiced our commitment to one another by sleeping, almost fitted together, or as Sam prefers to say, as one flesh. That evening, I carried for my caddie, by holding her tightly. I gave myself to her through my embrace, and she gave herself to me through her acceptance. In fact, I held her close, as if she were indeed, mine, to have and to hold, forever do us part.

CHAPTER 10

A Graceful Round

....

For this day, The Wambaw Club seemed like a sun, rising up in the distance, and dawning upon a new life. We were making excellent progress, enveloped in the spartan confines of a brand new, midsized, Chevrolet rental. Just below Macon, Georgia, we had made the turn toward Savannah. In my mind, Macon, and the exit for Interstate 16, meant that we were halfway home.

I said, "Sam, years ago, I played in a golf tournament just south of here, in a town called Warner Robins. That town is best known for the military base. Along several of the holes, the only thing that separated the golfers from the army men was a chain-linked fence. I also remember a standing cooler full of ice cold RC Colas being provided on every tee. I recall drinking a whole bottle of that cola drink between every hole. I think of that golf tournament like fraternity initiation. I mean that you had to endure the tension of the tournament, the constant heckling from across the fence, and the self-induced sickness from drinking so many cola drinks in the hot sun. I was mostly glad to have finished that event, standing on two legs."

"Mon Chéri, do you have a golf story for every town that we will pass?"

"Of course—I have another from a town called Dublin, but I'm waiting until we approach that location before I tell it."

"Chéri, I have always known that you liked to play golf, but in light of the last few days, I am realizing that golf has been far more important than I first imagined."

"You might be right, but I'm sorry. I don't think games are supposed to be an important part of life."

"Mon Chéri, we have never spoken about your work in the way we have been discussing your golf."

"Work is work; I try to make that important. Golf is golf; I try to make that invisible."

"But, Chéri, your engagement with those two endeavors is exactly opposite of your description. I have learned far more about you from your involvement with a game than I have through your commitments at work."

"I don't think I look at it like that."

"Chéri, there is an obvious difference. I would like to understand the distinction."

"Honey, let me say this. There is a saying in recovery that goes, 'I didn't get into trouble every time I drank, but every time I got into trouble, I was drinking.' Now, as far as golf goes, I will say this, 'Golf doesn't provide glorious results every time I play, but every glorious thing that has come to me has been provided through golf.' Like this trip, and the job opportunity, for example. I suppose I have acquired a few stories through work, but not opportunities. Like I said, work is work."

"Your proverb makes me sad, Chéri."

"Why?"

"I think that we have something glorious, together, but we were not introduced through golf."

"Not true! The only reason that I was in the laundry that day was to wash the clothes that I wanted to wear for a golf event. Remember, I told you about it that first night, while we were having dessert."

"D'accord, merci."

"That's another perfect example of weirdly delightful connections between life and golf."

"Un autre exemple, s'il te plaît."

"Alright, remember that tournament that I watch on television, in the spring, called The Masters?"

"Oui, bien sûr. For that one, I must become as a church mouse, who is mourning the death of the Pope."

"It's not that bad."

"Mon Chéri, this year I went to the shop on Sunday."

"No you didn't. Really?"

"Mon Dieu, Chéri. When I returned, I recall that you asked what I thought about the ruling on the playoff hole that I did not see, because I was not at home to watch."

"I can't believe that I did that. Are you sure? Well, if I did, I'm sorry. You can watch the whole thing, with me, next year."

"Dis moi, Chéri."

"Right, well, that particular tournament is special for some unknowable reason. Each year, that course becomes like a stage, which produces, with uncanny consistency, some type of unexpected, but extraordinary, performance. And, I might add that, on occasion, some of the magical effervescence which envelops that peculiar theater has overflowed its prestigious confines and landed directly in my lap. For example, some years ago, I received a surprise gift of tickets to the final day of the tournament. Wait ... never mind that story, please."

"Non, Chéri, dis moi, s'il te plaît."

"Sam, I don't think that I should tell that story. It's not that bad, but after hearing your story last night, I'm afraid that I might hurt your feelings."

"C'est bon, Mon Chéri. Dangling curiosity is always more pleasant than the truth."

"Sam, I'm trying to be nice."

"Oui, yes, I see that, but I am also seeing many other things, as well."

"Alright, but don't get mad. This happened a long time ago. I met a girl...."

"Oh la la, I should have known. Now I am heartbroken and very angry."

"Stop it, Sam. I'm trying to be serious and thoughtful."

"Allez-y, s'il te plaît."

"Years ago, there was a dance club in Atlanta which was frequented by so many friends from high school and college that I rarely saw a strange face. Nevertheless, on one Saturday night, during the weekend of the Master's Golf Tournament, I met a young lady, who I did not know. We talked and danced for a good while. We hit it off, as they say. Anyway, like Cinderella at midnight, she said that she needed to go home. And, being the gentleman that I am, I offered to be her chauffer."

"Mon Chéri, this happened during your previous life, n'est-ce pas?"

"Oui, Madame, why do you ask?"

"I have not heard stories of a gentleman from those days."

"I appreciate the subtle reminder. May I continue?"

"S'il te plaît."

"Of course she agreed...."

"Of course she did."

"Stop it, just listen quietly, please. Naturally, after we arrived, I escorted her to the apartment. At the door, she did something strange. She told me to wait, while she went inside. I waited, of course. After a few moments, she returned, but she did not invite me inside. She stood in the frame of the door, halfway inside and half outside the apartment. I recall her offering these words:

"I am grateful that you would bring me home. And, I suspect that you thought that you might receive a gift, in return for your trouble. I have a gift for you, but it's not the gift that you may have been expecting. I like you, Jack, but I don't really know you. However, I recall that you said that you like golf. Well, I don't. So, here is your gift for bringing me home. I want you to have my tickets to The Masters golf tournament. They're good for tomorrow, the final round. My uncle sends me these badges every year, and every year, I try to avoid the occasion. It's too crowded, and I never know what the weather will do.'

"She handed me two clubhouse badges for the final round of the tournament. She kissed me lightly on the lips, smiled, said goodnight, and retreated behind the door of her apartment."

"Mon Chéri, what was the gift that you were expecting?"

"That's not the point of the story, and that just happens to be way off the mark."

"Je vois, mais ton histoire est aussi proche du bord!"

"So, do you like it? Can you see what I mean? I got free tickets to the show."

"Chéri, you are standing upon the edge of a steep cliff, n'est-ce pas?"

"Come on, it's innocent, and sorta cool too, right? How about this…just forget that story. I'll redeem myself through one final tale. You'll see. This one is much better."

"Is this story about girls?"

"If you would listen closely, you will find that my stories are not about girls."

"I have been listening closely, too closely, as a matter of fact. I am seeing between the lines, as they say."

"There is no space between the lines in my stories. Just listen. This one does not have any girls."

"Allez-y, Chéri."

"Do you remember when I went home to Atlanta, for that surprise trip, just after we met that first year?"

"Oui, bien sûr"

"Well, I played golf with Dad, and Val, while I was at home. After that round, I met an old friend, who I hadn't seen in a long time. We had a nice reunion that afternoon. Anyway, that evening, he called the house, and asked me if I might be available to join him for a round of golf at Augusta National. Sam, no one gets invited to play golf on The Masters course. That club might be the most exclusive of all golf clubs in history. This was a once in a lifetime invitation. I had to go, and I had to change my plans to make it happen. No one believed me, of course, including me, as a matter of fact. Mom was furious, as usual. Even 'C' was angry because I had to borrow her car for the trip.

"I left the house at the crack of dawn. Along the drive, I began to consider whether the invitation might be a cruel trick, played against a likely sucker. I mean, like I said, no one gets to play that golf course. These visions became evermore vivid and threatening as I drew nearer to the club. My heart was literally racing as I pulled into the drive. They call that drive Magnolia Lane.

"Just past the entrance, I stopped abreast of the guard house. While I waited, I became aware of my recent history and my present appearance. On one hand, my memories of that golf club began to fashion a lamentable résumé. On the other, I realized that I was a mature male, who was basically driving a child's second hand automobile. Viciously sarcastic accusations began to fly about, inside my mind. The silent voice chided about grandiose assumptions of being accepted at this particular gate.

Soon enough, the sentry approached my window.

"He asked, politely, 'May I help you?'

"I spoke, as if I might be trying to enter an amusement park. 'Yes, I'm here to play golf.'

"I actually saw him snicker.

"Once again, politely, the guard asked, 'May I have your name, sir?'

"Shakily, I said, 'Yes, sir. I'm Jack Weatherlow.'

"The watchman left my vehicle, presumably, to check his schedule. His absence seemed to last for hours.

"Upon his return, he said, quite curtly, 'I'm sorry. I don't see your name on my list.'

"Several opposing sensations were inspired by this report. Most immediately, I suppose that I felt validated, as you say. I was, quite clearly, the unassuming victim of a merciless swindle. I also felt angry. My heart rate, once again, accelerated. In addition, I felt something like humiliation, but far worse. I felt as if my body were sinking into the hollow darkness of a comprehensive shame. This miserable transformation was apparently visible and contagious. I observed a similar change, enveloping my conscientious custodian. However, his alteration seemed to produce an opposing demeanor. Rather than a cold dismissal, I heard an unexpected question, which I took as a voluntary act of compassion.

"He asked, 'Do you have a member's name, sir?'

"I had to think for a moment. Once again, stupidly, I offered the name that I had been given.

"Armed with this information, the now charitable lookout made another visit to the gatehouse. Another seemingly interminable period of waiting ensued.

"He carried a smile with his return. Through the window, he said, 'Good morning, Mr. Weatherlow. Welcome to Augusta. May I direct you to the cabin?'"

"Mon Chéri, I am sad that you thought that you would not be accepted, even after having been invited."

"Thank you, my love, I was feeling anxious about telling that piece of this story. I thought you might think that I was foolish and petty."

"Non, Chéri, that gatehouse oversees everything that you do. Allez-y, s'il te plaît."

"Alright, and I'll be quick, but you need some background. I would say that most people who play golf envision a round of golf at Augusta National as the most precious but unobtainable invitation in all of the game, throughout the entire world. As a kid, my foremost ambition was to play golf in The Masters tournament. I've heard that same goal shared countless times, and regardless of my company or location. But, there I was, being welcomed into the realm of dreams. A dream was actually coming true. To say the least, the experience was surreal. Nevertheless, I have more history to disclose.

"When I was at college, one of the springtime social events involved traveling from school to The Masters golf tournament for the Wednesday practice round. Tickets were easy to acquire in those days, especially for the practice rounds. During practice round days, the general atmosphere is less restrictive than on an actual tournament day. Anyway, we always attended on Wednesday, before the actual tournament began. In fact, I recall thinking that half the college had skipped that day of classes to attend that round of golf. We would congregate behind the sixteenth green for a makeshift party, with all our friends. Oh, and back then, we all dressed up. Everyone wore some splashy spring outfit for the event. Wednesday at Augusta was one of the premier social events of the spring semester.

"We made that day into our own party. However, we were mixed and blended into the larger crowd. That particular day always drew an audience that was comparable to those of a regular tournament day. We stood shoulder to shoulder, behind the sixteenth green. Here is the reason that I am adding this information to my story.

"On one occasion, I suppose that I was swept up by the celebration and atmosphere. In other words, I had a lot to drink. At some point, late in the afternoon, while the party was rocking, out of all those people, attending that tournament, behind that green, two tournament officials singled me out as the wildest and most unruly reveler. They sifted through the throng and took me by both elbows. They escorted me away from our crowd, and they asked me whether I would prefer to leave the tournament grounds on my own, or whether I would like to be escorted. They were polite, in spite of their predicament.

"Sam, I had been thrown out of the very place to which I had attached a measure of esteem that had no peer. Even now, after all these years, my words are like escaping prisoners. They elope from a morose shame, but are hunted by a steadfast pride, and that sense prevails, beside the memorialized embarrassment that I absorbed from every friend who comprised my favored collegiate society."

"Mon Chéri, what were you doing?"

"Sam, I don't remember a single charge."

"This is a sad story, Chéri, tell me a different one, s'il te plaît."

"Here's the end. That day at Augusta, as we took the first tee, I noticed that Jim and I were the only players. I saw no one across the entire landscape. Once again, the scene was surreal. I had no idea that we might have that entire course to ourselves. Like I said, that club is unusually special. However, before we began our play, we were joined at the tee by a host of men. Apparently, our morning tee time had inspired the curiosity of some of the members. They wanted to watch our tee shots. We actually waited on the tee for their arrival. We exchanged the customary round of greetings, and we spoke about course conditions.

"There were nine men in all. I recognized four gentlemen from service announcements, which were aired on television during the actual tournament. Two others were complete strangers, wearing business suits, and the three working professionals joined from the golf shop. In addition, there were two caddies, and two players. All in all, thirteen men stood together on that first tee. And, as I said, I saw no one else. I recall bantering back and forth with Jim about the honor of playing that first shot. I felt as if I might be teeing off in the real tournament.

"Eventually, Jim accepted the honor. He played first, but I don't recall his shot. I was feeling rattled, to say the least. I remember thinking that I might not be able to hit the ball at all, much less down that famous first fairway. However, and in spite of a rather oppressive atmosphere, I hit my drive, and I hit a second, after being invited by the gallery. Neither stroke was my best. I simply felt relieved by the fact that I had been able to produce anything along the lines of a recognizable golf stroke.

"Before departing the tee, I recall asking my caddie if we were all set. I wanted to practice speaking the name that he had given. My caddie had introduced himself, as 'Skinny' but he was not skinny. Sam, absolutely everything about that day seemed to demonstrate this same sort of mismatch between appearance and reality. I wanted to connect with Skinny, but moreover, I wanted to feel comfortable with something that was real. I mean, there I was, beginning an activity which had been common to my life for as long as I could remember, but I felt decidedly lost and soundly disturbed.

"Nevertheless, that name, that singular signal of affectionate acquaintance, seemed to summon out of the surrounding ceremonial fantasy. I saw my caddie as the only truly accessible point of reality, and as my only hope of unearned acceptance.

"Here's the thing, Sam. As I left that teeing ground, and I mean with the very first footfall, I felt as if I were being squeezed, or like I was being crushed. I felt actual weight and pressure bearing upon me from all sides. I felt as if I were a wet towel being twisted and wrung. That day, I felt the same sensation that I described to you, after Mom's viewing at the funeral home, in Atlanta. I had no foresight, and no workable defense. I was simply taken by a substantial, but invisible force.

"Moving out upon that glorious field, I closed my eyes. There I was, doing something that I had always wanted to do, but I could not look. I dropped my head, as if I might be watching my steps. In my mind, I hoped that I might become inconspicuous. In my heart, I wanted to disappear. There I was, beginning one of the most famous walks in the entire world, and rather than feeling delighted, I was sobbing, like a child. Who acts like that, Sam?

"After a moment, and once again, without the first note of expectation, I was cinched by an arm and a giant paw. I was startled. I was, actually, stone cold mortified, but I did not attempt to escape. Instead, I suppose I simply accepted my station, as would a wounded child. I trudged along, pressed by the ethereal force, and gripped by this physical force. Several steps later, I heard Skinny's voice.

"His words were shaped and ordered by the accustomed drawl of the Deep South. His voice was soft and sure.

"'Don't be frettin' too much now, ya hear. It's gon' be alright. I seen this kinda thing take befo'. Jus' let it be, and let it pass. You be awright, directly. Then we gon' have a good day. Don't you worry. I got you wit me today, Mr. Jack.'

"Who would say that? Who would do that, Sam?"

"Mon Chéri, you are upset."

"I'm sorry. I can't seem to tell this story without reliving the emotion of that moment. Do you see what I mean? Who acts like that?"

"Tout le monde le fait, Chéri. Your story is about experiencing the grace of God. You said as much at the beginning. The anxieties that you shared tell me that you were feeling unworthy, and guilty, as well. In your mind, you had not earned such a wonderful invitation, and your memory of former behaviors classified you as... I believe your term was DQ? You felt that you had been disqualified from participation. Nevertheless, and in spite of your scorecard, there you were, realizing a dream that had come true.

"I wonder how you might define God's grace in your story. Would you say that it was bestowed by your 'Once in a Lifetime Invitation'? Or perhaps, through the compassionate understanding shared by Mr. Skinny? In my opinion, neither of those possibilities provides an adequate interpretation. In fact, I don't believe that the Grace that you received had anything to do with golf, or caddies, or your famous course.

"Earlier, you described that course as a stage for extraordinary performances, and I suspect that you have classified this incident along those same lines. However, I will not. You may consider the stage for your story extraordinary, but the performance is quite common.

"Mon Chéri, the Grace that you received that day is God's promised gift of forgiveness. Your story is about the gospel, the good news of Jesus Christ. Through the life and death of the Son of God, our sins have been forgiven. Your story demonstrates that truth. And, I might add that, the crushing sensation that you felt on that day, and still feel on this day, emerges from the realization that your darkest notions of shame, and your purest conceptions of judgment, fall woefully short under the light of God's love."

"Sam, I don't know how you can see those things."

"Ton histoire est très claire, Mon Chéri."

"Sam, how can I agree with your words, but still have a hard time believing your words?"

"Mon Chéri, I see through eyes that have been trained and conditioned by the Church. I have an answer for my 'why' question. You see life unfolding through the teachings and experience of recovery. You see the reality of God's promise, but you are always asking, why? I find my peace through faith and you, by willingness. However, since I have come to know you, I am no longer convinced that one is more appropriate than the other. You are a worthy recipient, Mon Amour. And, Chéri, apparently, we share a mismatch between appearance and reality that is undoubtedly intended to blend together."

"Thank you. Maybe, in the future, I'll just keep doing my stuff, and you keep telling me what's happening."

"I accept your plan, Chéri."

"Listen ... do you see what I'm saying about golf? I can clearly see certain aspects of my life unfolding through the progress of a silly game. Does that sound crazy? I mean, do you see your life unfolding at the flower shop, or on the tennis court? Or, is it all the same, but different, like seeing life through Church eyes or recovery eyes?"

"Oui, Monsieur. You may see as you prefer."

"And, through your blending of views and lives, can you see what I was saying about caddies? Skinny was my caddie in the beginning, but I became his player after that first stroke. We belonged to one another, but at a level that was far deeper than the game that we were playing.

"That day was much like our day during the qualifier tournament. You were focused upon helping me, and I was focused upon helping you. At Augusta, in the beginning, at least, I hold no doubt that 'Skinny' was more concerned about my composure and well-being than he was about carrying my bag. And, as far as I was concerned, I was determined to honor his efforts, by acting like a gentleman and playing my best. We were a team, as I said. We were headed toward the same goal, but we were helping one another in different ways. My golf game simply unfolded underneath those endeavors.

"The shocking realization is that neither effort was primarily focused upon golf, despite the fact that we were engaged in that very exercise, along the fairways and greens, of, arguably, the most prestigious golf course in the world. Now that is truly extraordinary, n'est-ce pas?"

"Do not try to be funny Chéri. You have learned something, n'est-ce pas?"

Through a chuckle I returned, "Sam, speaking of caddies, when I said that I was helping you and you were helping me, that's just another way of saying that I was focused upon your welfare and you were focused upon mine. The same goes for my story between Skinny and me, but now, I'm wondering if that type of outward focused attention isn't the same thing as giving myself, or you giving yourself, or Skinny giving of his self?"

"Oui, yes. C'est ça."

"Well, if that's true, then isn't all that the same as 'knowing' one another?"

"C'est vrai, Chéri."

"…but, I thought that 'knowing' was only between you and me."

"Non, Chéri, the episodes that you have described are the same as what we do, but we are committed to one another at a far deeper level. I hope that we 'know' one another more comprehensively than you might ever 'know' your caddie."

"Of course, but what's the point of 'knowing' another person, other than your husband or wife?"

"Mon Chéri, the act of 'knowing' another person, may include many things, but primarily, 'to know' another is to become connected and enveloped by the spirit of God."

"Why would I want to do that with a stranger, or almost a stranger?"

"C'est dommage, Chéri, your words are those of an orphan who does not know that he belongs. You belong, Mon Amour, and you will feel your place when you embrace and are embraced by another."

"Can't I feel that on my own? I mean, can't I feel the spirit of God, by myself?"

"You can, and you may, but the connection produced through 'knowing' another makes the feeling of the flow readily apparent. Each component of God's creation stems from the flowing current of God's love, Mon Amour. You are a part of that flow, in solitude or in connection, but you, more than most, must be reminded that you are not alone.

"You said yourself that your tournament round, with me by your side, was easier. I suppose that your round at The Masters golf course was the same, with Mr. Skinny by your side. You say that you see your life through a round of golf. That too is connection, and a part of the flow. You may travel upon your journey alone, but the ride is much more rewarding when you realize that you are a part of something wonderful, rather than simply moving along on your own."

"Thank you, my love. I actually think I understand. But, listen. I need a little caddie work, right now, please. Take a look at that map. I think we should have turned, back there. We may be flowing along, together, on God's river, but just because you 'know' me, and I 'know' you, doesn't mean that we know where we're going."

"Mon Dieu, Chéri."

CHAPTER 11

Wambaw

....

The final leg of our physical journey placed Sam and me upon a narrow two lane highway. That transfer was much like departing an open plain for a secluded tunnel. The local route seemed to burrow through the surrounding woodland. Mossy tree limbs stitched a shady ceiling and thriving jungle thatched constricting walls. For too long a time, I saw no indication of human life. An anxious sense, like claustrophobia, displaced my eager determination and my partner's softening peace. Under this uneasy affliction, we jumped at the first sight of an oasis, rising against the thicket. Without orders, I veered into an open expanse that hosted an ancient service station.

I left Samantha outside, stretching like a cat, underneath a patch of light falling between High Test and Regular. Inside, I found an attendant, relaxing behind an empty display counter. The glass case and my human contact wore the smudge tan and pungent perfume of oil and grease. My inquiry was met by a familiar answer—I was lost. I was informed that I had missed the sign and the turn by four miles.

"Yeah, I knows abou-tat place. It's kindly secret or sump'n a'—the like. I ain't been n'ere m'self, but I know where h'it is. They's a sign, by a side road, off t'-the right, 'bout four miles back. H'it ain't got no name on it, just a number. I'd tell ya, but I cain't 'member it right-offhand-now. Look close, you'll see it."

Armed with those coordinates, I crunched back across the sand and shell parking lot. I called to my basking bride.

"We missed by a few miles. I knew it. We need to turn around, and we need to look for an address marker next to the road."

"Do you know the number, Chéri?"

"I'm sure it's listed on my letter, but I don't think we'll be choosing between many alternatives. Did you see anything along that last stretch of road?"

"I saw only jungle from my side, Chéri."

"Don't worry, I think I understand now."

"Qu'est-ce que c'est?"

"You'll see ... let's just look for the sign."

On the road, I chirped, "Scout it out now, ya'heeya!"

"Mon Chéri...."

"I'm sorry, that's Southern for, 'Please look for the sign, dear.'"

"Non, you are not sorry, but excited to be at home again."

As the local language allows, 'we ran up along that sign before too long.'

I announced the find; "There it is."

"Mon Chéri, I see your sign, but there is nothing else... just a dirt road, leading into the jungle."

"This is it! You'll see."

I left the two-lane blacktop, in favor of a narrow ribbon of smooth sand. Just beyond the entrance, our vista opened upon an endless pine forest. We coasted along a soft roadbed, further cushioned by tufts of pine needles that appeared as woven, but tattered, remnants of cinnamon carpet. A lone palmetto bush made an occasional appearance, as if on patrol, among a numberless collection of columnar tree trunks. I felt no sense of confinement. In fact, I practiced dodging pine cones. After a time, I stopped the car.

I said, "Roll down your window. Just listen and smell."

"Mon Chéri, we should not be stopping."

"Just for a second, we're fine. I promise."

As expected, I entertained the soothing sense of sound and smell. The wind soughed through the upper pine boughs, a crow cawed at odd intervals, and the air was suffused with the refreshing aroma of evergreen rosin.

"Chéri, I think your homeland is lovely, but I do not think that this land is our land."

"Let's just go a little further. I can turn around anywhere inside these woods."

"We cannot push this car, Mon Chéri."

"We're not getting stuck, I promise."

Soon enough, our roadway curved around and passed over a brackish channel. That overpass featured the first signs of distinctly human invasion. The road was bordered by a low wall of rosy bricks that appeared to be leaching lime through a heavy slather of excess mortar. Beyond this bridge the sandy roadbed widened. We proceeded along a straight path for a distance. The next curve took us north again. Beyond that turn, we could see the edge of the wood. At that point, we noticed a considerable change in our forest and our sandy thoroughfare.

We had acquired a sort of border fence on both sides, constructed of stout trunks of gnarly 'live oak' trees. Their snaking limbs entwined above our heads to form a canopy. We also approached a structure, resting in a clear glade. It occupied an island of grass, which apparently distinguished coming from going. A collection of flag poles fronted the little house. I could see their cloth snapping in the breeze.

Samantha announced, "Mon Chéri, your gatehouse awaits."

"Thank you."

I stopped the car next to a stalwart cabana fashioned from pinkish bricks. The attendant exited promptly. He was wearing pleated knickers of a creamy linen material. I saw argyle socks, and white buck shoes. He wore a white golf shirt with a pointed collar and loose sleeves. The shirt featured an embroidered emblem on the left breast. It was a capital letter 'W' in copperplate block, stitched from pine green thread, fronting a golden threaded design that suggested some sort of plant.

He spoke, while bending toward my open window. His words were cheerful and reassuring.

"Welcome to the Wambaw Club. My name is Mike, and you must be the Weatherlows. We've been expecting your arrival. I hope that you found us without too much trouble."

I was dazzled. Samantha poked me underneath my ribs. I jumped.

"You're exactly right, Mike, and yes, we found you without any trouble. Thank you."

"Mr. Weatherlow, please follow the drive out toward the big house. Park wherever you like. You'll find Missy's desk inside, just beyond the foyer. Missy will show you to your accommodations. I hope to see you again, and I hope that you and Mrs. Weatherlow enjoy your time with us this weekend."

"Thank you, Mike, you've been very kind."

"You're welcome, sir. If I can be of any assistance during your stay, please let me know."

"I will, and again, thank you."

Pulling away, Sam asked, "How did he know us, Chéri?"

"Your French accent of course. It gave us away immediately."

"I said nothing."

"He's well-trained. He can tell."

"Stop it, Chéri. You are scaring me."

"I'm teasing, my love. Mike is simply demonstrating the art of customer service. Don't you feel special? I'm sure that you do the same thing with some of your customers, and I try to do the same with mine."

"I suppose, but they are not traveling hundreds of miles to our store. And, we are not customers."

"We are for this trip, but afterward, we should consider that, at the club, the members are the customers. I would bet that Mike knows every member, and calls each, by name, at that gate, every time."

The drive led us toward the front of the big house. There were two sandy rotaries fronting the house, such that the figure of a numerical eight might have been seen from the sky. One giant old oak stood in the middle of lower round and more flags centered the upper. We circled around the upper rotary and parked underneath the ranging boughs of a live oak. Our resting place was sheltered by the limbs and curtained by shrouds of Spanish moss.

My first visual inspection of the big house inspired a sense of puzzlement. The architecture was of a colonial revival design, fashioned from the overly iced and leaching pink brick that we had seen along the entrance drive. The structure was familiar. I had seen many homes built of that style. I suppose that I was expecting something like what I had seen in the movies. I noticed eight windows on two levels across the front. I saw four chimney stacks stationed at the corners of the main section.

The edifice rested on a berm or knoll above the drive. Thick blades of St. Augustine grass carpeted the surrounding ground, between beds of flowers and wild azaleas. A brick wall extended from each wing, but featured white gates near the center point of each length. Brick stairs led from the drive toward a large overhanging portico, but were sunken, rather than standing upon the rising terrain. A brass and glass chandelier swung from heavy chains, over the porch and above a large single door. With gloss over grain, the woodwork appeared somewhat nautical.

The heavy front door swung open without a single creak. We met Missy just inside. She rose from her desk, and she shined as we entered. Missy was a lovely middle-aged woman, dressed in a summer suit of blue chambray. She came around immediately, and took our hands, one in each of hers. Strangely, Missy spoke to me first.

"Good afternoon, Jack, and welcome, Samantha. You both look wonderful. I will assume that your journey was pleasant."

In the next moment, an elderly black man appeared by our side. He introduced himself as Benji. We exchanged greetings, but he did not linger in conversation. He asked about our bags. He took my keys and left our company for the Chevrolet.

Prior to making our way to our quarters, Missy provided a short tour of the big house. Besides several leather seating arrangements, and numerous oriental rugs, absolutely everything cast the polished sheen of varnished mahogany. I also took note of the decorations and artifacts that we passed. Each room was themed by memorials taken from the game of golf. I felt as if I were moving from one type of hole to another as we strolled along our tour.

Although the house seemed huge, with the high ceilings and an accessibility provided by arched passageways, I counted eight distinct spaces on the lower floor. I wondered. My curiosity was quelled in short order. Along with the tour, we were receiving a brief history lesson, concerning the house and property. Missy allowed that the surrounding land once served as a rice plantation. This fact affirmed my suspicions about the entrance marker.

She added that Wambaw was a part of a larger estate, owned by a single family, but was separated from the primary property, and controlled by an arm of that family who held conflicting political opinions. I noticed that she spoke presently, about events which had transpired inside a distant history. She also noted that Wambaw had supported eight rice fields. Her short course in rice cultivation offered that those fields had been fed by a single trunk, or water gate, which opened into the Moon River. Missy used the same adage, which I recalled from my telephone call with Mr. Woodson.

"One lies as all lie."

Our bedroom accommodations occupied the northwestern corner of the second floor. It featured two windows and a door. The western window looked out toward the practice facilities and the forest in the distance. Our northern window looked over the proshop villa and the golf course. Our inner doorway opened upon a sprawling porch, which ran along the entire back side of the house. There was a solid door and an old style screen door, opening upon the covered promenade.

The porch was a part of the house, rather than an addition. I stepped across a floor which was tiled in broken terra cotta. At the edge, I hung myself over a substantial balustrade for further inspection. The whole affair was supported upon round columns, and everything about that porch featured a façade of the same aging, Wambaw brick.

Missy joined me as I hoisted myself back to human level.

She said, "Jack, we would like you to see all the grounds during your visit. If you will notice, we have arranged for you to have that green golf cart, down there by the hitching post. It's all yours, for the entire weekend. It's kinda special, really, we only have eight, in all."

I said, "Of course, eight … right … Thank you, Missy."

"Well, I'll let you two settle in. Just relax and make yourself comfortable. If you need anything, I'll be around until eight. That's when dinner gets started. And, please use the telephone. Just pick it up, and I'll be on the other end. Anything, you might like, just ask. I think I hear Benji inside with your things. We're delighted to have you with us. Please take your time. Au revoir, for now…"

She glowed behind a sunny smile, before leaving us on the porch. I passed Sam a look of apology.

Alone on the porch, I offered, "I don't remember discussing your heritage with anyone at this club."

Sam offered, "I said, Bonjour Missy. Do you think…?"

"That must be the reason, but that's a pretty big step."

"She was sweet, Chéri, and also, very perceptive."

"I was kidding before. I mean about the accent thing, you know…?"

"Oui, Monsieur. Laisser aller, s'il te plaît."

"I suppose that she meant that remark as a kindness, but I feel invaded, or something."

"Let it go, Chéri. Missy was trying to make us feel comfortable."

"Well, I'm alright, if you're alright. What do you think so far?"

"Mon Chéri, everything is very lovely, but how do you feel?"

"Sam, it's perfect, and cool too. Did you notice that the number eight is everywhere? Did you see our room number? I'd bet we're staying in number eight! I'm not sure how that fits with golf, but I like the mystery. I know that the course will be spectacular. Mr. Woodson said that they built everything around a common love of the game. I mean, why would you have these fantastic facilities around a mediocre golf course?"

"Non, Chéri, how do you feel about being here?"

"I feel comfortable. It's kinda homey. I did feel that creepy, off-limits to kids sensation a few times, but for the most part, I feel like everything is meant to be used, rather than admired."

"S'il te plaît, are you feeling like a guest, or as a member, in this moment?"

"Well, a guest, I guess. I mean, that's what we are…for the moment."

"Oui je sais, but I am asking you to imagine a day in our future, when you are associated by employment, rather than membership. How do you think you will feel?"

"Sam, do we have to talk about this now?"

"Oui, I think we must. Your sense of belonging is the very reason we are visiting this lovely club."

"I'm hoping that I will feel like I do at the hotel, if you must know. I don't belong to the hotel, but that doesn't seem to matter. I work there, and I belong there, through my service. I think that this place will be the same."

"Mon Chéri, do you recall my observations of your behavior at your golf tournament?"

"Of course I do, but…"

"Chéri, I watched you change. You became more confident and assured as we entered the atmosphere of that tournament and that club."

"I'm not so sure that I agree with your assessment. I'm not all that confident at golf tournaments, but thank you."

"Non, Chéri, you were different there than in most any other situation that I have seen."

"Come on, what are you talking about? I feel pretty confident around you—always."

"Merci, but I am your wife."

"Honey, I'm not sure where we're heading."

"Mon Chéri, you have called your game of golf, the 'Game of Life' and you have called it your 'First Wife.'"

"Please don't pay any attention to that—like I said, I try to make golf invisible. You will never have to contend with her for my affections."

"Arrête ça s'il te plaît. I am not playing at the moment."

"I see that—I think."

"Mon Chéri, at home, the hotel is not intimately connected to your favorite pastime."

"I agree, but what are you trying to say?"

"Mon Chéri, here at this club you will be serving the members and their guests while they are doing what you love most. You will be watching from the sidelines most of the time. You would be like the manager of your high school basketball team. I remember your stories about that particular club."

"Sam, I kinda like this place. I mean, this club is pretty cool and look out there…"

"Chéri, you must accept your place inside this club."

"I know that, honey. Here's an idea—maybe I'll think about my job here as if I were a caddie. That might be nice."

"Mon Chéri, I recall what you said about caddies, but Mon Amour, I think of you as a player rather than a caddie. And I might remind you of my comments from your tournament."

"Qualifier, my love…"

"I am being serious. And I want you to be honest with yourself for a moment. Can you accept a role as a full-time caddie?"

"Mr. Woodson said that I would be given certain privileges."

"But, those privileges are offered to guests of the club."

"I was thinking of those privileges in a good way."

"But Mon Chéri, I am thinking of your comments about your childhood golf club. You said that you realized that your fascination with the club was not the same as your love of the game."

"I don't think that matters in this case."

"Mon Chéri, you will not be a member or a guest of this club. You will be an actual team manager with assignments and tasks to perform for all the real 'players.' I do not think you can consider yourself in terms of a helper or teammate, as you were saying about caddying."

"Sam, I fully understand the fact that I am looking at a job."

"But Chéri, in this job you will be excluded from the very activity in which you have found your sense of place and belonging."

"Dammit Sam, a moment ago, I was feeling pretty good about this setup. How did you ever remember those stories about the basketball team? But, you're right. I thought about the manager of our basketball team during every practice and certainly every game. I always wondered whether he considered himself as a real member of the team. I never asked. I liked him. He did his job well. And, I might even say that he provided a touch of comfort and compassion whenever coach was furious or we were having a bad game. But still, he wasn't a player. And since 'we' are apparently being brutally honest, I don't think I would have done his job."

"Pourquoi, Chéri?"

"Sam, I hate to say. I was glad that I was a player and not a manager, but I'm not proud of those feelings. And Sam, the fact that I hold that notion makes me feel like a terrible person.

"It's like you just said, I've always thought of myself as a player rather than a caddie. Our basketball manager was a permanent caddie for our team. I can caddie, and I have, but I suppose that I accepted that job because I knew it was temporary, and I didn't have to own that identity."

"Vas-y, s'il te plaît."

"I suppose that I take something from the memberships that I choose to claim. I need the connection that is provided. I am more me through my associations than I am when I am alone. In fact, the way I see it, something funny happens whenever people join together in some type of recognizable association. I mean like my basketball team, or some type of honor society, or this club, and even in church, too. Hey, remember last year—how about your episode with The Garden Club?"

"Oui, yes, I will never forget, but I don't want to talk about that right now."

"I understand, but I think that experience is exactly like what you suspect will happen here at Wambaw. Do you know that the basketball team was probably the first official 'club' that I ever joined?"

"Pourquoi, 'club'?"

"Club, team, association, league, call it what you will, but I don't think it really matters. Basketball teams, golf clubs, churches, Spanish honor societies, or garden clubs are all the same at base. Here's my point—something happened to me after I made the basketball team. I knew it ahead of time, but I didn't realize until later.

"Athletes were well received in my school. The basketball team was a private organization that was recognized by the general public in my school. After I made that team, my standing in that academic society was forever different by public declaration. In other words, that private athletic membership afforded a measure of publicly recognized prestige.

"And that's my point. I mean the public prestige. I became a member of the basketball team in an actual way, but also through public acceptance and notoriety. I was given an identity through that association. I liked that identity."

"And that, Mon Chéri, is the point of my questioning."

"Sam, do you see that as wrong on my part?"

"I want you to be who you are."

"Stop it, Sam—please. I have never known what that particular statement means. Do you remember my story about Mom and the alligator shirt? I wanted one of those shirts with an alligator on the breast. When I asked Mom about getting one she flew into a rage. She said that I would never have one as long as she was alive. She said that I would become who I was without trying to 'fit in' or 'join' or 'look' like all the other guys. I was ten years old. I had no idea who I was at that time, but I liked a particular group of guys that always seemed to be wearing that type of shirt. I thought that damned thing was some type of magic key or something.

"I was looking for a path in my particular jungle. Pick a path, any path—I don't know. How do you know which way to go without some type of direction? How do you know who you are without ever having done anything? Mom wore me out about that single issue through all my years at home. Be yourself. Be an individual. But all I heard was 'be alone.'

"I often pictured my mother's request in terms of outer space. I suppose she wanted me to be like one of those lonely comets that make a spectacular appearance once every hundred years. For my part, I wanted to be a star among all the others, but a shining star, nonetheless. That comet is an orphan thing. I wanted a place and a home."

"Je suis désolé, Chéri."

"And, speaking of who I am, do you realize that I have been forever changed since we were married? I am your husband, and you are my wife. I am different now. I might even say that you and I have formed our own tiny little club with a very exclusive membership roster."

"La Vache! Marriage is not a club."

"Why not? You chose me, and I chose you, but only after we met certain requirements for membership. My basketball team membership was no different."

"Arrête ça—Chéri. You did not fall in love with your basketball team."

"That's correct in more ways than you know, but think about this for a second. At first, I found the basketball team appealing, but I couldn't simply join. Membership in that club was based upon certain qualifications. I had to perform various tasks with a superior measure of proficiency. You know—dribbling and shooting the ball, running fast, and not least, a desire to play my best. In other words, I had to demonstrate my capabilities and my commitment toward a mutually recognized aspiration. And, I'm being careful here…I was only accepted as a member after successfully completing a mandatory period of courtship."

"Tu m'énerves!"

"I understand, but hang on, for a moment longer, please. And I appreciate your patience, my love.

"Keep in mind that you and I must be relatively successful at honoring this same sort of requirement in order to belong together. We must demonstrate some measure of proficiency toward the achievement of particular standards of a personal nature. I mean, besides that fact that I love you and you love me (I think) I also like you for a number of reasons, and I think that you like me as well. You are appealing to me in many ways, and I hope that I am appealing to you, even though this talk might be detrimental to my membership status at the moment."

"Mon Chéri, explain your meaning of relatively successful, s'il te plaît."

"Well, at the moment, I think that we're on different sides of this particular discussion. I might say that 'we' as in our small club are relatively successful with regard to this endeavor. Through our love for one another, we offer patience and willingness during our arguments. That is a part of our relationship and a qualification of our bond inside our association. We trust one another to honor the other's opinion.

"However, my point is this: I have become different over the course of our marriage. I am exactly who you married, but I am also more than I was. Now, think about this. Since the time of our official marriage, or since acquiring our 'club' status, we have enjoyed certain rights and privileges that are afforded to legally wedded couples. For instance, we are Mr. and Mrs. Weatherlow to the government.

"Our little club carries standing and esteem inside our larger community. Our identities inside the larger world have been changed. I am who I was, but still, different in a public view. And that, my love, is the unusual aspect of all human association. When we gather or commit ourselves to a communal effort, that private congregation inspires a public assessment. The person that I am in private is inescapably affected in some way by the person perceived by the public."

"Now, I am confused."

"Here's an example. You and I are married, both in spirit and legal definition. I belong to you and you belong to me. We are together. When you shared your story about the way Nicholas treated you in Paris, I went a little insane. In fact, I feel that same tension rising at this very moment. Those feelings resulted from our private connection, but also, I think, from our publicly recognized association. Had I been simply friends, I may have felt something similar, but not to the same degree of pain and rage. That story made me angry, but I also felt as if I had been harmed, personally, as you were. Lastly, I suppose that, if I were simply a passing acquaintance and I had heard that story as a bystander, I would have felt something, but different, still. My point is that my association with you has shaped my person. I am something of me, alone, but something more and different, as a member of our marriage club."

"Merci beaucoup, Mon Amour."

"Sam, I hope I don't sound angry, but I am frustrated. The notion of whether to join or go it alone has been the central issue of my life ever since I asked for that stupid alligator shirt. The primary voice of power in my life proclaimed that joining or belonging was wrong. It wasn't only that shirt, but being with friends, in any organized way, was wrong. Her condemnation whispers in my ear all the time. I have lived my life in irreconcilable defiance of that unforgettable order.

"I like the feeling of belonging that has been inspired by the associations that I have known. I liked belonging to the basketball team, and I like belonging to you. However, I also feel defective or out of line in some way. Like I said, that conflict is the story of my life."

"Mon Chéri, do you feel this same thing with me?"

"I do not, and please don't give that remark another thought. In the end, I think that Mom and I are both correct. I don't think that I ever really needed to belong anywhere in particular. In other words, there have been many groups, or clubs, or places in which I thought I needed to belong. However, in the cases where I was excluded, I found that I was really no less for the wear, and sometimes, after I made the team or was accepted as a member, I realized I didn't really need or want to belong where I found myself. But listen, if we keep this up, we're never going to get out there to see any of the grounds."

"Mon Cheri, do you need this club?"

"Honey, if you're asking about our club, the answer is unequivocally yes, but if you're asking about Wambaw, I don't know. Let's just remember what you said, in the beginning. We're looking, rather than searching."

With these words, Samantha stepped toward my position on the porch. She snaked her arms around my waist, and gazed at my face underneath dark brows, shaded by unruly bangs. She cinched me close, and spoke.

"Mon Chéri, I am thinking that I need to re-evaluate your qualifications for membership in our club."

"Oh really? Are you saying that you no longer find me appealing?"

"Non, Monsieur. I am wondering if you are capable of following our mutual aspiration."

"Are you saying that I need prove my capabilities?"

"Oui, Monsieur. I do not like to think that my teammate is only relatively successful."

"I see, but I thought that we weren't judging by performance metrics."

"Non, Chéri, my team has very strict requirements for membership. I am holding tryouts before supper. I would like to see how you perform."

"Can I warm up first?"

"Non, Chéri. I am the one who will be warming up. You should be ready when I return."

"Ok coach, I won't let you down."

CHAPTER 12

Lucky Chance

....

"Mon Chéri. I have given you something this afternoon."

"Honey, can we change that thought around, somehow? Sometimes, I feel a little creepy when you say that."

"I will not. I will always give myself to you, and I hope that you will do the same, but that is not my meaning, on this occasion."

"In that case, I have no idea what you mean."

"Tu verras, Chéri."

"I will see? I've already seen, and done, too. Tell me, please."

"Plus tard, s'il te plaît. We have other concerns at the moment."

"I don't. Tell me."

"Plus tard."

The telephone rang. I took the call from my side of our bed. I recognized Missy's voice. She relayed information concerning our supper plans with Mr. Woodson. Her words instantly enveloped me with that odd sense of freedom, which sometimes accompanies unfortunate news.

Mr. Woodson was being held over in Atlanta. Missy offered his sincere apologies, but promised that all would be made right across the following day and evening. She suggested that I take the opportunity to explore the club, at length and at my leisure. We exchanged kindnesses and cordial farewells, and I returned the receiver to its cradle.

"Well, Mr. Woodson is stuck in Atlanta. We're free for the entire evening."

I watched my bride smile, and sigh, and stretch her arms in invitation. She formed the figure of a snow angel, only underneath, rather than above the covers.

"Are you offering another secret gift, by chance?"

"Non, Chéri, I am feeling happy. We can do anything we like for the remainder of this day."

"Hey, that's right! We should take that golf cart for spin before dark, and we can search for your mystery gift."

This suggestion inspired an immediate sulk. Once again, my bride shifted and transformed beneath the sheets. She closed her entire body, as if a hand becoming a fist. I watched her turn away. I took this gesture as a call to action. I rolled on top of her curling body, pinned her to the mattress and applied a resuscitating kiss. After a moment, Samantha acquiesced to my plan, but only under the condition that she be allowed time to prepare for the remainder of the evening.

From the bathroom, I heard, "Mon Chéri, today, I have readied myself for three separate events, but all you have done is straighten your hair and change outfits."

"We're on our own, remember. How can I help you?"

"Non, Chéri, you are the one who is causing all the trouble."

"I'm not the one who is hiding secret gifts."

"My gift does not require you to change clothes."

Samantha wore a dress cut from a swingy cloth, dyed in the soft blue color of a robin's egg. Her shoulders were covered by a thin cotton sweater loosely entwined about her neck. She wore her ivory locks in a ponytail that hung heavily, down her back, but framed her face at the sides like velvet theater curtains. She wore pink on her lips, and dust over her eyes. I saw lapis jewels glinting beneath tugging bangs and tamed brows. Her expression seemed inquisitive, as if she were a woodland creature, peering out of the dark.

Sam wore shoes that seemed to have been designed for this single outfit. They were leather flats, finished with a sharp toe and a small, wide bow across the vamp. The smooth calfskin of the shoe matched the color and drape of her dress, and the rough suede of the bow collected the hue and texture of her sweater.

I said, "Honey, I'm not sure those shoes are good for hiking."

"Hiking!? I'm not hiking a single step. Where are you planning to explore?"

"I want to see the golf course. It might be wet."

"Did I miss the rain?"

"No, my dear, I mean, sprinklers."

"Mon Chéri, I will trust you to keep me dry, from sprinklers."

I found three golf clubs standing in one of the bag slots at the rear of the green cart. They were loosely secured by the bag strap. Apparently, I had been afforded a five iron, a wedge and a putter. The clubs had been taken from an older set of Spalding blades. The putter was a common, center shafted Bullseye. I found a sleeve of Titleist golf balls resting in the tray inside the cart. We stopped by the shop, along a sandy lane, leading toward the course. I told Sam that we needed a scorecard, and a few initial directions.

The hour had just ticked beyond six o'clock. Activity around the shop was minimal, to say the least. I assumed that most of the players had finished their rounds, and that most of the staff had departed. We entered an enclosure that appeared identical to the front room of the big house. We met the first assistant inside the shop. He turned from his straightening duties after hearing the door. I noticed large mahogany cabinets along the back wall of the room. A host of lovely golfing accessories were being offered as if books in a library.

I introduced our afternoon pairing, and provided verbal credentials. The young golf pro acted as if he knew Samantha and me. He seemed to have been waiting for our arrival. We spoke together for a time, before he offered the course. He gave simple travel directions, but specific meteorological advice concerning the setting sun. I took note of his explanation.

Eight holes moved north, away from the club, two traveled west, and eight holes moved south, and back toward our temporary home. He also allowed that we would have the course to ourselves. We exchanged farewells and departed for our first adventure.

"Mon Chéri, are you planning to play golf with only three clubs?"

"No, not really, but yes, I think that we should play a few holes. You'll be amazed at how well we can play with these three clubs."

"By saying 'we' do you mean that I should play, as well?"

"Of course! We'll have a little tournament, you against me."

"That does not sound fair, and I am not playing in these shoes."

"Don't worry, I'll make it fair, and we're going to play barefooted. There's nothing better than walking barefoot on golf course grass. You'll love it."

"Mon Chéri, I thought we were exploring."

"We are! We'll see everything, but only play every other hole."

We finished our negotiations while riding along the first fairway. I explained that bare feet were not included on any list of approved golfing apparel that I had ever seen. As described, the sun was sinking behind the trees off our left shoulders. The opposing view, across the marsh captured my attention. The briny sea breeze seemed to be commanding an invasion. An army of brackish waves were marching toward dry land. Their argent crests seemed to flash in synchronized communication with the aquatic reeds, which were signaling, first green, and then gold.

Along with the information concerning their meager fleet of golf carts, I had been informed that Wambaw was determined to foster the tradition of walking the golf course. I also understood that the club hosted an active caddie program, in support of this particular preference. Therefore, the course did not feature constructed pathways for golf carts. There were no substantial hills to negotiate, and the soil underneath the turf grass provided a robust foundation. Moving away from the proshop, I bore witness to these points, through an expansive vista. We entered upon a very special page of Earth, which displayed little sign of unnecessary human invasion. Under rights of permission and invitation I drove our green transport with the freedom of a pencil point, moving along an unblemished and unlined paper.

I had informed Samantha that we would begin our play at the second hole. That starting point provided for an initial view of our surroundings, and a comfortable distance away from more discerning eyes. Nearing the first green, I looked on, as she prepared for our match. In this case, the procedure was rather simple. The only requirement was the removal of her shoes. Nevertheless, I often found the process of disrobing feet inordinately captivating. Her ministrations seemed to carry the weight of liturgical steps, which led toward a reverential conclusion. In that regard, I am guilty of whatever crime is involved.

Once free of her delightful shoes, she tucked them against the bench. She stretched her legs, and rested her lovely feet upon the dash of the cart. Under this distracting spell, I failed to notice a short wall of leaching pink bricks that designated the teeing ground for the second hole. The wide tire on the right front of our cart simply thumped over the obstruction. There was a jolt. I saw Samantha bounce. The shock refocused my attention, and I stopped the cart with one wheel resting on the tee.

"Chéri!"

"I'm sorry. Are you alright?"

"Oui, yes, but you have hit something with the golf car."

"I see that now."

"Mon Chéri, did you not see?"

"I did not, but I do now. But, we're here... on the tee, I mean."

I backed off the tee bricks, and repositioned our ride, facing in the direction of the second green. I attempted to offer an osculation to placate the mishap, but my target departed before the kiss was ever launched. I exited, as well. I joined Samantha on the tee and we surveyed the second hole.

Spying our target, I offered, "This track might be called a 'Links' golf course."

"Is this course different than other courses?"

"No, but yes, I think so—a links course is the oldest type of golf course. They usually reside along the sea coast."

"But, Chéri, this course is not old."

"That name concerns the land, upon which the course resides, rather than the age of the course. I suppose the first golf courses were chosen rather than constructed."

"What does that mean?"

"I haven't really studied the history of the game, but, do you remember my story about hitting the pine cones around in my back yard? When I imagine the first golf games that were ever played, I envision several men doing something similar, but along the sea coast in Scotland. Of course, that's just my opinion, I don't really know."

"Oui, yes, I can see that same image. Men have invented a game to occupy their time and attention, and keep them away from home."

"I don't think that escape from home is the cornerstone of the game, my love."

"Why do you play, Chéri?"

"I play for many reasons, I suppose, but there is one inspiration in particular that never seems to change and keeps me coming back to the course. It's pretty simple, really. There is something deeply satisfying about producing a score or a single shot that ends up exactly as I planned. I suppose that golf affords me the opportunity, however fleeting that may be, to experience the sensation of performing like the guys on television. And, I think that, unlike other sports, or work, a round golf affords anyone and everyone that same opportunity, regardless of skill or devotion to the game."

"I cannot play golf like the television professionals."

"No, but if you consider any single shot, you, and anyone else, might play that one shot exactly like the pros on television. Consider a hole-in-one, for example. That shot is widely considered the most fantastic feat in the game, but everyone has at least a fleeting chance of producing that same piece of perfection. The sensation that I am describing has often been termed the experience of god-like performance. However, I won't go that far. I prefer to call it seductive marvel. I'm not certain that any other endeavor comes close."

"Voila! And, now I understand my competition, and, as you say, your first wife."

"What are you talking about?"

"I can think of another seductive marvel that you find deeply satisfying."

"And, what might that be, Professor?"

"Perhaps, we began this game before we ever reached the tee."

"I can't believe you sometimes! That's not the same, at all."

"Tu te moques de moi? Your feelings seem to be exactly the same. You have called this game your first wife. You spend long hours together. You buy her gifts, and you chase her all the way to the state of Georgia. I know of many occasions when you have felt deeply satisfied after an engagement, together. And, I also recall other times, you feel downcast and miserable.

"This game is your mistress, Mon Chéri. She is your trusted companion. Who has remained faithful to you from the beginning? She has been by your side, regardless of the road that you have taken. You feel at home on the golf course … n'est pas? This game is your seductive marvel, Chéri."

"Please don't say that. I mean it! I've done terrible, ugly things on the golf course that I would never do to you."

"Merci. I am grateful to have avoided the sight of such things, and I hope that I never hurt you in a way that might inspire such a response."

"I don't feel hurt. I feel cheated."

"They are the same, Mon Chéri. But, why do say cheated?"

"Well, let's look at it like this: if I brought you flowers one day … not flowers, I guess, but another type of gift. You wouldn't just throw it in the trash, and tell me to fuck off."

"Mon Chéri!"

"I'm sorry, but that's exactly what I mean. You would never do that, but golf can do that, and quite often, as a matter of fact. I mean that, when I hit a shot that I know to be well played in every respect, and the result is something far different, I tend to go a little crazy. But still, and in my defense, that has to happen several times before I become truly unhinged. That's what I call being cheated. I can pretty much accept the occasions when I have failed to provide my best. I can accept my missteps most of the time, but when I've done something right, I expect to be rewarded in kind. That's why it's not the same."

"Ah, Oui. Mon Chéri, that story makes me feel sad, but I also understand."

"Why? What do you understand?"

"Part of the reason that you play golf, Mon Amour.… Your game, or your mistress, has provided certain things that have been missing in your life. You have developed a relationship with this game. You are not simply a participant. You expect a type of human intimacy when you play. But, like I said, and unlike your game, I understand. Nevertheless, she cannot love you as you expect. She cannot return your affection, in kind, and as you wish."

"Stop it. You're making me sound like some kind of freaky lunatic."

"Mon Chéri, you said yourself that you feel cheated when your good behavior is not fairly recognized, and you compared that experience to our relationship. You expect something from your golf wife that she cannot provide. You are looking for human compassion and justice inside an environment that is, perhaps, something that approaches god-like status. In fact, your comment about god-like performance might be more accurate than you think. Inside the game, and out here on the course, you experience a purity, or sense of excellence, that lies beyond most human endeavors.

"I would say that the game you love is actually an interactive involvement with the power and movement of God's creation. A moment ago, you described, rather crudely, the notion that golf is not fair. I believe that you might apply that same description to life, in general. You and I have experienced our share of undeserved upheaval and tragedy in our lives. However, you also suggested that everyone is afforded the opportunity to achieve the same level of perfection that is demonstrated by a devoted professional. Perhaps, you are saying that, in addition to disaster, our lives provide moments of unwarranted and unexpected blessing or grace. While I will not say that everything works toward an equitable arrangement, I will say that whether playing golf or living life, everyone will experience a measure of both, misfortune and good fortune. Each day you play your beloved game, you voluntarily agree to enter into an experience that is very similar to a journey upon God's river of creation.

"Mon Chéri, your mistress is loving and faithful in her presence and acceptance. And, I might add that, of all the marvels offered by your mistress game, you find those two attributes most seductively attractive. That is the reason that you play golf, Mon Amour. You have said as much through your stories, and regardless of the field. Whether you were playing childhood games in your backyard, or walking along the fairways at Augusta National. The game is always available, and always accepting, regardless of your performance, be that as a prize winner, or something far less appealing."

"So, I'm right when I think of golf as my first wife."

"Oui et non, Chéri. I think that you might be better served by thinking of golf as your first experience with God. As I said, you are attracted to the unconditional acceptance and eternal presence of the game, but from that welcoming sense of hospitality you project and expect to receive the human sensations of love and compassion. God's spirit presides over all humanity, but the sensual affections for which you long must be provided by human hands, rather than the surrounding world. You are, in your game, as you have been in your life, an orphan child, searching for his place.

"I have accepted the role of God's hands and feet in your life. I will provide the warmth and touch that you desire, but God will provide the eternal presence and acceptance that you crave. I will be here as long as time allows, but God will always remain by your side, after I have departed."

"Please don't say that, either. Can we just hit a few shots? Good grief, I thought that I was the crazy person out here. This little talk can't be good for my game."

Laughing gently, Sam offered a simple affirmation. "Ça va."

I took the tee. I hit a little, three quarter five iron, almost squarely. My shot sailed straight and true, and landed softly along the right hand side of the green. We moved to Samantha's tee. She played a fuller swing with the same club, but her shot fell short and left of the green. She chipped up, and two putted for, bogey four. I performed a rather stalwart first putt that passed the cup, but managed to recover by sinking a four footer for par, three. We rode together along the third fairway. At the fourth hole, we played our balls, once again.

We followed this drill for a number of holes, skipping the odd numbers and playing along the even numbered holes. I felt quite proud of my Sam. She played her shots and accepted her scores with patience and humility. I actually used her sense of peace as a guide and as an inspiration to endure the limitations from our slim menagerie of golfing implements.

Samantha played tennis during her school years, and continues to play in her free time away from the shop. However, she plays, rather than practices. In her own words, she has other things to do. She is an athlete in my view, but her manner is decidedly passive. She possesses the raw talent and stalwart ability that enables her to participate with the graceful ease of one who devotes considerable time and attention to the endeavor. I am a secret admirer, in this regard.

In addition, Sam is left handed. She plays tennis from that side of the world. With affection, I call her a south paw. I learned that particular descriptor from my grandfather, who favored that sobriquet, when speaking of left-handed baseball pitchers of his day. Nevertheless, Sam plays golf, right handed. I suppose that I was her first teacher, and being that I am right handed, I simply taught her the swing mechanics from that position.

These notions populated the audience of my mind, as I watched her shot sailing away from the tenth tee. I took her ability to 'switch-hit' as an example of the grace and ease which Samantha routinely exhibits during our occasional athletic perambulations. Given the offset distance in our teeing grounds, we found our golf balls resting almost side-by-side, near the center of the tenth fairway.

Momentarily, we were called away by an insistent beckoning from the surrounding environment. We both heard, or felt, the gentle summons, and we took pause from our activities. The sun was setting, below the trees in the distance, and directly behind the tenth green. Shocks of golden brilliance shown like giant flashlights, peeking through entangled limbs, hung with Spanish moss. I imagined a great gallery of wise old men, secretly watching our play from the shadows. Off our right, the black water river seemed to be melting along a chocolate path. We saw a white egret flash a tawny sheen before coasting to a silent stop, along the shoreline. I hugged my bride and we both drew deeply from the salty air.

Sam said, "Je t'aime beaucoup, Mon Chéri."

I answered softly, "Je t'aime beaucoup, Samantha Weatherlow."

Standing there in our moment of private reverie I recalled the strange motto that I had been offered by Mr. Woodson and Missy.

I asked, "Hey, Sam, do you remember that slogan that Missy offered when we arrived? She said, 'One lies as all lie.'"

"Je ne sais pas, Chéri."

"Well, I think that I've figured it out. Look around here. Everywhere you step the grass is the same length. And it's all of the same type too. Even the golf cart rides on the same turf from which we play. I've only seen one or two bunkers on any given hole, and the grass was cut just the same around each one. That pond, we passed back there on number five, was the same, too. Unless, you're playing from the sand, each and every shot plays from the same type of lie."

"Pourquoi?"

"I don't know, but it's kind of nice, really. It's like being given an unexpected gift. You don't have to thrash your ball out of the hay, if you miss the fairway."

Sam questioned upon a note of earnest, "How many holes remain in our match?"

I answered, "We should probably get back to the house before dark. So, I think we'll play every third hole from this point. We'll play ten, thirteen, sixteen and then eighteen … so four."

"How do we stand?"

"I haven't been keeping track."

"Mon Chéri, I know, that you know, exactly how we stand. Do not try to fool me."

"Well, maybe…Ok, if we were to score by match play, you're three down. If we are playing medal play, then we're not as close."

"Pourquoi le difference?"

"Match play scores by holes, and medal play scores by strokes. For example, on the last hole you scored a seven, and

I scored a five, so in match play, you lose that one hole, but in medal play, you drop two shots to my par, five. Does that make sense? In match play, each hole represents a separate contest. I mean that, even if you had scored a ten against my five, you still only lose that one hole. In a medal play match we would record every stroke, working toward a total number at the end of the round."

"Oui, yes, I understand. And, I also understand that we are playing a match play game."

"Oui, Madame, that was my original plan."

I watched Sam begin to take her address for the next shot. She seemed inspired, and her manner seemed to set, like hardening glue. I watched her lovely bare feet settle into the plush green turf of the fairway. I noticed the beginning of her backswing, but fell victim to the enchanting spell of shifting feet, whirling skirts and flowing hair. I actually lost track of her golf ball, but was quickly called to attention by the sound of celebration.

I heard, "Oh La La, et Voila!"

I peered toward the backlit green. I thought I saw a white speck, lying near the hole, but just to the right.

I answered, "Wow! That looks like a great shot!"

I heard, "Merci."

In the next instant, I felt the rubber grip of the five iron club catching the hairs along my arm. I sensed something like smug satisfaction as I took the club for my shot. I attempted to manufacture a short iron shot using that longer club. I struck the ball cleanly. As I watched it sailing, I instantly knew that I had hit the shot too briskly. At the green, I chipped up toward the hole, and two putted for bogey five. Samantha followed, by sinking a five footer for birdie, three.

I watched my determined bride transform into an avid golfer. After she extracted her golf ball from the hole, she turned in my direction. She applied a tiny kiss upon the surface of that tiny white orb, while bouncing her eyebrows and grinning broadly. The intensity of her delight radiated as if she were defying the setting sun.

I spoke quickly, "Congratulations, my love. Well played, indeed. And, see there, like I said, anyone and everyone can play just like the guys on television."

"What does that mean?"

"I'm cheering for you, of course. That's what it means."

"You are not. You are teasing me."

"No I'm not! This is a perfect example of what we were talking about, just now!"

"Oui, yes, but you are also saying that my birdie was a lucky chance."

"Come on, that's not what I mean. You did it, still the same. It's great, but ..."

"... but what?"

I dropped the flagstick, which I had been holding, while Samantha performed her putt. It clattered against the surface of the green. I stepped quickly toward her spot, and I gathered her, firmly into my arms. She struggled, but being that her hands were engaged with her golf ball and putter, she simply turned away. I looked down, searching for her face.

I said, "You feel it, don't you? You feel the 'seductive marvel' that I mentioned, and you feel the sense of satisfaction. I'd bet that, right now, you're thinking that this is easy, and you are looking ahead, in anticipation of the next chance."

"That is why I am angry. You say, chance, as if my score was all luck."

"That is not what I mean. Let me ask you this? Why haven't you scored a birdie on any of the other holes? And, don't try to tell me that you weren't trying."

"Let me go!"

"I won't. Please listen. I'll try to do better. Now... you've done something marvelous, but not miraculous. You feel the rightful pride that comes from legitimate success, rather than the surprising elation, which accompanies a lucky chance. Better?"

"D'accord, merci."

"So why do you play, my love?"

"To be with you."

"Merci, but why else?"

"That is my only reason."

"Ok, but now you can understand why I play."

"Ça va, oui. I know exactly why you play this game, and I have said as much already."

"Which is it then, seductive marvel or lucky chance?"

"Neither—you play golf for an entirely different reason."

"What about us? Aren't we a perfect example of a lucky chance? I mean we met in a laundry room. How does that happen?"

This comment inspired an unexpected flurry of activity. Sam extricated herself from my playful embrace. She stepped away just beyond my reach. Her expression was determined.

Sam exclaimed, "Bon Sang, Chéri! That is not what I am saying!"

Jovially, I asked, "Then, our marriage is not based upon a seductive marvel?"

"Non, Chéri, and if it is, then you are far more clever than I can see."

"Thank you, I appreciate the credit for cunning and deceit. However, I do, in fact, think that of our entire relationship as a seductive marvel. You happen to be quite lovely, and you're smart, easy going, amazingly patient, and very seductive— like right now for instance. In fact, I might just call off this entire match."

"Chéri, we are discussing the reason you play the game of golf."

"Right and I like what you said earlier, but now you know why I really play. You felt it when you made your birdie. Regardless of whether we call it seductive marvel or lucky chance, I play for that glorious sensation. And, I might add, it happens all the time if you're paying attention. Like I said, a round of golf is like a small life lived in its entirety, from birth until death, from the first tee to the last green. Bad things happen along the way, but that feeling of elation and fulfillment that follow one glorious stroke, or hole, or score, is far more inspiring than the disasters are discouraging. And, sometimes, the marvels of the game are truly fantastic and even unexpected.

"That's the reason that I play this game, and I suppose that's the reason that I do most anything in my life. Hell, I drank liquor for that very reason. That stuff is a seductive marvel. The first years of my drinking career were like one long series of lucky chances. I thought good things were happening to me all the time, and I associated those things with my drinking. And, if I'm being totally honest, I should also admit that I looked at relationships through that same light.

"Do you recall the expression that I used when I described Mom's notion of my place in this world? I imagined myself in the form of a glorious comet steaking through a giant sky filled with common stars. In reality, that notion is like fashioning a life that appears as one long birdie hole at the golf course. I thought that was what Mom meant by being myself."

"Ça me rend triste, Chéri."

"Sam, I'm not trying to make you feel sad."

Samantha continued, "If you will recall, I do not believe that we can be truly defined by any single image which we choose from the longer string of experiences that fill our journey in life. You, however, are attempting to define your entire existence using one very special or spectacular picture. Our lives are ever moving and constantly evolving. We are never fixed and still as you prefer to imagine."

"I remember, and, if you will remember, I like that idea."

"You say that, but you believe differently. Mon Chéri, your reason for playing your game is nothing more than faithful obedience to your mother's conception of individuality. You feel a need to become outstanding in some way. For example, you need to become your comet in the sky. You need to become like a birdie score in golf. You need to live within the feeling of seductive marvel.

"And, I will add that your image of that comet in the sky is far more appropriate than you realize. That comet doesn't seem to belong to the regular sky. To see it, you have to look at the right time. By your definition, it is a worthy spectacle. It is exactly like your notion of seductive marvel or my idea of lucky chance."

"Right, and that's why I play."

"Mon Chéri, you see your comet as a wonderful image, but it is also a fleeting aberration. Your comet is not always available or present. When you choose to define yourself by one particular snapshot image, you fail to see, or be seen, within the bigger picture that actually exists.

"Mon Chéri, I might be looking on from a different perspective. I might be looking at a bigger picture of the sky. And, from that point of view, your spectacular comet appears as a common star among the millions of others. Your preference for one very particular image has kept you feeling separate from everyone and everything throughout your entire life."

"Sam, how did my question inspire this impromptu critique of my life?"

"Mon Chéri, you said that you play this game for one reason. And you believe that same reason is the sole motivation for everything you do in life. I am explaining why you are mistaken."

"All I'm hearing is the mistaken part."

"Mon Amour, over the past few days you have revealed something of yourself through the game that you love to play. I know you better now. And with respect to that knowledge, I can say with confidence that you are correct. You do, in fact, play this game for one reason."

"Now we're back on track. Thank you, my love."

"I am not finished. Mon Chéri, you have confused two endeavors all your life. You believe that an extraordinary performance will produce an acceptable status. You have been taught to believe that you must become that marvelous comet streaking through the sky, but your greatest longing is to know that you belong as one of the stars above. Your game is seductive through its potential for performance, but it is most appealing through its invitation to participate. Par is the reason you play your game, Chéri. Par is one reason, but it is also every reason. You have mentioned it all evening, on every hole and in every story you have shared. Par offers your open invitation to participate and it establishes your necessary measure of performance."

"Thank you, my love. That's a good answer, but I don't think par is as friendly as you think. Par is not so much an invitation to play as it is a benchmark for performance. I suppose most people think of par, in general terms—as in a state of acceptable balance. They say, 'par for the course' as if everything in the world is exactly as it should be. However, in golf, par is really a marker of excellence. It represents the ultimate number of strokes that are allowed on every hole and across each round. In fact, when I shoot even-par, I feel the same feeling that you felt when you made your birdie. More often than not, scoring par is a seductive marvel in itself."

"Mon Chéri, par is a requested measure. It is not issued as an ultimatum or a demand."

"Once again, my love, you are correct, but not in the way you are thinking. Do you recall my par on number six? I got up and down out of the front bunker? I didn't play that hole exactly as planned. Then again, we don't have a full set of clubs. And that same hole, number six, was too long for your best shots. So, for you, par was out of reach under the circumstances. Nevertheless, you played that hole very well, and I would bet that you consider your bogey a success. I certainly do. I might even say that your play on that hole was better than mine, even though I matched the scorecard par and you did not."

"You are making my point, Chéri. You do not make a perfect par on every hole, or across every round, as you say, but you always return to your game to play and to compete."

"That's true, but I am striving for that perfection. I like that kind of challenge. Look, for most players, scoring par is considered as an achievement rather than a mundane chore. The statistics suggest that most of the golfers in the world do not score anywhere near par. That value, or that number, exists for each hole and for every round, but for some reason, par always rests on the razor edge of success and failure. Par always appears attainable, but is rarely accomplished without difficulty. That's why par, in golf, is a term which is attached to the notion of excellence."

"Mon Amour, I would say that everyone who plays this game with any sense of commitment, and even those who join their husbands for a few holes in the afternoon, plays the game of golf out of some type of reference to par."

"I don't know about that. Some people say they play for fun or fellowship."

"But, everyone marvels at any shot that is perceived to be of excellent quality, even if that stroke is well beyond the respected bounds of quantity."

"Ok, but now you're making my point. There's an old saying that goes, 'while there's a thousand ways to make par, there's a million ways to miss.' Even the pros on television don't make par on every hole. And, if you will recall, you have asked me about par on every hole, even though you don't really play."

"Merci. What is the origin of par?"

"I have no idea. I've always taken it for granted. It's just there. It's listed on the scorecard and on the tee of every hole that I've ever played. As an educated guess, I would say that par evolved along with the game. We didn't just step out of the barn onto an eighteen-hole course, you know."

"Exactement, Mon Chéri! Par simply exists. It has little to do with the number on the scorecard. It matters, but at the same time, it doesn't. Par is a term that designates quality as well as quantity, and as I mentioned, it is a request rather than a demand."

"That's not true. Par does matter. You just said that we all play against some reference to par. And you recognized that in my qualifier event. You asked if I wasn't really competing against par instead of the other players."

"Once again, Mon Amour, you are confusing performance and participation. If you do not or cannot make par on any particular occasion, the game always invites you to return for another try. Your stories about your tournaments on the course, and your escapades off the course, are my proof."

"That's true … but, honey, it's just not that simple."

"Mon Chéri, why do you say you belong to this game? The reason is that you always have a companion and a competitor when you play. You are never alone on the golf course. And, I should add that par, as your companion or competitor, always provides a trustworthy communion. Invitation and trust and requested performance are virtues of welcome and hospitality—n'est pas? That is why you play your game, Mon Amour."

"Sam, I'm not sure that I agree."

"Chéri, you are an orphan at heart. It is a sweet heart, but a lonely one. I understand, and I feel that same yearning on many occasions. Do you realize that the only other place about which you announce a legitimate sense of attachment and belonging is inside your program of recovery?"

"That's right. I do feel like I belong there."

"Why do you feel like you belong there?"

"We're all trying to stay sober."

"Oui, yes, I agree, but why do you feel connected to that group of people?"

"I don't know. I've never really thought about it. We just seem to belong together. I just thought that we were bound by the common effort to stay sober."

"Chéri, might we consider that common effort to be par for your recovery game?"

"Come on!"

"C'est vrai! Think about it. Your steps are your golf holes, and par is sobriety."

"But, Sam, we have to stay sober."

"No you don't. That is a measure of performance. You desire and you prefer to make par, but if you don't or can't, you are always invited back for another attempt."

"Sam, the stakes in recovery are far higher than posting a poor score."

"Mon Chéri, I am speaking of the underlying principle that determines where you feel accepted in this world."

"Ok, I can agree with that notion, but still, drinking and making bogey don't seem to equate very well."

"What does your program say about membership or inclusion?"

"The only requirement for membership is a desire to stop drinking."

"Oui je sais, and what else have you shared with me about performance?"

"You mean the comment about progress over perfection…."

"Voila! And, are your steps not listed as suggestions rather than ultimatums?"

"Yes, that is also true."

"In recovery you are always invited to participate. Your performance is requested, and you find your communion with other members to be trustworthy."

"Damn, that's why I feel like I belong in recovery."

"Chéri, now you understand why you play both your beloved games. When you are streaking through the sky like your comet, you are performing, and when you consider that your comet is simply one of the stars that fill the sky, you are participating. Your presence as a participant is preferred over your performance.

"And Chéri, you are playing one other game that you seem to enjoy, and that game just happens to work in a similar fashion. I happen to prefer your participation with me over and above your ability to perform."

"What does that mean?"

"Do you realize that you rarely 'take' me for your pleasure when we make love?"

"Wait! What? Stop it! What are you talking about?"

"C'est vrai!"

"How does that have anything to do with why I play golf?"

"Everything, Mon Amour. You do not make love with me for the sole reason of experiencing your seductive marvel. I do not doubt that you enjoy that lovely sensation, but just like your other games, you do not participate for that reason alone. You have always wanted to 'know' me, Chéri. Every time and even since our first time together. That is your most fervent desire, Mon Amour. In fact, your engagement in our game has provided my understanding for your participation in all your other games."

"Damn it, Sam. I always end up feeling creepy when you talk about 'knowing' one another."

"Chéri, to 'know' me is to participate and belong and love. Knowing one another invites and accepts and requests. Performance and seductive marvel are glaçage sur le gateau."

"Ok, I get it, I think, but I'm also thinking that I might just change things around in the future, just so you don't think you know what you think you know."

"Tu pouvez faire tout ce que tu choissez."

"That's exactly right, whatever you said. Now can we just play golf, please?"

"Mon Chéri, how many more birdies do I need to win our match?"

"That is yet to be seen, my love. I might card a few birdies myself."

"Nous verrons, Chéri."

"Hey, how would I say 'lucky chance' in French?

"Pourquoi me fais-tu en colère?"

"Don't be upset, please."

"Pourquoi?"

"Just indulge me. S'il te plaît… just for a moment, you'll see.

"Heureux hasard."

"Is that a name, or the thing, 'lucky chance'?"

"That is the thing, Chéri. Pourquoi?"

"What if I wanted to say the name, like Lucky Chance Casino, but in feminine?"

"Mon Chéri, qu'est-ce que tu veux?"

"S'il te plaît."

"Peut-être, Chance Chanceuse."

"Merci, you are my Chance Chanceuse."

"What does that mean?"

"I met you by a lucky chance. I did it, or rather, we did it, but anything might have happened. You are a special birdie in my game of life."

CHAPTER 13

An Interview at the Club

....

Returning to our room after dinner, I noticed that an evening favor had been delivered. I saw a silver tray resting on the credenza. The tray was of an oblong shape. A tiny crystal flute vase rested in the center, and was flanked on either side by small porcelain dishes. Each of the dishes was covered by a dusty pink doily that matched the color of a long-stem rosebud, which had been inserted into the vase. The ultimate surprise was a familiar sight. Sam and I had each received a large strawberry, dipped in chocolate. A tiny envelope was leaning against the flute.

Being that I am a hotel man, I took notice of these details, and along that same line, common feelings of delight and gratitude were accompanied by a sense of curiosity. I pondered over production mechanics. How were these items procured, and who had prepared and provisioned our thoughtful gift?

Back at the hotel, I simply ordered such things from the bakery kitchen. I filled out a requisition slip and submitted the document to the food and beverage manager. I expected my request to be fulfilled. I gave no thought to the availability of strawberries, or chocolate dip. Nor did I typically concern myself with presentation amenities, such as silver trays and dishes, and flowers and doilies. I saw a part of my new job being unveiled in our room, and I wondered whether I would consider such things, in the future, and on my own. Apparently, my survey exceeded an unannounced time limit.

I heard, "Qu'est-ce que c'est?"

"I'm sorry. I was just wondering about our surprise."

"Pourquoi, Chéri?"

"Our evening favor would be a typical item on my list of responsibilities here at Wambaw. Someone has to do the work behind this little delight. Who brought the tray? Who prepared the strawberries? Is this a special favor, or is this gift standard for all guests of the big house? I'm trying to imagine the process taking shape in this small place."

"I will help you, if necessary. I do this kind of thing all the time. Our rose is lovely."

"Thank you, my love. Let's see what news is in the note."

I read the note aloud, while Samantha was changing for the evening.

'Mr. and Mrs. Jackson Weatherlow

The honor of your presence is requested for Breakfast in the Club Room. Buffet service will be provided at eight.'

Cordially,
Mr. Henry Woodson.

I heard, "That sounds lovely, Chéri. I will be ready."

"This note is a nice touch, and also, part of my new job. Do you remember seeing the Club Room?"

"Je ne sais pas."

That next morning, Samantha selected a seasonal ensemble. I chose standard attire. We were dressy, but a step down from formal. Samantha's dress was of a design that hugged her body and fell just above her knees. It was cut from a cloth which featured a design that might be described as an enlarged X-Ray photograph of a collection of seashells. The pattern color was tuned toward a faded turquoise with the imbedded images outlined by a soft yellow hue. I wore banker grey slacks, in summer wool, with a white shirt and a navy blazer. During the process of dressing, I was surprised by a gift from my bride. Her present was a neck tie, crafted in silk, featuring regimental stripes that seemed to complement the colors of her dress. My colors were bold, while hers were subtle. I wore brown tassel loafers and Sam wore kitten heel pumps in navy.

We found the Club Room off the main dining area. A coffee service stood guard just to the side of the left hand entrance. The inner space appeared to be a Sun Room of sorts, fixed along the golf course side of the big house. The exterior partition featured an array of windows encased by lacquered hardwood. We found them open, as we arrived. We stood for a moment, gazing across a panoramic vista, overlooking the course and the distant marsh, and we breathed the pungent freshening of morning sea air.

The inner wall featured a fireplace, formed of the leaching pink brick. A buffet station had been installed on either side of the hearth. Finally, a large rectangular table dominated the center of the room. I saw eight upholstered chairs and eight place settings waiting. Sam noticed the flowers and greenery decorating the space. The far corners of the room were occupied by giant earthen pots, in which small palms were rooted. The table featured a centerpiece that was an amalgam of local flora.

"Mon Chéri, this room is delightful. I feel as if we were entering our flower shop."

"There is something strangely homey about this room. I wonder who looks after this stuff."

"I am certain that you will have all your answers by the end of the day."

"I think the answer is standing right next to you, right now, but who is doing this work at present, and why do they need me?"

"Arrête ça. I would like a cup of coffee, s'il te plaît."

"… At your service, Madame."

I poured two cups of coffee from a medium-sized urn. I would have preferred a Coca-Cola, but I imagined that announcing such a preference might be interpreted as a juvenile persuasion. I noticed that the service equipment was quite elegant in substance and appearance. The coffee steamed nicely from the spigot, it delivered a pleasant aroma and presented an appealing color inside the cup. I inserted three cubes of sugar into one of the cups, and left the other, straight black, in honor of Samantha's preference. Turning from the service, I heard cheery voices over multiple footfalls.

I wheeled around, as if a machine moving precisely from one position to another. I was also rendered somewhat witless, and partially paralyzed. I felt my thumbs and forefingers automatically clamp together, along the edges of two delicate saucers. My brain and my voice seemed as if they were vital components in the simple process of keeping two cups of coffee aloft. A gentle clattering of metal spoons upon china plates provided the only evidence of activity from my station. I observed six figures moving in my direction, and I glimpsed another form, off my left, skulking behind a doorframe.

Momentarily, my shy partner recovered her courage. She took her place by my side, and with a nimble hand, she relieved me of one of the cups. I felt my voice being released and returned to normal duties. We stood together for a second, before taking a synchronized step toward a jovial cadre of hosts and inspectors.

Our greeting party was composed of three men and three women. I assumed that they might be paired as husbands and wives. I attempted to recognize Mr. Woodson's wife, or Janie, as he had mentioned. She represented the inspiration behind this whole affair, and we had been necessarily acquainted for a few moments in time. None of the approaching faces seemed familiar. The context of the occasion was vastly different.

My attention was quickly drawn to the fact that the men were wearing identical blazers. Those jackets were, at least to my eye, the inescapable focal point of the approaching group. Based on the visible wrinkles, I judged that the blazers had been crafted from pure linen. The cloth was pink, but the hue was soft, almost relaxing. Watching the approaching party was like listening to the easy rhythms of an acoustic jazz trio. I decided upon matching the color of the blazers with that of pink lemonade. In addition, each of the jackets featured an embroidered crest on the left breast pocket. The stitching displayed a copperplate 'W' in green, fronting the fruited rice stem, in gold, overlaying a background of sky blue.

Each of the ladies wore a summer shift of a personal selection, which complemented the season and our surrounding environment. I thought that Samantha might feel that she had chosen an outfit that blended well with her morning company. I placed my free hand lightly against the lower portion of her back. She passed me a reassuring smile, before we engaged in formal greetings.

I heard a single voice. The tone was slightly familiar.

"Good morning, Weatherlows! We're glad you're here."

We shook hands all around, with the single exception being demonstrated by Mrs. Woodson. Janie took my free hand between both palms. She administered a type of matriarchal embrace through her hands. Her greeting was like a hug, which communicated joyful remembrance and sincere gratitude. I felt as if I were standing in the company of my best friend's mother, who always seemed to welcome my presence.

In the midst of the ensuing persiflage, I noticed Samantha's nose twitch, following a sip of her coffee. Apparently, she had taken the cup with the sugar. We switched our coffees as we made our way into the Club Room. During this initial round of introductions, Sam and I came to distinguish our hosts at the Wambaw Club. They were respectively, Henry and Janie Woodson, of Atlanta, and Savannah, Georgia, Steve and Barbara Newsome, of Atlanta, and Ponte Vedra Beach, Florida, and Talbot and Emily Overcash, of Atlanta and Sea Island, Georgia.

Before long, Henry Woodson directed our party toward the breakfast service.

He announced, "Now, I've asked Ophelia to prepare some of her special breakfast delights this morning. Please take a look, along the buffet, but if you don't see anything that suits your taste, just let Maria know. And don't feel shy. I want you both to know that, underneath all that you see at The Wambaw Club, our essential purpose is to renew one's sense of welcome and comfort in the world. And, we try to honor that by accommodating certain personal pleasures and preferences."

That statement ignited a small display of fireworks inside my brain, and rather than inspiring any hint of welcome or comfort, I felt a shivery frisson of terror pass through my body. Personally, the thought of asking for something different than what was being offered was an indulgence of fantastic proportions. Every meal that I recalled from formative experience was accompanied by the threat of personal harm, but that accoutrement only became compulsory after the fare du jour had been declared unacceptable. In addition, I imagined managing huge inventories of peculiar goods, and deciphering complicated charts connecting those preferred delicacies with names. In the midst of this grim reverie, I felt small fingers collecting my right hand.

Most of our crowd found the buffet offering sufficiently satisfying. Mrs. Newsome ordered a special omelet from the kitchen, something that included fruit, of all things. After finding our seats at the large center table, we began our meal, and the first round of this interview.

Henry spoke first, "Jack, Samantha, we want you to know that we are delighted that you would consider joining us here at Wambaw. We realize that the shift in location is a big step, but we also think that, perhaps, you both might consider such a move under the notions of returning home.

However, please forgive me, I'm already jumping ahead of myself. Our primary objective for this weekend is to become better acquainted...."

I felt a persistent, but unexpected, sense of acceptance prevailing across the extent of our breakfast meeting. However, while I sat listening to the recollections of various family histories and gainful endeavors of our hosts, I felt myself involuntarily evolving. The physical alterations were vague, but the emotional shift was like continents separating during antediluvian times. I felt myself rejecting the more appealing distinctions of peer and member, while gravitating toward the far less attractive roles of prospective employee, and perpetual guest.

Such a depressing transformation might have been avoided had I not internalized a basic sense of welcome and hospitality through the golf clubs, which had provided a special type of nurturing throughout my formative years. I did not feel as if I were being personally excluded, nor did I sense that I was being seen as a member of a lower caste of this particular slice of society, yet, at the same time, I clearly understood that I could not be one of these people.

I considered that at least a piece of my state of puzzlement was being inspired by the respective age differential between parties. Sam and I were, of course, the youngest members of our gathering. We were not kids, by any observation, but the chronological distance between our apparent ages and those of our hosts might be more accurately compared to that which separates a mother and child, rather than the eons which segregate dinosaurs from human beings. In other words, I pictured our group as adult children sitting before a gathering of parents.

This image was being encouraged by an unexpected sensation that I had been receiving throughout the deliberation process. I felt something like a sideways embrace being administered, and I also detected a bit of coaching and support being shared. The presence of these small graces suggested that a type of parental compassion was wafting through the Club Room.

Not long into our discussion, I might have said that Samantha and I were being characterized as familial travelers, setting out upon our adventures in life. Nevertheless, the presence of this sense of legitimate concern between strangers produced a balanced scale, matching pleasant reassurance on one side, with fidgety curiosity on the other. And, between those forces, I entertained a watchful state of perplexity.

Before long, I began to envision the club as a sailing ship, upon which each and all hands played a part, and held stake, in the ultimate goal of a pleasant voyage. And through this image, I looked toward my prospective duties, as if I might be joining a crew or team. These pictures stood in stark contrast to my original predictions. I suppose I was expecting to be evaluated as a candidate who might be serving on a different kind of ship; a luxurious ocean liner, to be more precise. I was expecting to serve patrons who held first-class passage for a glorious cruise. I performed that very role at the hotel, and I accepted the associated duties.

I had simply projected that same image upon the Wambaw Club. However, I found myself discussing service duties with a group of people, who were, under a different light, like guests of my hotel. I did not discuss my responsibilities with temporary guests of the hotel. This was another peculiarity, which was the primary nugget of my percolating suspicion.

Soon enough, I began to realize that I had mischaracterized this club. My error had been subtle, but also profound. The hotel provided permanent spaces for temporary patrons, but The Wambaw Club, provided temporary spaces, for permanent members. My experience involved patronage, rather than membership, or a better description might read, renters, as opposed to owners. This understanding enabled me to relax, but also inspired a previously unimagined opportunity for concern. And, I wondered—how does one care for the temporary spaces, which belong to permanent owners?

The men of our group were the apparent and official title holders of the Wambaw Club. Mr. Henry Woodson held title as the Membership Chairman. He acted in the capacity of a public relations manager for the club. He promoted the club in certain circles of society. Mr. Newsome was the club President. As far as I could tell, he managed the financial responsibilities of the club. Finally, Mr. Overcash claimed title to Secretary of the club. He was the most enigmatic member of my self-styled sailing crew.

During breakfast, Mr. Overcash delivered an unexpected and uninterrupted speech, which was like a lecture on golf club operation and maintenance. Through that talk, he revealed a comprehensive library of esoteric knowledge. I heard about everything from nozzle water-pressure readings on course sprinklers to a special supplier of beef from Savannah. I learned about mower clip settings, and bunker densities. I was informed of the preferred particularities in provisions for stationery, and sheeting, and seedlings and shrubbery. I quickly understood that Mr. Overcash was the de facto sovereign of the club. However, rather than feeling enlightened and informed, I wondered, once again, why my services were desired or required at the Wambaw Club.

This particular question was growing evermore confusing, underneath the sensation that I was feeling all the more comfortable in the company of my hosts. This mental dilemma was proving difficult to resolve. I had foreseen this occasion of interviews as a sort of wintery day, rather chilly and taking place underneath a hanging overcast. However, the general atmosphere of our meeting seemed to be moving forward beneath clearing skies. The concerning aspect of this unexpected change of season was that I was not accustomed to such ranging miscalculations between prediction and reality, where human interaction was concerned. Therefore, I added this set of conflicting sensations to the other pairs, which were being inspired by my hosts. In simple terms, while my hosts seemed to be offering the dawning illumination of hope, I rested beneath the shade of my own cloud of uncertainty.

Prior to adjourning, my attention was drawn toward a familiar song. I heard English lyrics, being carried upon a French melody. Samantha was answering a direct inquiry concerning her personal endeavors. She was describing our flower shop to the ladies. Her voice, and her words, became a part of the warming sunlight, which had eluded my weather predictions. More practically, I was awakened to Samantha's presence by my side. I hadn't forgotten that she was there, but I had temporarily abandoned our connecting thread. I realized that, through my overt performance and my covert deliberations, I had become waywardly distracted. Over the course of that transitory moment of clarity, I felt both shamefully shocked, and remarkably reassured. I saw a smile curving in my direction, and I accepted the invitation to reconnect with my permanent partner, in life and in this meeting.

Watching from this fully wakeful state, I thought I detected clouds of confusion forming over the other side of our table. A shadow seemed to fall across listening faces. However, I judged that the conundrum being presented was unexpected, rather than disturbing. It seemed to inspire their curiosity, rather than discourage further investigation. As for me, I felt another piece of my own puzzle being fitted into its proper place.

I had not considered the image of a wedded couple in the midst of an interview for gainful employment. To say the least, Samantha commands certain assets that are both seductive and marvelous. I had observed the enchanting effects of her delightful French accent, on many occasions. However, that accent is rarely provided without substance. She is, more often than not, ready and willing to offer a clever idea, and a unique perspective.

While Sam spoke, I recalled her classification of this opportunity. She had stated that we were looking, rather than searching. And, with that thought in mind, I realized that I had not only forgotten our connection, but her counsel, as well. I recalled a feeling of settled security underneath that advice. Samantha and I did not need anything from this club or these people. In her words, we possessed something worthy of offer. We had come as prospective givers, rather than needy takers.

That simple notion stood in stark contrast to my personal history. Every employment opportunity that I had ever entertained had resulted from a rather involved episode of searching. I sought a place of employment, from which I might spend my time and service, in order to acquire what I needed. I thought about employment in the same way that I thought about athletics. I earned my place on the team, in either case. In my mind, my position was necessary to the team, but my person was not.

I had never been recruited for my particular talent or ability. I simply tried out, and tried hard. I made the team, but my presence was always dependent upon my performance. Quite literally, before Samantha's suggestion, I had never considered that I might possess a particular or peculiar talent or skill, from which a coach or an employer might find delight and value. The notion that I might possess the right to choose, and to give of myself, had never crossed my mind.

Once again, I goggled over the extent of my wanderings, but I also marveled at the serenity, which seemed to flow from the recovered memory of Samantha's simple counsel. And, from that state of mind, I realized that I had settled the most confounding element of my morning deliberations. I sat back in my chair, feeling peaceful and present in the moment, and I admired the woman who was dedicated to the task of shifting my worldly status from fleeting to fixed, or from temporary to permanent.

Following a brief question and answer session regarding the flower shop and Samantha's personal history, Mr. Woodson … Henry, suggested that we adjourn for the time being, in order to accommodate more particular engagements.

He offered, "Jack … Samantha, I'm going to take the liberty to speak for our side of the table. I think that we all agree that our little breakfast gathering has served as a delightful opening for our weekend together. And, I ... or we, hope that you feel the same."

"... Now, we need to do a few things over the course of the morning, and this afternoon. Jack ... Steve, Talbot and I would like to steal you away from Samantha for a while. We're going on a little inspection tour of the facilities around the house and the golf course. And, we'd like to introduce you to the staff, but especially Jimmy Thompson, our head professional, and Bob Goddard, our greens superintendent. I think the girls have planned some type of outing with Samantha. Honey, aren't ya'll headed up toward Savannah?"

"Henry, you know good and well where we're headed. And, I think that's about all that any of you boys need to know. Now ... all I need to know is when you are expecting us back at the club?"

Mr. Woodson refocused upon me after that question. His words were carried upon a tone, which suggested, secret confidence, "Jack, we're holding a little golf event, this evening. We call it The Sundowner Special. Only eight holes ... four out and four back. You'll see. And afterwards, we'll have dinner on the patio, next to the proshop. If I remember correctly, the theme is a sort of Hawaiian luau barbeque. It's our first event of the season, and you and Samantha are our honorary guests."

As we huddled with our respective pairings for the afternoon, I felt as if I were saying goodbye to my parents after being installed as a freshman at college. I passed Samantha an expression that blended regret and apology. In addition to my feeble efforts at weather forecasting, I did not anticipate surrendering Samantha to the processes of inspection and approval. Apparently, both members of the Weatherlow team were being evaluated as potential candidates for acceptance at the Wambaw Club.

The ladies' group adjourned first. I followed Samantha's departure with my eyes. By my appraisal, she was a courageous trooper. I watched her moving away, with the other ladies, across the glossy planks of the main dining room floor. With each step, she rose slightly on her toes. Her hair bounced with each footfall, and she swayed, and flowed, in her signature gate.

Mr. Newsome remarked, unexpectedly, "Jack … Samantha is a very lovely lady."

I returned, but curiously, "Thank you."

Mr. Woodson announced, "Let's begin with the proshop. This way, gentlemen …."

The afternoon session was much like our breakfast meeting. I felt as if I were being directed by Mr. Woodson, observed by Mr. Newsome and educated by Mr. Overcash. Once again, during our afternoon session, I did not feel as if I were being evaluated as a candidate for employment. Neither did I imagine that I was being vetted as a prospective member. On the contrary, I felt as if I might have been the newest member of the Wambaw Club, fully fledged and duly accepted. I felt as if I were being introduced to the wonders of my new association.

There seemed to be no end to the intricacies of Mr. Overcash's involvement and oversight of the club. My opinion about points of operation was never solicited. Nevertheless, I felt obligated to offer some type of comment. On various occasions, I provided stories, taken from my experiences at the hotel. I inserted certain eccentric comparisons, or life examples, which corresponded with Mr. Overcash's elaborations on specific operating procedures. I wasn't trying to be funny, but clever. I wanted my hosts to know that I understood the business of keeping house for finicky guests. Those precisely targeted anecdotes were my way of giving of my talent and experience.

We enjoyed lunch on the patio off the western side of the proshop. During our second meal together, I learned more about the respective histories of my hosts. I held no doubt that these gentlemen had been successful in all their endeavors. Most of all, I learned that these men took immense pride in their golf club. And once again, I felt the conflicting disturbance created by clashing sensations of inclusion and exclusion. I felt the comfortable embrace provided by fatherly figures, but all I had ever known under that particular watch was that acceptance was contingent upon performance. We ended our afternoon session on the lower porch at the rear of the big house. My hosts shared a bottle of red wine, while I sipped a Coca-Cola. No one asked a single question.

The ladies returned before long, and under female orders, our gathering was temporarily disbanded in order to make preparations for the evening. Our tee time for the Sundowner's Special event was scheduled for 6 p.m. Everything about our day seemed exceptionally smooth, and well received on both sides; even the actual weather appeared to be unusually cooperative.

Samantha flopped across our bed as soon as we entered our freshened room. I paused, momentarily, as if I were back at the hotel. I was inspecting the cleaning work. Through a peripheral glance, I noticed two arms being upheld, silently imploring my presence.

I slid along Samantha's side. I propped my head on my elbow and looked over her smiling face. Her eyes were closed, and her arms fell limply along her sides.

I inquired, "Well … how was it? You were pretty brave down there. I didn't expect that you were going to be interviewed as well."

"Mon Chéri, I spend most of my days around women who are exactly like these ladies. I was not afraid or worried."

"Well, I was. What did you do?"

"First of all, we just drove all around Savannah. The ladies wanted to show me the city. Everything that I saw was very beautiful. Some parts reminded me of Paris. Later, we walked along the waterfront, by the river, and we visited the City Market. I also saw the old graveyard, and they showed me where movies had been made. I like Savannah, Chéri. It is a comfortable place that reminds me of my home."

"That doesn't sound so bad …."

"Mon Chéri, my day was lovely. We went to Janie's home for lunch. My visit was expected. Janie held a reception party, just for me. We ate salads with shrimp and crab and strawberries, and I drank champagne mixed with orange juice. They called that drink a mimosa. We all drank mimosas. They were delicious, but now I feel a little tired…."

"Yes, I see that … But, there was a party at Janie's house? I don't understand."

"Chéri, Mr. and Mrs. Woodson live here during the winter. They have a home in the old section of Savannah. Their house is like this club. I was reminded of the older homes in Ward Estates, at home, but without the surrounding property. Like Paris, everything inside Savannah is very close.

"We mingled in the garden behind their house, and on the porch, in back. Janie has a rose garden, surrounding a koi pond, with a fountain. I saw many varieties. Every hedge was manicured. The aroma of camellia, and jasmine, and magnolia filled the air, and there were mimosas too."

"Yes, I know about the mimosas."

"Have you seen their garden?"

"No, I haven't seen their garden."

"Then how do you know about the mimosas?"

"I can see them, right now. They're lying right here, on our bed."

"I am not a tree, Chéri."

"Never mind, I'm sorry. Who was there?"

"Janie's friends were there. Most of the ladies that I met live in the city. Some said they were members of the club. I even met one lady who owns a flower shop. I would like to see it, if we have time, before we depart."

"This is amazing! I had no idea."

"You can have this job if you would like. Janie told me that. She likes you. You saved her life. Until today, I did not know that you were her hero."

"I didn't save her life, but I did save her nightgown, and a few other things. But, don't get any ideas."

"Not ideas, Chéri, images. I like to see you as a hero."

"Well, good, you may think of me as a hero, but that's all. Look… do you think you can play golf again, but later, this evening?"

"Oui, yes, bien sûr."

I allowed our conversation to dissipate into total silence. I lay there on my back, next to my sleeping bride. I entertained former images from college. I recalled that resting between certain raucous events was once a rather common practice. With or without my date, we would take an hour or two to recover and recharge between 'fête du jour' and 'soirée.' Samantha was dozing, while I peacefully pondered the previous proceedings.

I recalled a summary history of my prospective endeavors, and I recognized that, on each occasion, I was haunted by separate streams of anxiety. The first always concerns acquisition. The underlying fear comes from the possibility that I will not be chosen to perform my preferred pursuit. The second concerns performance. Once the desired activity is acquired, my idling fear shifts gears and begins to question my ability to provide the actual performance that I have been awarded. Lying next to my bride, I felt that precise shift taking place.

I had taken Samantha's advice about this position as fact. I recalled acquiescing to the wishes of my bride, on many occasions. I had often accommodated her preferred desire, when I was planning an entirely different course of action. For the case at hand, I thought Janie's wishes might very well represent the deciding vote in my favor. I wondered whether the unexpected sense of welcome and inclusion that I had perceived throughout our engagement was not wholly inspired by Janie's preference. I allowed that consideration to rise and wane as I slipped away for a short nap.

I was aroused by a light tapping sound, emanating from the outside of the inside door to our room. I rose and responded. At the door, a female attendant offered that I might consider the time, and begin to prepare for the evening. I thanked her, and returned to the bed and my sleeping bride. This touch of grace was another service that was not common at my hotel, but was, in my mind, a masterful gesture of courtesy.

I hovered over pink lips, emitting wisps of musky breath. I touched my lips against hers. I aroused a flicker of life. There was an attempted hug, a shrug, a soft suggestion, and a whimper. Thirty minutes later, Samantha and I were entering the proshop.

CHAPTER 14

The Sundown Special

....

The players for our twilight event had gathered on the patio, next to the proshop. Jimmy Thompson was making announcements to the field. As expected, we would be playing a Fort Lauderdale format, all players would hit, but the best stroke would be selected as the ball in play.

Prior to our tee time, Sam and I were presented to the select throng. We were, after all, the guests of honor. Once again, Henry and Janie were our escorts and directors. We mingled together for a while, enjoying delightful refreshments. I met the head bartender. His name was simply Sundown, and his special offering for the evening was called The Sundown Special; a plunge of vodka, mixed with a flood of Fresca, inside a highball glass, and garnished with a thick slice of lime. I knew that drink from former days. Samantha thought it was delicious. I took a Coca-Cola instead.

The staging area around the proshop appeared as if a parade might be starting. I noticed all eight golf carts decorated with palm fronds. The stalks were fixed atop the roofs, with the fronds hanging over the front and sides. Our electric chariots appeared as mobile jungle blinds. I also saw eight men, wearing white jump suits, standing as if sentries. Apparently, one man was assigned to each cart, and each seemed to be guarding two golf bags. I suspected that the ladies were to be the riders and the men, walkers, beside the caddie.

Our communal cart was affixed with a large placard, which featured a numeral like those found hanging upon a theater marquee. The front of our cart displayed the number, one. That number designated our first hole of play. I also noticed that our cart had been loaded with two fully stocked golf bags.

During the process of taking her seat, Samantha asked, "Qui sont ces?"

"Yours, I suppose, but only for the evening, they must belong to a member who isn't playing."

There was a prevailing sense of confusion as the field dispersed. Some of the ladies took off, without allowing their caddie to board for the customary courtesy ride to the assigned starting hole. Afterward, we waited, in order to allow for travel times to respective starting holes. I spoke with our caddie in those few minutes, and I brought Ginger around to meet Samantha. Ginger, or rather, Walter G. Barrow, Jr., was a resident of Savannah, and earning money for college at Georgia Southern. He was beginning in the fall.

The event was eventually and formally started by a real shotgun blast. Jimmy Thompson held the thing aloft, and pointed toward the marsh. He pulled both triggers and discharged each barrel of the side-by-side gun. Samantha jumped, even after having been prepared. I felt a crushing grip being applied to my hand.

I heard, "J'ai peur, Chéri."

"Please don't worry. I'm sure things will settle down."

At some point in the midst of all these preparations, I noticed an old style biplane flying in the distance, over the marsh side of the course. I watched it patrolling, and moving, as if in slow motion. It glowed like flames of fire, when descending through the rays of the setting sun. I thought the sight gave a touch of panache to the event.

I heard Henry remark, "That's Newsome flying that thing. He's a pilot, more than a golfer."

While watching the ladies putting on the second green, I finally inquired about the odd design of this peculiar eight-hole tournament.

Henry replied, "This is the first tournament of the year! We always play eight holes to begin the new season. We play one through four going out, then cross over to fifteen and finish on eighteen. We play par to thirty-four in this event."

"Yes, I see, but, why just eight? I mean, we all begin from different locations on the course. Our group is the only group that will finish back at the house. Everyone will still need to motor in, from their own finishing hole. I don't see the benefit."

"Jack, there is no tangible benefit. This tournament is symbolic. The first official tournament ... the beginning of our golf season ... renewal, and rebirth ... the number eight has always been associated with some type of new beginning... always, and all over the world."

Hearing that remark was like watching the sun stutter-step its descent. I felt, rather than saw, a special illumination. A window opened inside my consciousness.

I said, very softly, "I see ..."

Walking with Samantha, I asked, "Honey, what do you know about the number eight?"

"Qu'est-ce qu c'est?"

"Eight, or numbers in general, do they have other meanings?"

"Oui, yes, bien sûr. Numerology is significant in many faiths, perhaps, all faiths."

"What does the number eight mean? I mean, we've seen that number everywhere around here."

"I do not understand, Chéri?"

"First of all, golf tournaments are not eight holes in length. Mr. Woodson, I'm sorry, Henry, just told me that we are playing an eight-hole tournament because this is the first tournament of the year. He said that it symbolizes the renewal and rebirth of the season for golf at Wambaw."

"Oh la la! Je vois…Perhaps, he is thinking about the Resurrection."

"What? Now, I don't understand. What are you talking about?"

"The Christ, Mon Amour; Jesus rose from the dead eight days after he entered Jerusalem."

"Really? Who would count that?"

"Everyone who cares to know, Mon Chéri."

"That's it then, isn't it? That's why everything is eight around here. This place, the land, eight rice fields, eight golf carts, eight chairs at the table this morning, eight-hole golf tournaments … everything is eight. This whole place has risen from the dead to become something new …."

"You are scaring me again."

And, as if by some supernatural cue, we watched our airborne patrol deploy his sprayer device, and leading a trail of white smoke, he began to form the number eight, high above our heads. It took shape, a perfect eight, hanging in the sky, but also, sideways to our view, like the symbol for infinity.

Although newly awake, my golf game apparently went to sleep. My drive on the following hole moved like that cherry-red biplane. It soared high and turned eastward toward the ocean, but fell short into the marsh, while the biplane dove and disappeared below the tree tops. Nevertheless, we recovered quickly. I might say that our team began to coalesce over the following holes. Sam hit a great drive, Janie made a putt, and Henry knocked an approach shot stiff. As for me, I was considered the most accomplished player, and as such, expected to hit various shots, longer and more accurately than my teammates. We were four under par after our seventh hole. Henry offered that five under would definitely place, and six under might win. We needed a birdie or an eagle on our final hole.

Over the course of the round, Sam had become slightly perturbed by the format. She didn't like the fact that my drive was almost always chosen by the team. As I approached the eighteenth tee, she asserted her sense of affront in indecipherable French.

"Pourquoi Devrais-je Frapper!"

"I'm sorry?"

"Why should I hit? We always use your drive?"

"We need you! You always hit a good one."

"Non! We have taken your drive on every hole."

"No we haven't, remember? I hit it into the gundge back on three, and we used yours."

"But, if you hit a good shot, mine will not be better."

"Look, it's just the way it is in a Fort Lauderdale tournament. One more hole, ok?"

"Peut-être, nous verrons."

As planned, our final hole was the final hole on the course, number eighteen. It was a meandering par five that played rather long. It appeared almost like the entrance drive that led to the big house, but as a pristine carpet of grass, rather than sand and shells, moving between lagoons and live oaks. Unfortunately, in this case, I hit a good drive from the tee. Subsequently, and in keeping with her protest, Sam decided to forego her tee shot. Luckily, Janie Woodson saw that Samantha's idea was quite sound.

Under gloaming skies, we prepared to play our approach shots from the fairway. Janie hit first, and Samantha followed. Sam hit a nice layup ball, which came to rest in the middle of the fairway, approximately, 100 hundred yards short of the green. Henry's shot curved away into the limbs of a waiting oak.

I paused, as I began to address my next shot. I was distracted by the commanding sound of a vigorous internal combustion engine. There was a robust whine. A muscular buzz alerted my senses, as if I were being called to attention by a gigantic bee. I turned back, toward the sound, in the direction of the tee and the distant sea.

I saw an airplane approaching, but different than the former. It seemed to be aligning with the fairway. This aircraft was no lazy biplane. I stood there somewhat paralyzed, but compelled by the sight. The distant image resolved rather quickly. I observed a World War II vintage, P-51 Mustang, bearing down on our positions. The aircraft was finished in a striking yellow color, which gleamed like a varnished banana peel. The Mustang leveled off, near the teeing ground, and barely above the upper branches of the live oaks. I stood there, as if by order, rather than choice, mouth agape, frozen in place, trembling slightly, awed by delight and fear.

In a matter of seconds, the Mustang 'strafed' our fairway. I actually saw the pilot waving, through the glass cockpit, as he passed. Approaching the big house, he turned straight up, and rolled into the darkening sky using a corkscrew maneuver. After a moment, he was gone, and like an incoming tide, a disheveled peace filled his disconcerting wake.

I heard a complaint, "Damn that Newsome! I gave him the approval for the Curtiss, but not the Mustang. Are you folks alright?"

"Henry, I want to go in, please. I don't think I can hit another shot."

I felt, arms encircling my waist, and the deliberate press of a forehead against my back. I shifted and turned like that Mustang, a grounded corkscrew maneuver intended to avoid breaking needful contact.

I said, softly, "It's alright. He's gone. Hey, look here…."

I heard, "What was that, Mon Amour?"

"Part of the ceremony, I suppose. It's over now, don't worry."

"May we finish now?"

"Of course, my love… just a few more shots."

Henry calmed Janie. And returning to my shot, I played a rather scrappy, low ball, but straight and solid. It rolled up—some ten yards from the front of the green. We chose that ball, chipped up, all but Janie, who waited behind the fronds of her jungle cart. We proceeded to two-putt as a team, for a par five. We carded a four under score of thirty, for our round.

We collected near the proshop, among a host of other golfers who were coming in from different holes. Out of the ensuing melee, I heard an immediate cacophony of vociferous complaints being issued by the female participants. Henry gave a general announcement meant to sooth an agitated tribe. Afterward, we all headed for a darkened patio, which was being illuminated by standing torches. Waiters in white coats stood among the tables holding trays with prepared drinks. I thought I heard glasses chattering against one another.

Gradually, nerves were soothed and souls emerged from cover. Fellowship was coaxed to life by a combination of soft Hawaiian melodies and an easy flow of alcohol. Steve Newsome arrived, after a time. He was soundly and roundly reprimanded by the ladies, but I noticed that the men said nothing of any substance. Sam mingled with the ladies, but stood back while the others made their pleas to a deaf justice.

We enjoyed a supper defined by heavy hors d'oeuvres. There was roast pig, which I have always found to be a surprisingly delicious offering, despite the rather medieval presentation. There were the expected delicacies, accompanied by a host of familiar southern salad dishes. In the end, I decided the luau theme was accomplished mostly by music and torches, and the pig. I wondered if any of my surrounding crowd had actually attended a true Hawaiian luau.

In the midst of the festivities, I was invited back to the Club Room, inside the big house. I was joined by my three hosts. The large table from breakfast had been replaced by three smaller round top tables. All of which displayed four place settings. Once again, I wondered about the setup work. We sat around one of the tables, Henry Woodson, Steve Newsome, Talbot Overcash and Jack Weatherlow.

Henry said, "Jack, first of all, I should say that tonight has been a different sort of interview. You might say that we have been showing our stuff to you.

"In fact, I might say that, while I cooked the food, Talbot prepared the tables, and Steve provided the entertainment. In other words, Steve holds title and deed to this place. He pretty much does as he pleases. And, as you have seen, he prefers to fly his planes. Over time, Talbot and I have convinced him to avoid using the fairways as landing strips. That particular grace is better for the course, and also enables us to maintain a relatively low profile before the authorities.

"I feel fairly certain that you have recognized that Talbot keeps the place spic and span. He likes that sort of thing, and he is just the sort of drill sergeant that can keep the troops in line. As for me, I am the self-appointed host of our little getaway. I like to keep the guests happy. Like I said, Talbot sets everything up, while I prepare all the delicacies.

"Along those lines, I might say that this evening's event has been fairly common, but also somewhat special, but purely because of your presence. We like to do this sort of thing around here, and we do it quite frequently, although along varying lines of theme and entertainment. We may choose to be formal or casual. This is our club, the members are our friends, and we gather and we do as we please. Nevertheless, all that we do here at Wambaw is intended to foster the inspiration for rebirth and renewal. Our members may come in for a day, a single gathering, or perhaps, a week or more. The club is our vehicle for renewing our lives, but golf is our inspiration. We operate at ground level, under the old adage which says, we begin our lives on the first tee. We promote that notion through all we do at Wambaw.

"Therefore, here is our proposal. We have been looking toward the future. We are three, but also six, looking ahead. We have decided to become four, but also eight, for the future. We would like you and Samantha to become the minds, bodies and souls that make our team eight, and as such, you will represent our commitment to renewal and our vision for the future of Wambaw.

"We are growing older, and we must inevitably surrender the reigns to someone else. Our children are engaged with other pursuits that do not include the game of golf as a centerpiece of their lives. We would like you to join us here at Wambaw, as a fully vested, honorary member, but a working member, just like us. Don't worry, we understand your financial situation, Steve has been checking. Nonetheless, we see you exactly as was promised, the assistant secretary of the club, but only for the time being.

"We have employees here at the club, but our leadership comes from the bond of membership. You will invest in this club of your time and your talent, as a servant, but also underneath the commitment inspired by membership. Please don't concern yourself with buy-in fees or dues, we are considering your time and service as plentiful and proper currency in that respect. In addition, we are arranging a salary, and of course, an expense account.

"So, this is our proposition. You will work for the club, but underneath our guidance, until I suppose, we all agree to place you in full command of the ship. Now, we'd like to hear your answer, but not tonight, we have a party to attend. We'd like for you to consider this offer, and provide your answer, tomorrow. We have arranged for Samantha and yourself to have the day, all to yourselves. Visit Savannah, have lunch, and mingle with the natives, so to speak. We will meet for dinner tomorrow evening. We will convene at 8 p.m., once again, and in this very room, as a matter of fact. Now, unless you have a pressing issue for our discussion, let's all rejoin the party."

I felt as if I were, once again, staring at that incoming fighter plane. I was stunned, curious, confused and somewhat fearful. In addition, I was experiencing a type of mental eclipse. A moon, composed of flattered delight, was passing in front of the inner sunlight of logical sensibility. After a moment I deferred to simple training.

I offered, "I would first like to say, thank you, to one and all, Henry … Steve … Talbot. I am grateful, but I also feel quite honored."

I paused before adding, "However, and with all due respect, I feel somewhat confused. I can't remember feeling honored after a job interview, and I want to ask why or what I might have done to inspire your grace and trust in such generous proportion?"

Over the ensuing seconds of silence, I marveled over the words that had strung together with obvious precision, and apparent ease. I watched my hosts confer for a few seconds.

Henry spoke for the group, once again.

"Jack, I owe you a confession, but the following words are attached to something we term in the legal profession as 'due diligence.' I sincerely hope that you do not take offense from the following testimony. Wambaw is by legal definition a social organization, and by a consensus of opinion, we view our club under that distinction. I might say that our predominant concerns, with regard to the club, fall into a category that considers a human credential, in greater measure than business experience. In simple terms, we have done some research on you and your background, prior to your arrival. I hope you will not judge us harshly under this light. I will explain but I will offer several examples.

"First of all, Janie is by no means a sucker. I hold her appraisal of character in the highest esteem. Due to the list of reasons, which she presented to our entire group, you received our invitation to visit our club.

"Next, and if you will recall from a moment ago, I had Steve perform a sort of review of your financial situation, but nothing under the table, mind you. Everything we know has been gathered from public record, and personal extrapolation. In addition, I asked some questions, of a social nature, within certain circles of Atlanta. And, Talbot did some research into your history with the game.

"I'll review our little research report with an easy one. Perhaps, you remember a Mr. Johnny Monroe from ACC up in Atlanta, or perhaps, you remember him by a more familiar moniker. We call him Trilby or Trill. I might call your attention to his famous hat."

I blurted, "Yes, of course, I'll never forget him. He was caddie master at the club, when I was younger."

"Well, ole Trill's son, Johnny, is our caddie master. He takes care of the caddies and the bag department at Wambaw. Anyway, we asked about you through those links. Trill has retired, but he's still doing well, and he remembers you from the club. You were one of his favorite boys.

"Talbot is a member up there, but he plays more seriously than me. Through certain connections, which link together through his other club, on Sea Island, he discovered bits and pieces of your golf career."

Talbot Overcash spoke up, unexpectedly, "Congratulations, on your victories at Druid Hills, and in Dothan, and Charleston."

Henry offered, "See there, that's the kind of thing I'm trying to present. Now, for my part, I will add, through a mixture of delight and compassion. I happen to know various people who were pleasantly acquainted with your folks from younger days. Let me simply say that I am sorry about your mother. And, from a close friend, who just happens to be a member here at Wambaw, I know something about your own struggles. However, I also know about your dedication to recovery.

"I have an old friend in Atlanta, perhaps, my best friend of all time. We grew up together and schooled together, and we've stayed together for most of our lives. He's also a member here at Wambaw. I've seen him flying high and I've seen him crawling on all fours, as they say. I believe you know him, as a matter of fact. He's been around, and he's spent a considerable time in Kansas City.

"Now, even though I have his permission, I also want to pay honor to the rules of his other club. He frequents the High Ball Group down on Peachtree Street, every Wednesday evening at 8 p.m. ... funny how those things convene at eight, but, never mind that, for now. Perhaps you recall meeting him. He goes by Grant T. inside that particular club. And, through your own authorization, he has told me part of your story."

I expelled an audible gasp, as I realized that my personal interview at this club had been but a shadow behind an uncanny web of unlikely connections and the historical interview that had been taken in Atlanta.

"Jack, please bear with me for a moment. I'll offer our closing arguments with regard to your case. You will be the judge from this point forward, and I might add that we consider this particular case as closed to the public. We like you, Jack. You are a living example of renewal and rebirth. You have traveled a colorful road. You've made a few poor shots, but you've also encountered a few bad breaks. Nevertheless, and to your credit, you have recovered well, and we expect that, in time, you will, once again, finish at the top of our leaderboard. I hope you don't mind my golf analogies, I just happen to know that we share a special love for an activity that is more like life itself than any simple game.

"Now, consider the connections that brought you here. You made an unforgettably graceful impression on my Janie, but you did that from a displaced home, and inside a necessary endeavor. That is not an easy grace, in my mind. You once had a heart set upon a career in golf, but you ended up learning and serving in the hospitality industry. These traits, one and all, are the founding principles of our club. And, I shouldn't forget to add that, you have found a very astute and lovely partner in life. In fact, from what I've seen over this short amount of time, I could say that my Janie has met her match. Perhaps, you have not realized, but Samantha has kept me on a more respectable footing since your arrival. Let's just say that I like to enjoy myself, when I'm away from the office.

"So, there you have it. That's the way we see things. The membership and the job are yours, if you so choose. But, as

I mentioned, we want you to decide. That is, of course, you and Samantha. Now, if you feel settled, let's conclude our business back at the party with all the others."

I sat still and silent for a moment. The shady fog of flattery had disintegrated. I was fully awake and standing beneath the brilliant lights of full disclosure. However, in this case, my pause was a product of amazed incredulity, rather than stark terror. I frankly could not believe what I had just heard.

I spoke rather sheepishly, "Maybe, we should get back to the party. But, thank you...again, for everything."

I saw smiles transform tension. We rose together. We shook hands, all around. Henry took my shoulders with an arm, and we departed the Club Room for the party.

I found Samantha engaged in a conversation with several couples. I joined the fray, but along the outer rim of the huddle. I fitted my hands around her waist from behind, inside my curvy place, above her hips. She turned quickly, but smiled, and I was instantly filled with a sense of renewal. We remained in place for a few moments, but only until a suitable window of escape was opened. I stole her away, toward the tiny space reserved for dancing, in front of this evening's quartet. I took her by the waist once again, and we glided against one another, beside the smooth rhythms of a sultry Bossa Nova tune.

Finally, I heard, "Où tu étiez, s'il te plaît?"

"Secret meeting... I can't tell you."

"Arrête! Dis moi!"

"Nope, can't do it. I would be divulging ancient rites of initiation. But, if you're good, I'll show you the handshake, later, and in private."

"You are not funny, Mon Chéri. I have missed you, and I was worried."

"Don't worry. I'm right here. Everything is fine."

"Perhaps, I will steal you away from this party for my own purposes."

"I'm not stopping you. And, who knows, if your 'purposes' happen to include certain devious methods of coercion, I might even talk."

That remark inspired Samantha's signature response to my frustrating provocations, albeit, guarded and measured by the circumstance. I felt an open handed smack across my left shoulder. However, I might add that such a thing was 'Par' for our course. Both the aggravation and the amendment operated inside an ongoing game of courtship.

We found Henry and Janie at one of the tables. I offered our respects, and gratitude, but also, our goodnight. We shared a few comments about the day, and pledged our intentions to convene for supper the next evening. Samantha offered a hug to Janie, along with her gratitude. The ladies shared a moment of conversation. They held hands and laughed at their own secret confidences before we departed.

Back in our room, Samantha took the first turn in the bathroom. I slipped out of my golfing attire. I folded each article and placed them on my stack of dirty clothing.

I called out from the main salon, "Honey, I know this has been a long day. If you're tired, we could wait until the morning, before sharing certain private secrets. I haven't forgotten, you know."

"Oui je sais, Mon Amour, but I am feeling fine."

"Well, I mean, you have been attending parties all day."

"Oui, yes, but I have other things to do now."

"What other things? Hey, are you going to take a shower? I think I'll…"

In midsentence, I heard, "Close the lights, s'il te plaît."

With that comment, I turned toward the bathroom. Samantha appeared in the frame of the doorway. I saw a darkened image, backlit by the white light, refracting and reflecting around the tiled enclosure. For the third time in a single day, I stood there, as if by order, rather than choice, mouth slightly agape, frozen in place, trembling slightly, equally awed by delight and fear. On each occasion, highly irregular scenes of entirely different natures had produced identical sensations. This time, there was no aging fighter plane bearing down upon my position, nor a collection of fatherly figures applauding a curious compendium of questionable experience, but rather, I looked upon my bride, standing across the room, very still, quite solemn, original birthday style, without the first stitch of covering.

Samantha remained in place, while I performed the requested task.

Fumbling with one of the table lamps, I asked, "So, we're not taking showers?"

"Non, Chéri."

At last, I approached, and took her in my arms, but with caution, rather than hunger.

"Are you alright?"

She gripped me tightly, and pressed against me with peculiar urgency.

I asked, "What's wrong? What happened? It's ok, I'm right here."

She led me toward our bed, but said nothing.

After a rather lengthy appointment, we lay together, entwined, but recovered and resting; I spoke the first words, following an unexpectedly torrid engagement.

"Do you want to tell me now?"

"Non, Chéri."

"You have to. You haven't needed to 'know' me like this in a long time. Please, tell me. What happened tonight?"

"It's not just this evening, Chéri. Everything is different here. I have been looking, as we agreed, but I have been drifting, as well. Then, this afternoon, on the golf course, that yellow airplane seemed to pass directly through my body. There was a spiritual force in that sound and sight. I felt as if I had been torn away, and separated from you."

"Honey, please, why didn't you say anything?"

"I am interviewing too, Chéri."

"But, not with me, you're not. I've never known you to keep your feelings to yourself."

"As I said, I have been drifting, and tonight, I lost you for that time."

"I had to go, but I'm sorry. I should've said something. Everything happened so quickly."

"There is something that you love, here in this place, Chéri."

"What? What do you mean, golf? Please don't worry about that! Golf is like a weird cousin or something."

"Non, Chéri. I have seen it. This place and your game possess the possibility of restoring something in you that was, at one time, trusted and honored. You have told me on many occasions that your first and only source of connection in the entire world was provided through the game of golf at your childhood club."

"Yes, I have, but this is different. I would be working. This is a job."

"Oui, yes, but not just any job, this job represents the fulfillment of your oldest desire."

"… but that seems like a good thing to me."

"I have become afraid."

"I understand the Mustang. That was kinda scary, but that thing is long gone. I think you're feeling a little jealous."

I spoke those last words through a tinge of disparage, but that offhanded slight only served to inspire a fiery flare of determined defense. Samantha wriggled out of our embrace, but only to advance her position. She hovered above my face. I felt her breath, before I heard her words.

"Oui bien sur! I am jealous, but I am also afraid. I have never before needed to compete for your attention, or your love. That is why I needed to 'know' you tonight. I needed to know where you were, with me, not where you went inside this club."

I couldn't help myself. I said, "And, how did that little interview go?"

This time, I felt the mist from a chuff of disgust, before she pushed off my chest, and left me. Sam returned to the darkened bathroom. I lay there for a moment, reflecting on these latest proceedings. I tried to remember the last time that I had ruined one of our 'knowing' sessions, by inserting certain impulsive remarks in defense of my pride. However, on this occasion, I felt somewhat noble. I genuinely considered that I possessed the more virtuous position.

Nevertheless, I was quickly engulfed by a familiar restlessness. I began to squirm underneath an inescapable chorus of accusatory debate. Unanswerable questions accosted me like waves in the surf. Am I right? Am I wrong? Is she badly hurt? What about me? And, when will she return, or will she return? Those few moments, floating inside that silent darkness, became like hours of bobbing upon a turbulent ocean.

I did not typically invade the bath, while Sam was in place. Therefore, and after a time, I called from the bed. My tone was decidedly imploring.

"Will you come back, please? You don't have to see me. I need the bathroom for a second."

In the next instant, Samantha appeared. She padded softly toward our bed. She was wearing a nightgown. I excused myself, while she found her place. When I returned, she was propped upon her pillows. Her knees were pulled up, underneath the silky cloth of her gown. In the dark, I felt, rather than saw, the expression of her mood. At that point, heated flames of offense had been doused, and the chilly air of temporary divorce filled the atmosphere of our room. I am at best, a guerilla fighter where Samantha is concerned. I can manage a skirmish or two, but I have never possessed the supply lines, necessary for a prolonged war.

"Honey, please forgive me. I shouldn't have said that. But, do you really think that I would choose a game or a job, over you?"

"Non, my fear is that you will return to your old life. I am jealous because I cannot compete against the power of that former life. And I am also hurt, because I love you, and I don't want to lose you."

"We are not losing one another over a job. Besides, they probably wouldn't take me unless you were part of the deal. So, you're stuck with me. But, why would you think that I am returning to my old life? I haven't had the first thought about taking a drink. I promise, and, I might add that, it was easy too, even though drinking seemed to be the centerpiece of every activity."

"Mon Chéri, you have said, many times, that some addictions are accepted, some are condemned, and some are celebrated."

"I know, but I can't see how that applies."

"Mon Amour, everything you counted as fulfillment at one time in your life is being offered through the activities and instruments of this club. Every significant connection that you have ever known, throughout your entire life, has come through this game, and your childhood club. In comparison, I am a secondary source of fulfillment."

"That's not exactly right, but I'd rather not go down that particular road right now."

"I have not forgotten, but that point is like me, secondary. Your game has never abandoned you."

"Honey, please, I promise. Think about it. Has my involvement with the game ever before caused you to worry like this?"

"Non, Chéri...."

"... why is this so much different?"

"Eight."

"Eight?"

"Oui, bien sûr! Eight ... the special number for this club! The number for renewal, and restoration ... and, the number for the resurrection."

"But, you said yourself, that number is connected with Jesus. How can that be bad?"

"Mon Chéri, the world is filled with good and evil, but both forces serve to move the stars."

"Honey, what does that mean? What are you trying to say?"

"Chéri, I am not, la folle. This place can give you what you once knew and loved."

"Stop right there. That's what sounds crazy. Why is that scary?"

"… Mon Chéri, this club can restore you to the path that you once sought and admired, but that form of restoration or renewal is not progress. It means to return to what you once were."

"Please, Honey … aren't you always telling me that I haven't been changed by recovery but restored? Don't you say that, through recovery, I can once again be, exactly who I was meant to be? I thought that was good, but now you seem to be saying that being restored is bad. I don't think you can have it both ways."

"Non Chéri, your recovery allowed you to become who you were meant to be in order to live your life in freedom and fullness. The restoration offered here simply renews a previous exercise in bondage. At Wambaw, you are an alcoholic taking a job as a bartender."

"Now you're beginning to sound a little mean, too!"

"My words are the truth."

"Well, what if that just happens to be my calling? Think about it! Here we are, out of the clear blue sky, just like that! How or why would such a thing happen? Is it just a lucky chance, or did we do it ourselves?"

"Why would you consider doing such a thing?"

"We're looking, aren't we? Before today, I couldn't have dreamed of such an opportunity."

"After today, I have seen enough."

"What about your reception, and those ladies, and the mimosas. Didn't you say that you enjoyed all that?"

"Oui, merci, but that was a reception party, as you say. I was like a curious sort of niece or daughter, returning from boarding school, overseas. Those people will not become our friends."

"That is not how you described things in the beginning."

"I also said that I was drifting, Mon Amour. I see more clearly now."

"Damn It! So, I guess you've already decided everything, even though we don't know anything."

"Tell me about your secret meeting, s'il te plaît."

"I think that's beside the point, at the moment."

"I already know everything."

"Then what are we doing? Why are we fighting?"

"I am fighting for you, Jackson Weatherlow, the man that I have come to know as my love and my husband. I was afraid, before I became angry."

"I really can't see how this job has become so damned terrifying all of a sudden. Here's an idea. As long as we're going to allow numbers to guide our life, why not slogans and mottos too? How about that other saying? Remember? 'One lies as all lie,' those words pertain to the golf course, but if you apply them to this job, then you might say that this job is like any other job. That sounds peaceful and safe to me."

"That saying is not the spiritual foundation of this golf club."

"Oh my god, Sam, please…"

In the midst of my next volley, I heard a whimper. I turned, as Sam turned. She rolled herself into the shape of a small fist, and she began to emit a mewling sob. I took a risk, and moved toward her place. As I fitted myself behind her, she opened her clinch, rotated around and crushed me within a forceful embrace. I took her to me in a deliberate clutch. We clung together for a time, saying nothing, but vibrating beneath her active sorrow.

In time, I spoke softly, "May I ask you a question? It might sound disturbing, but that is not my intention. I want to know.

I heard, "Ça va."

"Did you 'know' me, in this bed, earlier tonight?"

"Oui, je te sentais avec moi."

"Good. I very much wanted to give myself to you tonight, and especially tonight, because I knew that you needed me. We were connected, right?"

"Oui, d'accord, Mon Amour."

"And, I did that, and we did that, in spite of all the excitement and even the drifting, right?"

"Oui, merci."

"Please remember that, Ok? Now, tomorrow is our day. No one at this club is expecting to see us until suppertime. We have the whole day to ourselves. Here's my plan. I want to spend the entire day, alone, with you, on the beach. We can go to a place called Tybee Island. You'll like it, I promise. We will decide about this job, by ourselves, out there on the sand. And, if you like, we will visit that flower shop that you mentioned. How does that sound?"

With those words, Sam turned up to meet my face.

Behind pink eyes, she chided, "I am your wife, not your daughter."

"I'm sorry. I chose my words with extra care, but that was for me, rather than you. My record this evening is not so good."

"Merci."

"Je t'aime, Samantha Weatherlow."

"Je t'aime, Jackson Weatherlow."

"Can I get you anything before we go to sleep?"

"Non Chéri, but you may give me your presence."

CHAPTER 15

Detours and Distractions

....

The problem with sobriety is that, once you wake up in the morning, that's as good as you're gonna feel, all day.' I recalled that acerbic quip, while pouring a cup of coffee for Samantha. In various instances, my personal history provided excerpts of profound wisdom. In this case, and after the activities of the previous day, I assumed that Samantha might be feeling somewhat foggy on this particular morning. I was hoping that a hot cup of black coffee might energize her mood and means. However, my initiative was not a product of hotel conditioning, but rather, an authentic gesture of loving care for my sleeping bride.

I found myself totally alone on my mission, and apparently the only active guest in the club. I had not seen a moving soul along my entire journey to the coffee station outside the Club Room. In fact, an eerie sort of silent stillness pervaded the public areas of the big house. Strangely, I did not feel out of place. I went about my task as if I were inside my own home. As expected, I found the coffee station arranged and readied for the morning. The caffeinated elixir poured from the spigot black and steamy.

I typically rose from bed before Samantha, but for this day, I had performed my morning chores behind ethereal purpose. I wanted to let her sleep. Friday had been a full day, to say the least, and I presumed that this day might hold much of the same. After slipping back into our room, I placed the hot coffee on the nightstand, along her side of the bed, and I sat down next to her slumbering form. After a moment, I touched my lips to hers, and spoke.

I whispered, "Good morning, my love."

I aroused a stir, a twist, and a whine.

Using words that had been emblazoned on my brain since early childhood, I murmured, in tones that were remarkably reminiscent of my father's voice.

"Rise and shine."

"Non, Chéri, come back to bed, s'il te plaît."

"Can't do it, we have places to go, secrets to tell and decisions to make."

"S'il te plaît, cinc minute."

"That won't help."

I watched a scene that included a few wrestling kicks, a prolonged grumble, a final flail of arms, a sigh, and finally, blue eyes, blinking in, dim light, behind tousled hair.

I said, "I brought you a coffee."

"Merci."

I queried, "Petit-déjeuner?"

"C'est dommage."

"Come on, we need to eat something. We're going to the beach. You'll need your strength."

"Oh la la! Malliot de bain!"

"What?"

"Mon Chéri, we have no bathing suits."

"Damn! You're right. I forgot all about that. Hey, I know … we can get one from one of those beach shops. We'll probably pass a million, on the way to Tybee."

"Mon Chéri, I am not wearing a tourist stop bathing suit."

"We aren't going to the beach at St. Tropez, we're in Georgia. The water will be green and the sand is sorta brown."

"Perhaps, Mon Chéri would like to see me parading around in wet tissue paper, but I prefer something more substantial."

"I already saw better'n that, last night."

This last remark proved to be more energizing than the black coffee. I received the standard form of correction across my right shoulder blade. I might have retaliated with a tackling hug to the mattress, but Sam was ready. As I turned, she bounced her brows, while taking a sip from her cup.

I passed her a smirky smile, and said, "Well, my love, what do you suggest?"

"I saw some shops in town, yesterday."

"Fine. We wouldn't want you to feel uncomfortable."

"Mon Amour, what time is our supper meeting this evening?"

"What else? 8 p.m. of course. Dinner at eight, as they say."

"Then, we have all day. I would like to visit the city first. We can shop for our suits, and have lunch before going to the beach. I might like to take a nap with you in the sand. We have never before spent a whole day together on the beach."

"Your wish is my command. Watch this…."

I moved toward the telephone, energized by an unusual sense of brazen confidence. I dialed and I waited. After a single ring, I heard Missy's voice.

I said, "Good morning, Missy. It's Jack Weatherlow."

I heard, "Good morning, Mr. Weatherlow, how may assist you?"

I offered, "Samantha and I have planned a little outing together. We're going to spend the day at the beach. I was wondering if I might arrange for a few supplies."

"Of course, and by all means. However, may I ask where you are planning to go?"

"I thought we would go into town first, and then I thought that Sam and I might visit Tybee Island."

"That sounds like a lovely plan, Mr. Weatherlow. And, if you would like, I can arrange for you to use the bungalow. We keep a place at Tybee for this very purpose. Please, don't worry about packing anything. I'll have your supplies installed while you travel. Would you like me to include any special amenities?"

I hesitated for a moment, out of surprise, and shock.

I answered, "A bottle of champagne would be nice—I think—a French vintage, if you can manage, but nothing spectacular, please."

I turned toward Samantha, after announcing this request. This time, I was bouncing my eyebrows. I was looking for a complementary cheer in support of grand gallantry. Instead, I saw vanilla hair slowly swishing, back and forth, and a cherubic face, hiding behind closed eyes.

Returning to the conversation, I corrected, "On second thought, I think we'll skip the champagne. Maybe, some soft drinks instead, a few bottles of Coca-Cola, and some chips, or crackers. I'll be happy to settle up when we return."

"You're already settled, Mr. Weatherlow. Just stop by my desk on your way out."

"Thank you, Missy, we'll be down shortly."

"You are most welcome. Please, take your time. I'll arrange everything."

Once again, I turned toward Samantha.

I said, "Do you feel alright? Would you rather stay around here?"

"Non Chéri, I feel fine. But, no champagne, s'il te plait."

"But, you always like champagne for celebrations. I thought we might celebrate today."

"Nous verrons. Merci, Chéri."

I did not pursue the implied discussion in that moment. I wanted to get on the road. However, I was attributing the intensity of the previous evening's debate to the effects of the collection of libations, which had accompanied that long day, and I was hoping that as the elixirs lost their glow, our negotiations might lose their heat.

Sam was nimble and efficient in her morning preparations. I was expecting the process to move more slowly. She was ready after a short time. Samantha chose a billowy shift in a smoky pink color, which appeared as would a large sack, but was fashioned from fine seersucker cloth, instead of paper. It hung at mid-thigh length, but I saw mostly dress. She wore a pair of raised sole huarache sandals. There was a golf tan line beginning around her ankle. Her vanilla hair was fluffed and full, but gathered in back in a single ponytail. Her tether was a pink grosgrain ribbon, which hung from a large bow and two bitter ends. She stepped toward me, as was her custom, unveiling a finished product.

Her face was toasty tan. I focused upon hawkish eyes casting a solemn gaze. Small cerulean seas were being buffeted by an uncommon storm. They were lifted by reaching lashes, shaded beneath brunette brows, but laden with an extra touch of gloss, and electrified by slivers of pink lightning. I gathered her close, but dodged her thoughts.

I asked, "I haven't seen this dress."

"I bought in in town, yesterday."

"But, I didn't see you with any packages yesterday?"

"I had it sent to our room, after we returned from the party."

"Why?"

"My dress is a preview of my secret gift."

"Tell me."

"Plus tard, Mon Chéri."

"So, I guess we're trading secrets today. Should we shake hands to seal the deal?"

"Non, un baiser c'est mieux, s'il te plaît."

I kissed her on the lips. She returned the gesture, but with an urgency that was both fully exciting and slightly arresting. After a moment, we exited our room and made our way toward Missy's station. An envelope inscribed with my name was waiting upon an unoccupied desk. I opened it. Inside, I found two notes, and a key. One note offered an address, and driving directions, the other was an invitation to explore and enjoy all that we found, and to lock up, but to leave everything for the cleaning staff. I passed the notes to Samantha, after having read them.

"Mon Chéri, did you know about this bungalow before today?"

"I did not."

"I thought Wambaw was a golf club."

"Me too, but I don't care. I've never had my own house at the beach before."

"Would you also be responsible for this house, in your job?"

"I suppose, but, isn't that something I should be saying?"

"We should know everything before we decide."

"I can't argue with that. But look, we have a whole day, and right now, all I'm thinking about is getting you into the ocean."

"Don't forget.... We need bathing suits."

The drive from Wambaw to Savannah was a bit more involved than I had imagined. We passed through uninhabited jungles, crossed several bridges, negotiated ever-growing patches of congestion, and finally searched for parking in the downtown area. I noticed that we had been driving for close to an hour, before settling the car in a public lot.

Samantha's bathing suit stop was located along Broughton Street. It was quaint, and densely packed, but beautifully arranged. I was not allowed to participate in the process of selection, nor was I invited to judge the fitting. And, being that her shop was a women's boutique, I wandered down the street in search of a more accommodating environment. I found a local haberdasher. My decision was simple. I picked a pair of printed trunks and returned, almost before I was missed.

Bags in hand, we ambled along the streets window shopping. After a time, we found a delightful café and settled there for lunch. We were seated at a table situated along the sidewalk. Sam remarked of the Parisian similarities, but gave exception to the heat and humidity. While waiting for our meals, I noticed a peculiar arrangement of tropical-looking plants, apparently standing guard along both sides of the sidewalk. This unusual oasis was approximately one block east, toward the ocean side of our café.

I inquired, "Did the lady who owned the flower shop mention the location of her shop?"

"Qu'est-ce que c'est?"

"You know, at the party yesterday. You met a lady who owned a flower shop."

"Oui, yes, I remember. She said that it was downtown, but I don't recall her mentioning the address."

"Well, I see something that looks promising. It's behind you, just down the street."

Sam turned in her wicker chair, as would a child. She spun around and placed both hands along the top rung of the ladder back design.

She said, "Mon Chéri, perhaps those palms belong to a flower shop."

"Do you recall that lady's name?"

"Non, Chéri, there were too many names from yesterday."

"Well, My Love, there was only one of you. We'll take a look after lunch."

We enjoyed local fare for our meal. Samantha chose the daily special, shrimp and grits. I chose from an upscale version of a blue plate menu. I ordered a crab cake, accompanied by sliced local tomatoes, and succotash. We shared our selections, and as a consequence of that exchange, I ate less crab than I would have preferred and more grits than I wanted. Over the meal, I confessed a certain type of snobbery which concerned grits and tomatoes. I offered that the only tomatoes worth eating, in the raw, were those which had been grown in the yard, and I added that grits were a breakfast staple not to be mixed or blended with anything but salt, pepper and butter.

Laughing gently, Sam remarked, "Oh la la! I did not know Mon Chéri was such a connoisseur of grits and tomatoes."

"And, once again, you can see that I'm not the caveman that you imagine."

"C'est bien, Mon Amour. And, I will love you, either way."

"Thank you, but keep that in mind, for later, when we're in the ocean. Let's go see that shop."

"Oui, merci, I am ready."

The plants I had seen were indeed marking the entrance to a flower shop. They were potted in containers that Sam called ornamental temporaries. Inside the shop, we found other plants, emerging from far more substantial containers, composed of terra cotta, and glazed clay. In fact, I felt as if we had entered a small botanical conservatory. A lush jungle surrounded on all sides, and hung from the ceiling. We found a variety of palms, fantastic species of orchids, and creeping, large-leaf vines of all sorts. Sam offered names, while I tried to dodge drips of water falling from unknown locations.

Toward the rear of the shop we found a more familiar type of display. I moved toward the coolers, but in search of their type and operation, rather than their contents. Sam admired various arrangements, which were resting upon, what appeared to be, antique credenzas, and sideboards, and tables. We were alone inside that shop for longer than I would have expected.

Sam said, "Mon Chéri, this shop is very lovely. There are many plants we do not stock."

"Hey, these coolers are the same as our new ones."

With that remark, a woman emerged from a curtained archway along the side of the coolers. I was alerted by her greeting, rather than her form.

"Good afternoon, may I help you folks find something."

I turned, feeling slightly embarrassed by the liberty of my position and uninvited intrusion. Samantha apparently turned as well.

I heard, "Well, what a wonderful surprise. Hello, Samantha, I'm so glad to see you again."

And, "And, lordy mercy, look who's here. You must be Jack. I've heard all about you, but I never thought I would ever have the pleasure. I haven't been to the golf club since losing my husband, and I don't plan to, anytime soon. I'm sorry, please forgive me, my name is Emma Waterson."

I heard, "Bonjour, Emma, mais, s'il te plaît, tu dois me pardoner."

Then, "I'm sorry, Emma. Please, you must forgive me. Jack and I should have announced ourselves."

"C'est bon! Tout est pardonné! But, don't imagine that I speak your language, my dear. I know a little of this, and a little of that, but all that amounts to a little bit of nothing."

"C'est dommage, mais merci. We are not exactly trespassers, but I was not certain of the location of your shop. We are explorers today, and may I say, everything that we have found is, tres magnifique!"

"Thank you, my dear. Can you stay awhile? If you two will give me a minute, I'm working on a few arrangements for a small dinner party this evening. I'm all alone today."

Sam looked at me through a gaze that nailed me to the glass cooler door. I could not escape. The smile that I returned was something I imagined a medieval page may have offered to a knight in shining armor, timid acknowledgement of a threatening order.

I heard, "Perhaps you do not recall, but Jack and I have a flower shop back home. I would like to volunteer our services. If, that is, you think we might offer more help than bother."

These words acted like a chemical reagent. I felt myself dissolving, into a state of existence one shade above transparency. I visualized the beach and the bungalow, receding into a panoramic vista of incalculable distance. I said nothing out of my enfeebled state. I understood that I occupied a precarious place, which teetered between surprise disaster and serious conflict. I took a moment of silence, in which to subject myself to a type of mental flogging, as payment and penalty for failing to anticipate this situation.

Ms. Waterson replied, "Actually, my dear, your assistance would be most welcome."

Sam said, "Let's take a look."

She whispered to me as she passed, "I haven't forgotten our outing. I will work as quickly as possible. You may help by watching the store. Call me if you need anything, s'il te plaît."

"As you wish, my liege."

"Mon Dieu, Chéri."

I received a chuff and a kiss, before positioning myself behind the cash register. That device was apparently as old as the furniture piece upon which it rested. It was mechanical rather than electric, and all but hidden beneath a jumbled menagerie of items, ranging from cash money to pruning snips. A crystal vase rose out of the clutter, supporting one long stem rose, in pink.

I decided to do exactly as I was told. I went to work, and as I surrendered to the situation, all sense of disaster evaporated. Before Sam reappeared, I had spoken to four different customers, and actually helped two make a real purchases. I rang up a $25.00 order for one dozen sweetheart roses in white, and $50.00 for some type of potted fern.

I heard a whisper in French, "Comment allez vous?"

I turned to reply, "Fine … just fine. And, I made two sales."

"Tres bien. I will be ready in a minute. Merci beaucoup, Chéri."

"You're welcome."

More precious time elapsed before the ladies emerged from the workrooms. Emma and Sam acted as if they were old friends, or rather, mother and daughter. I hung back, wrangling with a twitchy sense of anxiety. However, my gloomy predictions were delightfully dashed by an unexpected round of shared gratitude and a final farewell. Before I realized, Sam and I were on the sidewalk headed for the car. Over the course of our city walk and the remaining drive to the bungalow, Samantha shared the story of Emma Waterson.

"Mon Chéri, Ms. Emma's story is tragic. I feel so sad for her. I am grateful that you would allow me to help her today."

Listening, I wondered how I had allowed anything, but I found the recognition no less uplifting.

I replied through a cavalier tone, "Of course, my love. We had to stay."

"Chéri, Ms. Emma is not only alone for today but, toujours et pour toujours! Both her husband and her only daughter are dead. Her husband, Roger, died of a freak heart attack, while playing golf. He wasn't at Wambaw, but somewhere called Sea Island. That happened two years after she took full ownership of the shop. Then, two years ago, Emma's daughter was killed in an automobile accident."

"Slow down, honey. I'm confused. Did Emma lose her husband and her daughter two years ago?"

"Non, Chéri, just listen, s'il te plaît."

"I thought I was, but go slow."

"Roger bought that flower shop, as Emma's gift, for their twentieth wedding anniversary. That was fifteen years ago. Roger died two years after, in 1979.

"Now, Emma and Roger were married in 1957, and after two years, they had a daughter. Her name is, or perhaps, was, Anne Riley Waterson, she was born in 1959. She and I are almost the same age. Riley is Emma's maiden name. Anne was in her junior year of college at the University of Georgia, when Roger died."

"Oh my god, I was there at that same time! I might know her! What else do you know about her?"

"Not much, but I do know that she left school after the tragedy. She returned home for a year, in order to be with Emma. They worked together in the shop across that time. After that, Anne returned to school to finish her degree. After graduation, Anne returned home to Savannah. She spent the next eight years helping Emma in the shop. Eight years, Chéri!"

"Stop it!"

"Non, Chéri. That was the year that Anne was killed. Anne had gone to Sea Island to attend the wedding of two friends from school. That was in 1990. Apparently, she was all alone. Mon Chéri, Anne was returning home from the same place her father died. Emma said the weather was terrible that day. There was a terrific storm. No one knows what really happened, but Emma received a call from the State Police. Anne's car was found upside down in a culvert off the interstate highway, just north of a city called Darien."

"I'm sorry, honey. Good grief, you did more than arrange flowers today."

"I think you are right, Mon Amour."

"That is terrible. Is Emma doing alright?"

"She was insistent upon a sound emotional outlook, but she attributes her well-being to her shop and her love of flowers. She sees her shop as her protector and her flowers as her companions."

"That's good I guess, but that sounds a little lonely to me."

"Mon Chéri, she is surrounded and embraced by something she loves. That shop is her grace."

"If you say so, my love, but flowers for souls seems like a poor trade."

"Mon Chéri, this trade, as you say, is an inevitable destination along the course of everyone's life. I happen to believe that Emma is doing very well in her transition."

"Destination? Transition? Really—that sounds terrible."

"Would you prefer me to say that she is scoring a par on her course?"

"What? No, certainly not. How can you be so flippant about such a thing?"

"I have made a similar trade in my journey, and you have as well."

"I'd bet you'd change your tune if something happened to me."

"We have many years ahead of us, Mon Amour."

"See there, you're like, 'Well, that was nice, but ho hum, I guess it's time to move on.'"

Through a chuckle, I heard, "I will have a nice service for you, Chéri, and I will arrange all the flowers."

"That's good. Thanks. I had no idea that you could change roles as easily as words. Your transition from funeral director to comedienne was effortless."

Through laughter, Sam said, "C'est dommage, Chéri. When will we arrive at our beach destination?"

"I don't know. I kinda forgot what I was doing for a minute."

I felt a small palm caressing the top of my right thigh.

"Perhaps, after we arrive, you will find a lucky chance."

"What?"

"Ma oui, Chéri, you may never know what lies ahead."

"Hang on then, let me try to get through this traffic."

CHAPTER 16

A Day at the Beach

....

I n time, we found the bungalow. A Cape-styled home occupied the last lot on the south side of 8th Terrace. I parked underneath a raised porch. I failed to notice the overhanging flag, emblazoned with the club logo.

I said, "Well, I hope this is it."

"Mon Chéri, this must be right, everything is eight!"

"Yeah, I see that. Come on. Let's see what pleasures await our arrival."

We made our way through a lower gate, which was tentative at first, but finally receptive to my key. We climbed the stairs and entered the bungalow through a heavy wooden door, featuring a carved club logo. Pickled shellac had been burnished by the salt air. Inside we found an interior space finished in stark white. The only colors interrupting a dazzlingly antiseptic continuity were occasional splashes of sky and mint, provided by framed pictures and 'beachy' accessories.

The main floor was configured as one, great, flowing openness. The rear of the primary living space was dedicated to kitchen duties. I saw gleaming appliances tucked behind an island feature, all of which occupied the length of the rear wall. All around this space generous windows and sliding doors offered scenic views of the ocean.

There was a master bedroom located off the southern side of the great room. Through an archway along the far side of the kitchen, I found a landing area for stairs. One set led down into the garage and storage area. Another set led up toward a second floor. There were four bedrooms on that floor, each with a private bath. From there, a third staircase gave access to a widow's walk, porch area.

The ocean side of the house featured another wide porch, partially covered by fabric awnings, striped in alternating green and white panels. There were multiple collections of furniture spaced at intervals, all around the porch. I found a prepared tray of delicacy cold cuts in the refrigerator, along with six bottles of Coca-Cola, and an unordered bottle of French Champagne. I also found a large ceramic bowl, complete with fresh salad, and topped with a full layer of boiled shrimp.

By training, and habit, I reviewed the guest spaces far more closely than most men. Consequently, I lost track of Samantha during my inspection of the premises.

I called, "Hey Sam, where are you?"

"Une minute, s'il te plaît."

I took this remark as an opportunity. I offered, "Hey, I'll just change out here."

"Pouvez-tu attendes, s'il te plaît."

"Oui, Madame, I will wait."

Her words floated from behind a partially closed doorway, and inside the master bedroom. As requested, I waited, but I found a chair, across the living room, facing the bedroom door. My judgment seat was a low-profile club chair, upholstered in a heavy white on white brocade fabric.

More quickly than expected, Samantha emerged from her dressing space. She was wearing her new bathing attire. At first glance, I saw a suit, finished in a lapis blue color, which was, by all visible distinction, a perfect match for her eyes. The fit appeared to be of such precision that I had trouble discerning skin from fabric. However, I noticed a shimmer as she padded through showers of radiant sunlight. As she approached, she seemed to be dragging another garment, from the fingers of her left hand. This article hung like a towel, woven from gossamer cloth.

Her suit covered in a single wrap, but appeared as if it were being stretched between shoulders and hips. Every turn and curve of her body was accentuated by a thin iridescent fabric, but I saw all Samantha, from bare feet to pelvic crest. And, that particular view held steady as she twirled in front of my chair. Her suit plunged in the rear, such that her entire back was visible above the bottom brief. I was rendered somewhat stupid by the final vision. Her floppy straw hat seemed to be the most substantial covering of the entire ensemble.

I heard, "Qu'est-ce que tu penses?"

I said nothing, but slowly rose from my seat. I took her by the waist. I held her in my fingers, skin to skin. I peered into the pelagic fathoms of pondering eyes. My head knocked the hat loose. She tried to save it. I kissed her and pulled her close. And, we clung there together, breath to breath, for a long moment. She pushed me back. I allowed it.

"Are we going in the ocean?"

"Later."

"But, I am ready for our swim."

"But, I'm not."

"But, I am, and you have a new suit to wear."

"In a minute."

"Non, Chéri, we came for the ocean."

"The ocean will always be there."

"And, so will I, unless I miss the ocean."

This last remark broke the spell by which I had been enchanted. All of a sudden, rational thought returned to me as an accessible tool for living.

I said, "Ok, just give me a minute. I'll change and be right back. Oh, there's lots of good stuff in the refrigerator."

She tipped up on her toes and kissed me lightly on the lips. I bent to recover her hat. I watched her slide into her cover garment. I found my bag with the new suit and retired to the front bedroom.

Through the doorway, I heard, "I want to see your suit when you are ready."

"I'm not modeling my suit."

"I will be waiting in your chair."

We spent the afternoon together on the beach. We erected a small encampment just down from the house. We had an umbrella, and beach chairs, towels and snacks. The champagne made an unscheduled appearance, but that occurred toward the end of our stay. And, much like our entire trip, the occasion for our celebration was far removed from anything that I might have predicted.

In the same way that I prefer the game of golf, over many similar pursuits, I prefer to submerge myself in the ocean over all other varieties of aquatic activities. Salty surf, far outpaces, the offerings of swimming pools, lakes and rivers.

I am not partial to lake swimming, in the least. Rivers are fine as long as the water is swift and clear. And, as far as I'm concerned, a dip in the pool is like a bath. However, I find that immersing myself in the ocean, regardless of clarity or temperature, turbulence or placidity, is a seductively sensual experience. In fact, if I were to call upon the spiritual counsel of my bride, I would say that the difference between liquid environments is equivalent to the distance that separates 'knowing' one another from having sex.

These thoughts occupied my mind, as we struggled to free ourselves from the breakers. At chest depth, I began a casual float. I pondered as I watched my bride swimming against the outgoing tide. I felt peaceful and content in the salty water. Surprisingly, our decision about Wambaw was not pressing upon my mind. I might say that I felt present in the moment. In short order, I considered my thoughts about ocean swimming, and I realized that I had always thought this way about the ocean, but had never recognized such a thing before that instant. I suppose that Samantha more than anyone has served as my coach and mentor regarding the art of being present. To be fair, recovery first exposed me to the concept, through the admonishing slogan, 'One Day at a Time' but Samantha had made those words real and effective. I am no master, by any means, but she has inspired me to accept and enjoy the time at hand.

In support, I might add that, although I've played thousands of rounds of golf, I don't believe that I had ever been truly present for an entire round, until I met Sam. Before we became involved, or before we came to 'know' one another, all of life was focused upon an end result. In golf, I was always intent upon posting a score. I sought the recognition provided by a definitive marker, in far greater measure than the fulfillment offered through the journey. I was a snapshot man, before Samantha became the director of my film. And, once again, I came to realize something rather shameful. I considered that, while having sex is a temporary event, often referred to as 'scoring,' Samantha's term about 'knowing' suggests a type of mutual journey, which reaches toward permanency, or committed love.

I gathered her from the waves as she returned from her swim. I supported her in a suspended float position. After a time, I attempted to convince myself that we were in deep water, and I was aiding her efforts in turbulent seas. However, the fact was that I could not seem to keep from touching her in that sparkly suit, in that salty sudsy ocean tide. I honestly sought a clue or a sign, which might indicate her desire to alter our posture, but I detected nothing of the sort, and we remained as we were, partially fused in the surf.

Bobbing with the rolling water, Sam said, "Mon Chéri, I am ready to trade secrets now."

"I thought you already knew everything."

"I do, but you do not."

"So, you are aware of everyone who has had a hand in this deal?"

"Peut-être."

"Perhaps! I don't think you know as much as you think. Quid pro quo, my love, tell me your secret, and I'll tell more of mine."

"Ça va … something very special happened during our first evening at the club."

"That's not a confession."

"… But that is my secret."

"How did I miss it? We were together every minute."

"Oui, yes, we were, but what did we do, while together."

"I remember everything, clearly. We inspected the big house, and the proshop. We played golf! And, we had dinner."

"What else, Chéri?"

"Well … that too, but that was your idea…."

"Do you recall what I said that evening?"

"Of course…. That particular comment represents the bait, which has kept your fish tantalized by your deadly hook."

"Mon Dieu, Chéri. That was not my intention."

"Maybe not, but here we are."

"Oui, merci, and as you say … here we go. We are going to have a baby, Mon Amour."

"What!?"

"Oui Monsieur."

"That's nowhere near what we're talking about?"

"That is my secret gift for you, and us."

"Sam, that's not right. You can't say that."

"I can, Chéri. That day, I felt it. I know it."

"You can't know that from that… can you?"

"I know it, Mon Amour."

"Don't you have to go to the doctor, or take a test or something?"

"Oui, yes, we will take our tests, but I already know."

"I think you're making that up. That's your line in the sand. You're still upset with that business about eight, and renewals, or reverse renewals and thoughts of relapse on my part."

"Fais chier, Jackson Weatherlow!

This comment preceded a rather violent push and a splash. Off balance by the shove and confused by the odd exclamation, I submerged, briefly. After surfacing, and clearing my eyes, I saw Sam swimming.

I called out, "Where are you going?

"Come back... please!

I'm sorry...."

And finally, "Should you be swimming?"

She looked back, but toward an approaching wave, rather than me. She caught that wave, with exact timing, and vanished from my sight. After a moment, I watched her step up from shallow water. That was the last thing I saw before being pummeled by a different wave from my rear. I floated around for a time. I reflected upon my thoughts about ocean swimming, and decided that this would have never happened in a pool.

From a distance, I watched Samantha, resting in one of our chairs. I considered holding my position for a while longer. I thought that I might fare more favorably with the unseen denizens of the deep, as opposed to the visible menace that was lounging on dry land. Soon enough, I made my way to the shore. Sam had shifted to the front edge of her chair. She was toweling her hair. I flopped in the sand directly in front of her position. I stood upon my knees, but took her knees in my hands in effort to secure my station, and in hope of enlivening my exoneration.

I said, "I'm sorry, I didn't mean that."

The toweling continued.

"Look, I was worried about you last night. You haven't been that upset in a long time. That's what I meant to say."

She wrapped her towel around her neck and peered into my eyes. Her eyes glistened wet above a deeper sadness that I did not expect. I remained still and quiet, holding her knees.

"Mon Chéri, do you recall when I made my announcement about giving you a special gift? I offered my little secret before we knew anything about eight, and the meaning of that number at Wambaw. I knew everything, before I was made aware of the fact that this club is founded upon the spirit of renewal."

"Oh yeah! That's right! I remember now, but I wish I didn't. I'm sorry. I take it all back."

"I wanted to tell you two things today. I have revealed my first secret, but my second is that I want you to have this job if you prefer. I was going to say that I trust you, and that I also know that everything will work out for the best. But, now, I don't know if you trust me, and that must mean that you do not 'know' me, even after all our time together."

"No Sam, that's not right. Please don't say that. Don't think that. Ever since our first night together, I've tried my best to give myself to you, and I mean everything, mind, body and soul. Remember my question last night? I asked if you 'knew' me. You said, yes, you did 'know' me. That's the truth of this whole thing. You 'know' me, and I 'know' you. I'm sorry I said what I said, just now. I mean it. But, what you said out there in the water was so different than anything you've ever said, and different than anything I've ever expected. Do you really know? Can you really know?"

"I know it, Mon Amour."

"How can you know?"

"My 'knowing' flows from a special type of peace. Here... or there, in our room that first afternoon, I fell in love with you more deeply than I have ever known. How could that happen when I already love you with all my heart, and mind, and soul? I felt pleasure and happiness, but I also felt the joy of divine peace. I felt the satisfaction of a desire that I did not know I possessed. Afterward, I was, quite simply more than I was, before we came together. I have felt that twice with you, but never before, and only with you. That is how I know."

"That's a pretty good answer. I didn't expect that, either."

"Chéri, I cannot decide the time, but my time will be decided before long. I am growing older, and we decided before this opportunity was ever presented."

"I know that, but I didn't think, now, or here."

"Mon Chéri, men and women have been having children for thousands of years. No time has ever mattered, famine, war, peace, bliss, creation moves regardless of time."

"Sam, we have to live, and we have to decide how to live."

"We will live, regardless of our decision. That too is a part of everything."

"But, why now? It's too much…."

"Would you like to tell me your secret now?"

"I suppose, but first, I want to say this. You probably won't believe me, but I've felt something similar happening to me since we've been here. It's the same thing, but different, I suppose. Everywhere we've been, regardless of what we were doing, I've felt proud, or as you say, peacefully satisfied that you are mine. During this visit, I have felt that you were more, mine, than I have ever known, but in return, I have also tried to be more, yours, than ever before. I hope you don't mind that I think of you as mine. I just don't know any other way to say it. I mean that, you're mine, but I'm yours, as well. I am more than I was, as well. I know it, and I feel it."

"I am yours, Mon Amour, and you are mine."

"Thank you, my love. But, will you listen for a minute?"

"Oui, bien sûr."

"Honey, all my life, I've been looking for something that might fill the emptiness that I've always felt, in my heart or soul, or whatever. They told me last night that the job was mine, if I wanted. And, here's my secret. Mr. Woodson is best friends ... old best friends with Grant ... my Grant ... our Grant, from Kansas. Apparently, they've known each other since childhood. Grant recommended me for the job, after Mr. Woodson made some calls. He called it due diligence work. I mean, think of that! What are the chances of such a connection?

"After hearing that, I thought this job was like you, divinely ordained, or something. Not to mention that thing about eight, and renewal. Think of that, a divinely ordained job, dedicated to the renewal of our lives. I thought we had to take this job. I thought that I had finally found the answer to my longing.

"But then, last night, you were so worried that everything was wrong. You were upset, and I was upset. I was hoping that you were just feeling frightened about making such a big change in our lives. I was hoping that you might feel differently today, here at the beach. And, you do, I think, but here's the thing. While I was in the water, watching you swimming away, all alone, I began to see this whole trip under a different light.

"Honey, I think I came here out of habit; the habit of searching for satisfaction and fulfillment. Looking back, this trip is no different than every other thing that I've ever done, but with you, everything is different than before. I suppose I felt admired or needed when they called. I was enchanted by the fact that someone had called for me. And, as you have seen, everything seemed to be falling into place."

"Mon Chéri, we came here to look. We were never searching. And, we came here to give, if asked. We both agreed that we do not need anything from this club or these people."

"That's the thing, honey, regardless of what we decided, I am searching. I may not have been searching for the right job, but I am searching for happiness and fulfillment—seductive marvel, remember? I've always been searching for that. I've always been captivated by something new and wonderful. Like I said, it's my habit. However, out there in the water, I realized something else. That habit is like all other habits, or addictions. Inside my habit, I don't get to choose. I am a prisoner of whatever seems to promise new and more and better.

"I'm beginning to believe that the real gift of this whole trip is the club itself, Wambaw. They are prepared to give me everything that I ever thought I wanted. Everything we've found appears perfectly suited to fulfill my peculiar affections. Wambaw is the best of the best in my book, but nothing that I've seen seems to hold any claim upon my life. I don't feel a need, nor do I feel a pressing desire to possess anything that they are offering. I feel grateful, and somewhat flattered, but I do not feel compelled or imprisoned by my habit. I suppose that I feel a sense of freedom more than anything."

"That makes me happy, Chéri."

"I want you to be happy, more than anything."

"So what are you thinking?"

"Remember what you said last night? You said that I would be a bartender at Wambaw."

"Je suis désolé, Chéri."

"No, I think you're right. I would be a bartender here. Every day I would be mixing and mingling with all the things that have ever promised fulfillment and satisfaction in my life. I would have to pass by them every single day, without indulging their promises."

"Mon Chéri, this work would be exactly like your work at the hotel."

"Not exactly, I can always leave the hotel, but here, once I'm inside and on duty, I don't think that option applies."

"Peut-être pas, Chéri."

"I think the club thing about eight and renewal is real, but as far as I'm concerned that renewal has nothing to do with rice fields or golf. I mean, if everything hadn't been so perfectly wonderful, I might have missed the more profound message. The freedom that I have come to know through sobriety is overseeing this decision. I came out of habit, but like I said, everything is different. I think this job and this place are about deciding where to focus my heart and soul. I am free to choose, although I have been engaged in one of my habits. That's not normal. I've never known that power. I am living in the gift of renewal, by recognizing that I am free to choose.

"Honey, all I'm saying is that I realize that I already possess everything I've ever really wanted through you and us, but I don't think I could've seen that without this wonderful gift staring me in the face. And, I don't feel very proud of that remark. Out there in the water, my life appeared to me exactly as you described your golf shot on our first day. I saw this opportunity, and I looked across my entire life as if it were the product of one gigantic lucky chance, but none of this, or you, or us, would have been possible without God's gift of grace through recovery. I don't think I could've seen that without Wambaw offering such grand perfection. But, I suppose, you're going to say that you already knew everything that I've said, right?"

"I knew that Chéri, but you are the one who needed to know."

"I know that now."

"But Chéri, if you know that, then this job is glaçage sur la gateau!"

"What? I'm sorry...."

"Grace, Mon Amour, this job is your gift of grace. You may receive it freely."

"Do you believe that, for real?"

"Oui, yes, I know it to be real."

"What about Emma?"

"Qu'est-ce que c'est?"

"Emma Waterson, and her flower shop."

"Pourquoi, Chéri?"

"Sam, I've also thought about Emma. And, I believe that our little side trip, this morning, was a divinely inspired kick in the pants. Emma is alone, because of unspeakable tragedy, but as you mentioned, she has her store and her flowers. She has her second loves. We have that same store, honey. It's our store, but it's your store, and your heritage. That store has stood the test of time. It will be there if something happens to me."

"Ne dis pas ça!"

"... Emma's story, our story, how do those similarities converge and mingle across time and half the planet? What are the chances? That story was meant to help me decide to do what is right."

"And...?"

"Sam, if you're right, when?"

"Quand quoi, Chéri?"

"The baby."

"Next year; perhaps, January or February"

"That's a long time from now. How do you feel?"

"Mon Chéri, I feel fine. In fact, I may celebrate with a glass of champagne."

"We could be all set by then, I guess. Everything might be ok."

"Oui, d'accord, Mon Amour. Everything will work out, regardless. You may accept your job."

"But, have you really changed your mind?"

"I no longer feel like I'm losing you."

"That's weird, because that's the way I feel right now. Soon you'll be two people, and one that I don't even know."

Laughing, "Perhaps, I'm already two people, but we made that other person together, and he or she will be some of you and some of me, not a stranger."

"Which is it?"

"Ce qui?"

"Your baby."

"Our baby, our child, Chéri."

"Right, I meant that. I'm sorry, but do you know that too?"

"Non, Chéri. That will be our next secret. May I have my champagne, s'il te plait?"

❊ ❊ ❊

I called out to Samantha, from my sink in our bathroom. Hey Sam, "Did you take my razor blades?"

"Non, Chéri, but I have them. They are in my razor, on the little stand in the shower."

Hearing that answer, I began to wonder how much time I would require before I truly understood the depth of Samantha's commitment to giving and receiving. We gave and we received in this house, and through our lives, but to me, my razor blades always seemed to have been gifted without permission. Nevertheless, our arrangement instilled a sense of connected embrace that was far more fulfilling, and decidedly more satisfying, than any other strategy that I had ever known.

I heard, "Mon Chéri, you may have them if you need them."

I had no idea what kind of creams and emollients might be adhering to those fine blades, so I declined that gift.

I said, "Thank you, I'll manage."

I heard, "Don't forget to bring Savanne to the shop before you go to the golf course."

To Samantha, I said, "Of course, my love."

To the mirror, I said, "You know? She might prefer to stay here. I mean, she's been trying to figure out that bouncy thing on her crib for the longest time. She might just get it, if we leave her alone for a while."

These muted musings were interrupted, suddenly. I felt a shock, as if I had been caught.

I heard, "And, we're going to see that house on Wornall tomorrow. I would like to tell them when we will arrive."

I said, "Honey, it's a two day tournament. I won't know anything about tomorrow, until I finish playing today."

"Oui, merci. Everything will work out. I'll have everything ready for Savanne when you arrive. Je t'aime Chéri. Au-revoir."

To a closing door, I said, "Hey wait! Let's go downtown tonight. They're having that taste of Kansas City festival at Crown Center."

And finally, "I love you, Samantha Weatherlow."